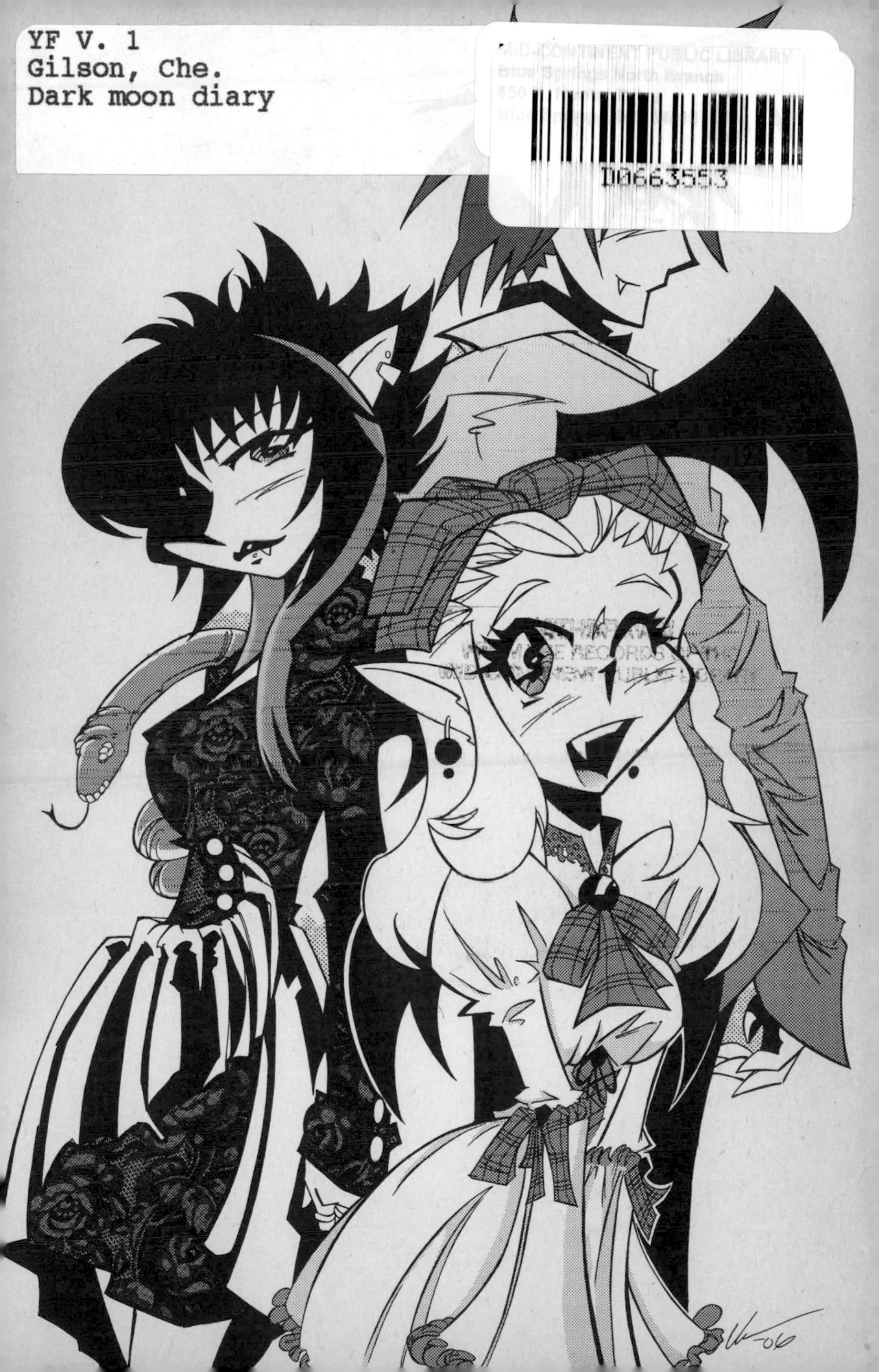

Dark Moon Diary Vol.1
Created by Che Gilson
Illustrated by Brett Uher

Lettering - Lucas Rivera
Inks and Tones - Mara Aum
Cover Design - Christian Lownds and Colin Graham

Editor - Troy Lewter
Digital Imaging Manager - Chris Buford
Pre-Production Supervisor - Erika Terriquez
Production Manager - Elisabeth Brizzi
Managing Editor - Vy Nguyen
Creative Director - Anne Marie Horne
Editor-in-Chief - Rob Tokar
Publisher - Mike Kiley
President and C.O.O. - John Parker
C.E.O. and Chief Creative Officer - Stuart Levy

A ⚙ **TOKYOPOP**® Manga

TOKYOPOP and ⚙ are trademarks or registered trademarks of TOKYOPOP Inc.

TOKYOPOP Inc.
5900 Wilshire Blvd. Suite 2000
Los Angeles, CA 90036

E-mail: info@TOKYOPOP.com
Come visit us online at www.TOKYOPOP.com

ISBN: 978-1-59532-844-1

First TOKYOPOP printing: September 2007
10 9 8 7 6 5 4 3 2 1
Printed in the USA

DARK MOON DIARY

Created by
Che Gilson

Illustrated by
Brett Uher

HAMBURG // LONDON // LOS ANGELES // TOKYO

Table of Contents

NACHTWALD

L.A.

Chapter One

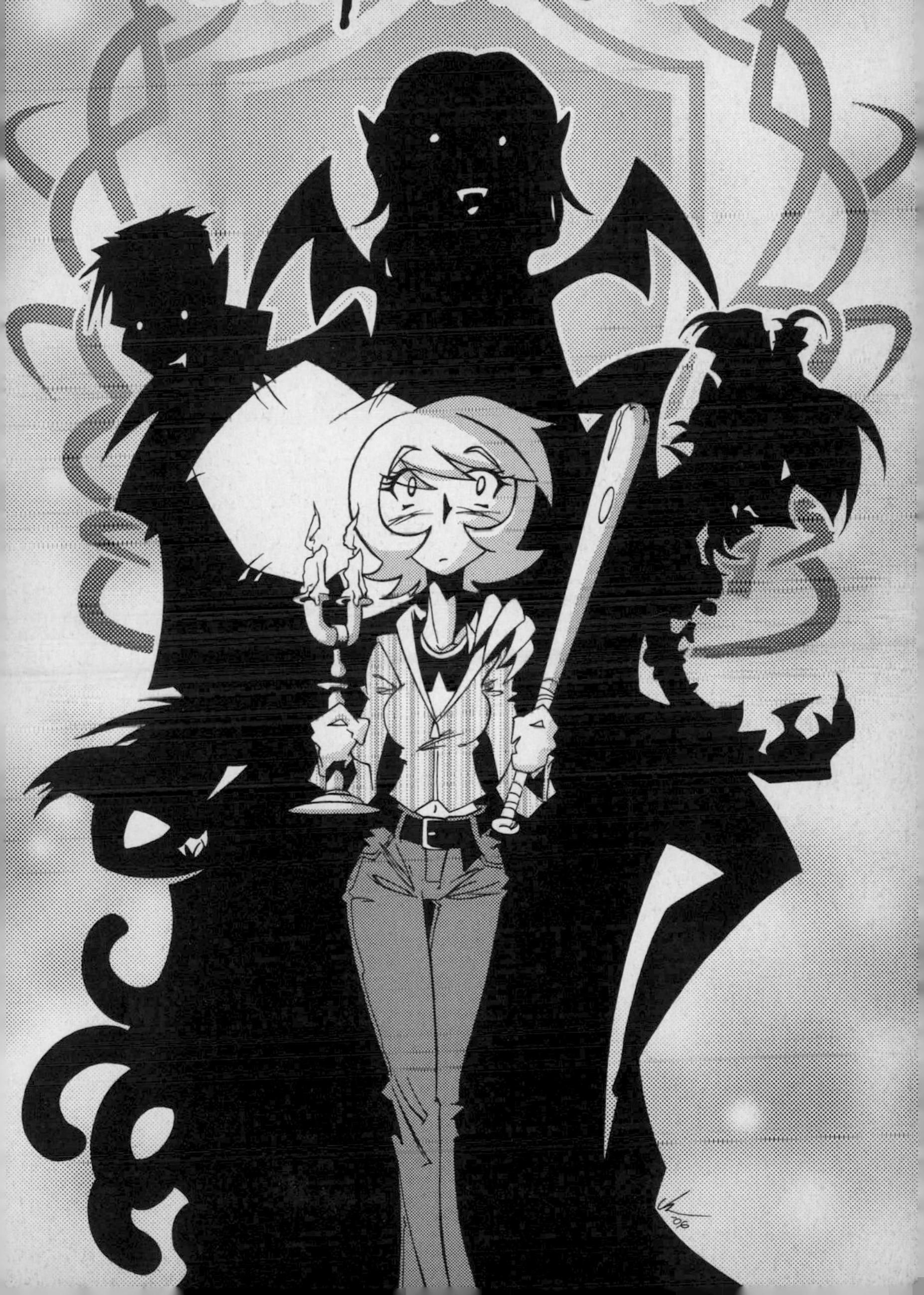

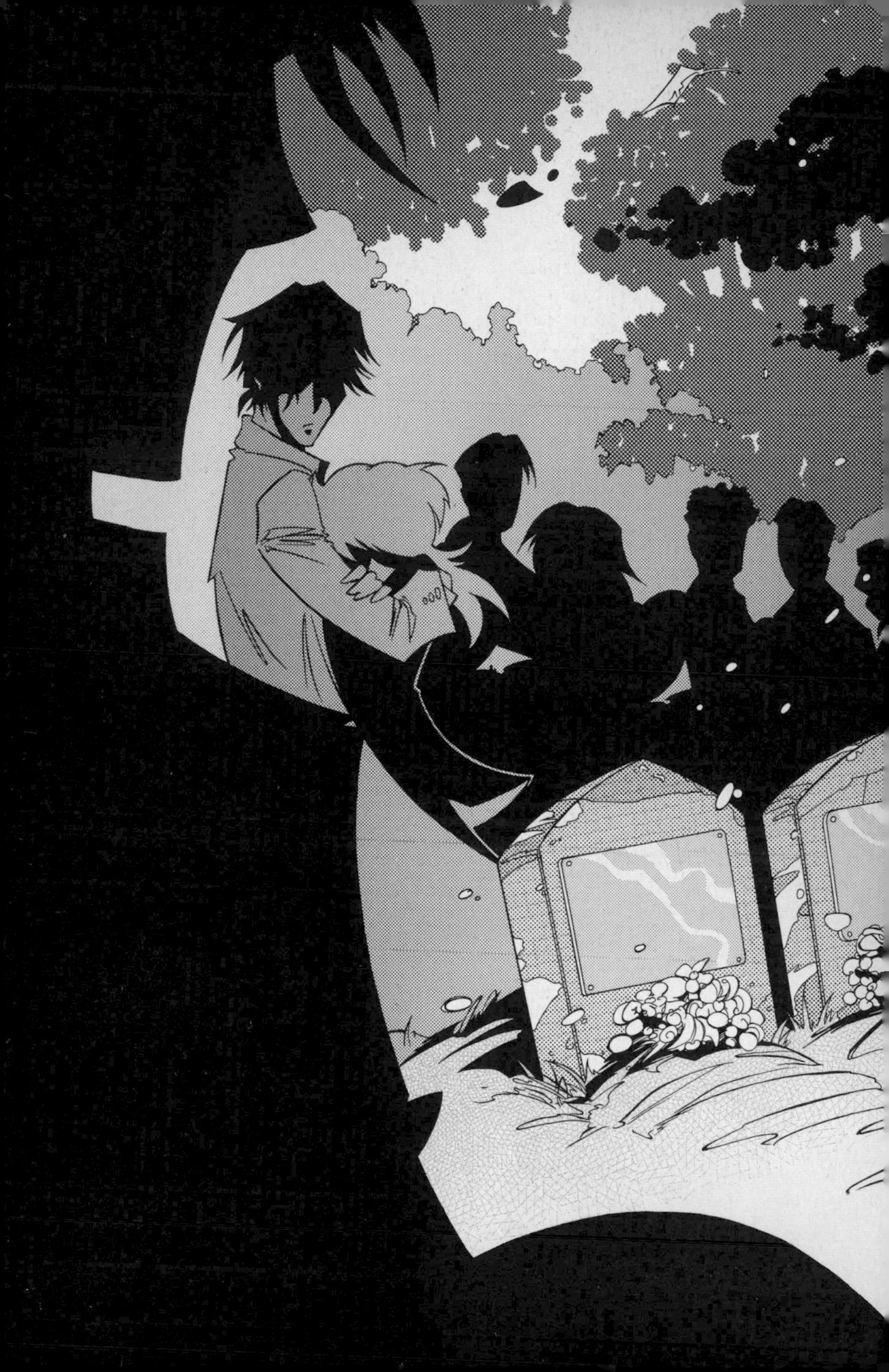

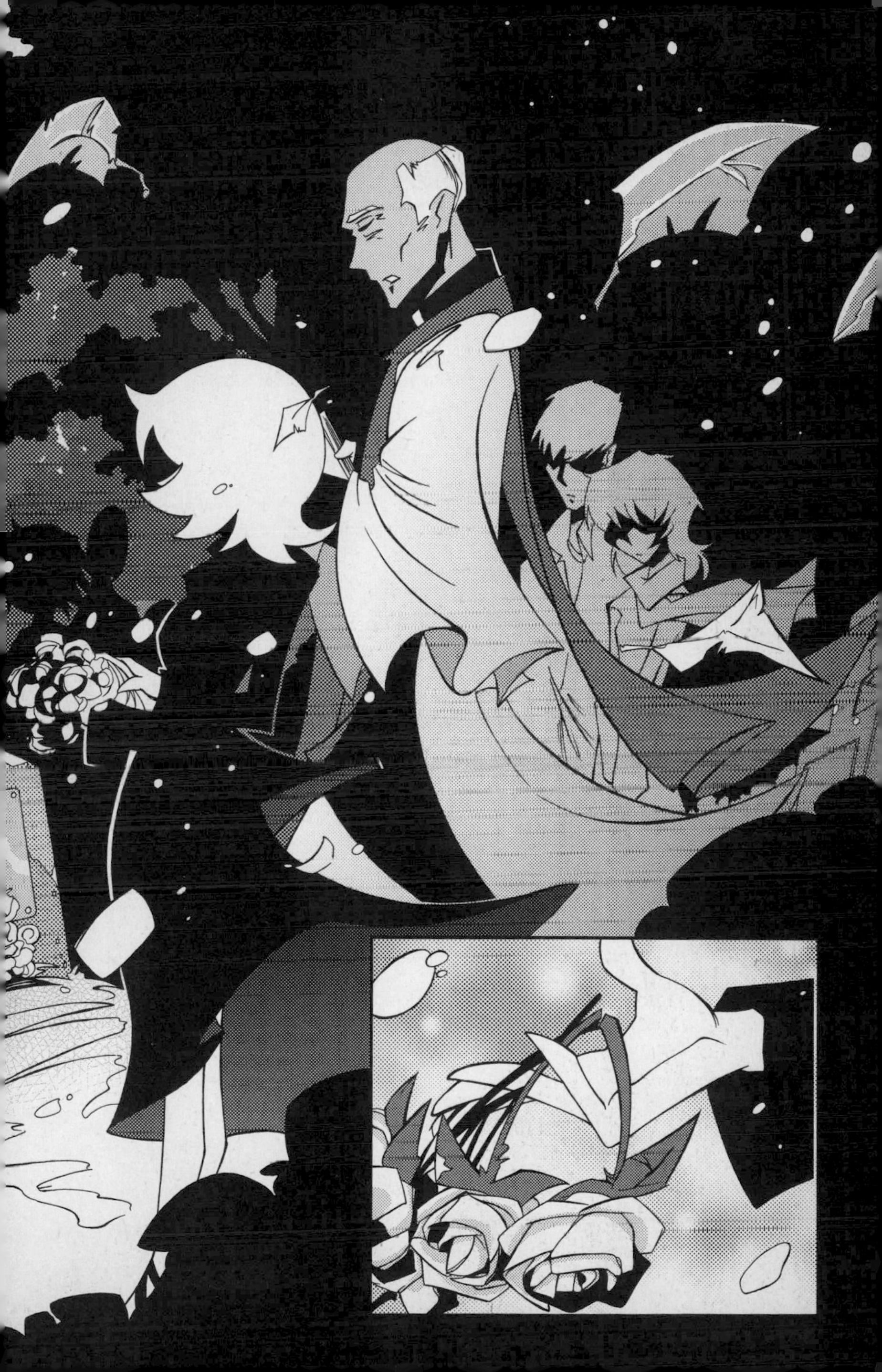

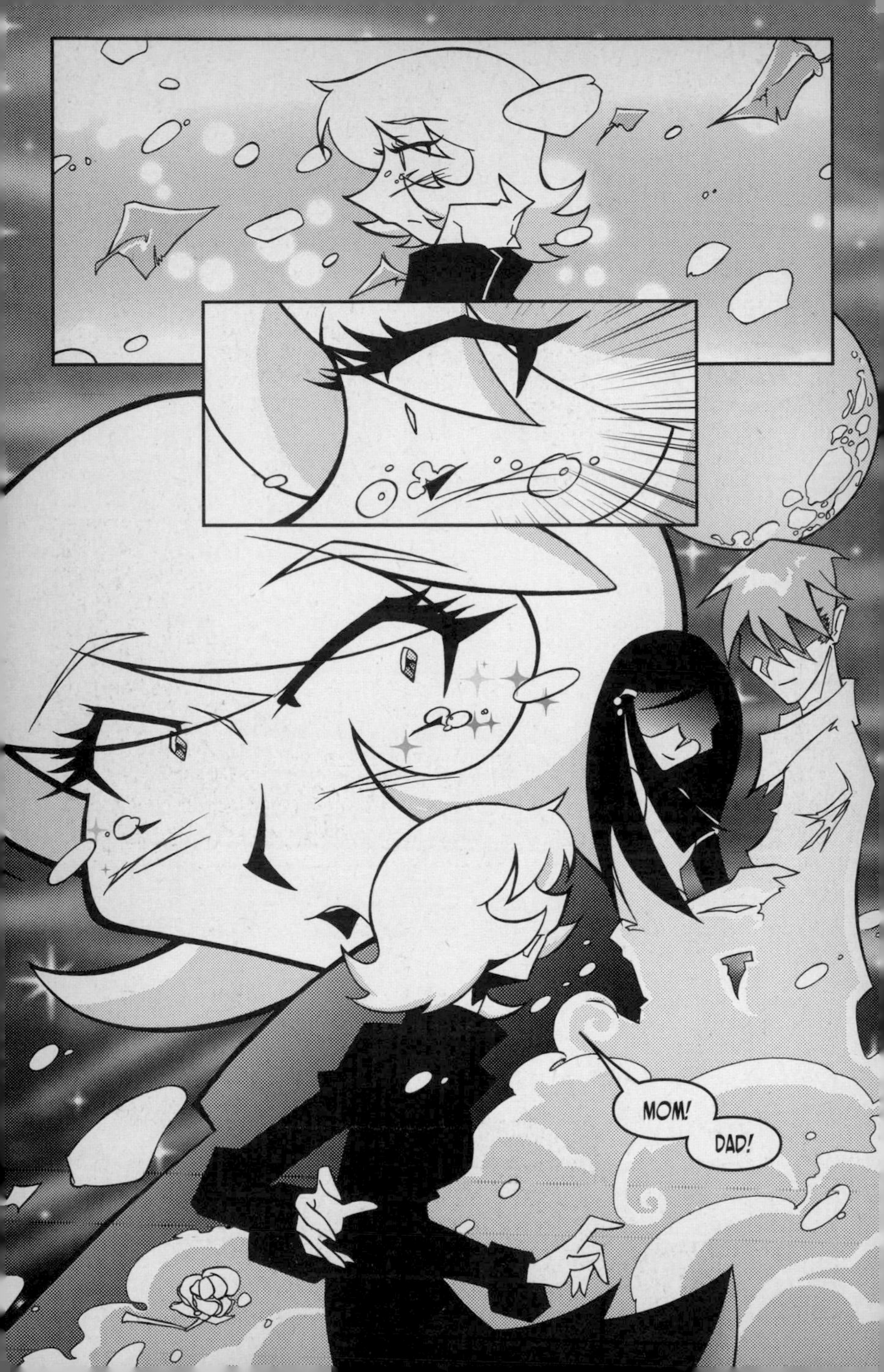
MOM!
DAD!

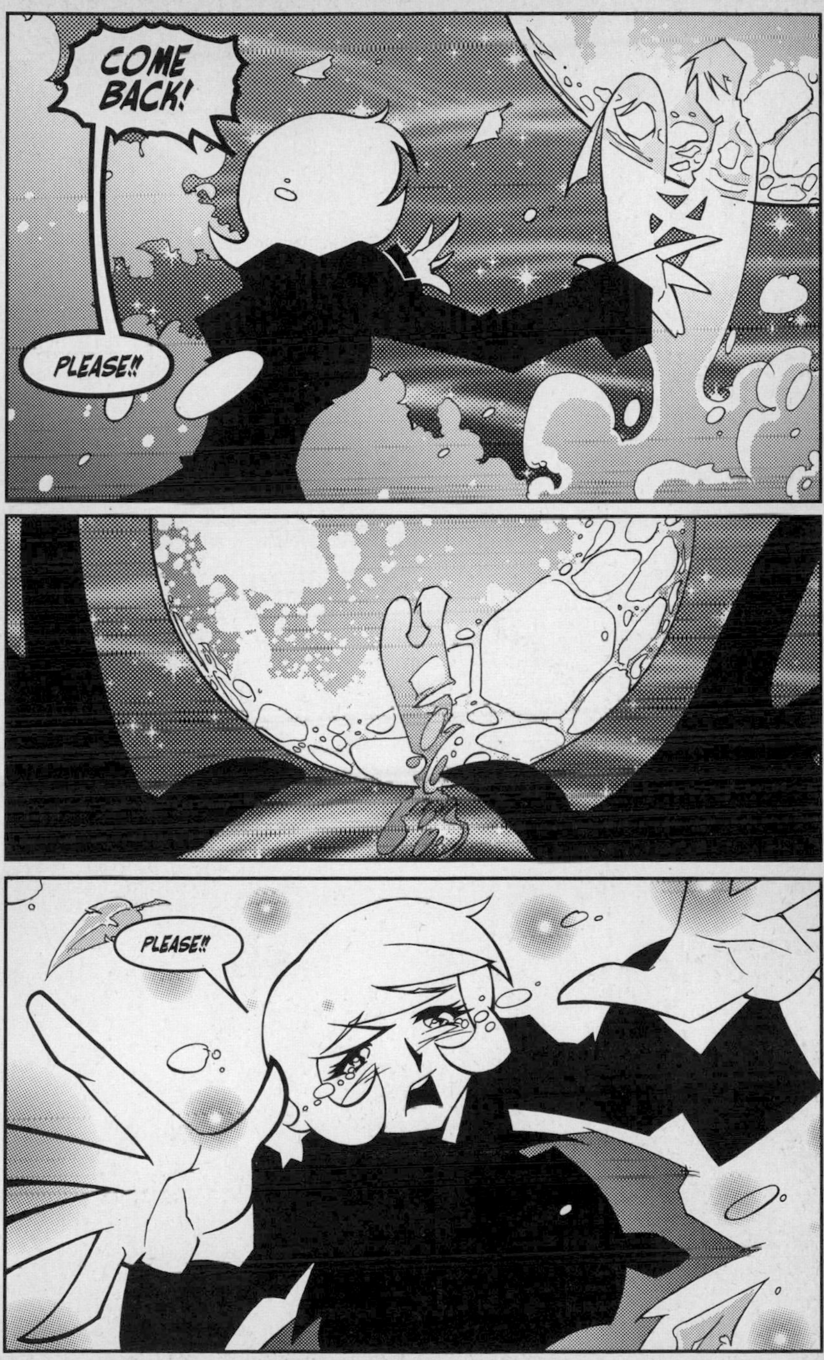
COME BACK!
PLEASE!!
PLEASE!!

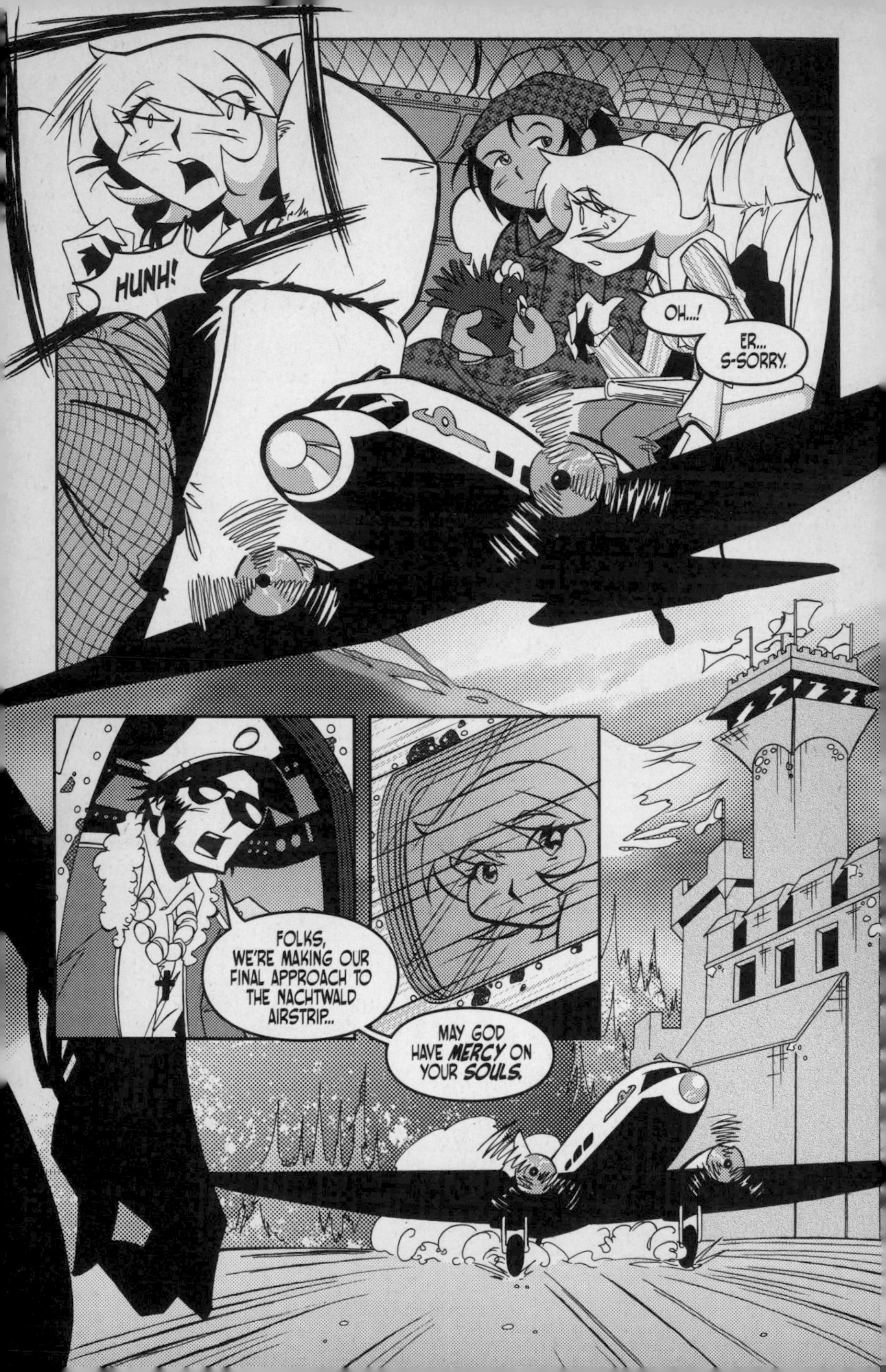
HUNH!
OH...!
ER... S-SORRY.
FOLKS, WE'RE MAKING OUR FINAL APPROACH TO THE NACHTWALD AIRSTRIP...
MAY GOD HAVE *MERCY* ON YOUR *SOULS.*

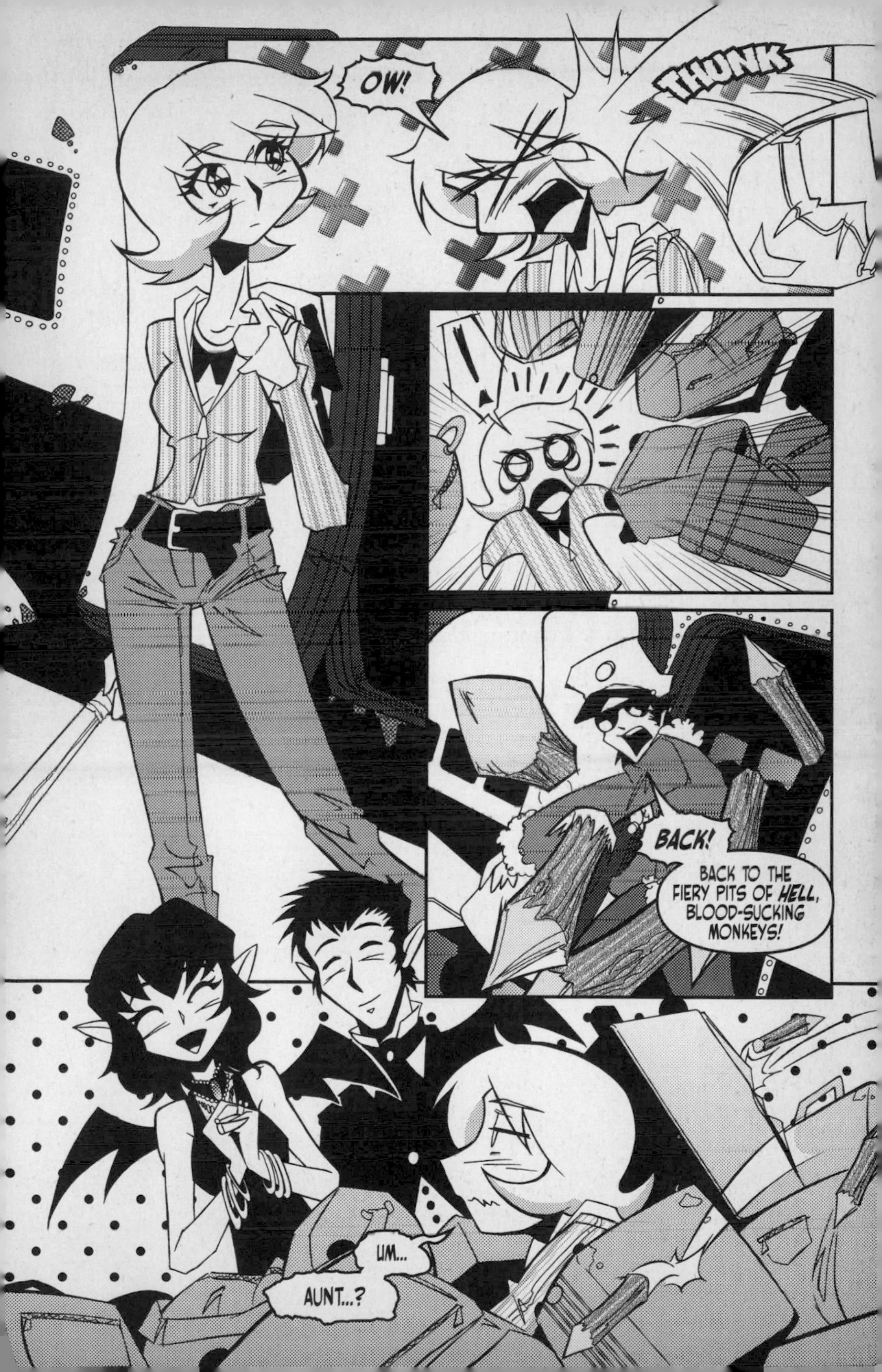
OW!
THUNK
BACK!
BACK TO THE FIERY PITS OF HELL, BLOOD-SUCKING MONKEYS!
UM...
AUNT...?

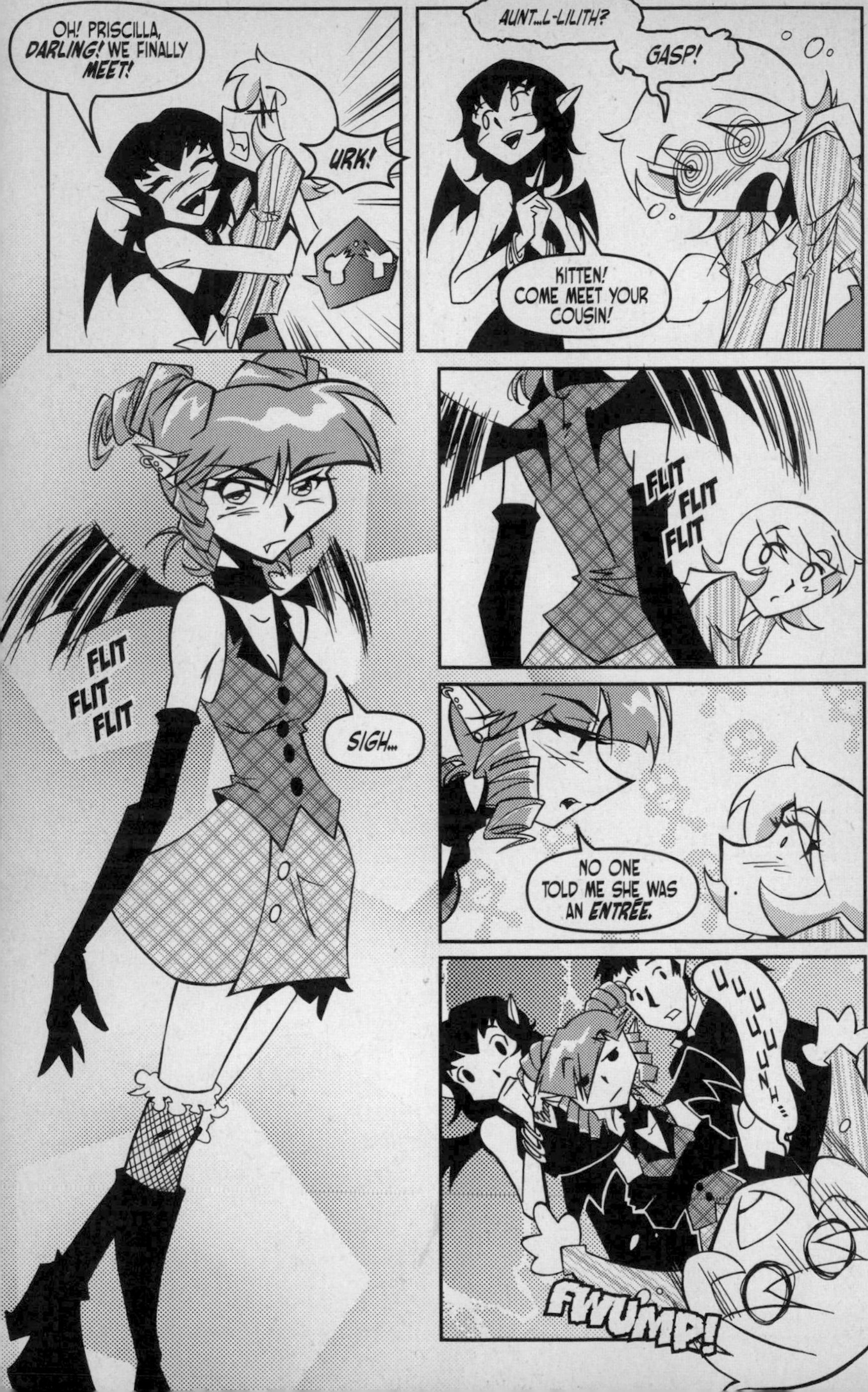
OH! PRISCILLA, DARLING! WE FINALLY MEET!
URK!
AUNT...L-LILITH?
GASP!
KITTEN! COME MEET YOUR COUSIN!
FLIT FLIT FLIT
SIGH...
FLIT FLIT FLIT
NO ONE TOLD ME SHE WAS AN ENTRÉE.
UUUUUUNH...
FWUMP!

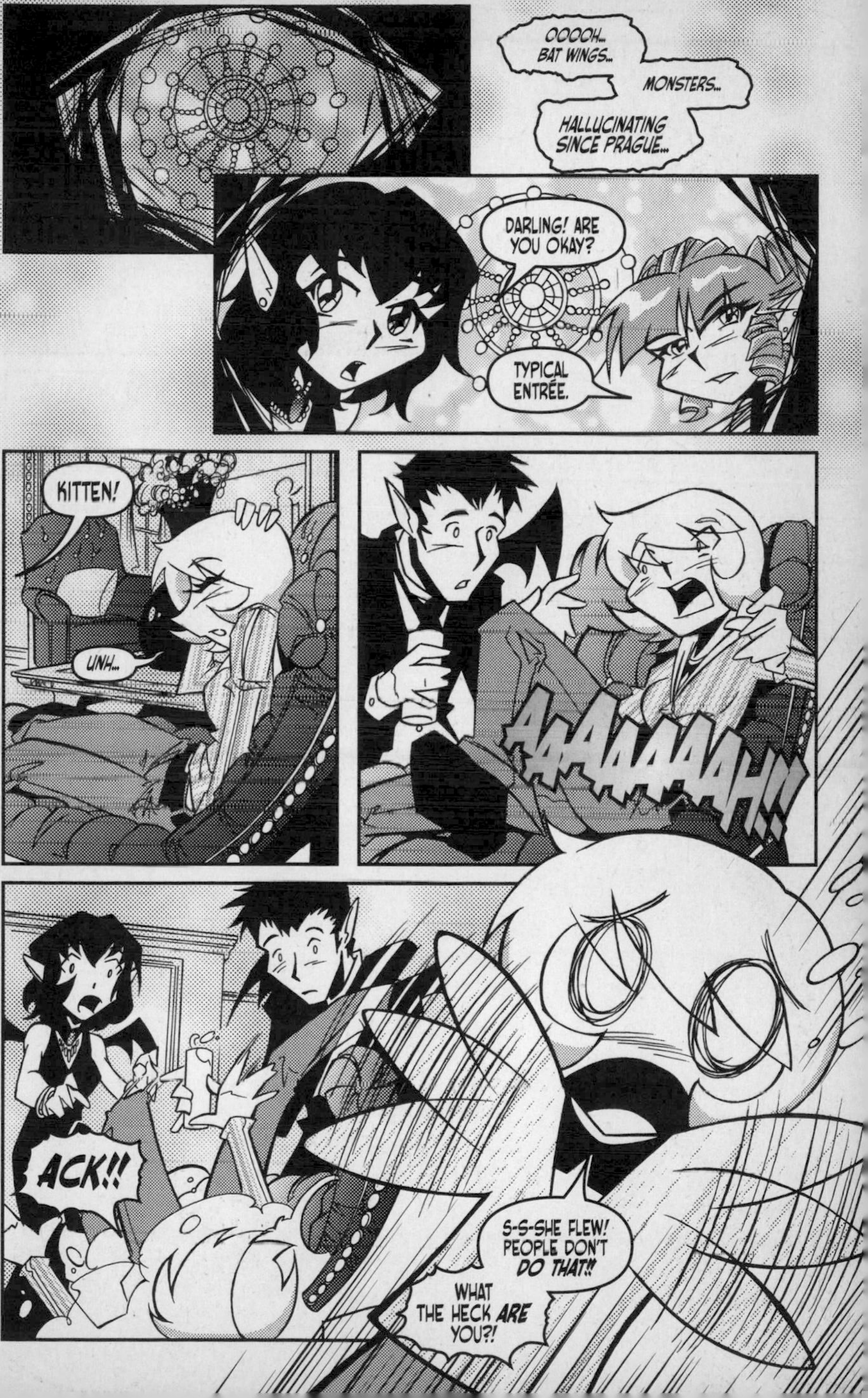
OOOOH... BAT WINGS...
MONSTERS...
HALLUCINATING SINCE PRAGUE...
DARLING! ARE YOU OKAY?
TYPICAL ENTRÉE.
KITTEN!
UNH...
AAAAAAAAH!!
ACK!!
S-S-SHE FLEW! PEOPLE DON'T DO THAT!!
WHAT THE HECK ARE YOU?!

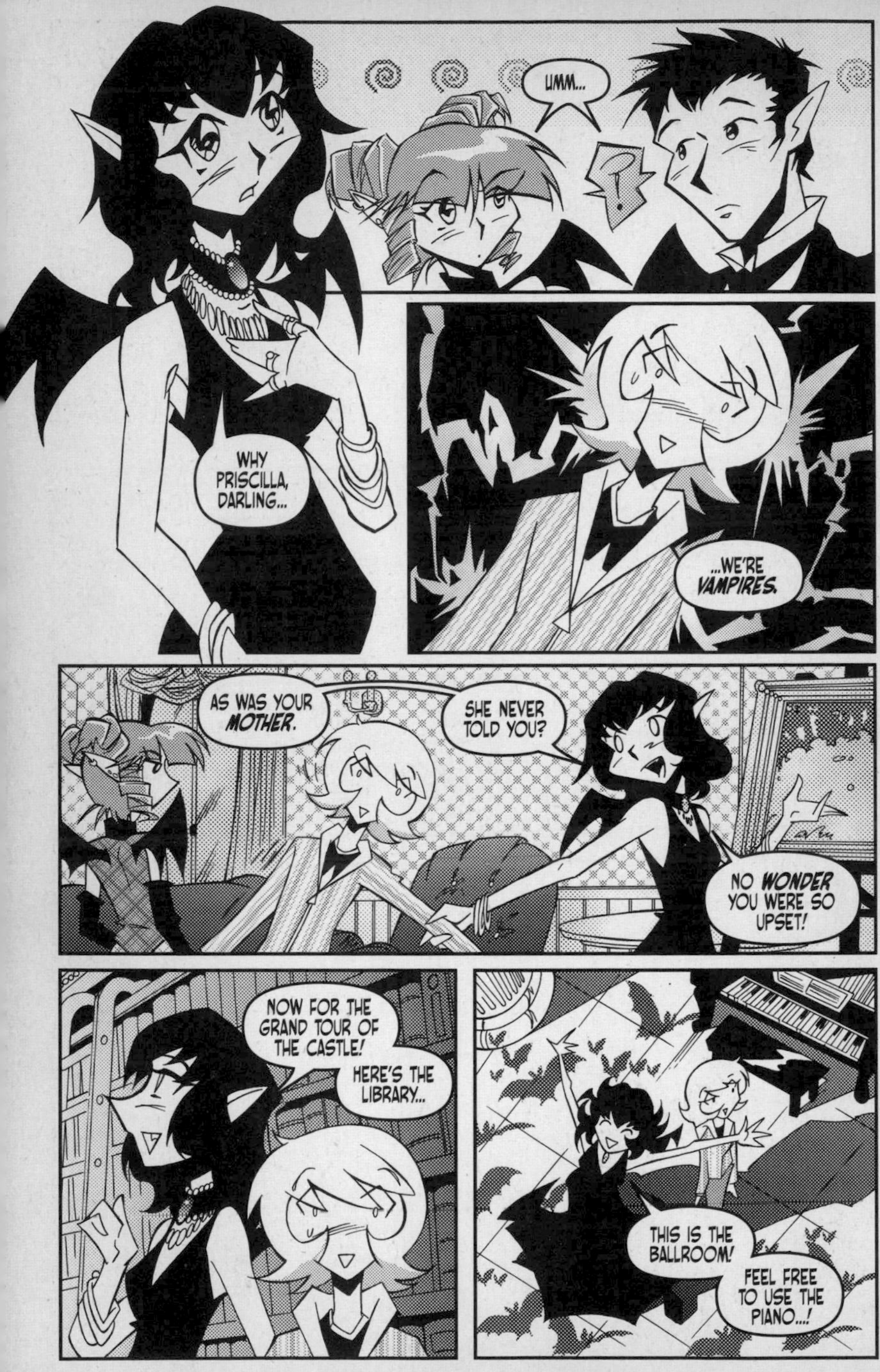
UMM...
WHY PRISCILLA, DARLING...
...WE'RE VAMPIRES.
AS WAS YOUR MOTHER.
SHE NEVER TOLD YOU?
NO WONDER YOU WERE SO UPSET!
NOW FOR THE GRAND TOUR OF THE CASTLE!
HERE'S THE LIBRARY...
THIS IS THE BALLROOM!
FEEL FREE TO USE THE PIANO...!

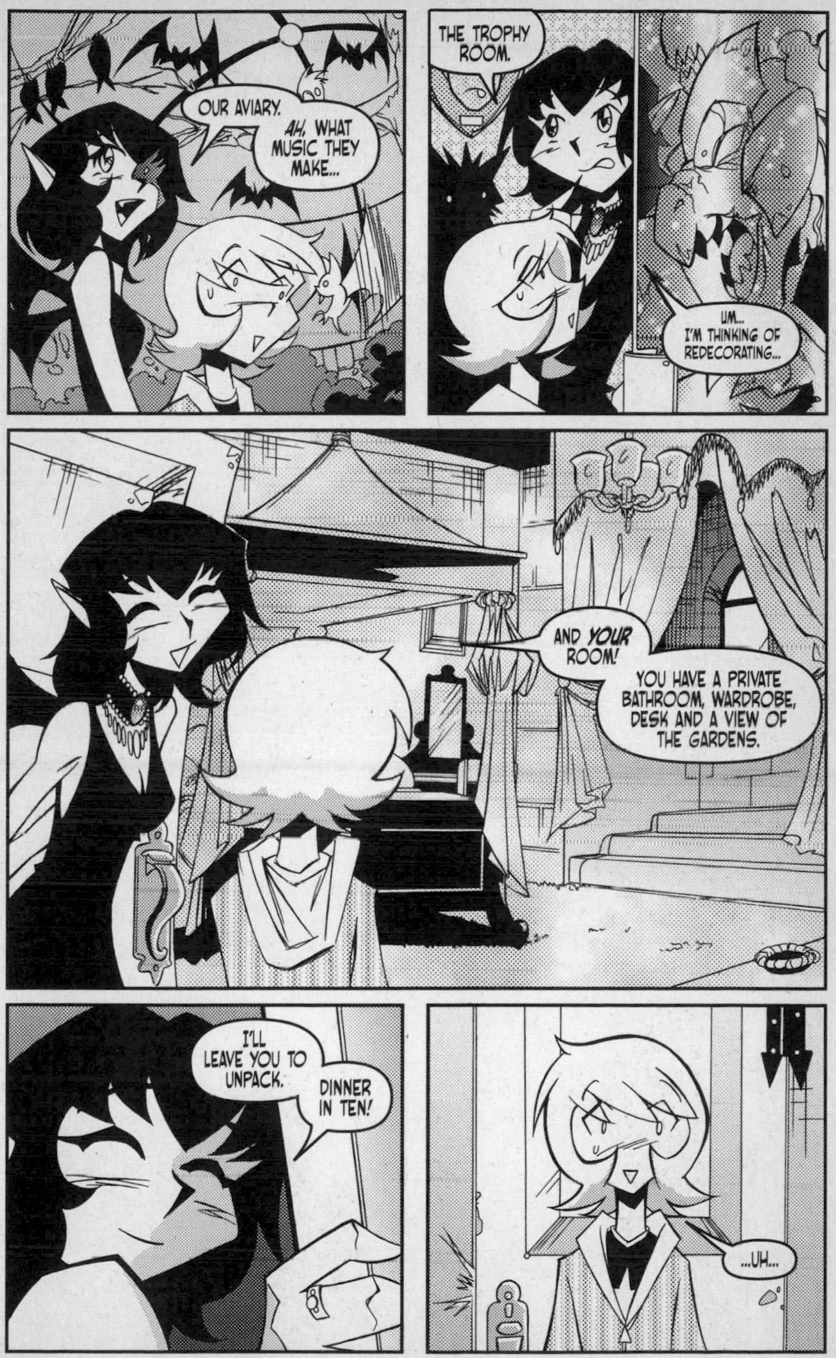
OUR AVIARY.
AH, WHAT MUSIC THEY MAKE...
THE TROPHY ROOM.
UM... I'M THINKING OF REDECORATING...
AND YOUR ROOM!
YOU HAVE A PRIVATE BATHROOM, WARDROBE, DESK AND A VIEW OF THE GARDENS.
I'LL LEAVE YOU TO UNPACK.
DINNER IN TEN!
...UH...

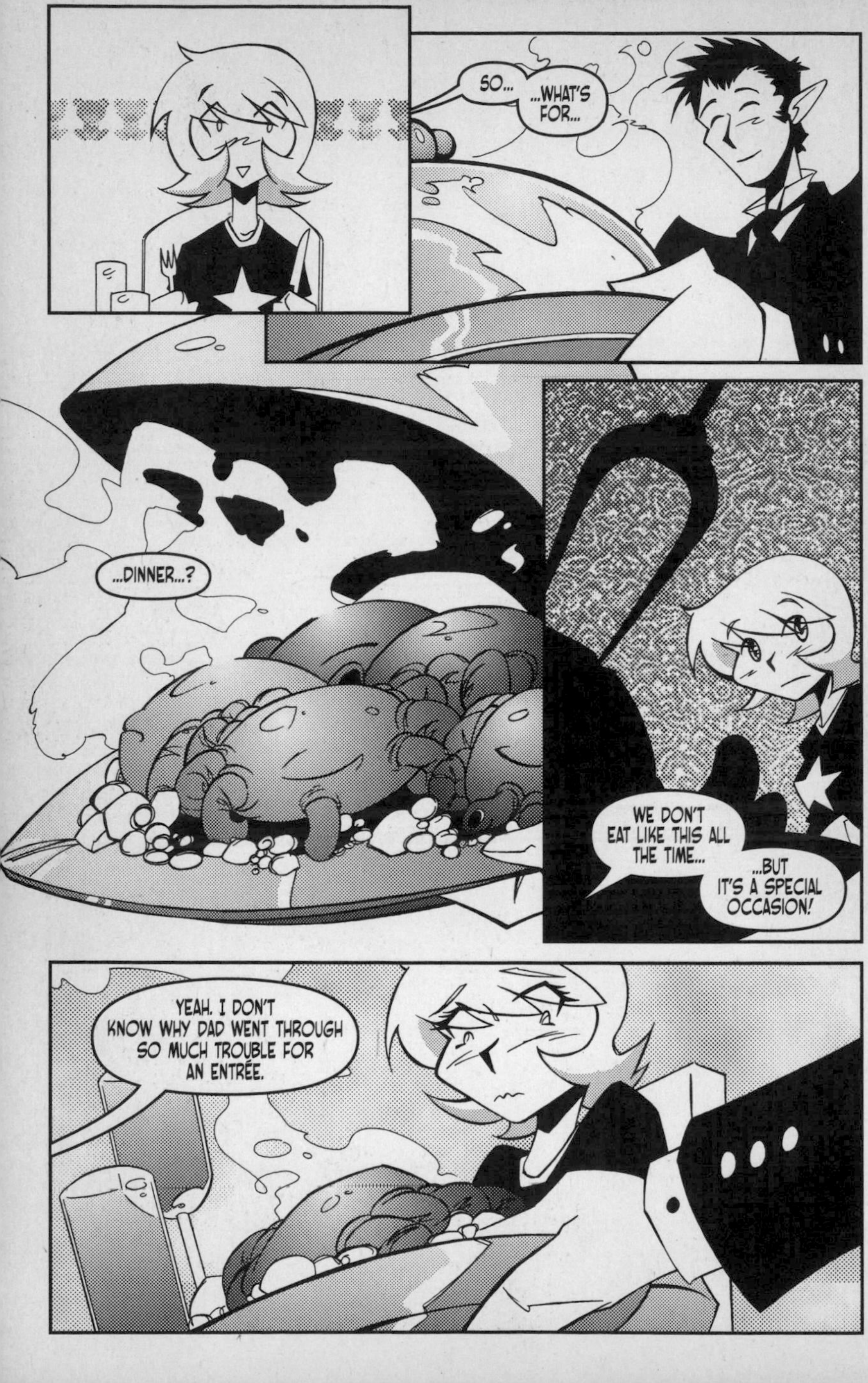
SO...
...WHAT'S FOR...
...DINNER...?
WE DON'T EAT LIKE THIS ALL THE TIME...
...BUT IT'S A SPECIAL OCCASION!
YEAH. I DON'T KNOW WHY DAD WENT THROUGH SO MUCH TROUBLE FOR AN ENTRÉE.

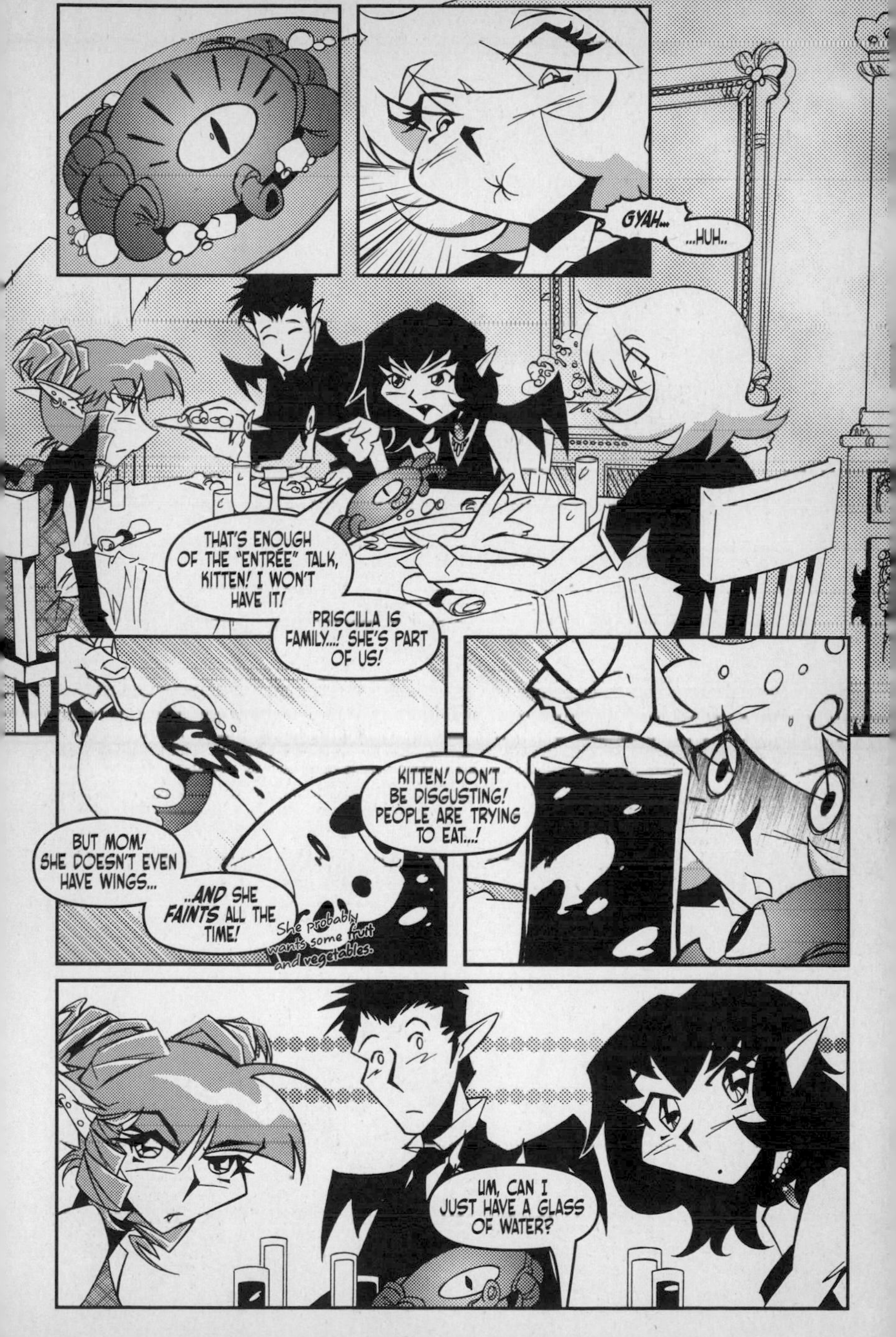
GYAH...
...HUH..
THAT'S ENOUGH OF THE "ENTRÉE" TALK, KITTEN! I WON'T HAVE IT!
PRISCILLA IS FAMILY...! SHE'S PART OF US!
BUT MOM! SHE DOESN'T EVEN HAVE WINGS...
...AND SHE FAINTS ALL THE TIME!
She probably wants some fruit and vegetables.
KITTEN! DON'T BE DISGUSTING! PEOPLE ARE TRYING TO EAT...!
UM, CAN I JUST HAVE A GLASS OF WATER?

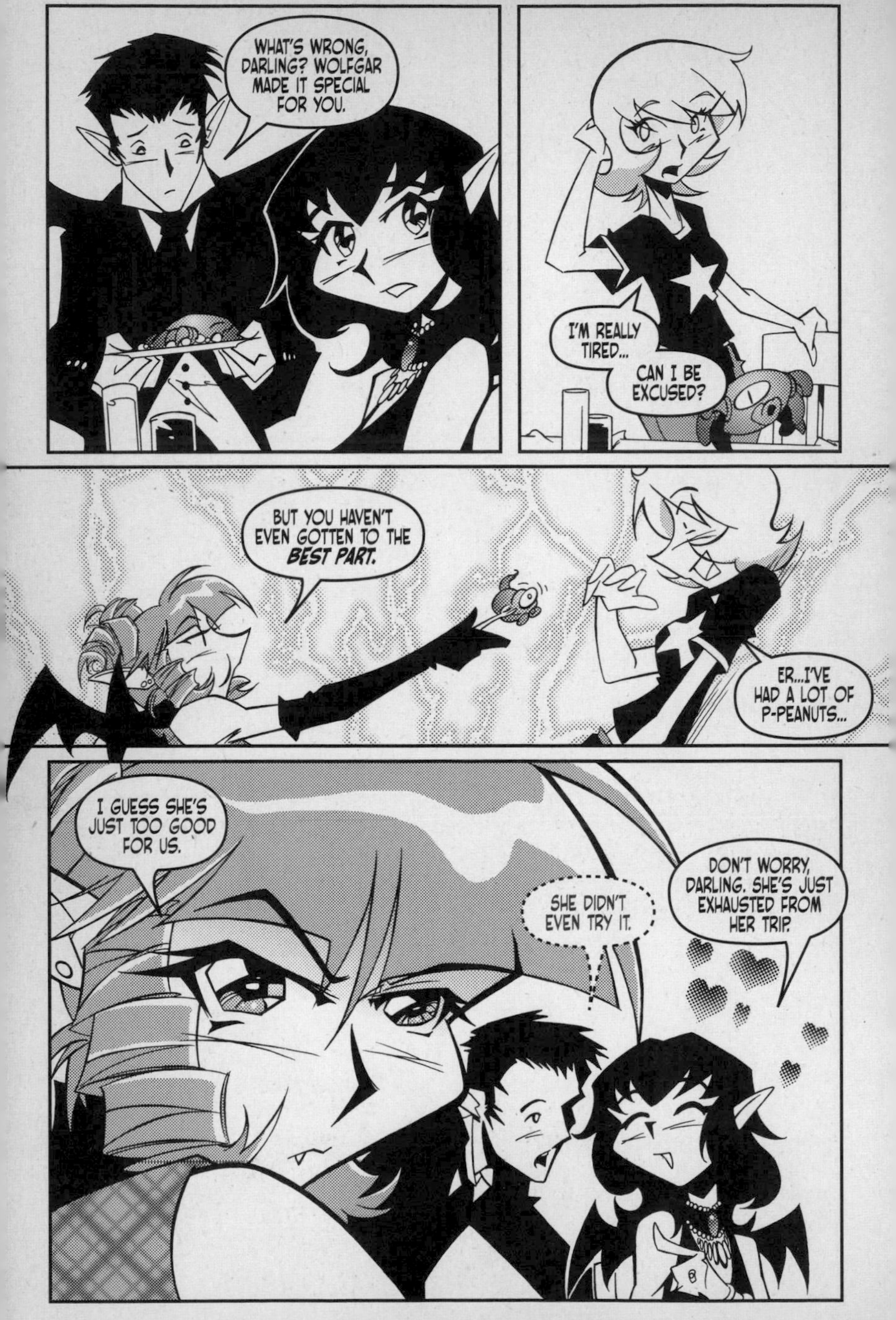
WHAT'S WRONG, DARLING? WOLFGAR MADE IT SPECIAL FOR YOU.
I'M REALLY TIRED...
CAN I BE EXCUSED?
BUT YOU HAVEN'T EVEN GOTTEN TO THE *BEST PART.*
ER...I'VE HAD A LOT OF P-PEANUTS...
I GUESS SHE'S JUST TOO GOOD FOR US.
SHE DIDN'T EVEN TRY IT.
DON'T WORRY, DARLING. SHE'S JUST EXHAUSTED FROM HER TRIP.

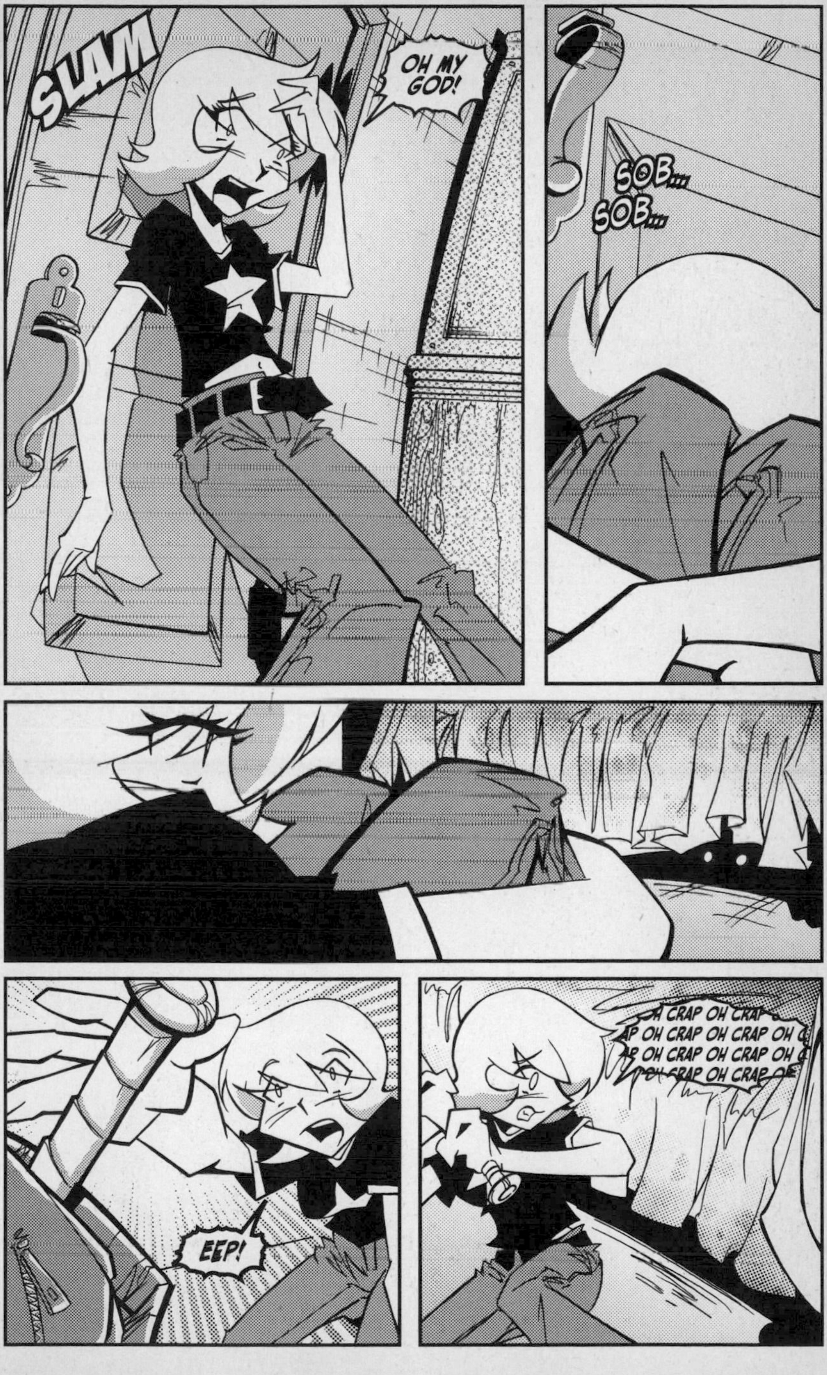
SLAM
OH MY GOD!
SOB... SOB...
EEP!
CRAP OH CRAP
OH CRAP OH CRAP OH
OH CRAP OH CRAP OH
CRAP OH CRAP

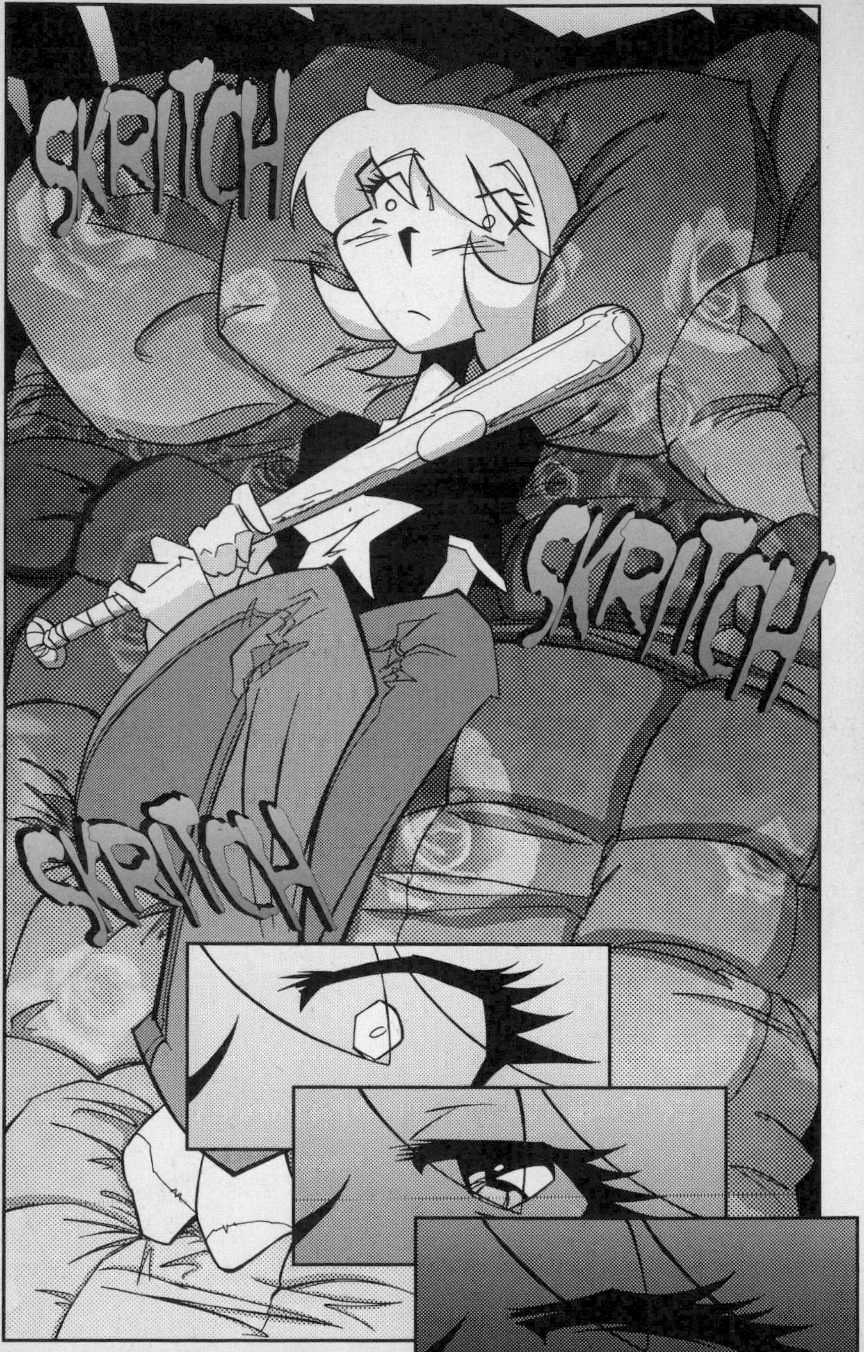
SKRITCH
SKRITCH
SKRITCH

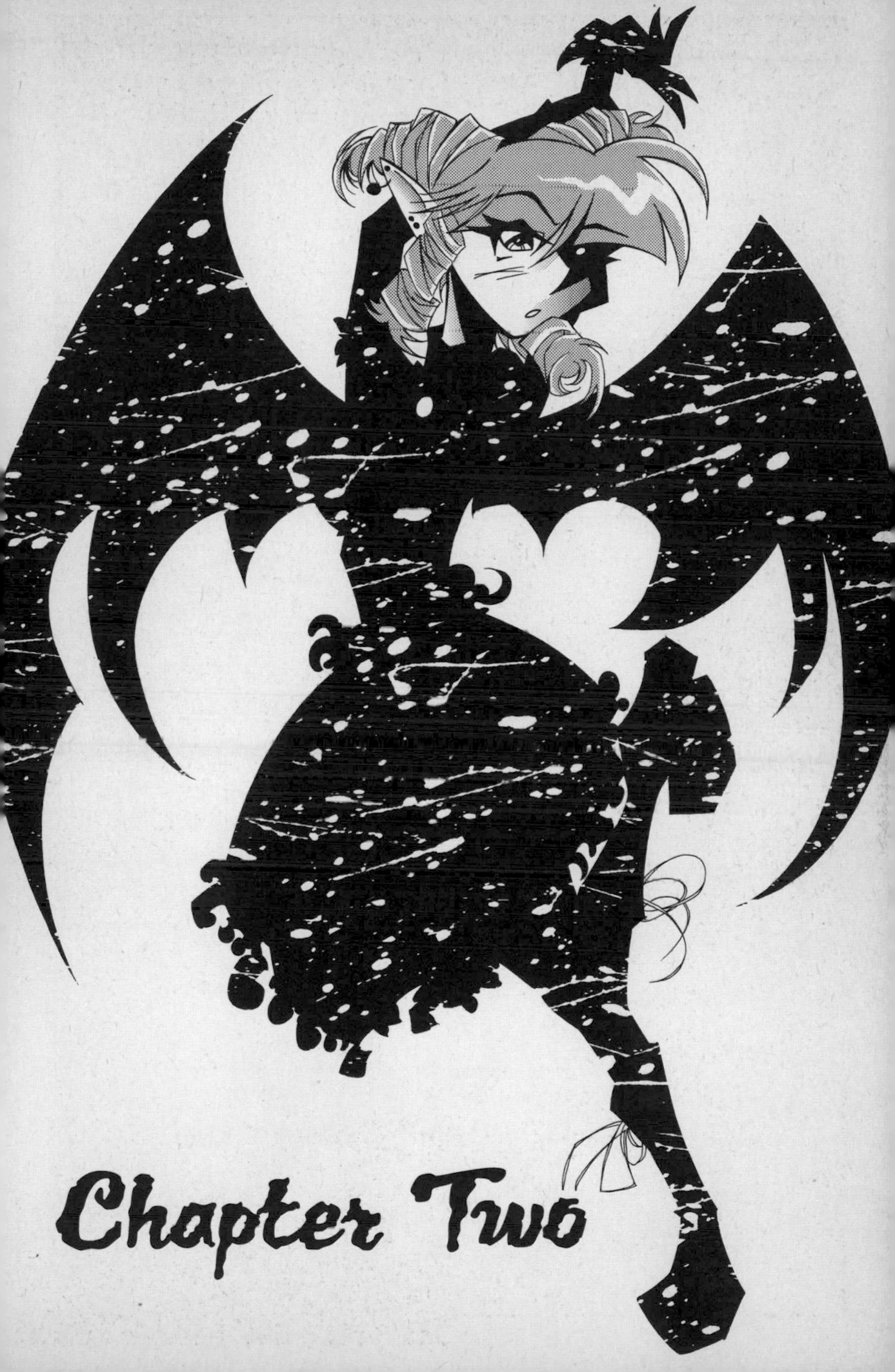

Chapter Two

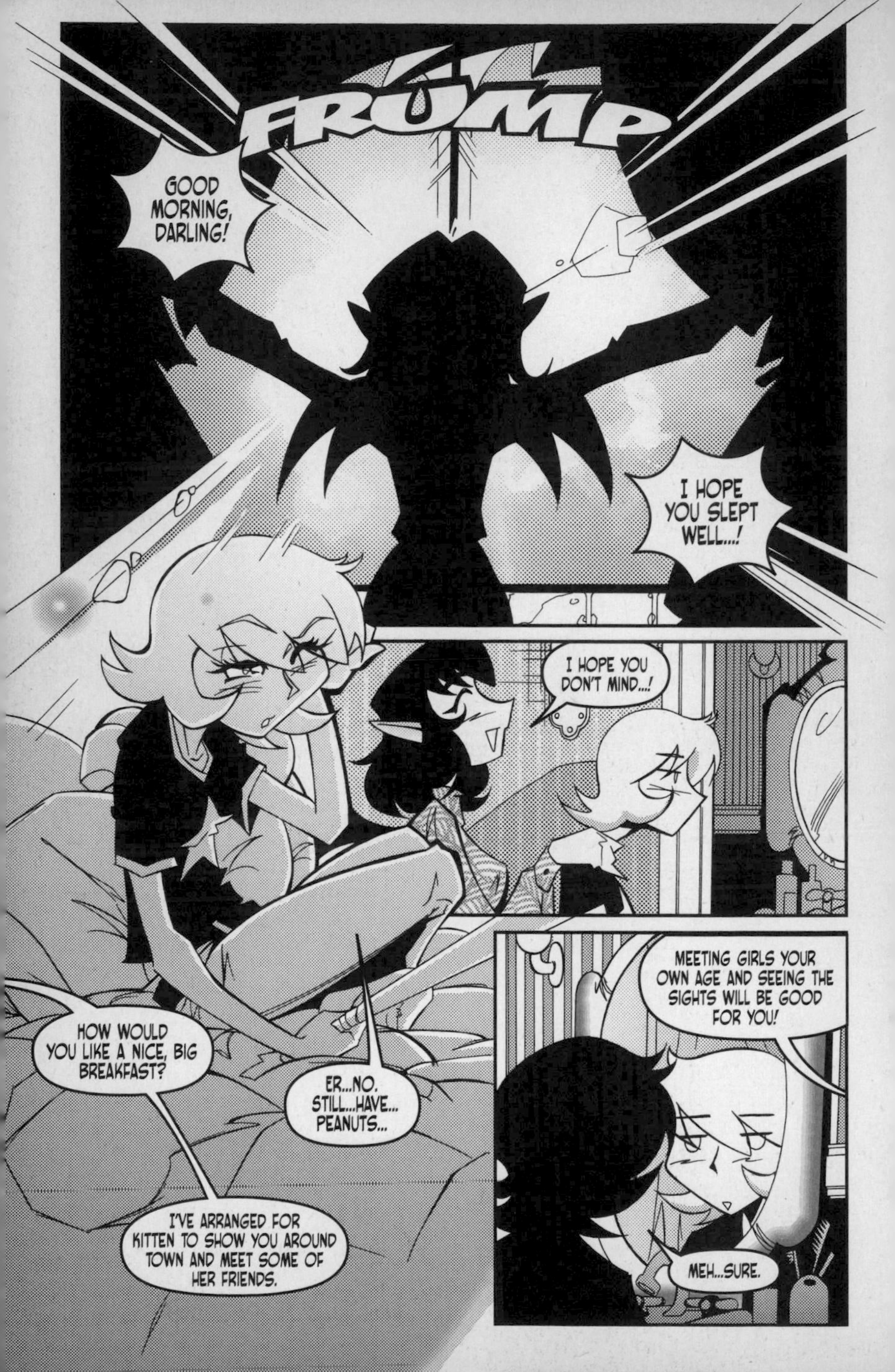
FRUMP
GOOD MORNING, DARLING!
I HOPE YOU SLEPT WELL...!
I HOPE YOU DON'T MIND...!
HOW WOULD YOU LIKE A NICE, BIG BREAKFAST?
ER...NO. STILL...HAVE... PEANUTS...
I'VE ARRANGED FOR KITTEN TO SHOW YOU AROUND TOWN AND MEET SOME OF HER FRIENDS.
MEETING GIRLS YOUR OWN AGE AND SEEING THE SIGHTS WILL BE GOOD FOR YOU!
MEH...SURE.

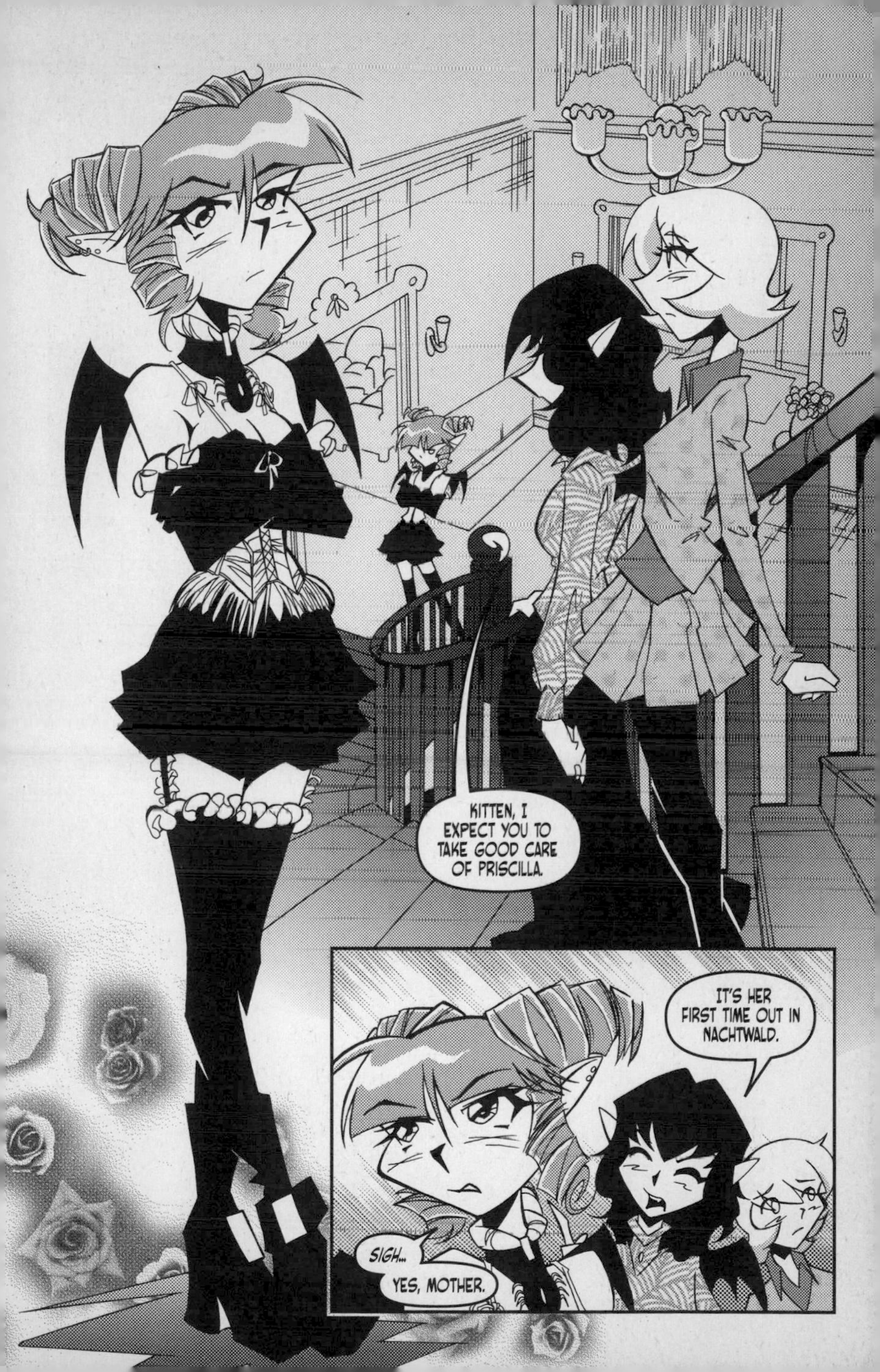
KITTEN, I EXPECT YOU TO TAKE GOOD CARE OF PRISCILLA.
IT'S HER FIRST TIME OUT IN NACHTWALD.
SIGH...
YES, MOTHER.

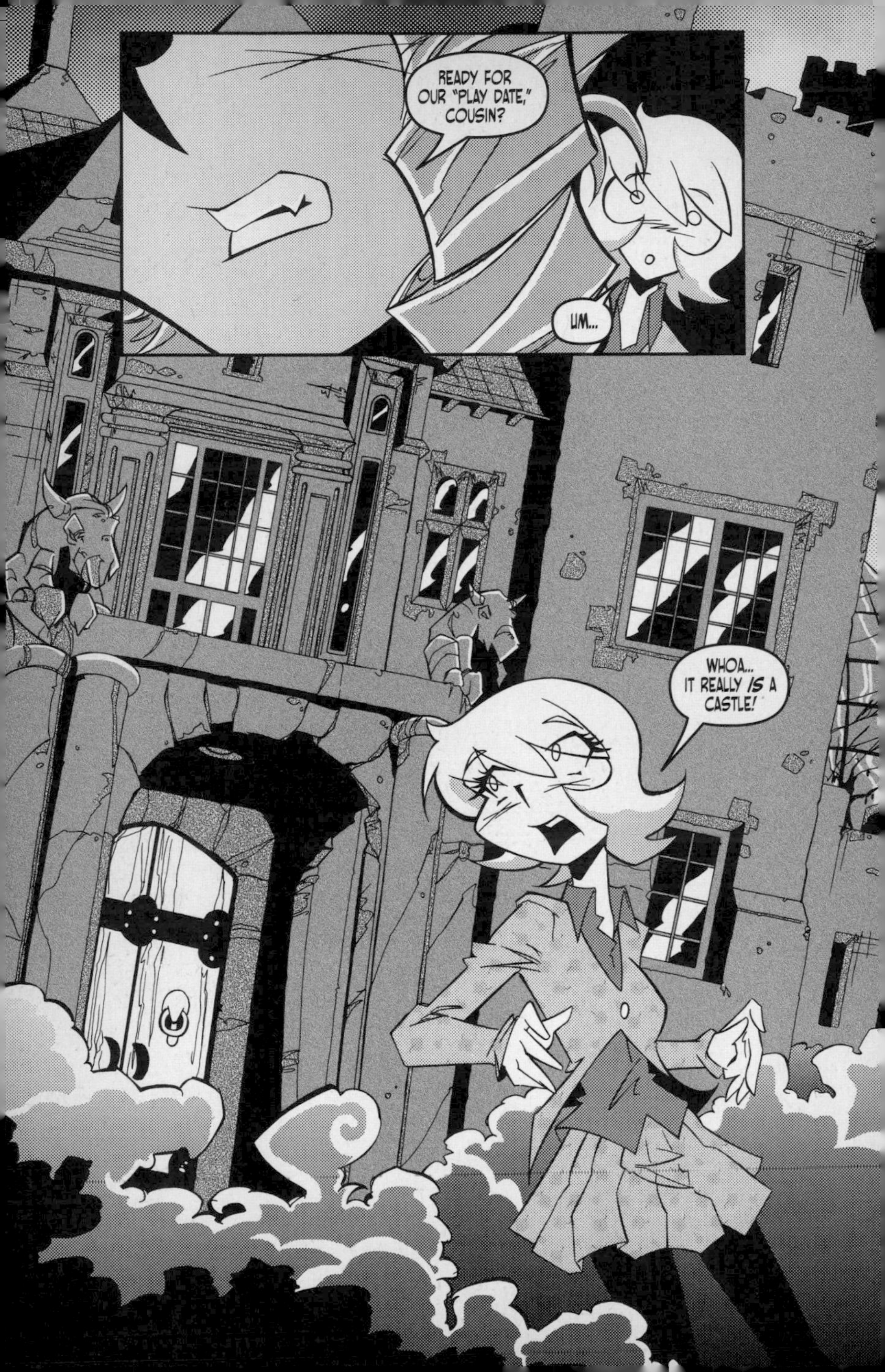
READY FOR OUR "PLAY DATE," COUSIN?
UM...
WHOA... IT REALLY *IS* A CASTLE!

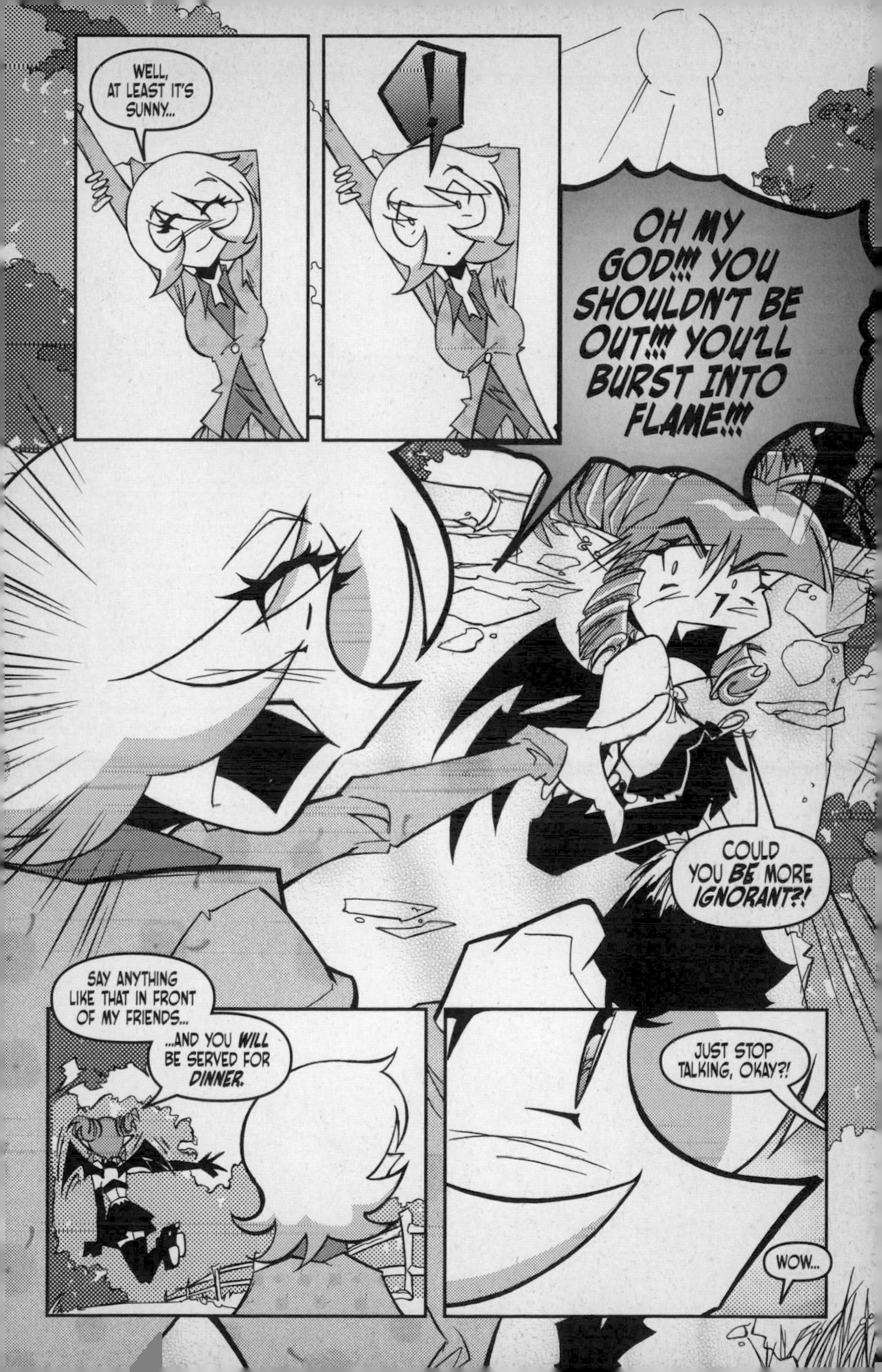
WELL, AT LEAST IT'S SUNNY...
!
OH MY GOD!!! YOU SHOULDN'T BE OUT!!! YOU'LL BURST INTO FLAME!!!
COULD YOU BE MORE IGNORANT?!
SAY ANYTHING LIKE THAT IN FRONT OF MY FRIENDS...
...AND YOU WILL BE SERVED FOR DINNER.
JUST STOP TALKING, OKAY?!
WOW...

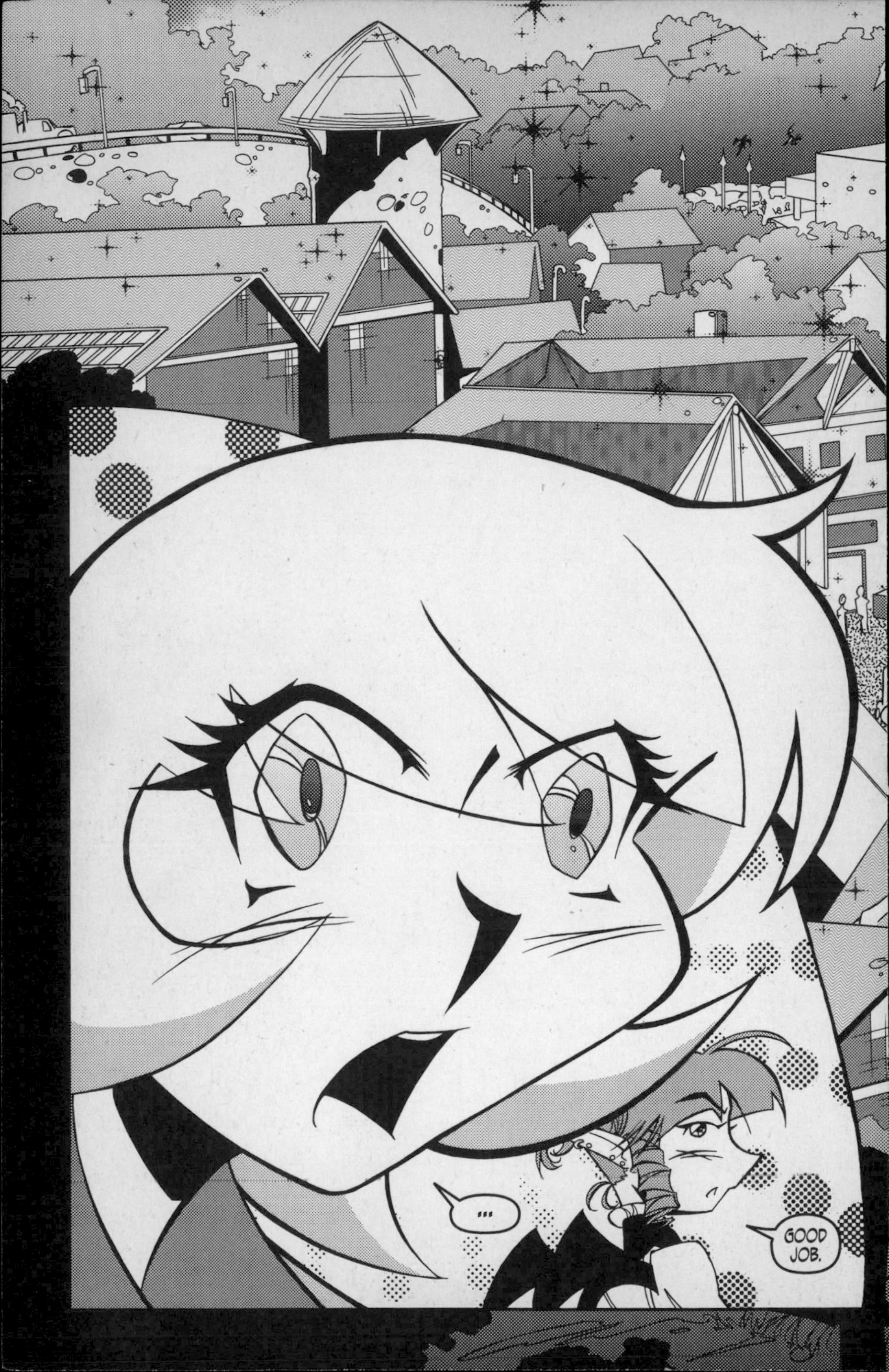
...
GOOD JOB.

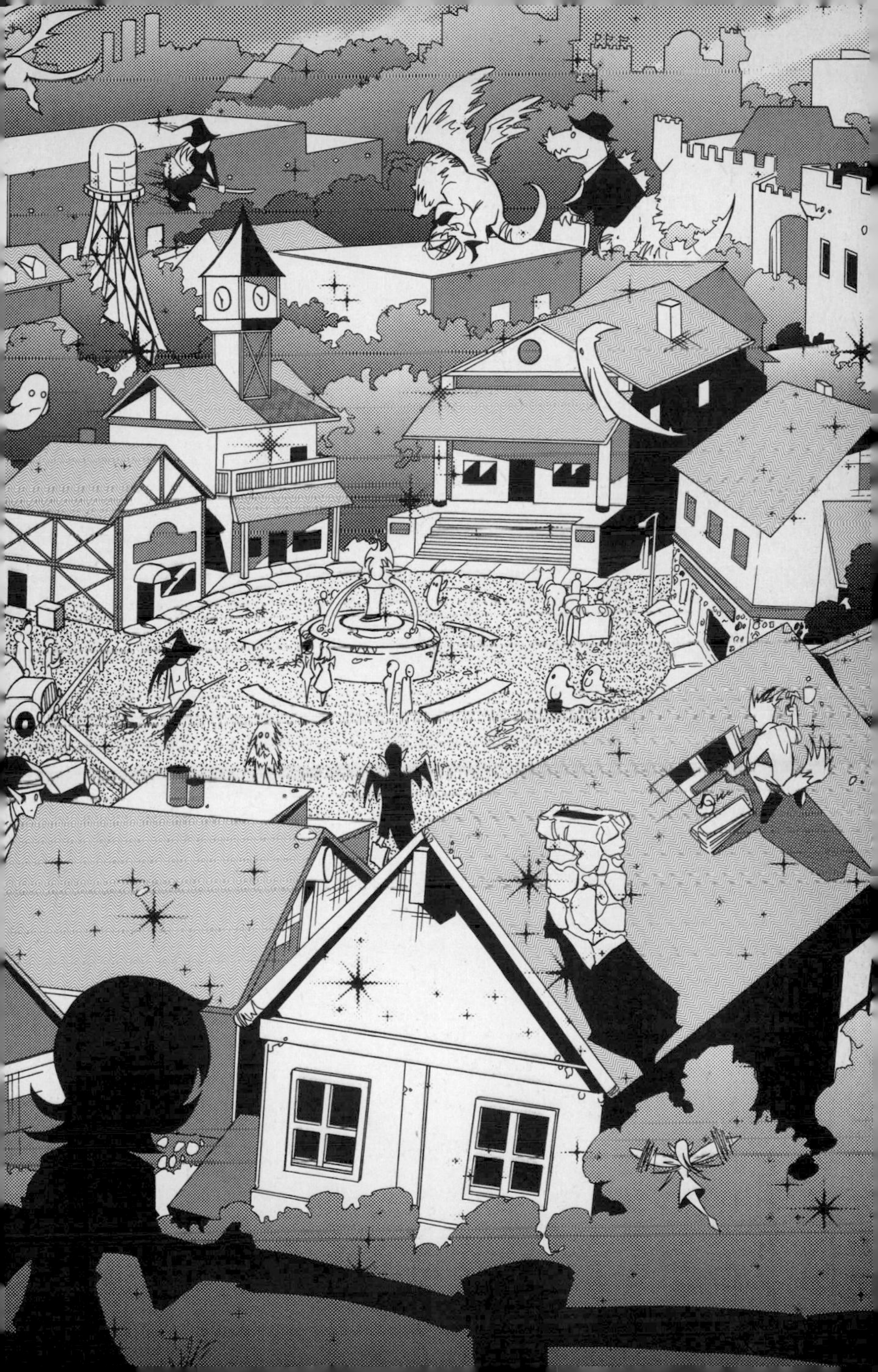

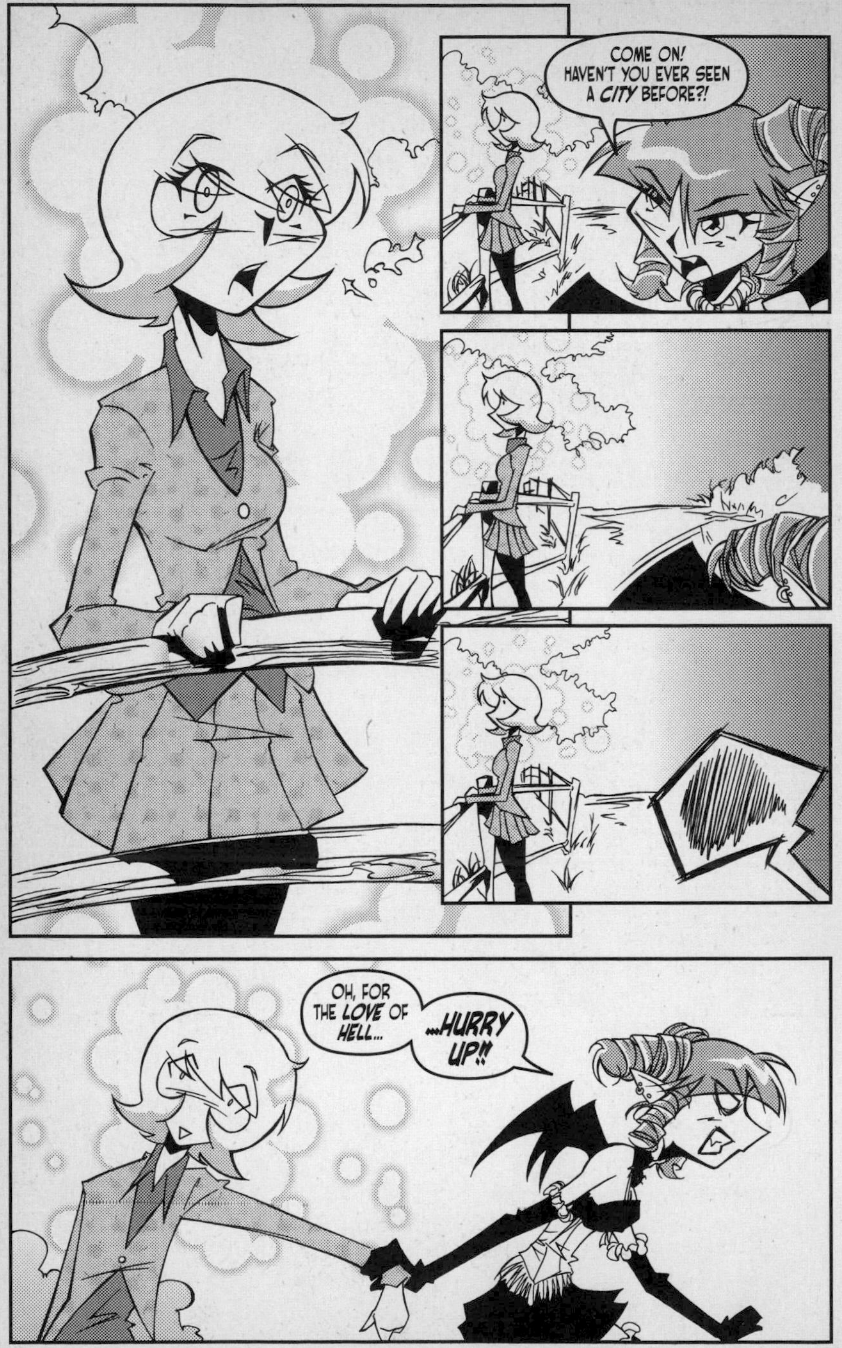
COME ON! HAVEN'T YOU EVER SEEN A *CITY* BEFORE?!
OH, FOR THE *LOVE* OF *HELL*...
...HURRY UP!!

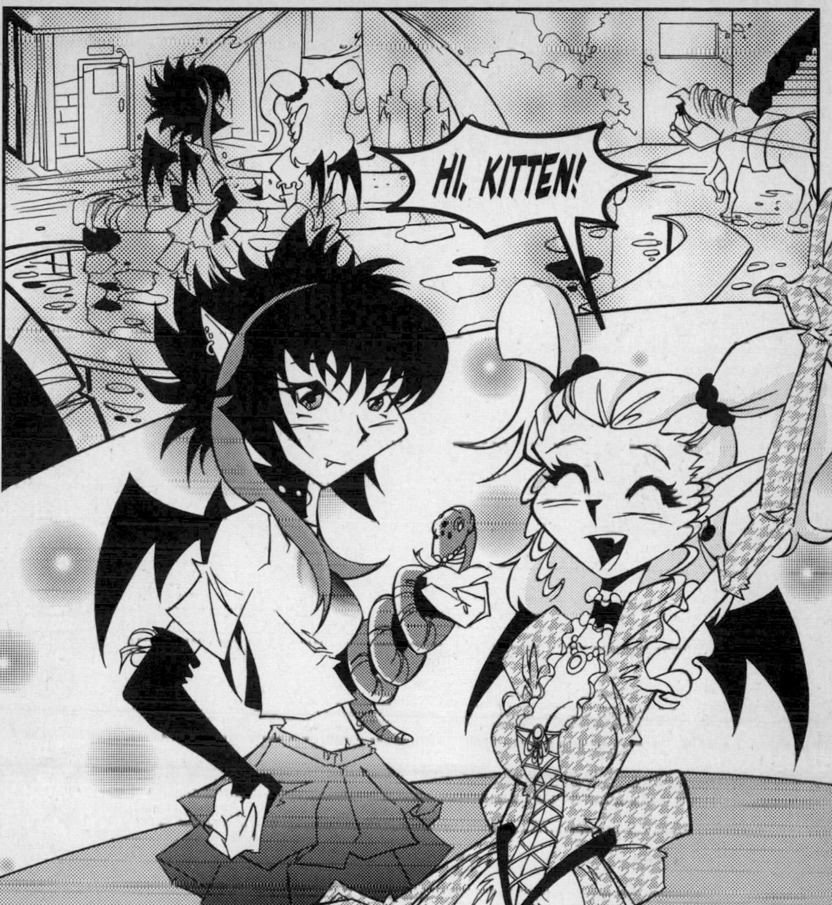
HI, KITTEN!

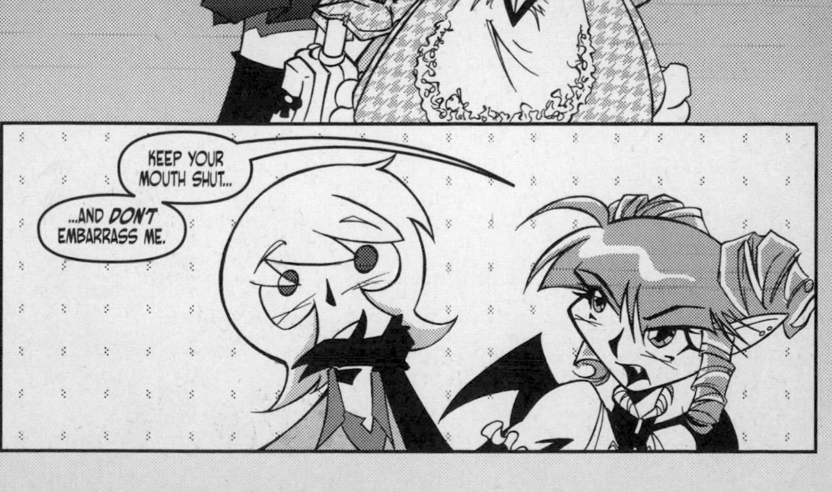
KEEP YOUR MOUTH SHUT...
...AND DON'T EMBARRASS ME.

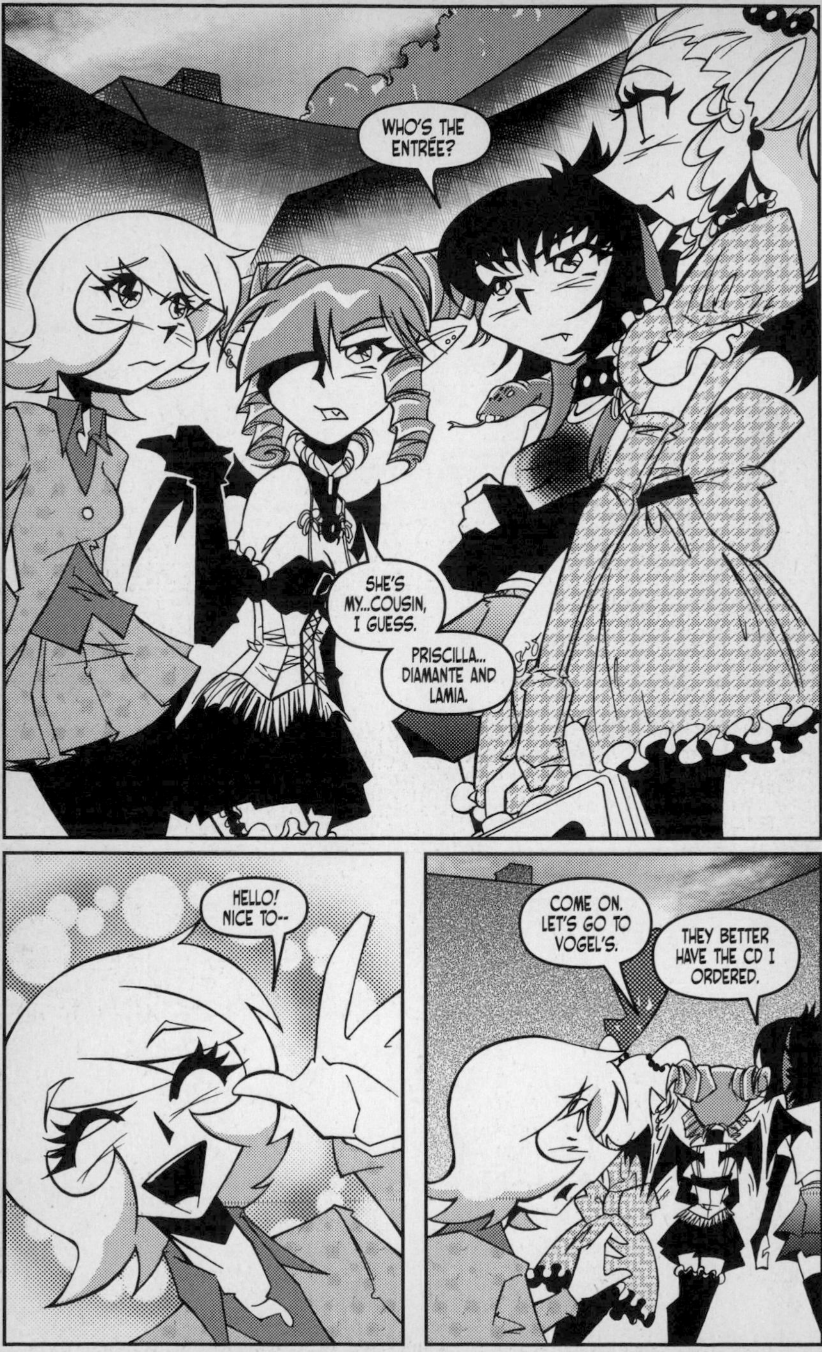
WHO'S THE ENTRÉE?
SHE'S MY...COUSIN, I GUESS.
PRISCILLA... DIAMANTE AND LAMIA.
HELLO! NICE TO--
COME ON. LET'S GO TO VOGEL'S.
THEY BETTER HAVE THE CD I ORDERED.

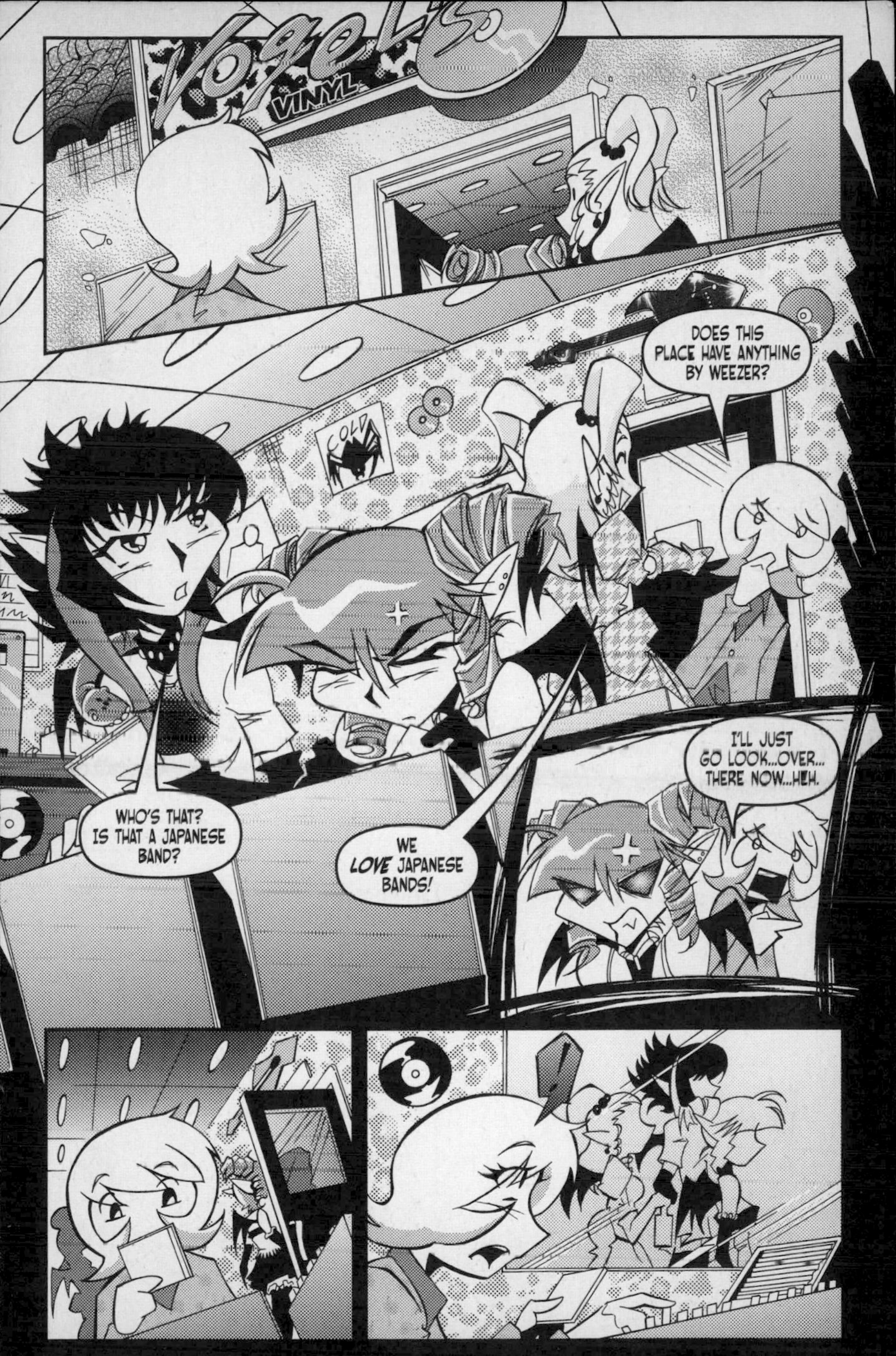
VOGEL'S
VINYL
DOES THIS PLACE HAVE ANYTHING BY WEEZER?
COLD
WHO'S THAT? IS THAT A JAPANESE BAND?
WE *LOVE* JAPANESE BANDS!
I'LL JUST GO LOOK...OVER... THERE NOW...HEH.

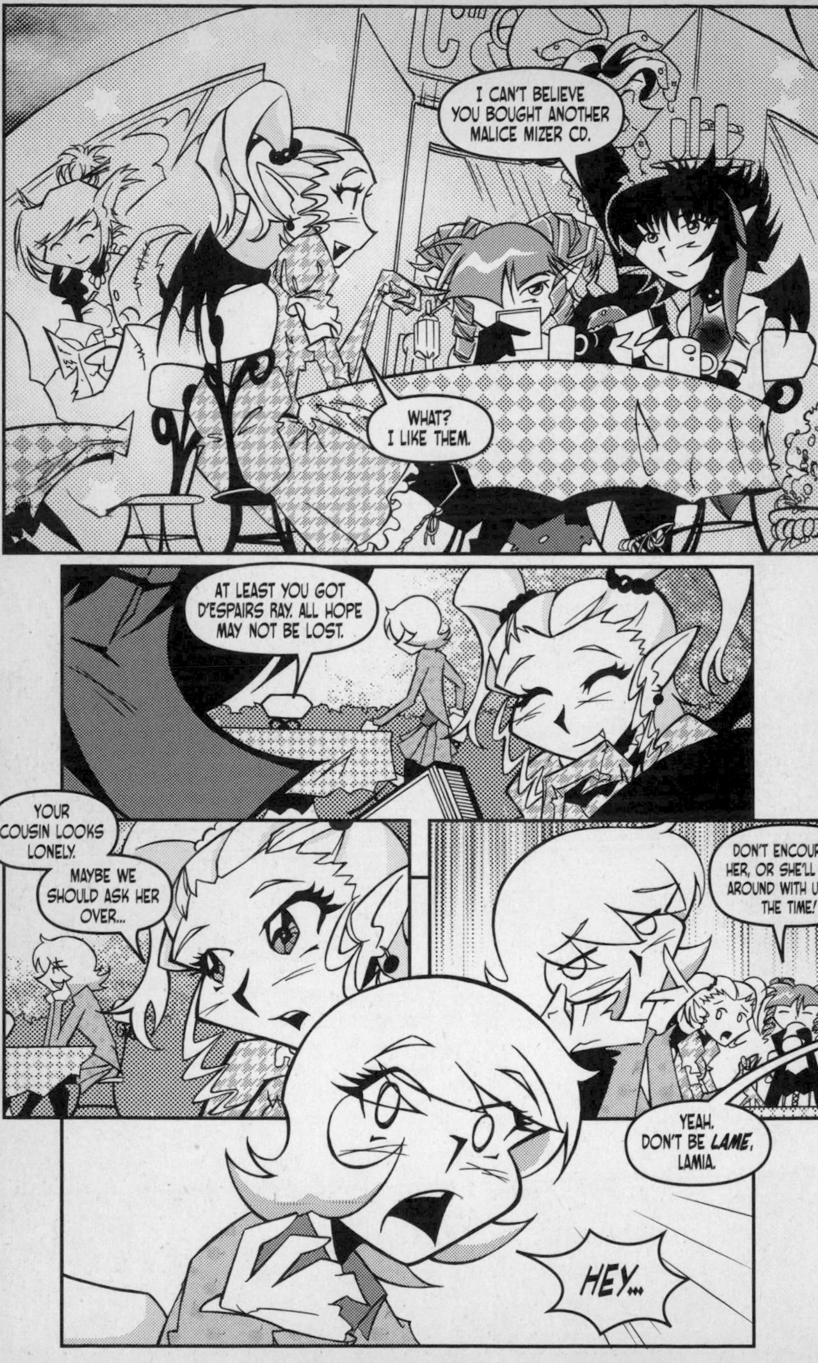
I CAN'T BELIEVE YOU BOUGHT ANOTHER MALICE MIZER CD.
WHAT? I LIKE THEM.
AT LEAST YOU GOT D'ESPAIRS RAY. ALL HOPE MAY NOT BE LOST.
YOUR COUSIN LOOKS LONELY.
MAYBE WE SHOULD ASK HER OVER...
DON'T ENCOURAGE HER, OR SHE'LL HANG AROUND WITH US ALL THE TIME!
YEAH. DON'T BE *LAME*, LAMIA.
HEY...

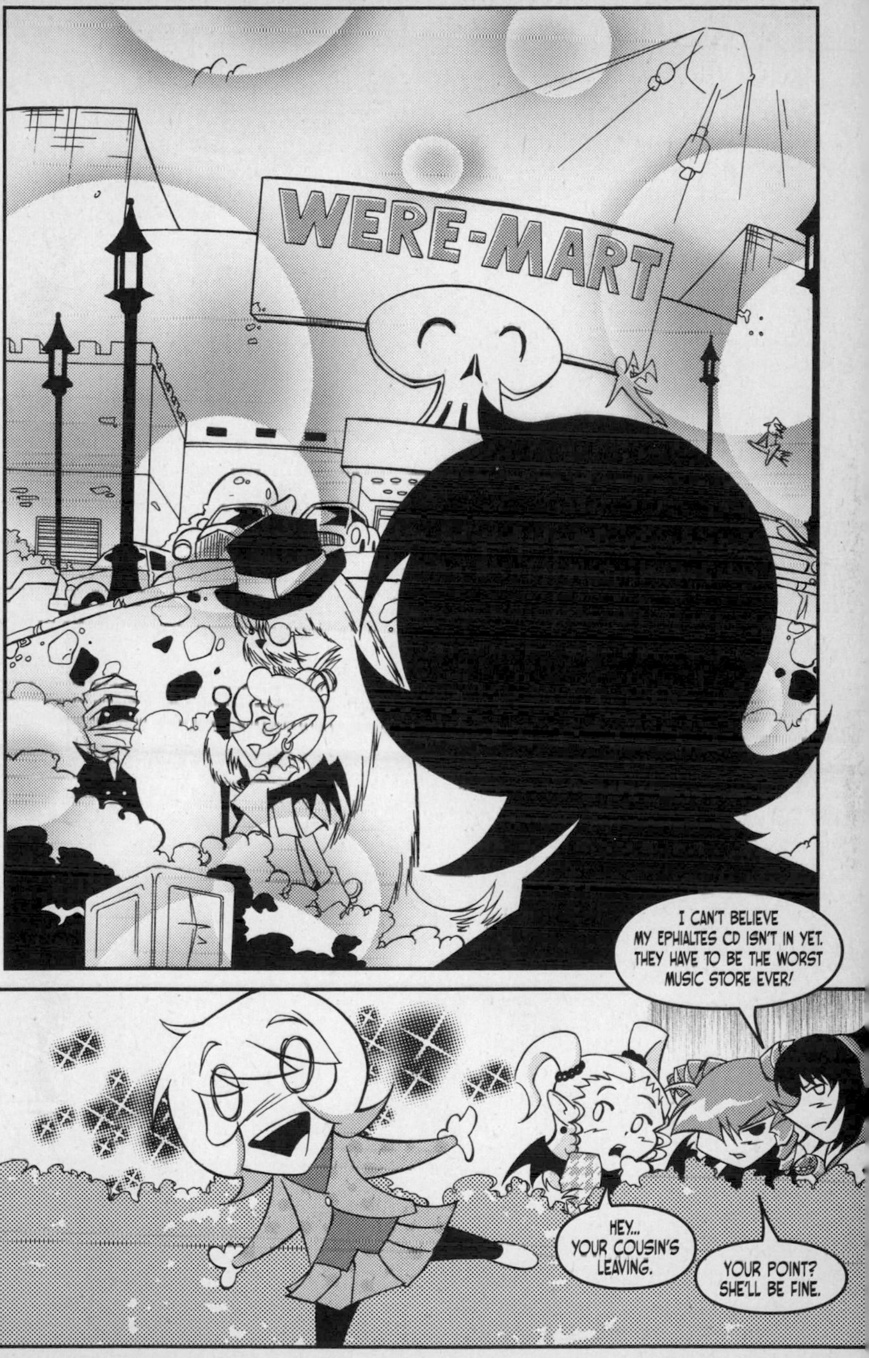
WERE-MART
I CAN'T BELIEVE MY EPHIALTES CD ISN'T IN YET. THEY HAVE TO BE THE WORST MUSIC STORE EVER!
HEY... YOUR COUSIN'S LEAVING.
YOUR POINT? SHE'LL BE FINE.

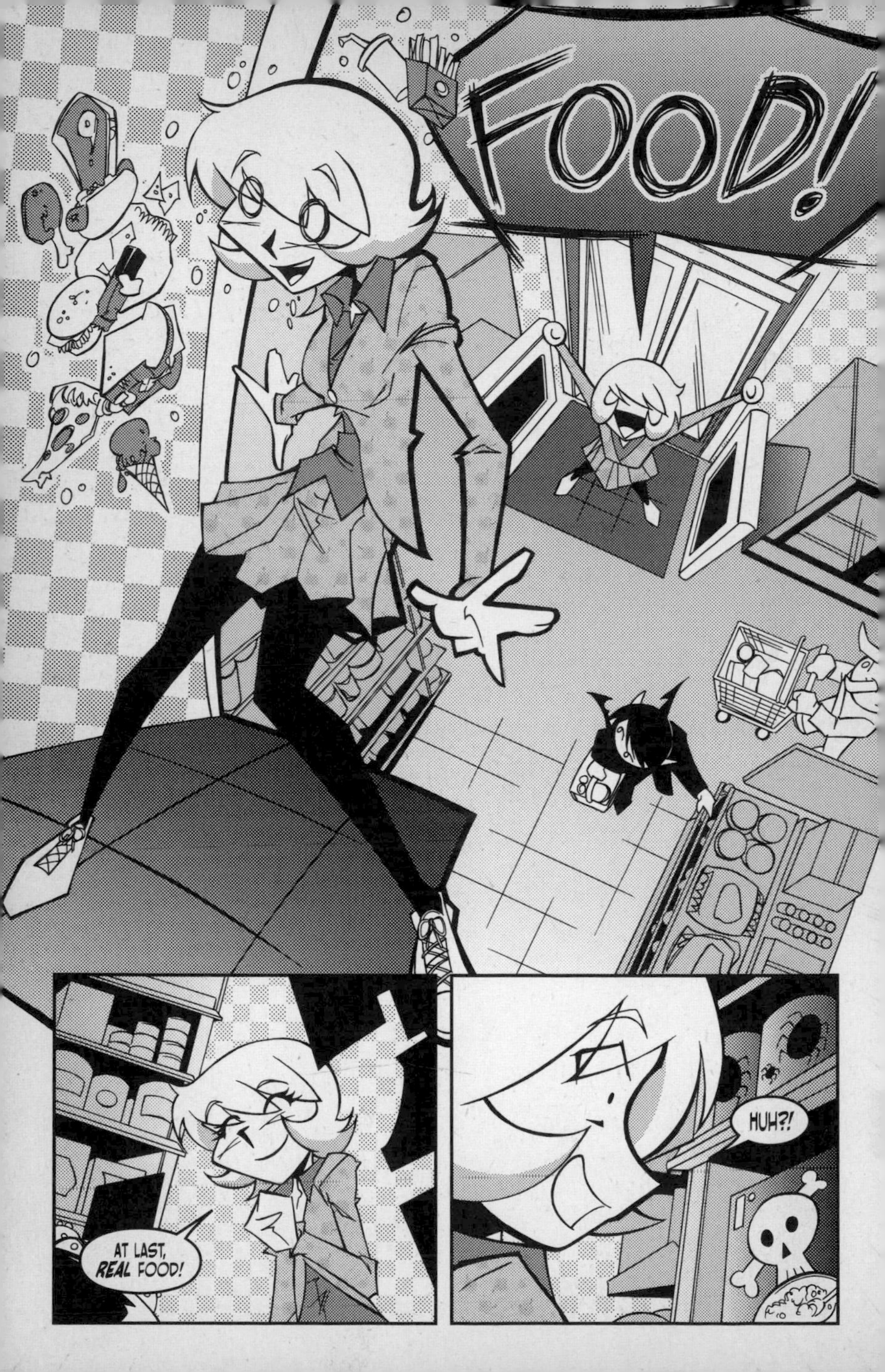
FOOD!
AT LAST, REAL FOOD!
HUH?!

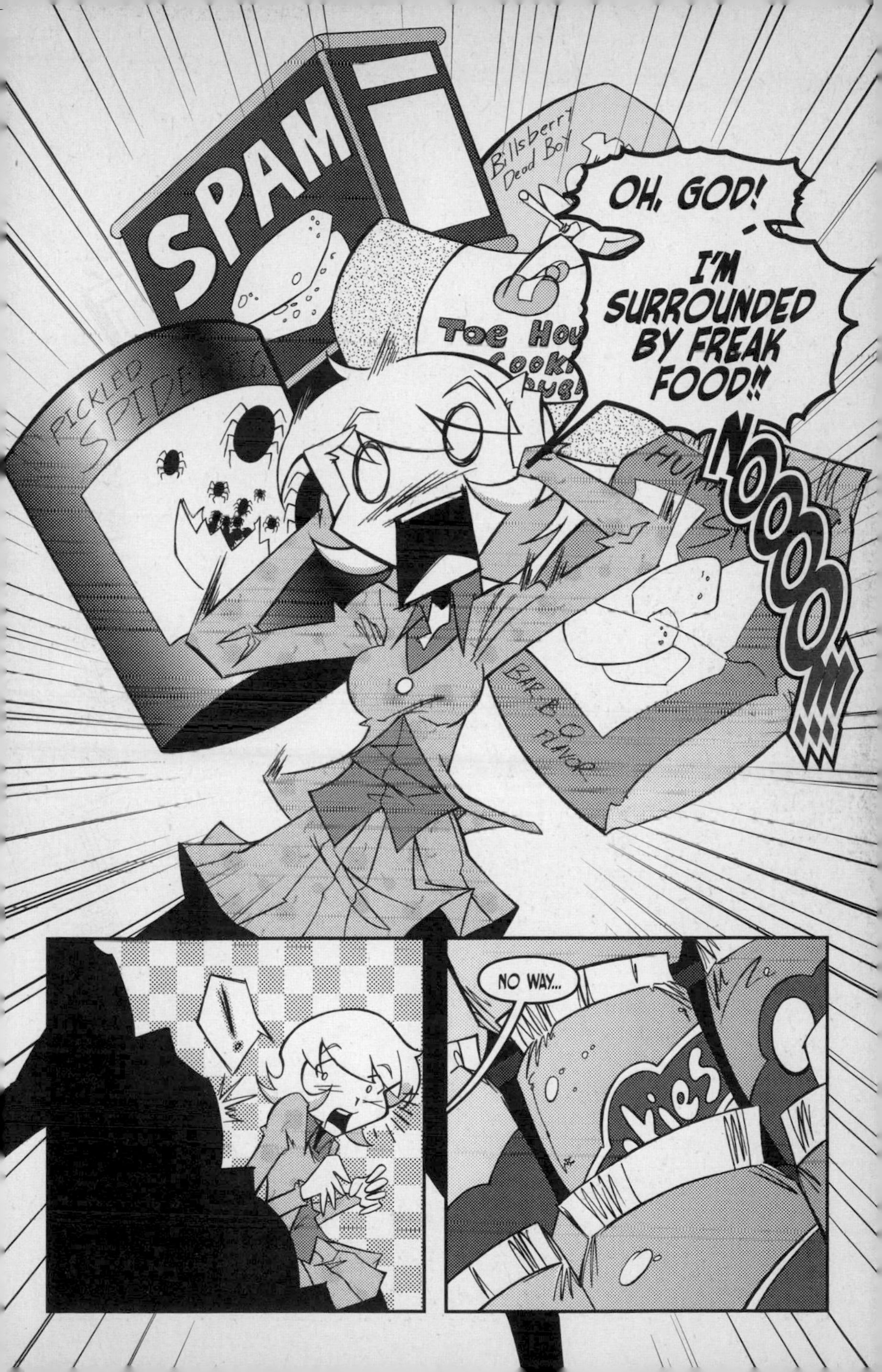
SPAM
Billsberry Dead Boy
Pickled
OH, GOD!
I'M SURROUNDED BY FREAK FOOD!!
NOOOOO!!
!
NO WAY...

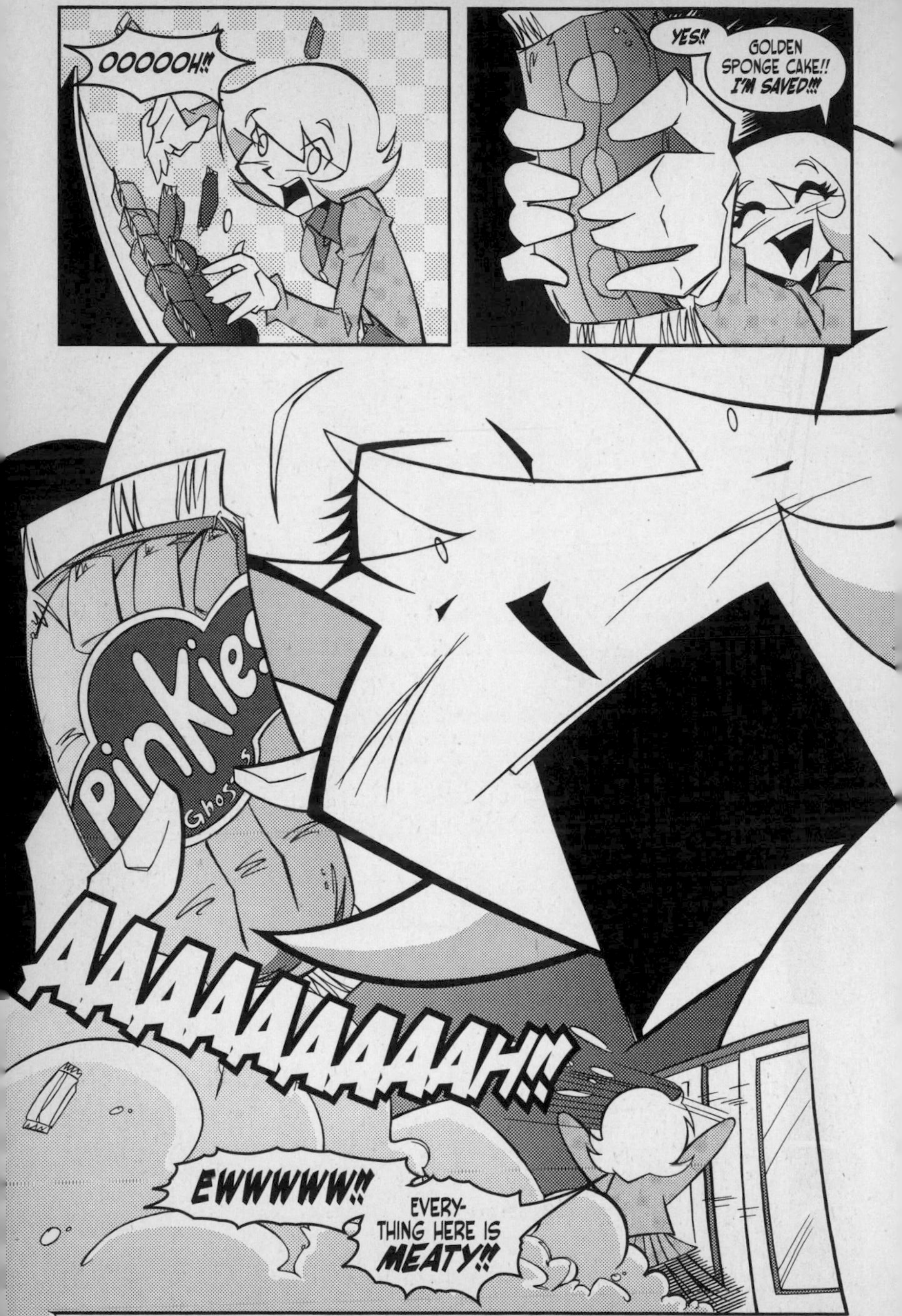

OOOOOH!!
YES!!
GOLDEN SPONGE CAKE!! I'M SAVED!!!
Pinkies
AAAAAAAAAH!!
EWWWWW!!
EVERY-THING HERE IS MEATY!!

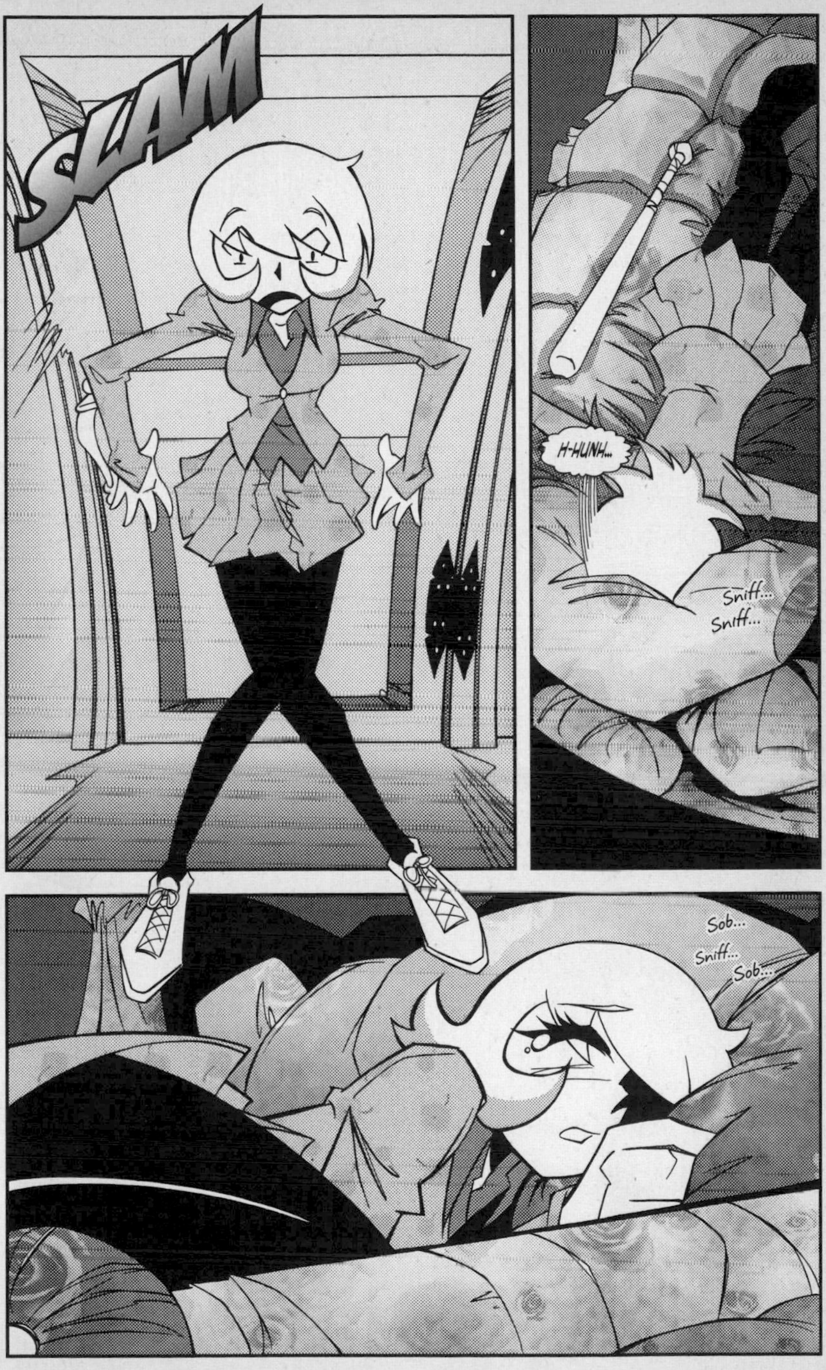
SLAM
H-HUNH...
Sniff...
Sniff...
Sob...
Sniff...
Sob...

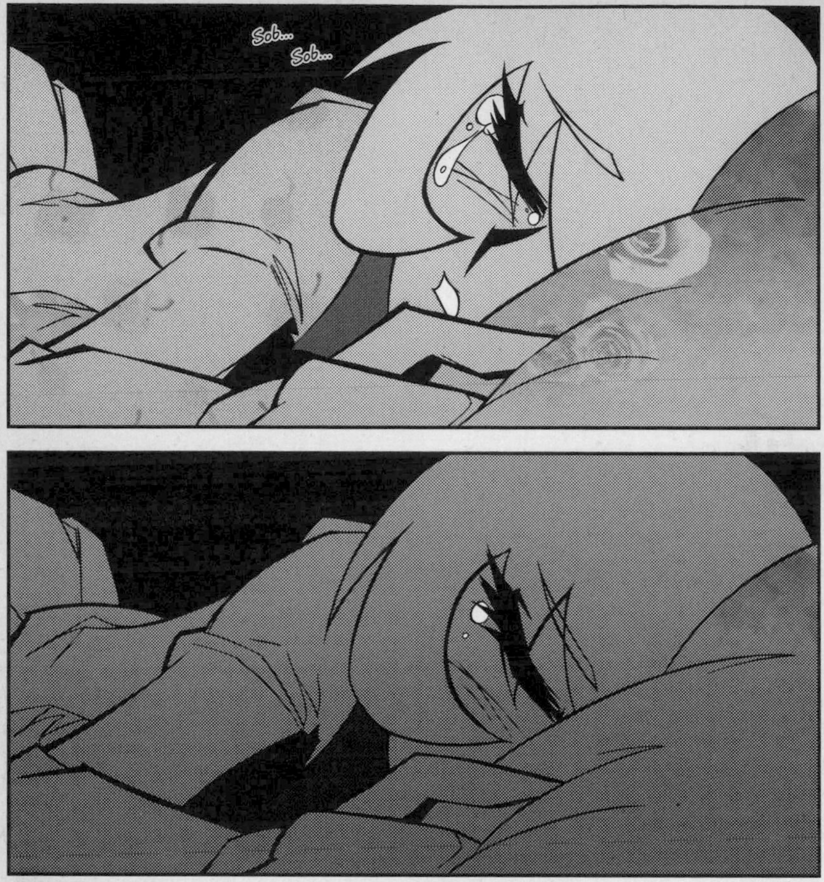
Sob…
Sob…

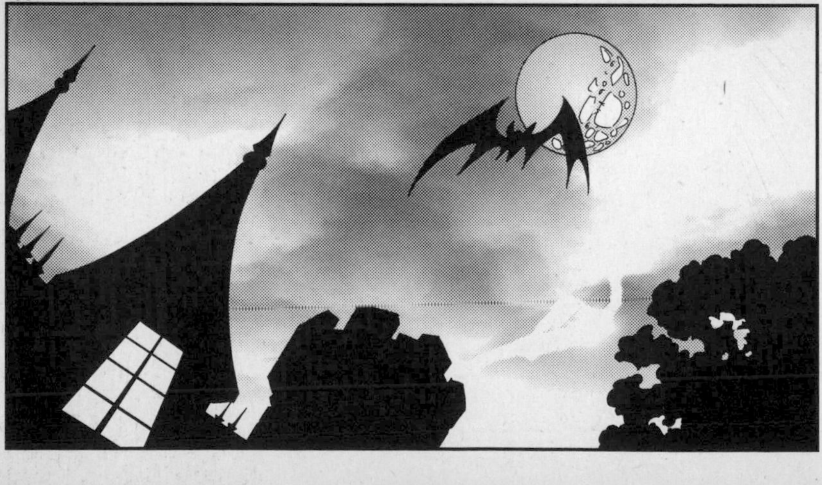

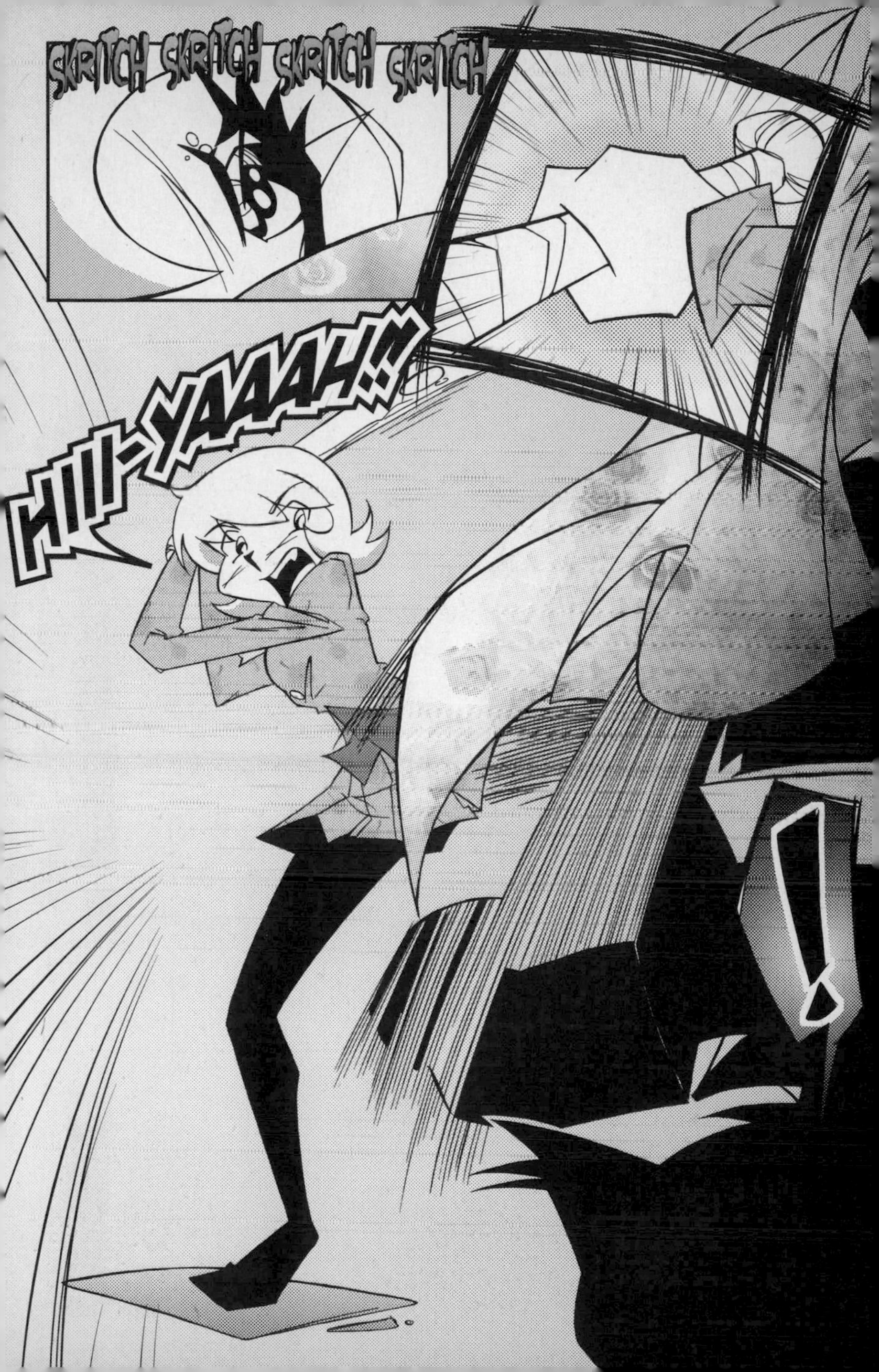
SKRITCH SKRITCH SKRITCH SKRITCH
HIII-YAAAAH!!
!

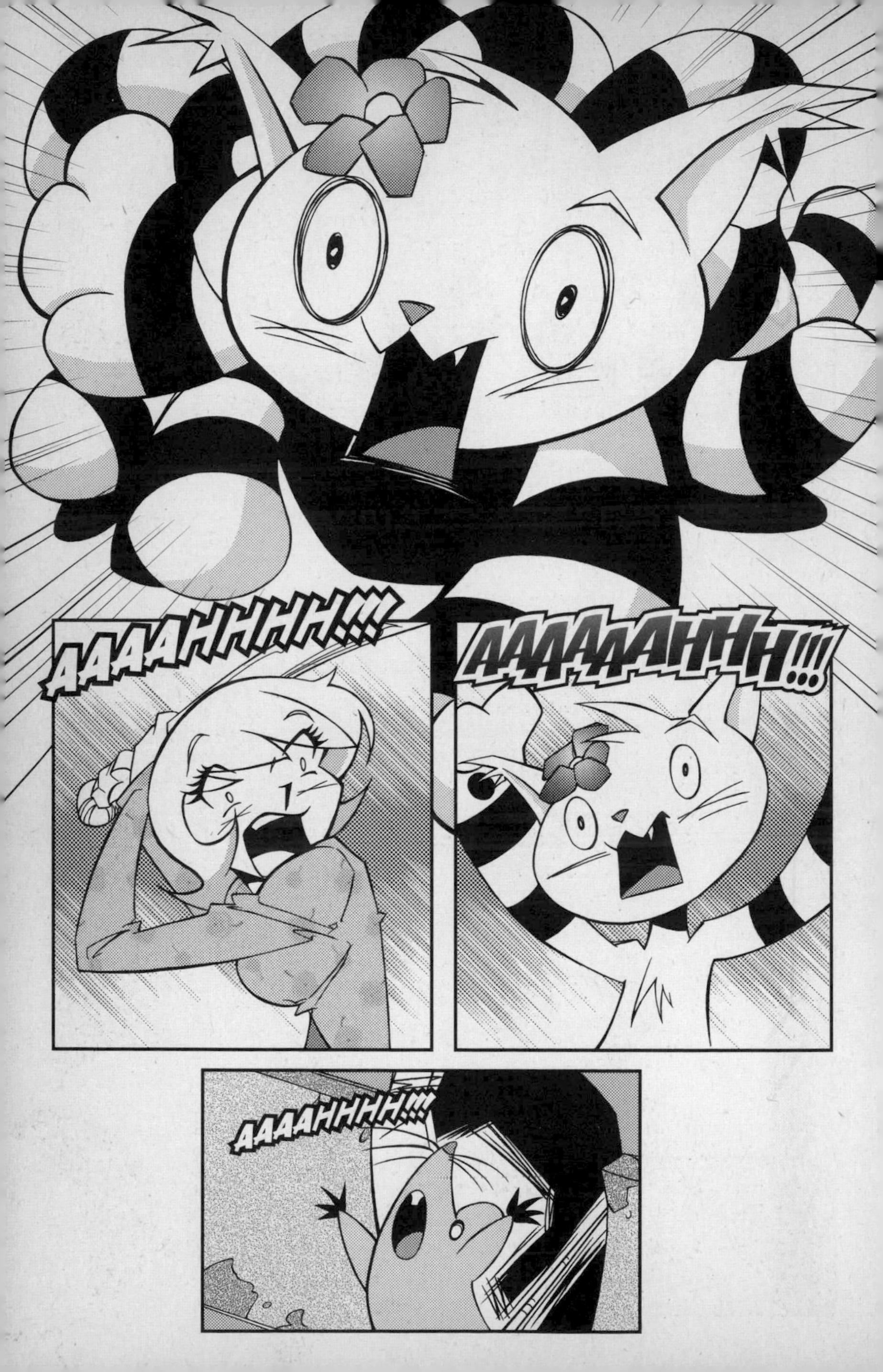
AAAAHHHHH!!!
AAAAAAAHHHH!!!
AAAAHHHH!!!

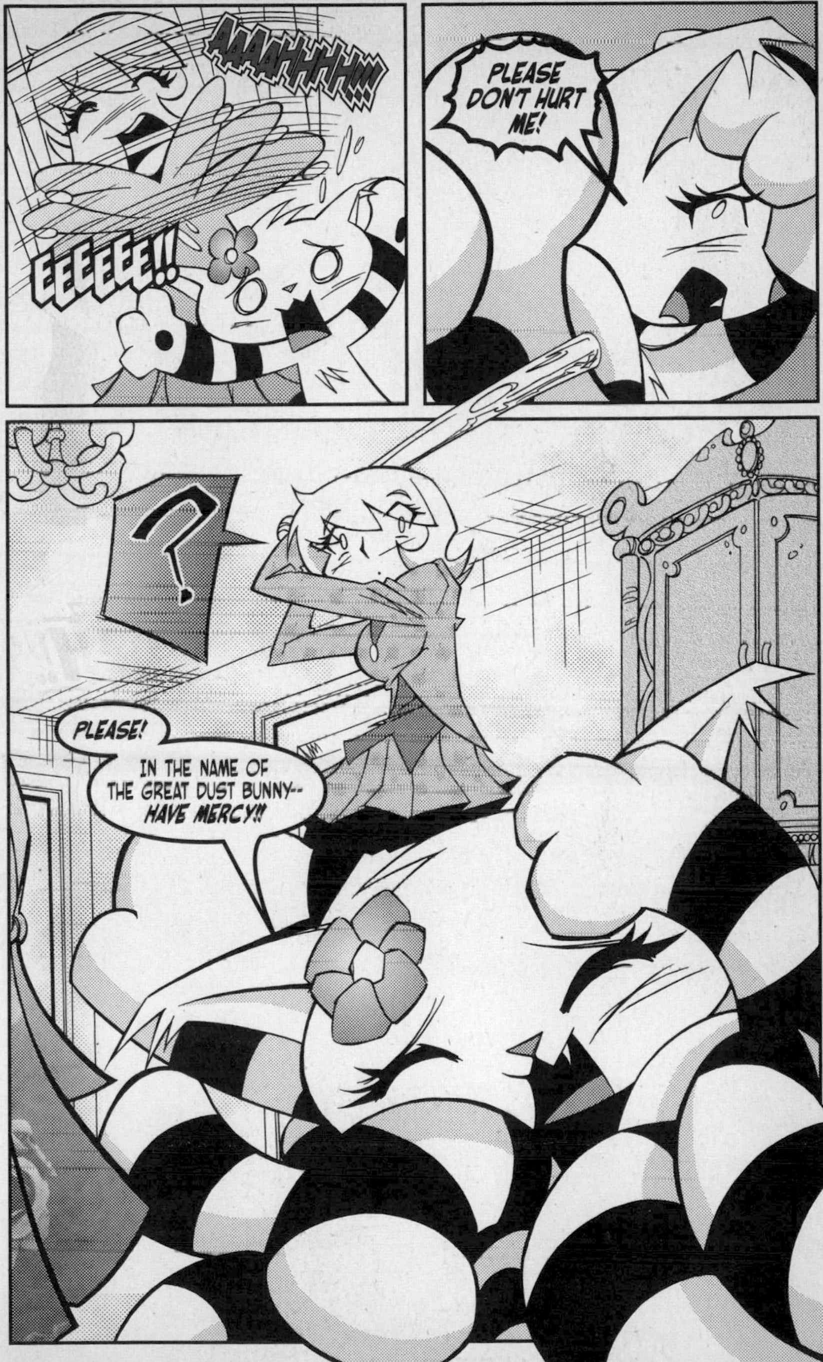
AAAAHHHH!!!
EEEEEE!!
PLEASE DON'T HURT ME!
?
PLEASE!
IN THE NAME OF THE GREAT DUST BUNNY-- HAVE MERCY!!

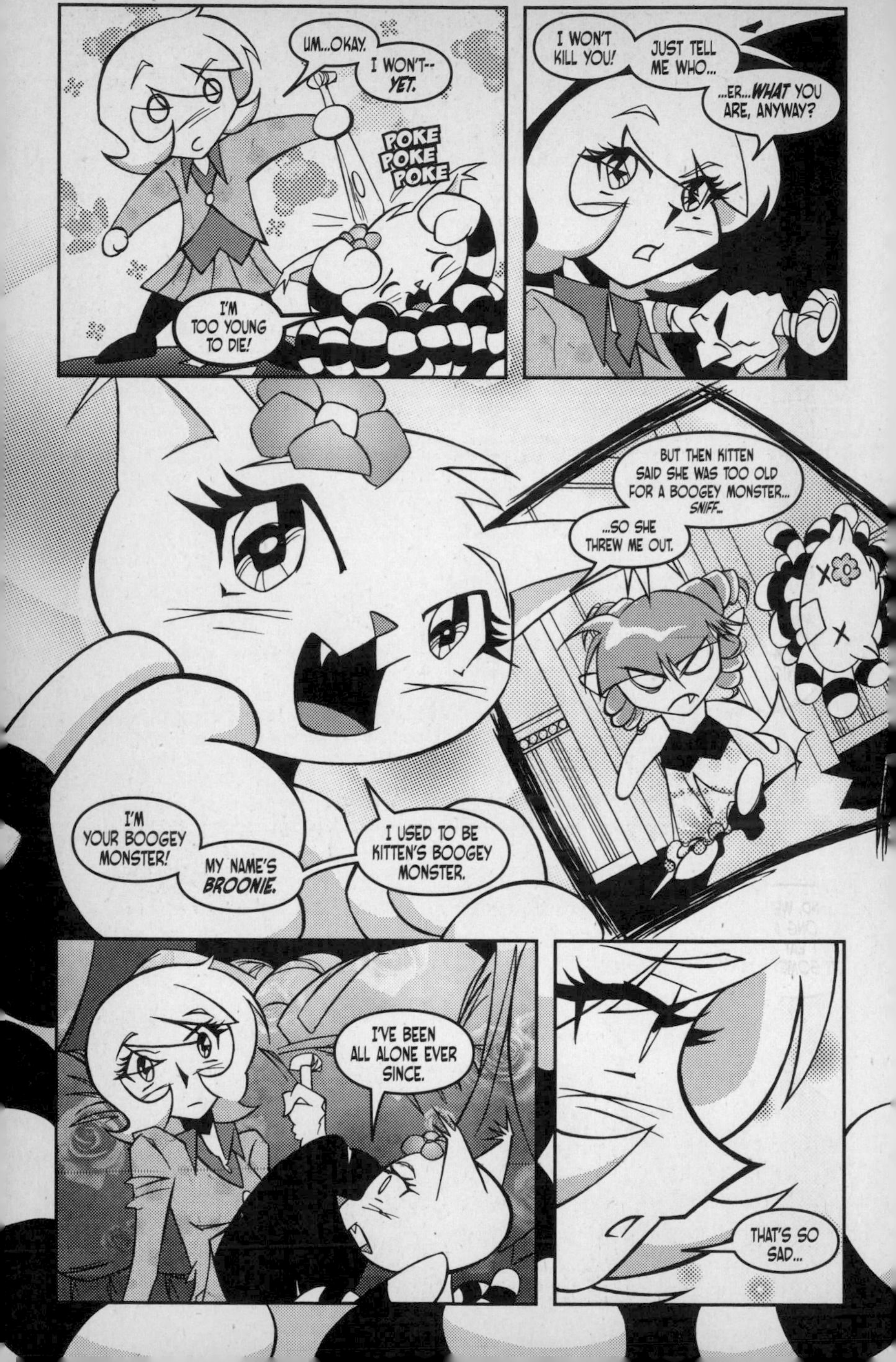
UM...OKAY.
I WON'T--
YET.
POKE POKE POKE
I'M TOO YOUNG TO DIE!
I WON'T KILL YOU!
JUST TELL ME WHO...
...ER...WHAT YOU ARE, ANYWAY?
I'M YOUR BOOGEY MONSTER!
MY NAME'S BROONIE.
I USED TO BE KITTEN'S BOOGEY MONSTER.
BUT THEN KITTEN SAID SHE WAS TOO OLD FOR A BOOGEY MONSTER... SNIFF...
...SO SHE THREW ME OUT.
I'VE BEEN ALL ALONE EVER SINCE.
THAT'S SO SAD...

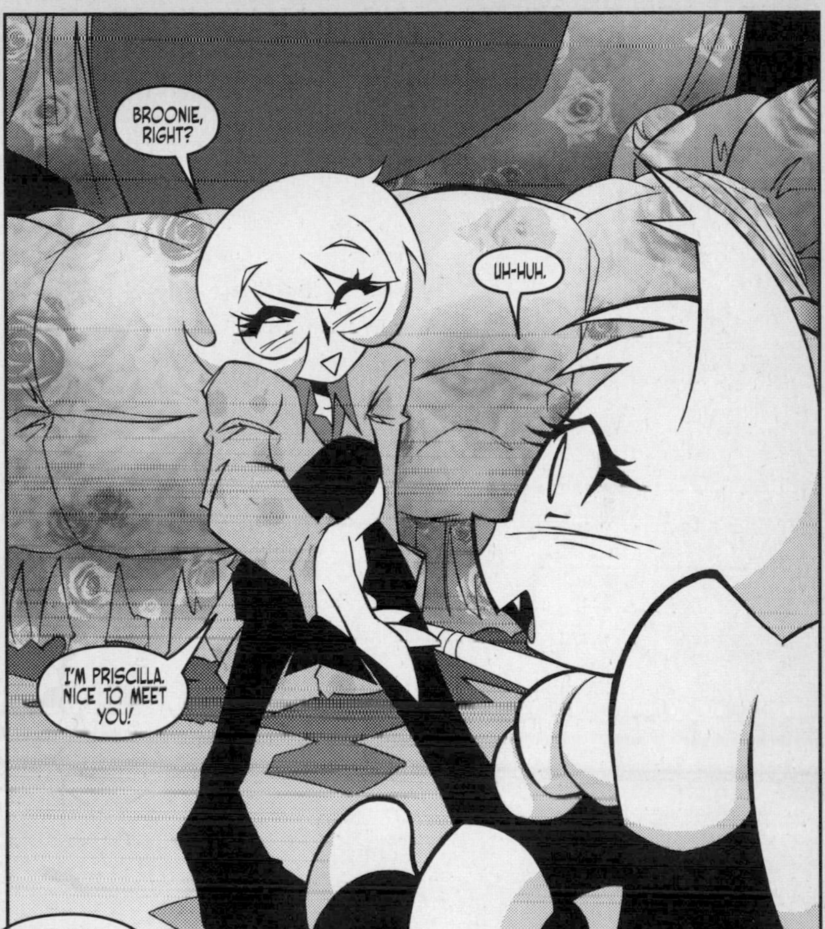
BROONIE, RIGHT?
UH-HUH.
I'M PRISCILLA. NICE TO MEET YOU!
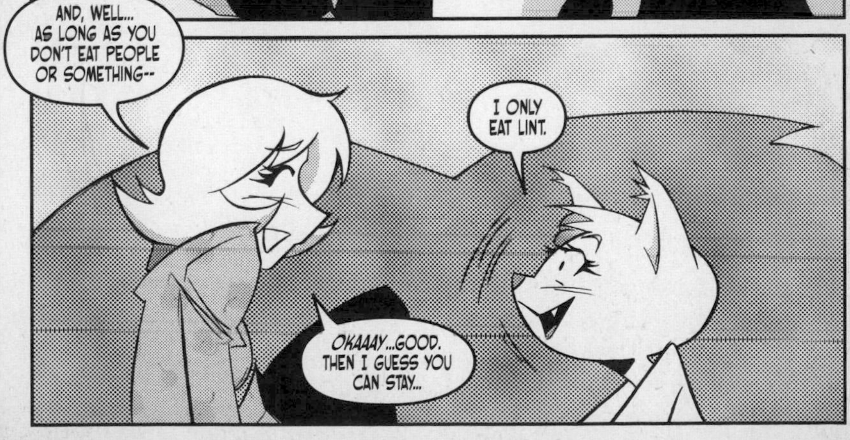
AND, WELL... AS LONG AS YOU DON'T EAT PEOPLE OR SOMETHING--
I ONLY EAT LINT.
OKAAAY...GOOD. THEN I GUESS YOU CAN STAY...

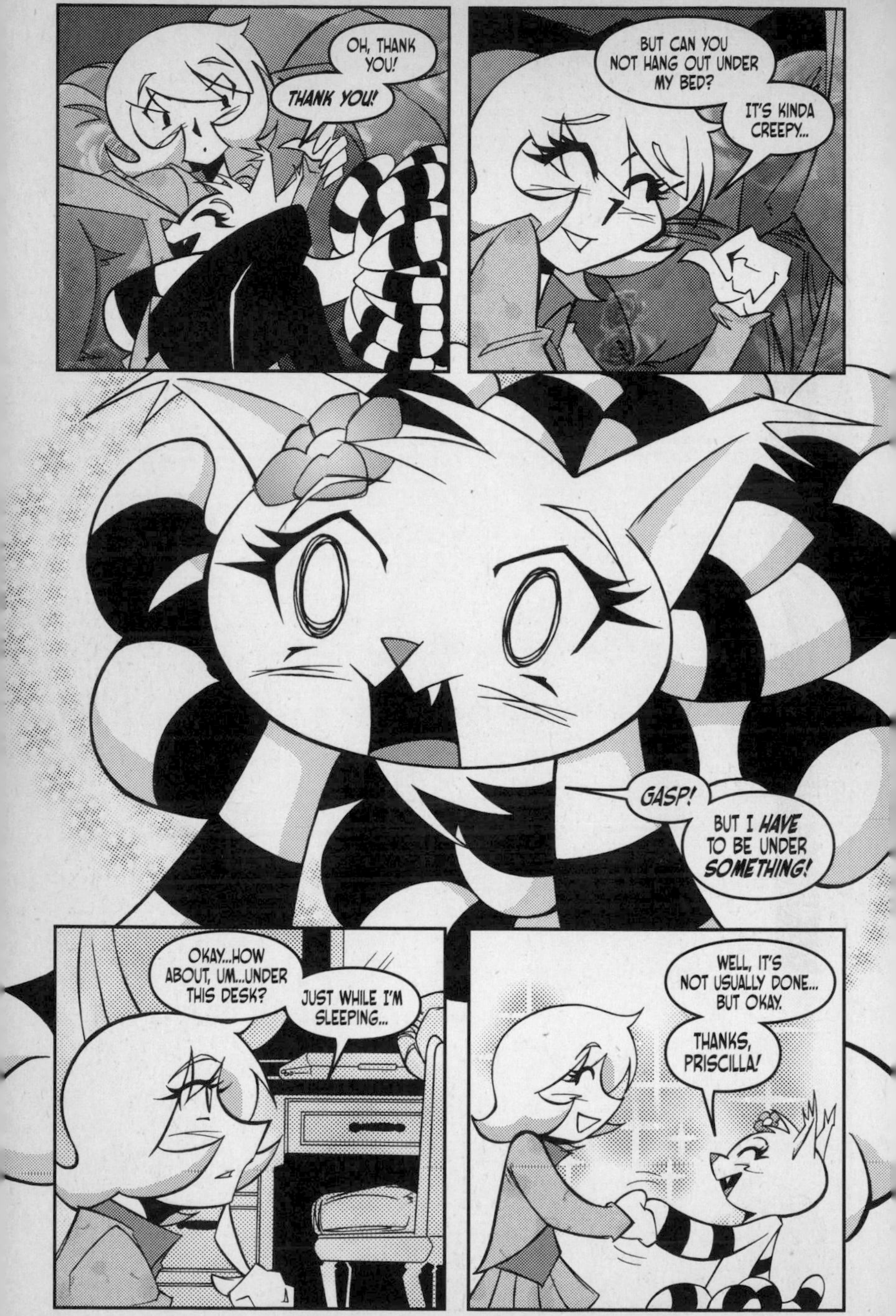
OH, THANK YOU!
THANK YOU!
BUT CAN YOU NOT HANG OUT UNDER MY BED?
IT'S KINDA CREEPY...
GASP!
BUT I HAVE TO BE UNDER SOMETHING!
OKAY...HOW ABOUT, UM...UNDER THIS DESK?
JUST WHILE I'M SLEEPING...
WELL, IT'S NOT USUALLY DONE... BUT OKAY.
THANKS, PRISCILLA!

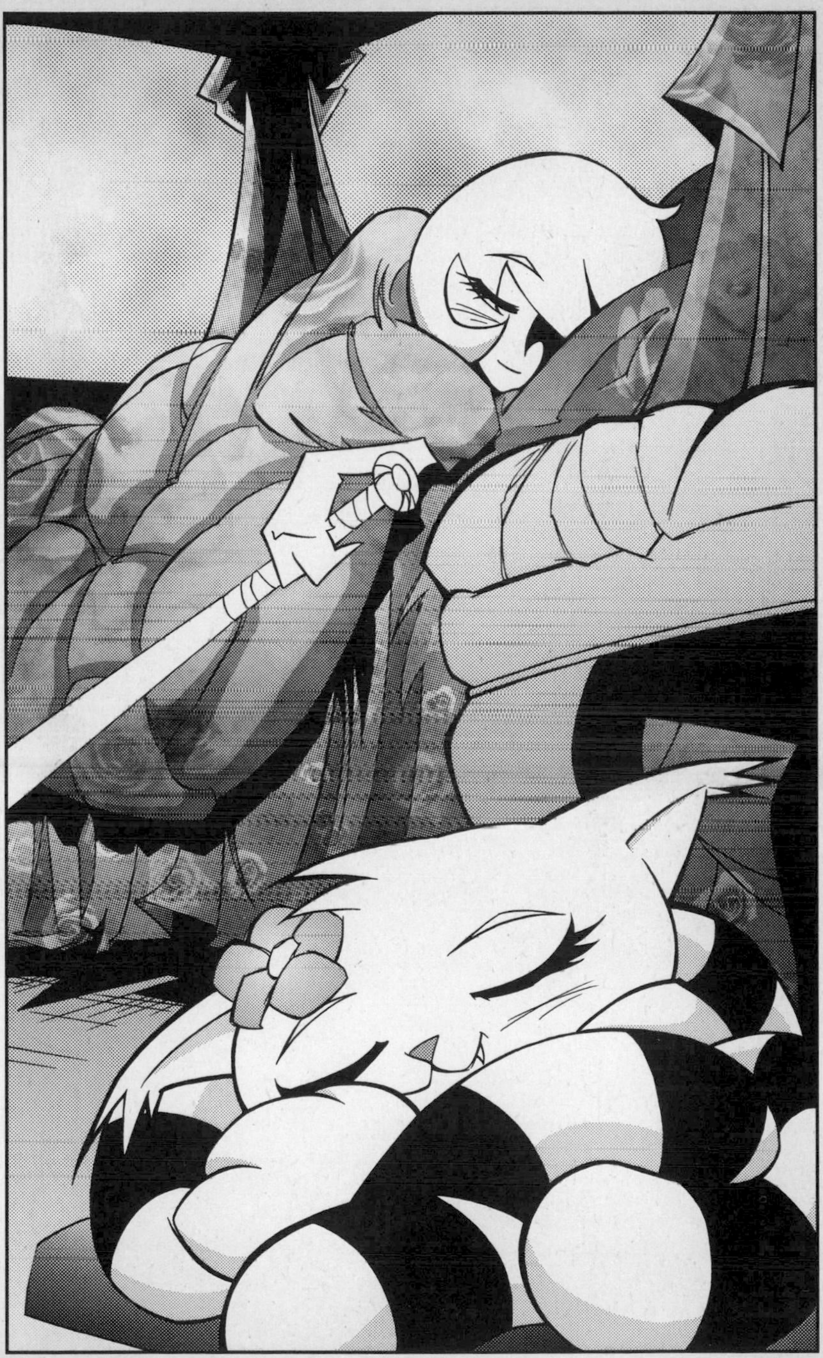

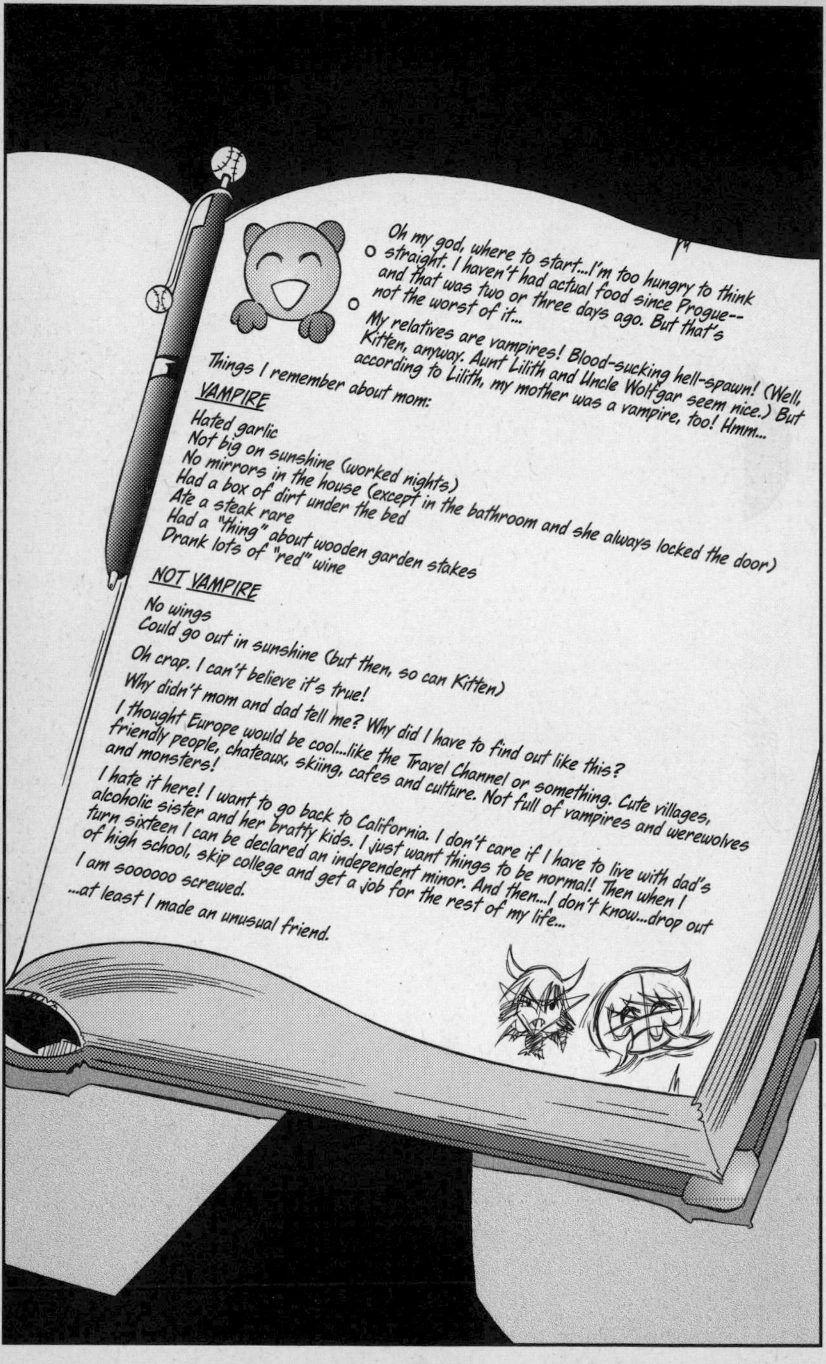
Oh my god, where to start...I'm too hungry to think straight. I haven't had actual food since Progue-- and that was two or three days ago. But that's not the worst of it...
My relatives are vampires! Blood-sucking hell-spawn! (Well, Kitten, anyway. Aunt Lilith and Uncle Wolfgar seem nice.) But according to Lilith, my mother was a vampire, too! Hmm...
Things I remember about mom:
VAMPIRE
Hated garlic
Not big on sunshine (worked nights)
No mirrors in the house (except in the bathroom and she always locked the door)
Had a box of dirt under the bed
Ate a steak rare
Had a "thing" about wooden garden stakes
Drank lots of "red" wine
NOT VAMPIRE
No wings
Could go out in sunshine (but then, so can Kitten)
Oh crap. I can't believe it's true!
Why didn't mom and dad tell me? Why did I have to find out like this?
I thought Europe would be cool...like the Travel Channel or something. Cute villages, friendly people, chateaux, skiing, cafes and culture. Not full of vampires and werewolves and monsters!
I hate it here! I want to go back to California. I don't care if I have to live with dad's alcoholic sister and her bratty kids. I just want things to be normal! Then when I turn sixteen I can be declared an independent minor. And then...I don't know...drop out of high school, skip college and get a job for the rest of my life...
I am soooooo screwed.
...at least I made an unusual friend.

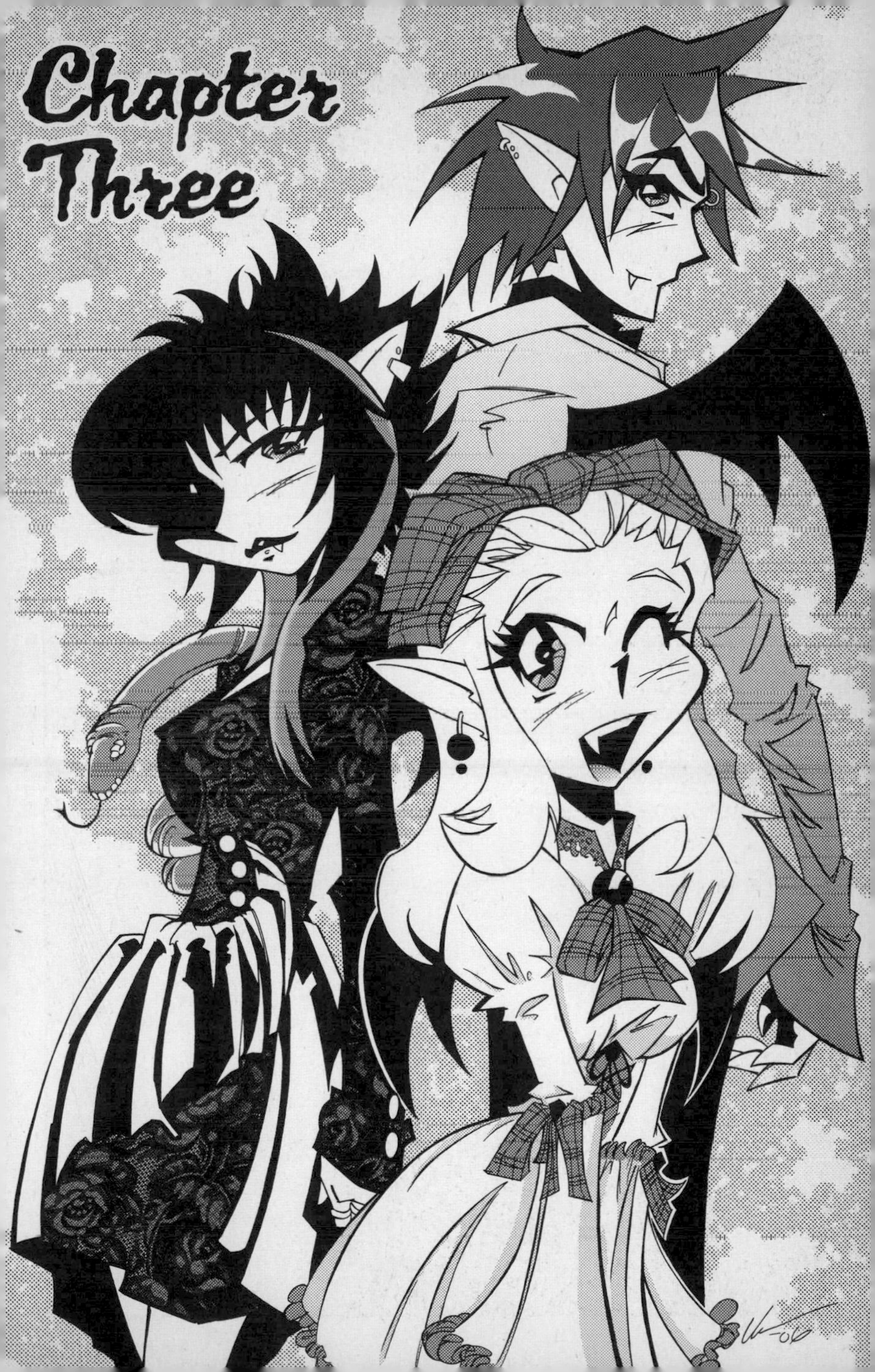
Chapter
Three

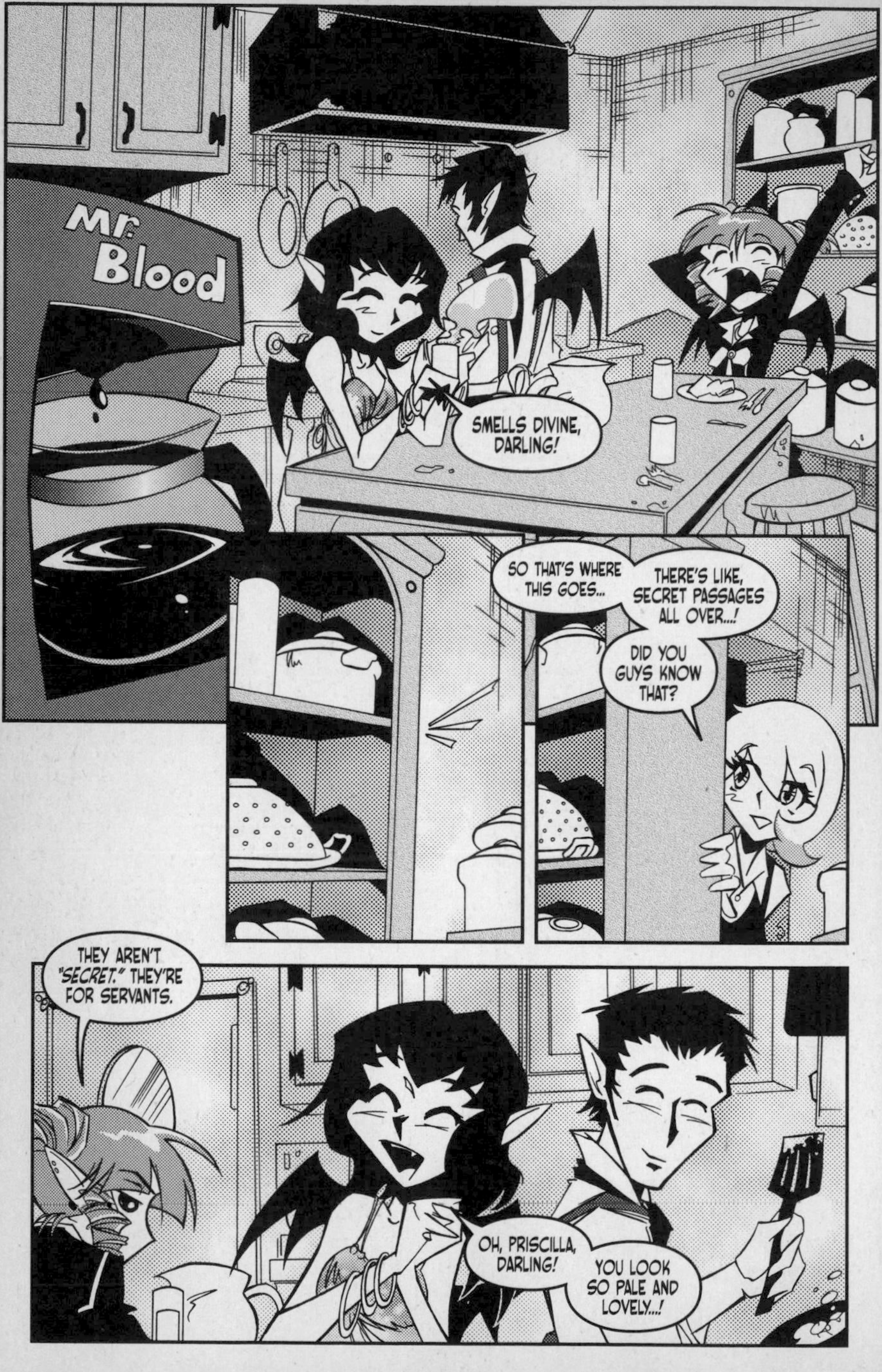
Mr. Blood
SMELLS DIVINE, DARLING!
SO THAT'S WHERE THIS GOES...
THERE'S LIKE, SECRET PASSAGES ALL OVER...!
DID YOU GUYS KNOW THAT?
THEY AREN'T "SECRET." THEY'RE FOR SERVANTS.
OH, PRISCILLA, DARLING!
YOU LOOK SO PALE AND LOVELY...!

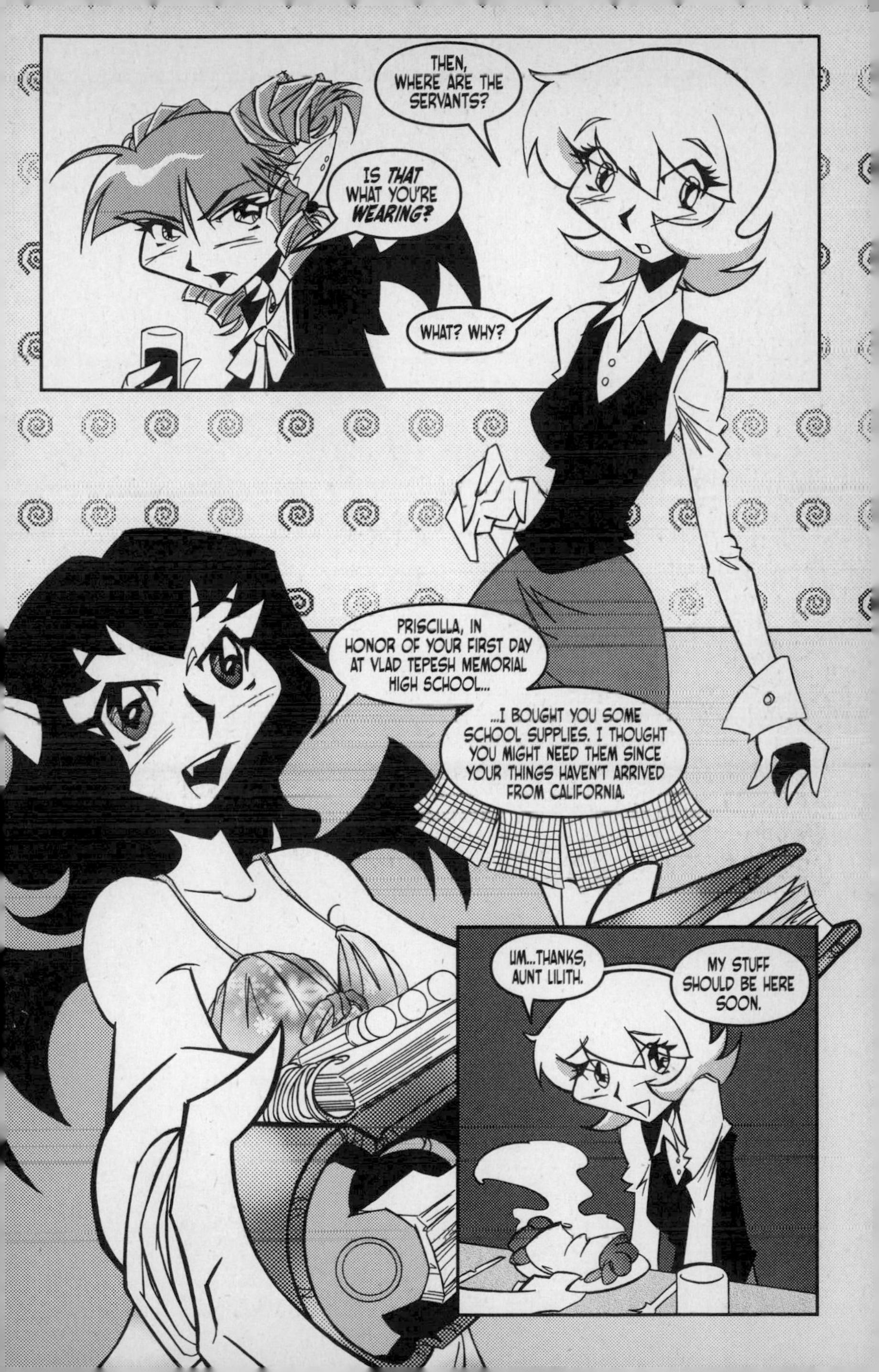
THEN, WHERE ARE THE SERVANTS?
IS *THAT* WHAT YOU'RE ***WEARING?***
WHAT? WHY?
PRISCILLA, IN HONOR OF YOUR FIRST DAY AT VLAD TEPESH MEMORIAL HIGH SCHOOL...
...I BOUGHT YOU SOME SCHOOL SUPPLIES. I THOUGHT YOU MIGHT NEED THEM SINCE YOUR THINGS HAVEN'T ARRIVED FROM CALIFORNIA.
UM...THANKS, AUNT LILITH.
MY STUFF SHOULD BE HERE SOON.

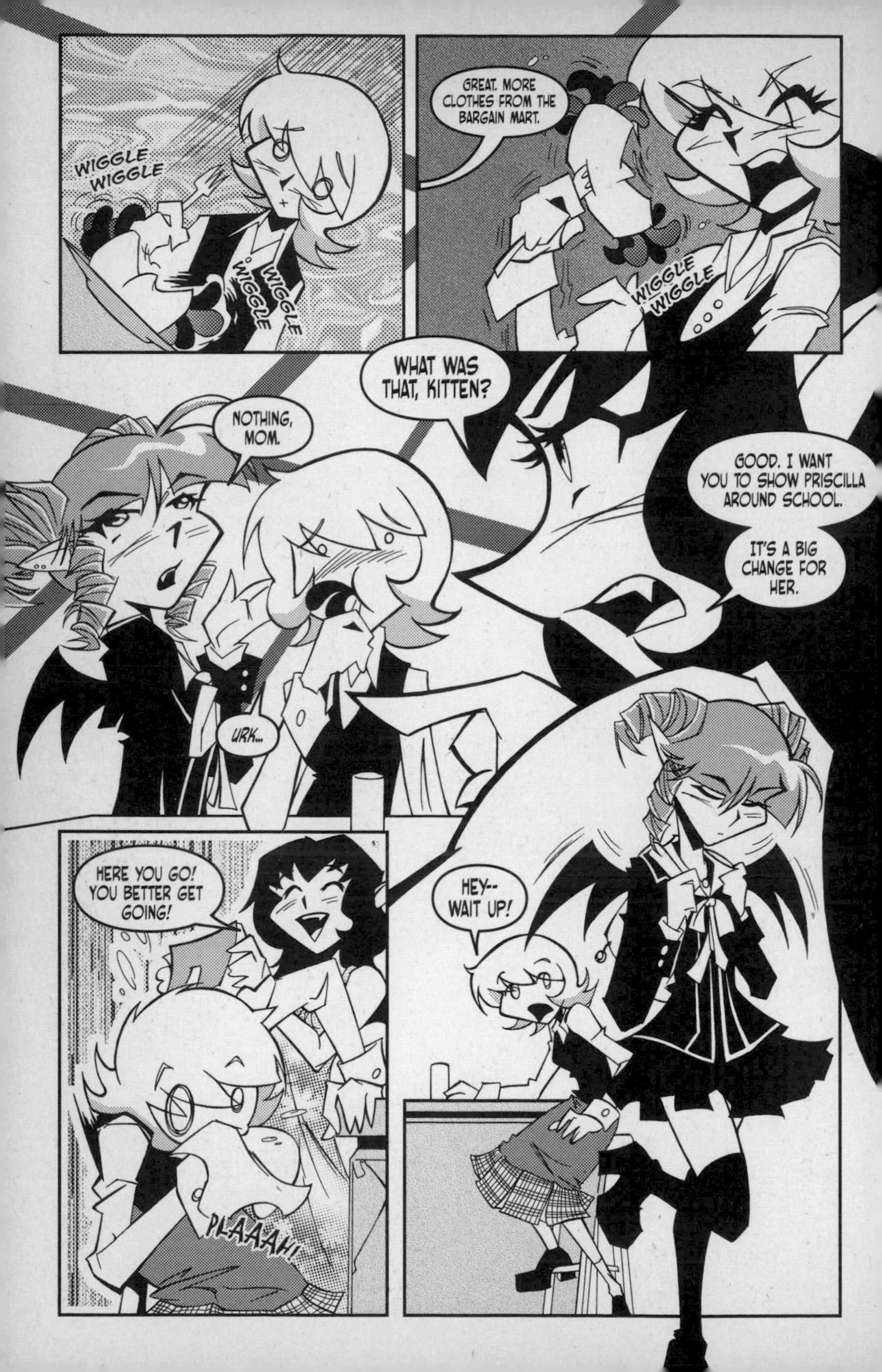
WIGGLE WIGGLE
WIGGLE WIGGLE
GREAT. MORE CLOTHES FROM THE BARGAIN MART.
WIGGLE WIGGLE
NOTHING, MOM.
WHAT WAS THAT, KITTEN?
GOOD. I WANT YOU TO SHOW PRISCILLA AROUND SCHOOL.
IT'S A BIG CHANGE FOR HER.
URK...
HERE YOU GO! YOU BETTER GET GOING!
PLAAAAH!
HEY-- WAIT UP!

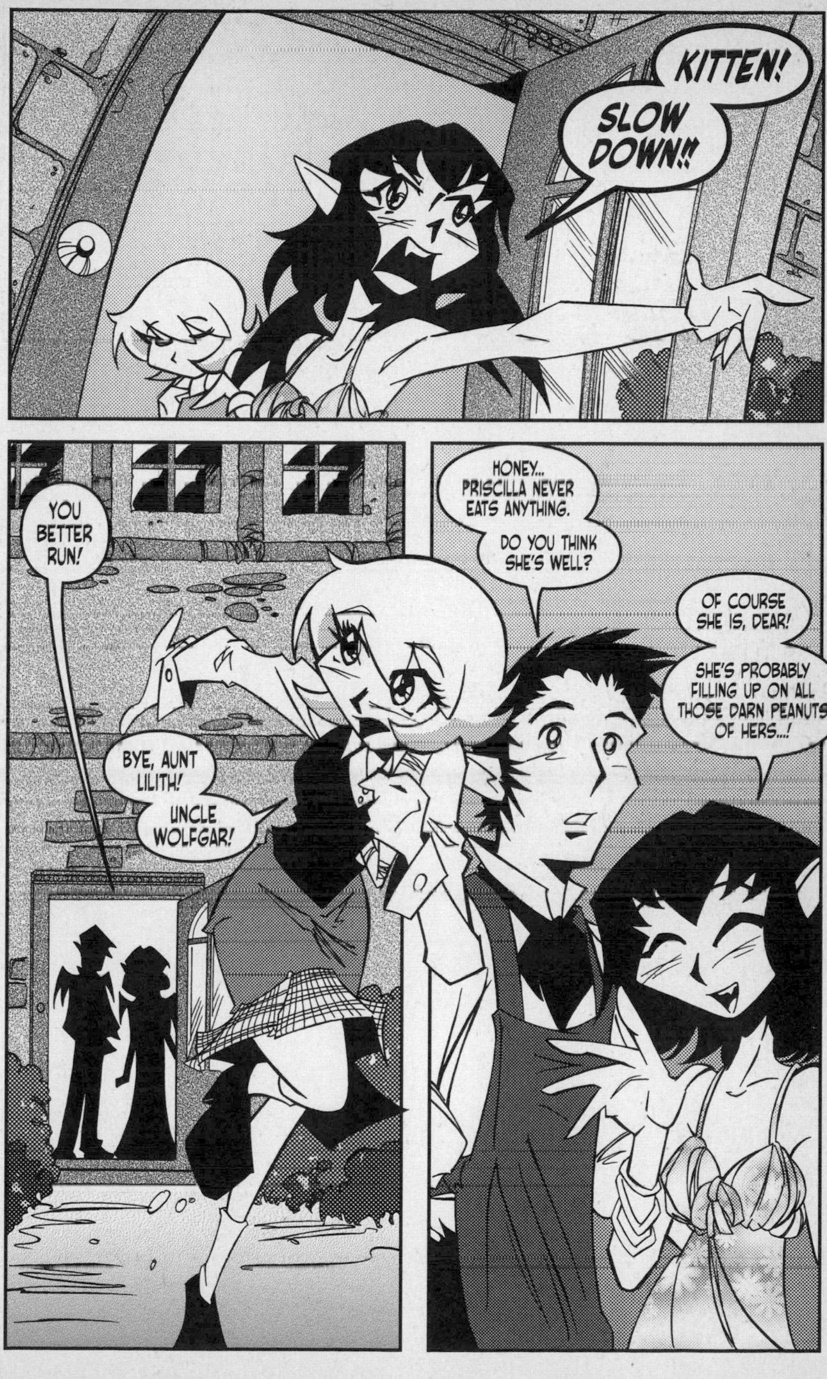
KITTEN!
SLOW DOWN!!
YOU BETTER RUN!
BYE, AUNT LILITH!
UNCLE WOLFGAR!
HONEY... PRISCILLA NEVER EATS ANYTHING.
DO YOU THINK SHE'S WELL?
OF COURSE SHE IS, DEAR!
SHE'S PROBABLY FILLING UP ON ALL THOSE DARN PEANUTS OF HERS...!

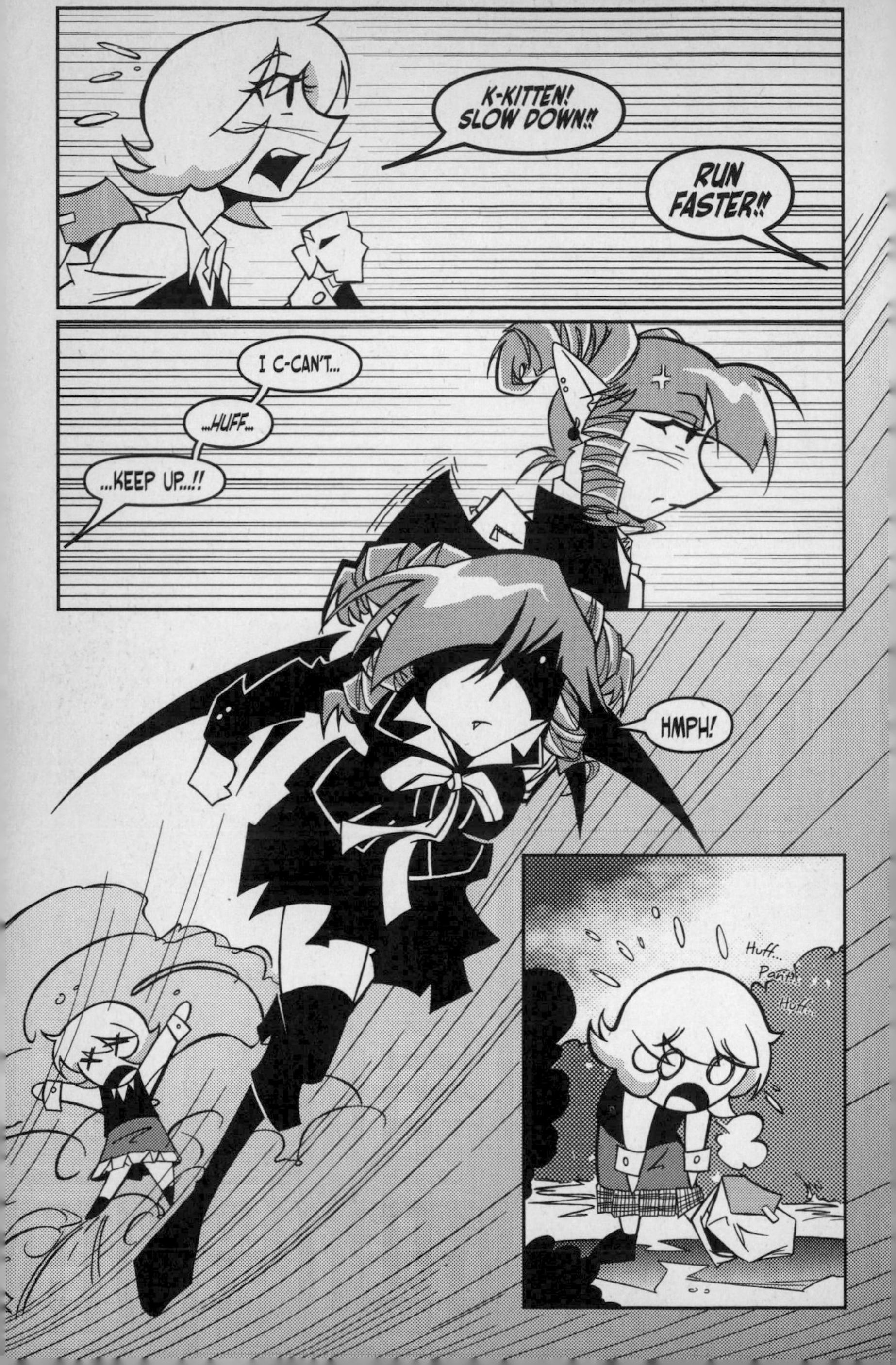
K-KITTEN! SLOW DOWN!!
RUN FASTER!!
I C-CAN'T...
...HUFF...
...KEEP UP...!!
HMPH!
Huff...
Pant!
Huff...

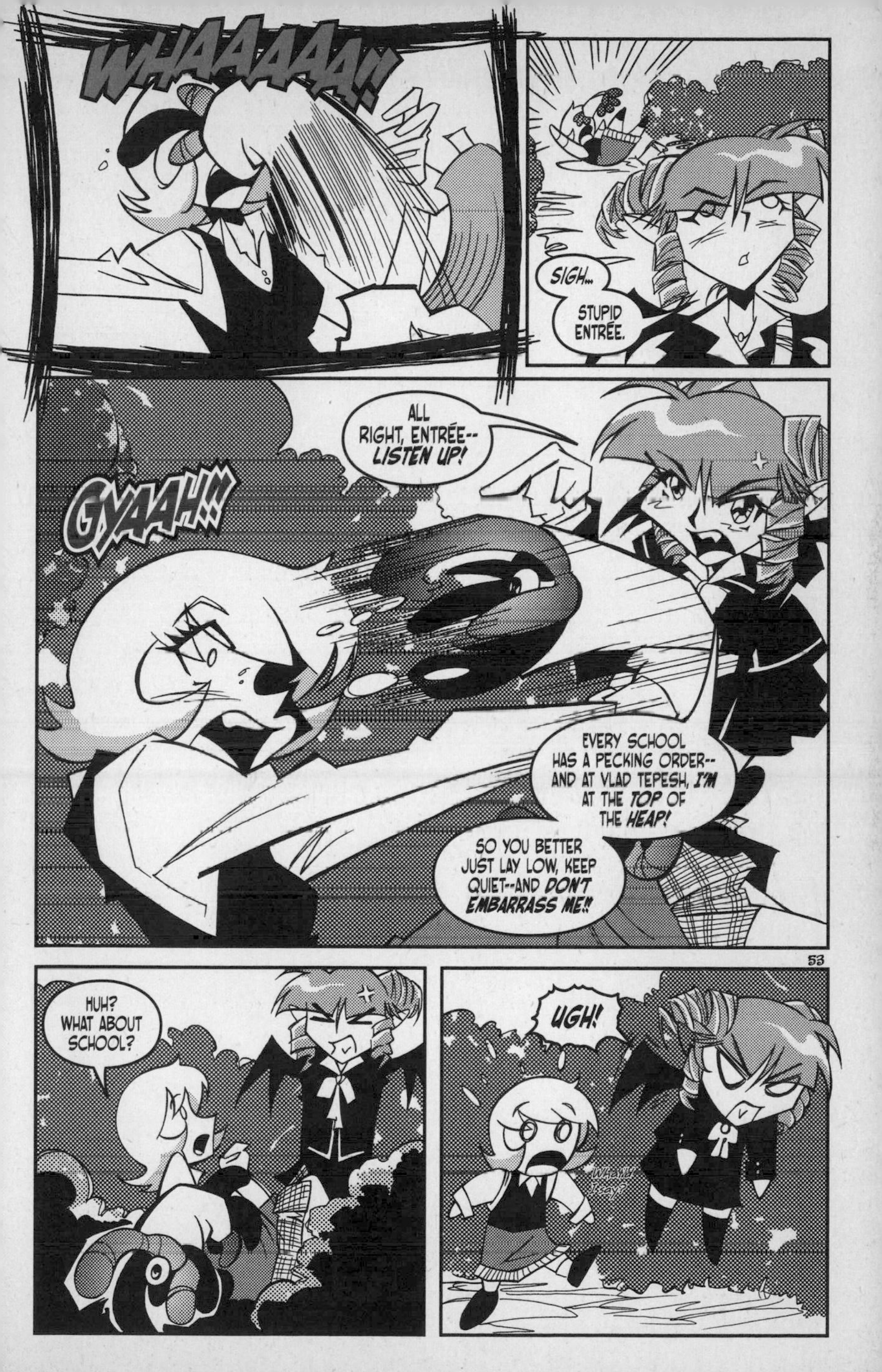
WHAAAAA!!
SIGH...
STUPID ENTRÉE.
ALL RIGHT, ENTRÉE-- LISTEN UP!
GYAAH!!
EVERY SCHOOL HAS A PECKING ORDER-- AND AT VLAD TEPESH, I'M AT THE TOP OF THE HEAP!
SO YOU BETTER JUST LAY LOW, KEEP QUIET--AND DON'T EMBARRASS ME!!
HUH? WHAT ABOUT SCHOOL?
UGH!

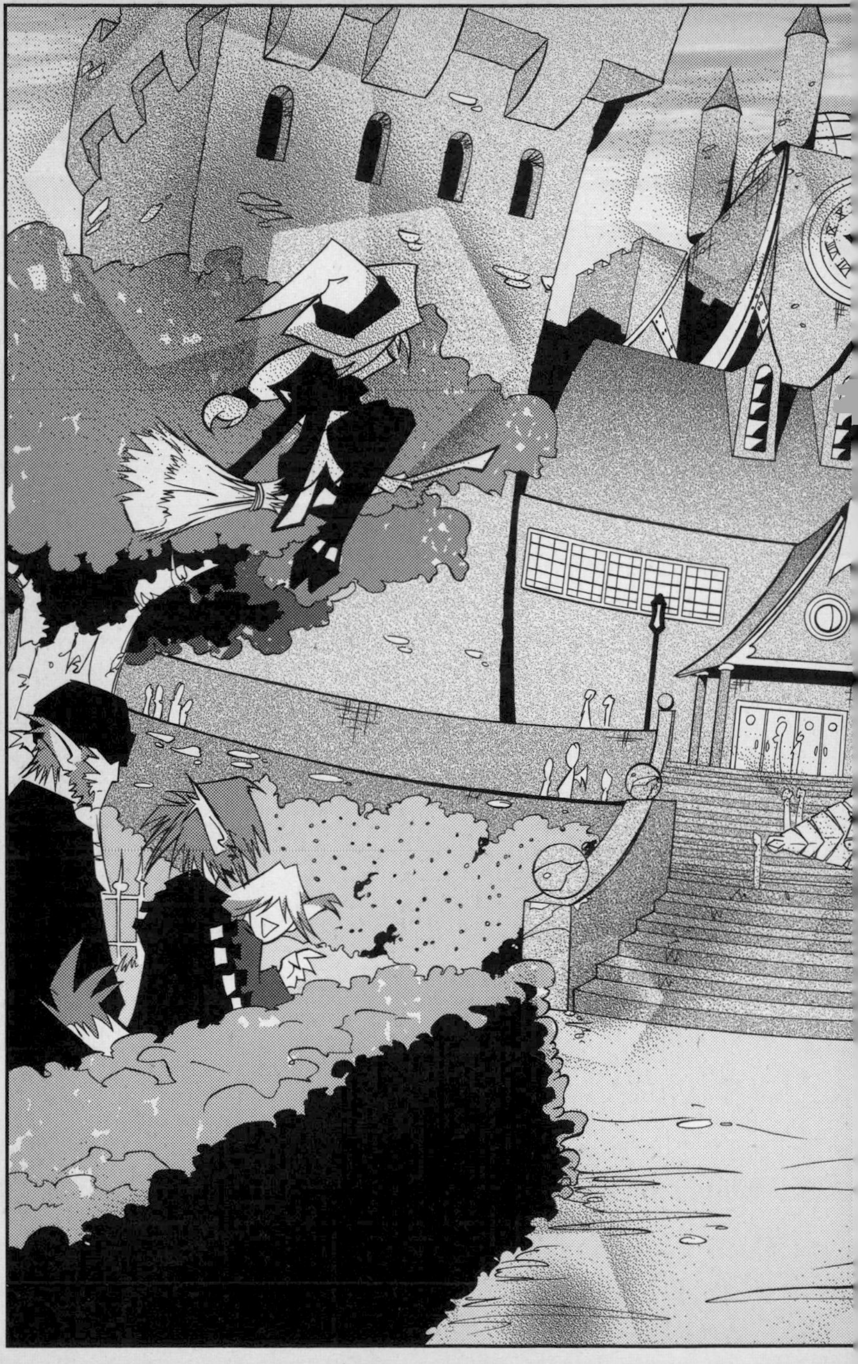

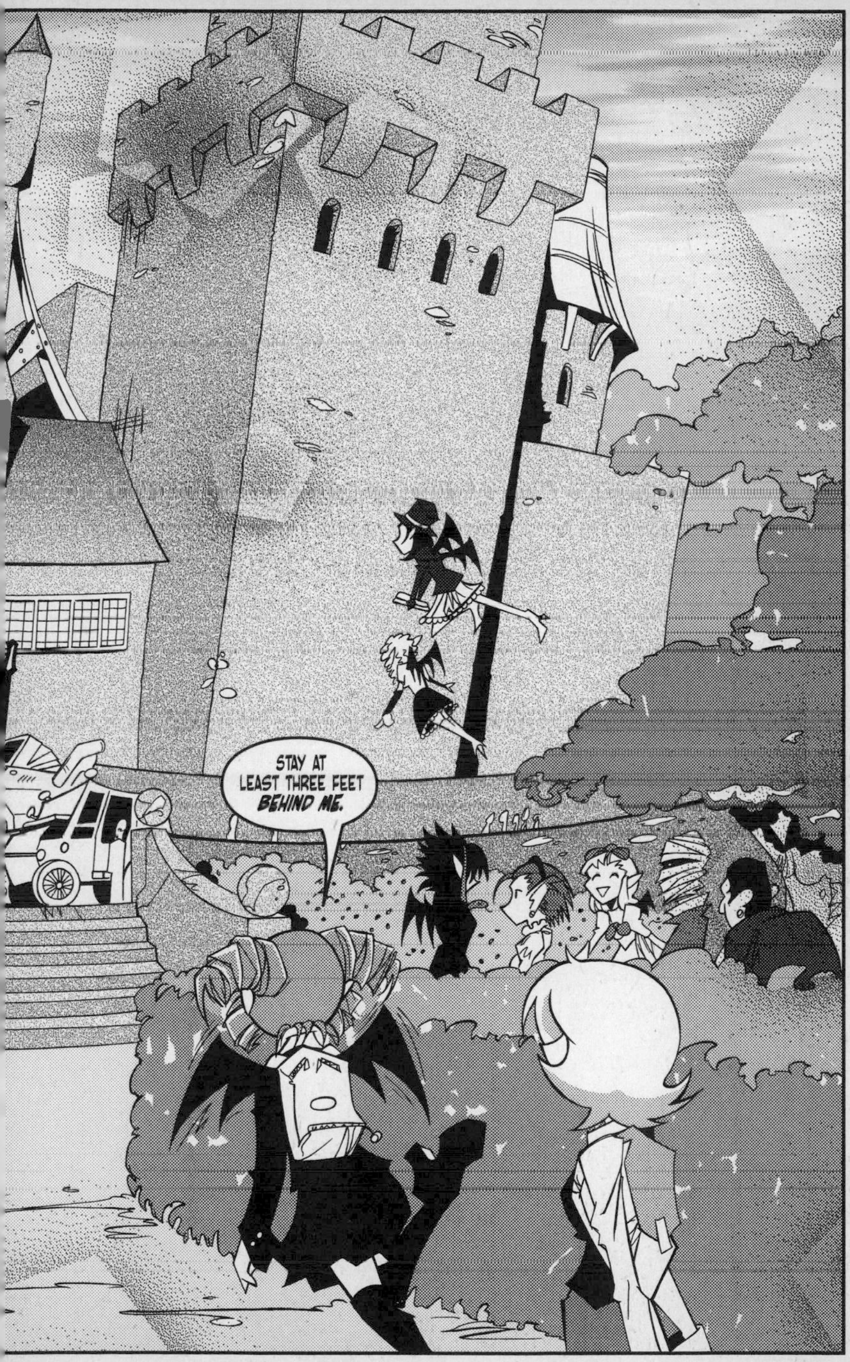
STAY AT LEAST THREE FEET BEHIND ME.

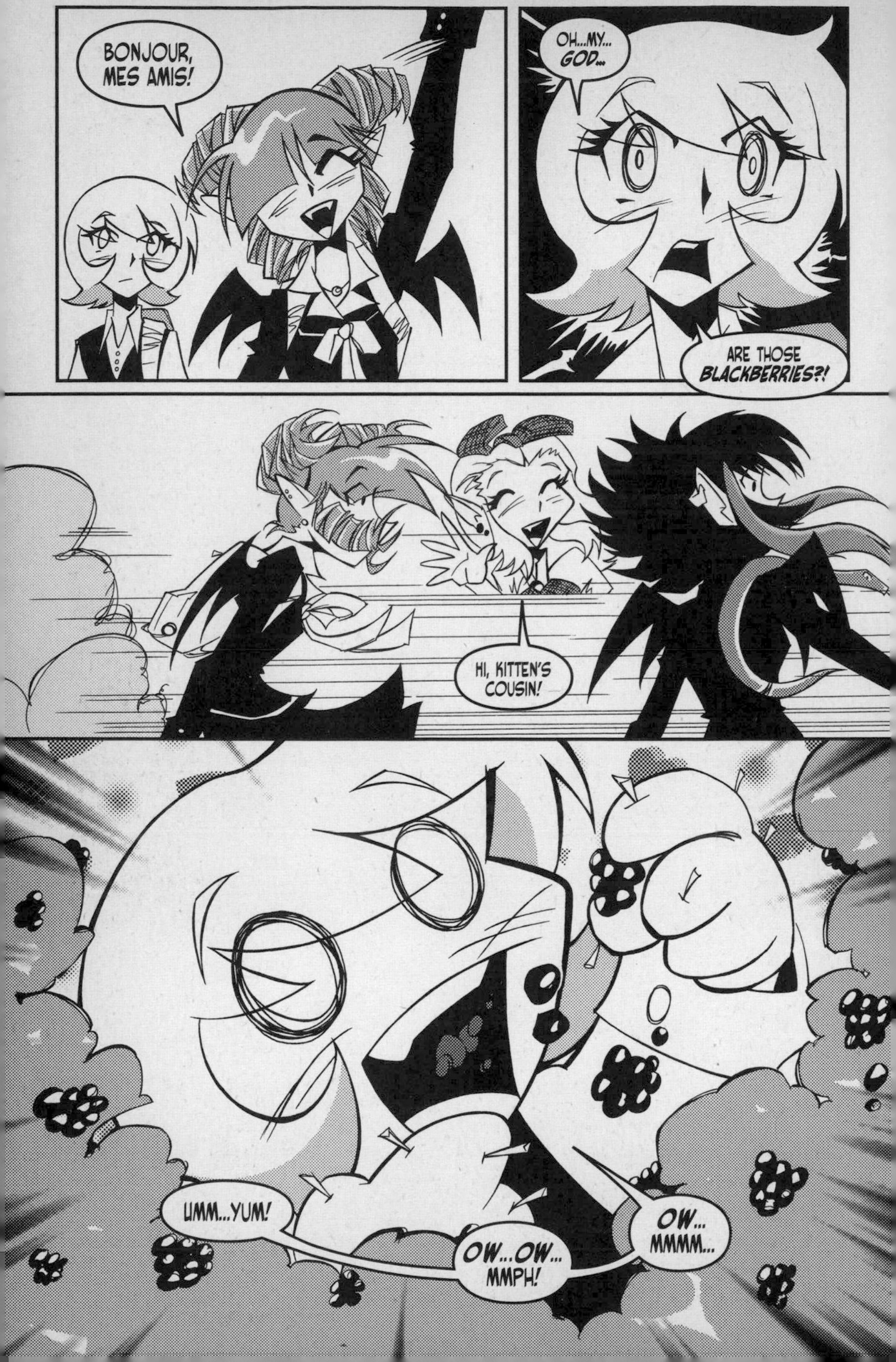
BONJOUR, MES AMIS!
OH...MY... GOD...
ARE THOSE BLACKBERRIES?!
HI, KITTEN'S COUSIN!
UMM...YUM!
OW...OW... MMPH!
OW... MMMM...

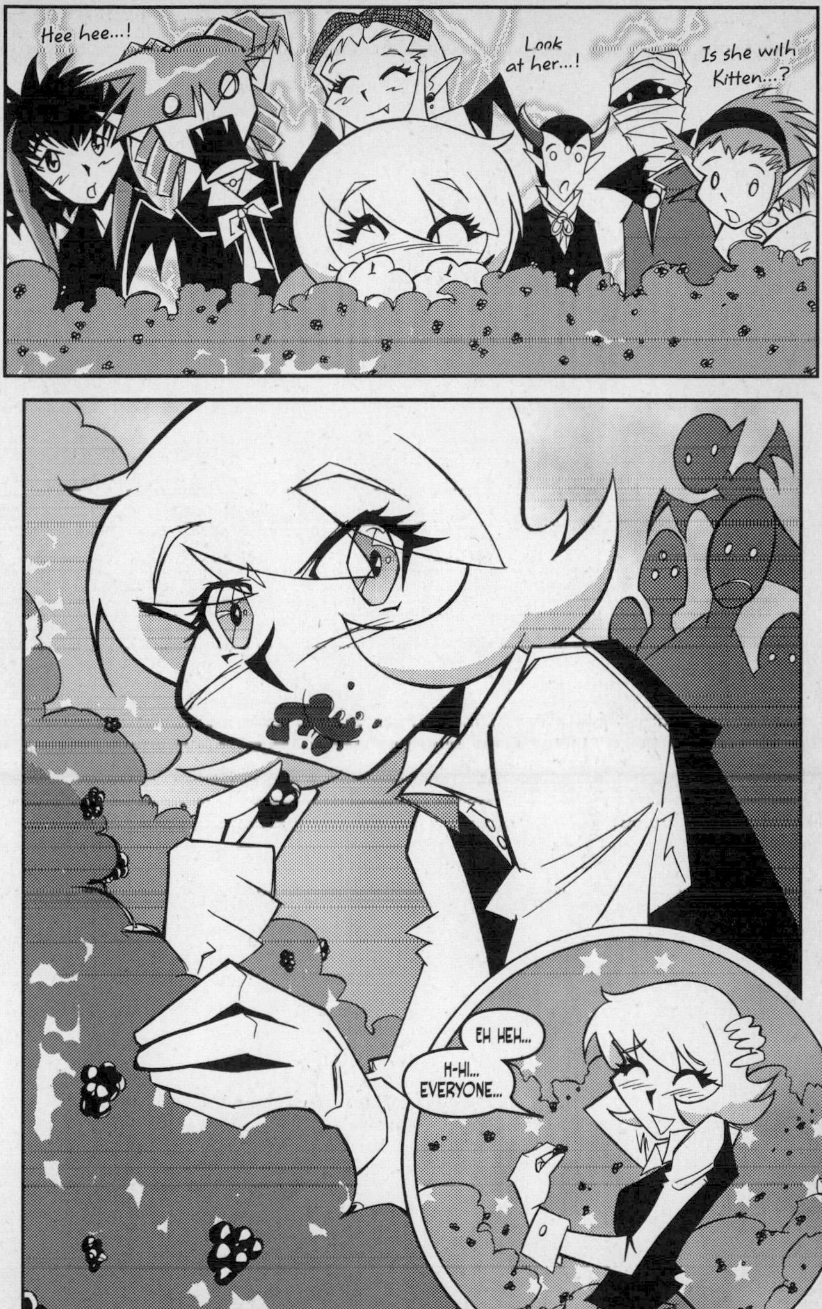
Hee hee...!
Look at her...!
Is she wilh Kitten...?
EH HEH...
H-HI... EVERYONE...

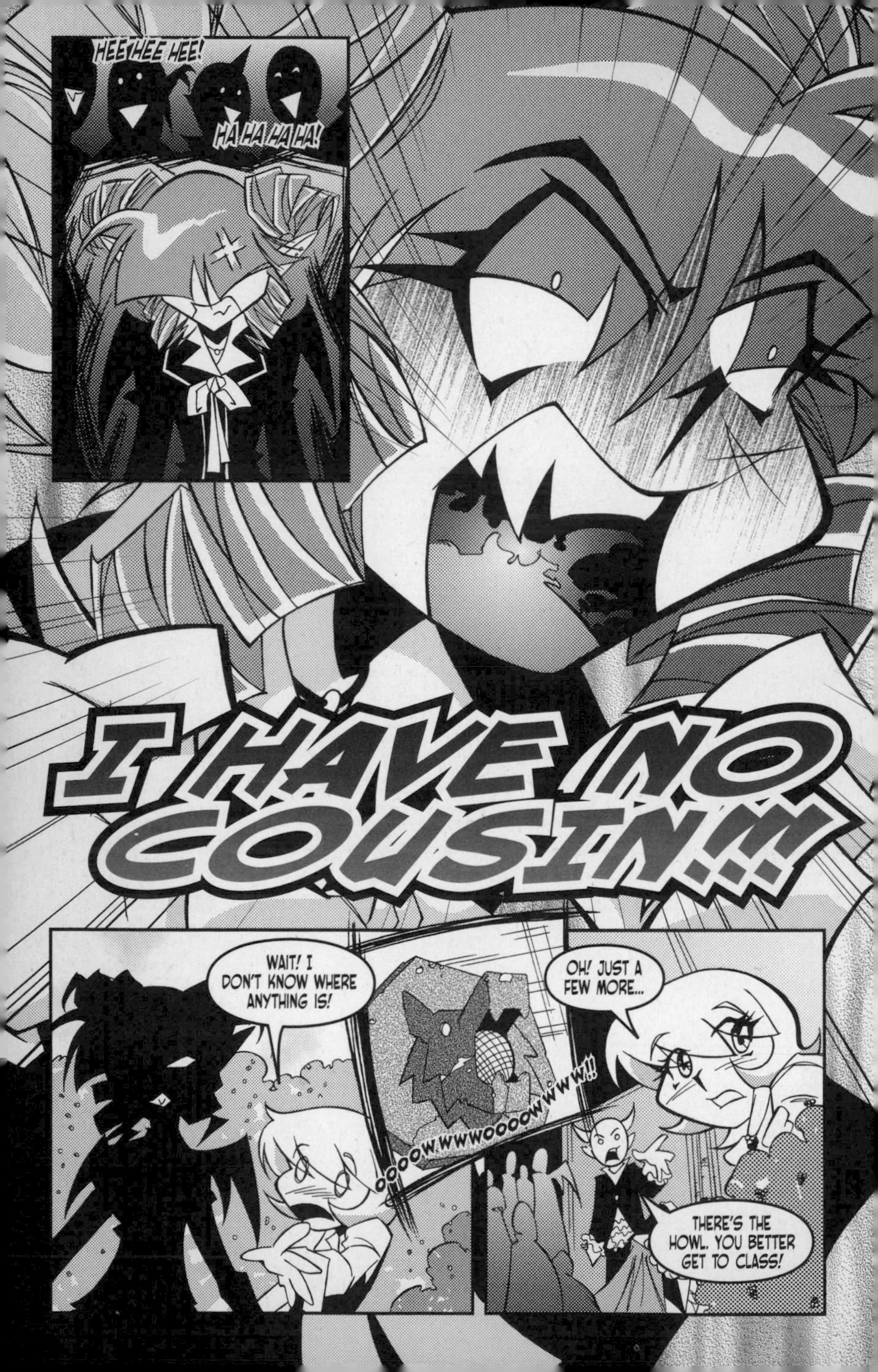
HEE HEE HEE!
HA HA HA HA!
I HAVE NO COUSIN!!!
WAIT! I DON'T KNOW WHERE ANYTHING IS!
OOOOWWWWOOOOWWWW!!
OH! JUST A FEW MORE...
THERE'S THE HOWL. YOU BETTER GET TO CLASS!

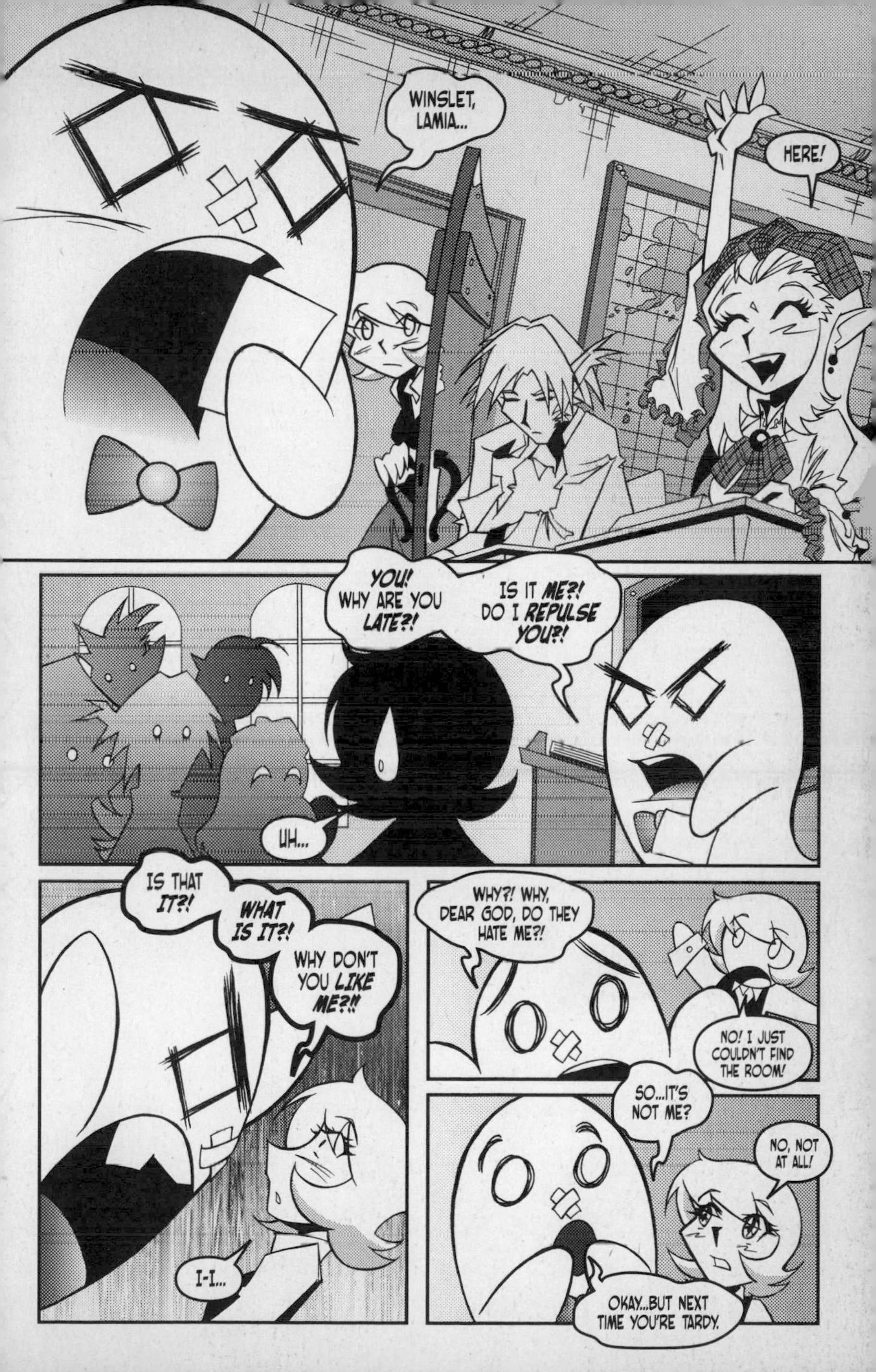
WINSLET, LAMIA...
HERE!
YOU! WHY ARE YOU LATE?!
IS IT ME?! DO I REPULSE YOU?!
UH...
IS THAT IT?!
WHAT IS IT?!
WHY DON'T YOU LIKE ME?!!
I-I...
WHY?! WHY, DEAR GOD, DO THEY HATE ME?!
NO! I JUST COULDN'T FIND THE ROOM!
SO...IT'S NOT ME?
NO, NOT AT ALL!
OKAY...BUT NEXT TIME YOU'RE TARDY.

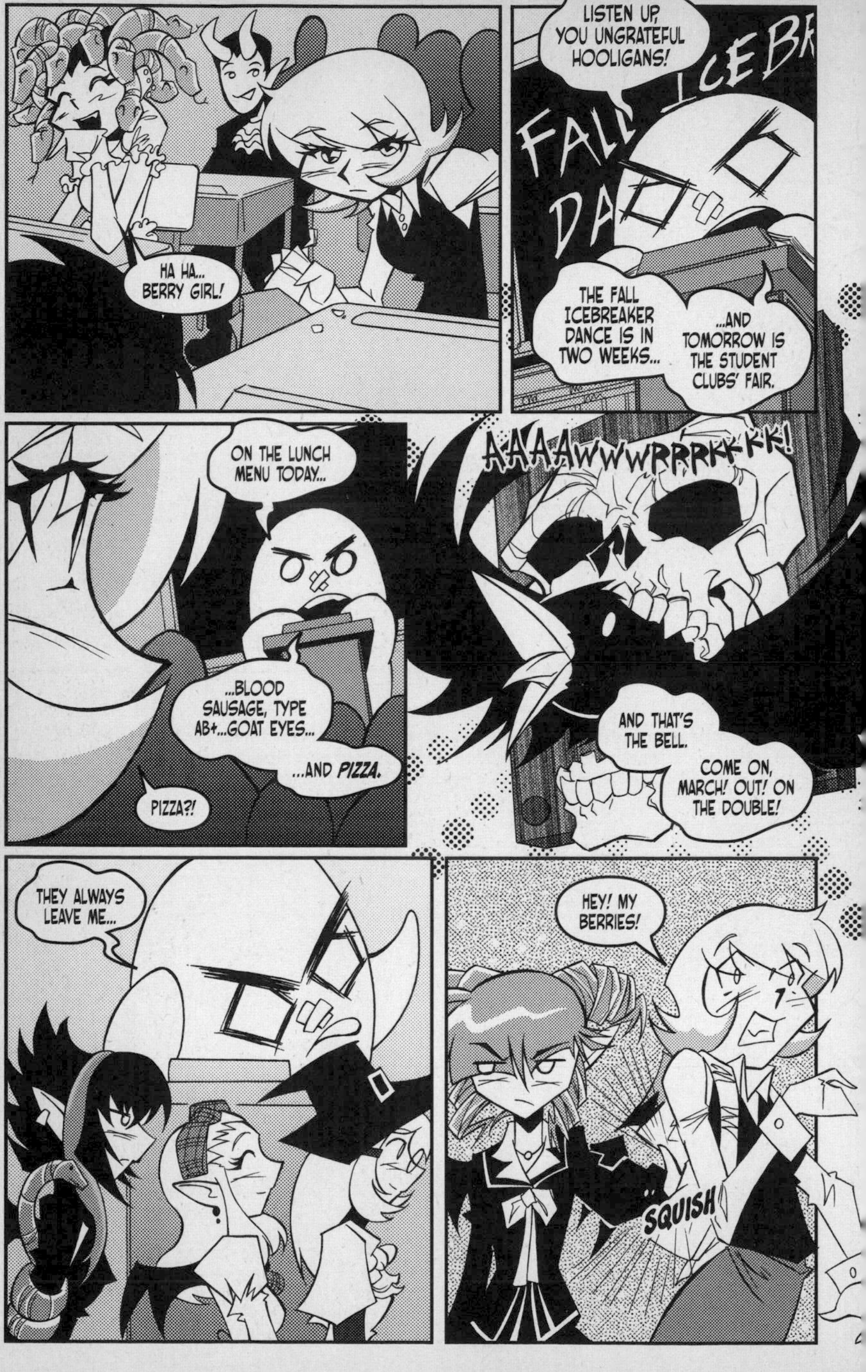
HA HA... BERRY GIRL!
LISTEN UP, YOU UNGRATEFUL HOOLIGANS!
FALL ICEBR
DA
THE FALL ICEBREAKER DANCE IS IN TWO WEEKS...
...AND TOMORROW IS THE STUDENT CLUBS' FAIR.
ON THE LUNCH MENU TODAY...
...BLOOD SAUSAGE, TYPE AB+...GOAT EYES...
...AND PIZZA.
PIZZA?!
AAAAWWWRRRKKKK!
AND THAT'S THE BELL.
COME ON, MARCH! OUT! ON THE DOUBLE!
THEY ALWAYS LEAVE ME...
HEY! MY BERRIES!
SQUISH

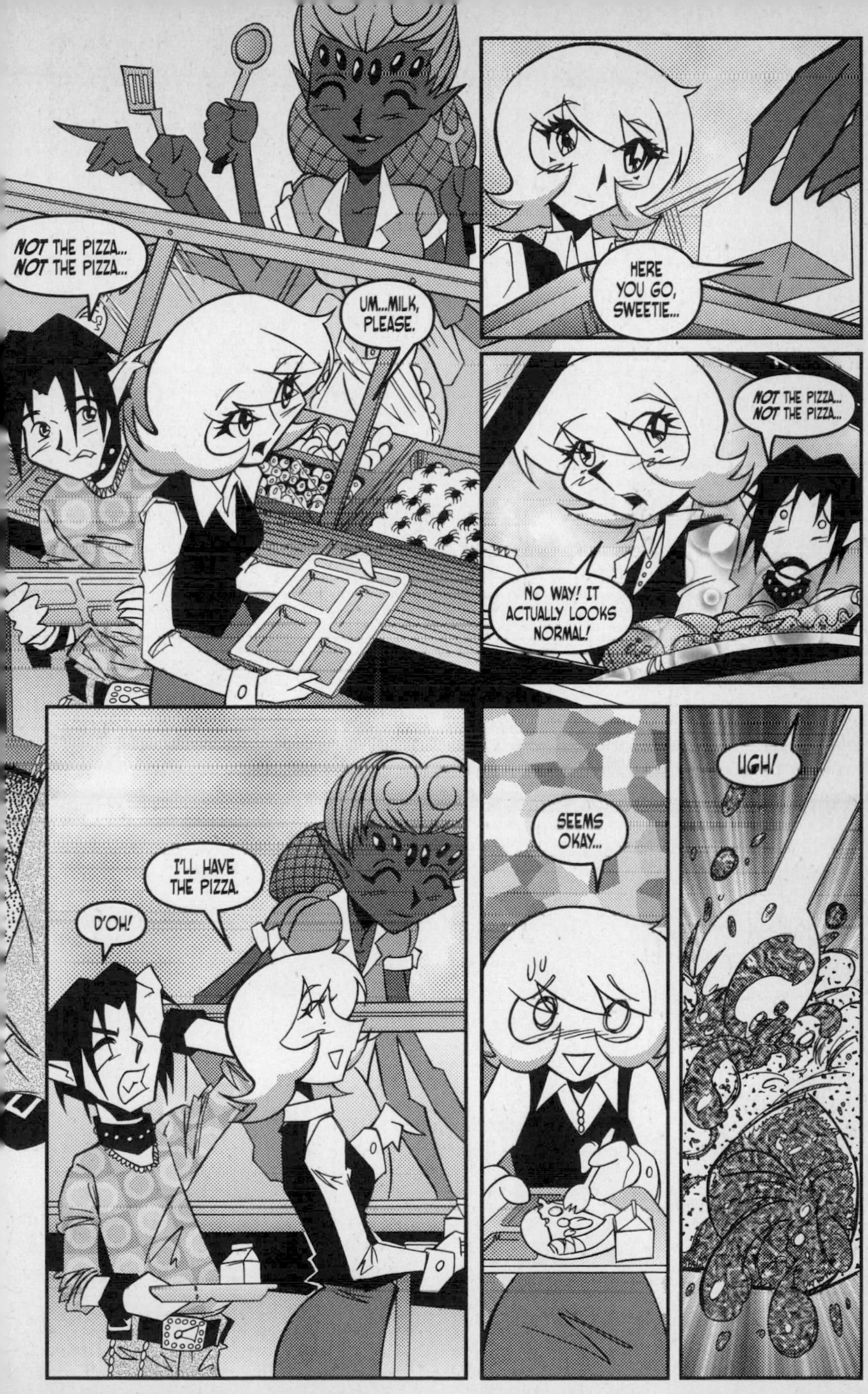

NOT THE PIZZA... NOT THE PIZZA...
UM...MILK, PLEASE.
HERE YOU GO, SWEETIE...
NOT THE PIZZA... NOT THE PIZZA...
NO WAY! IT ACTUALLY LOOKS NORMAL!
I'LL HAVE THE PIZZA.
D'OH!
SEEMS OKAY...
UGH!

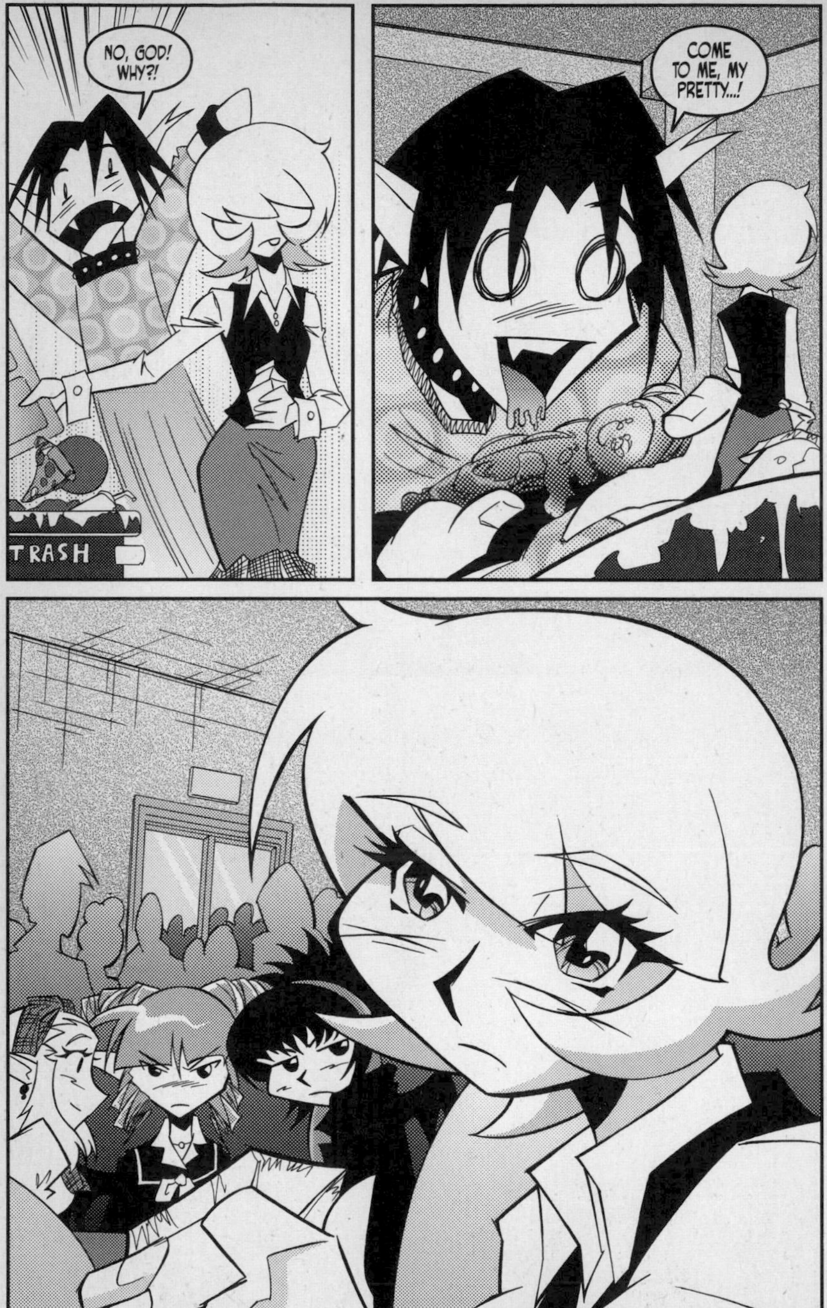
NO, GOD! WHY?!
TRASH
COME TO ME, MY PRETTY...!

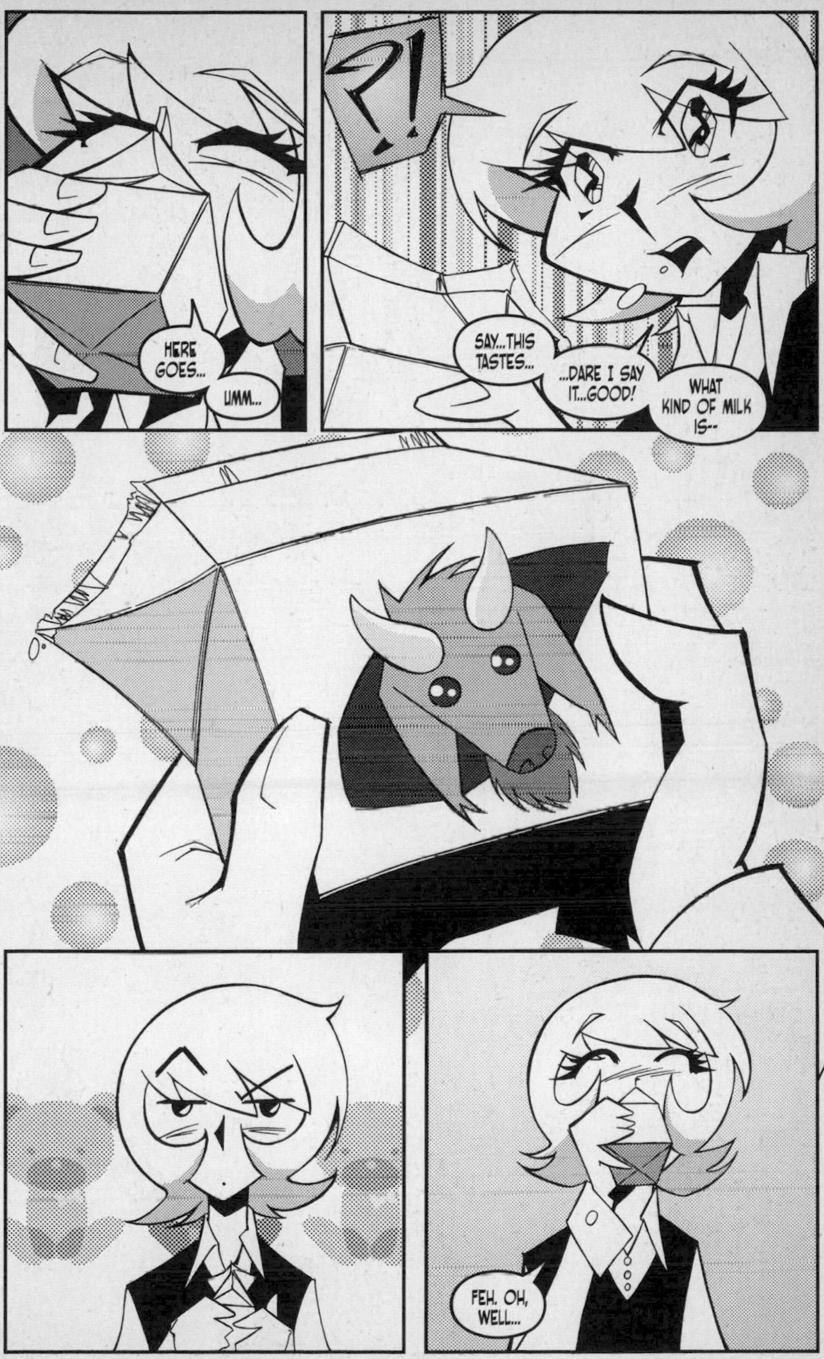
HERE GOES...
UMM...
?!
SAY...THIS TASTES...
...DARE I SAY IT...GOOD!
WHAT KIND OF MILK IS--
FEH. OH, WELL...

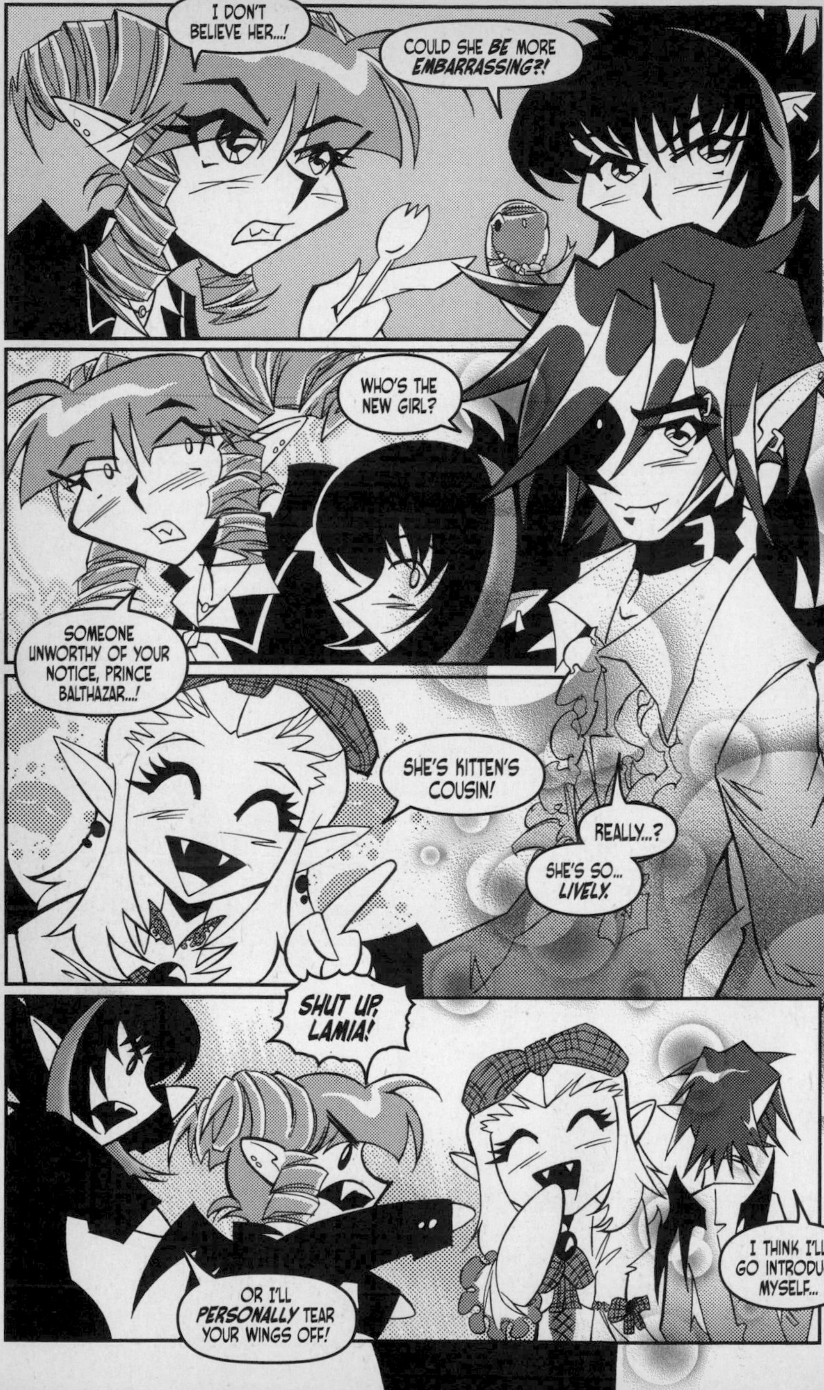
I DON'T BELIEVE HER...!
COULD SHE *BE* MORE *EMBARRASSING?!*
WHO'S THE NEW GIRL?
SOMEONE UNWORTHY OF YOUR NOTICE, PRINCE BALTHAZAR...!
SHE'S KITTEN'S COUSIN!
REALLY...?
SHE'S SO... *LIVELY.*
SHUT UP, LAMIA!
OR I'LL *PERSONALLY* TEAR YOUR WINGS OFF!
I THINK I'LL GO INTRODUCE MYSELF...

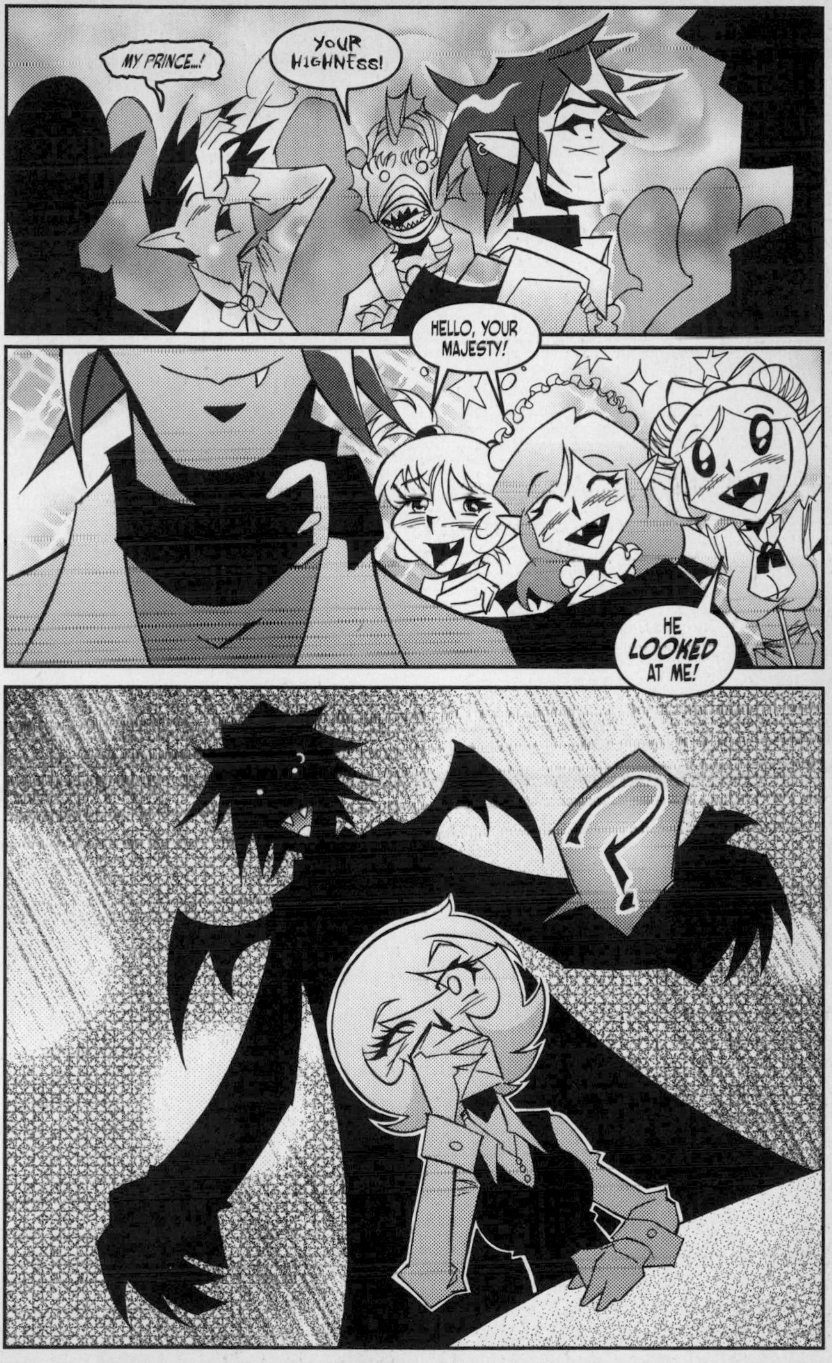
MY PRINCE...!
YOUR HIGHNESS!
HELLO, YOUR MAJESTY!
HE LOOKED AT ME!

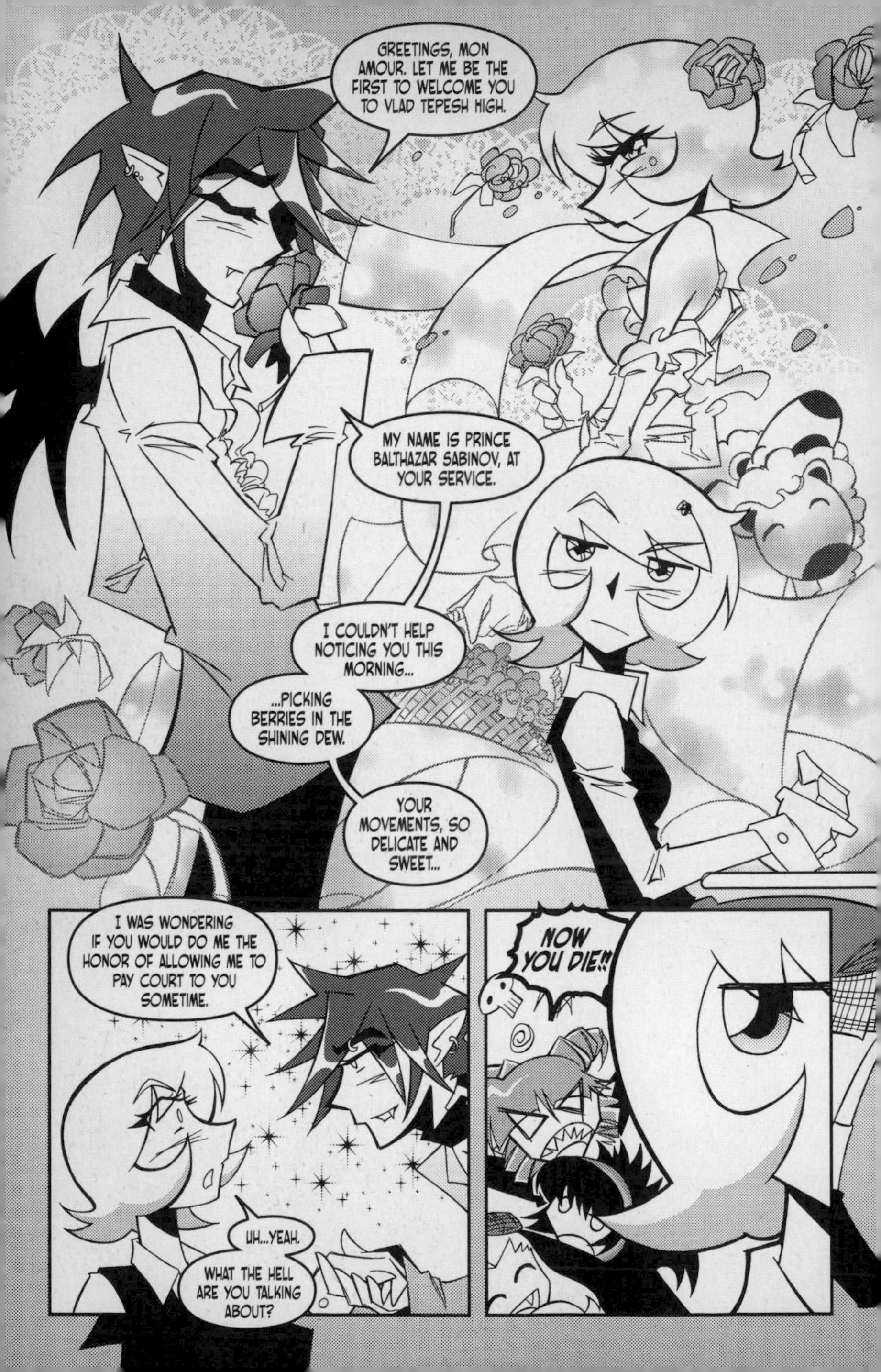
GREETINGS, MON AMOUR. LET ME BE THE FIRST TO WELCOME YOU TO VLAD TEPESH HIGH.
MY NAME IS PRINCE BALTHAZAR SABINOV, AT YOUR SERVICE.
I COULDN'T HELP NOTICING YOU THIS MORNING...
...PICKING BERRIES IN THE SHINING DEW.
YOUR MOVEMENTS, SO DELICATE AND SWEET...
I WAS WONDERING IF YOU WOULD DO ME THE HONOR OF ALLOWING ME TO PAY COURT TO YOU SOMETIME.
UH...YEAH.
WHAT THE HELL ARE YOU TALKING ABOUT?
NOW YOU DIE!!

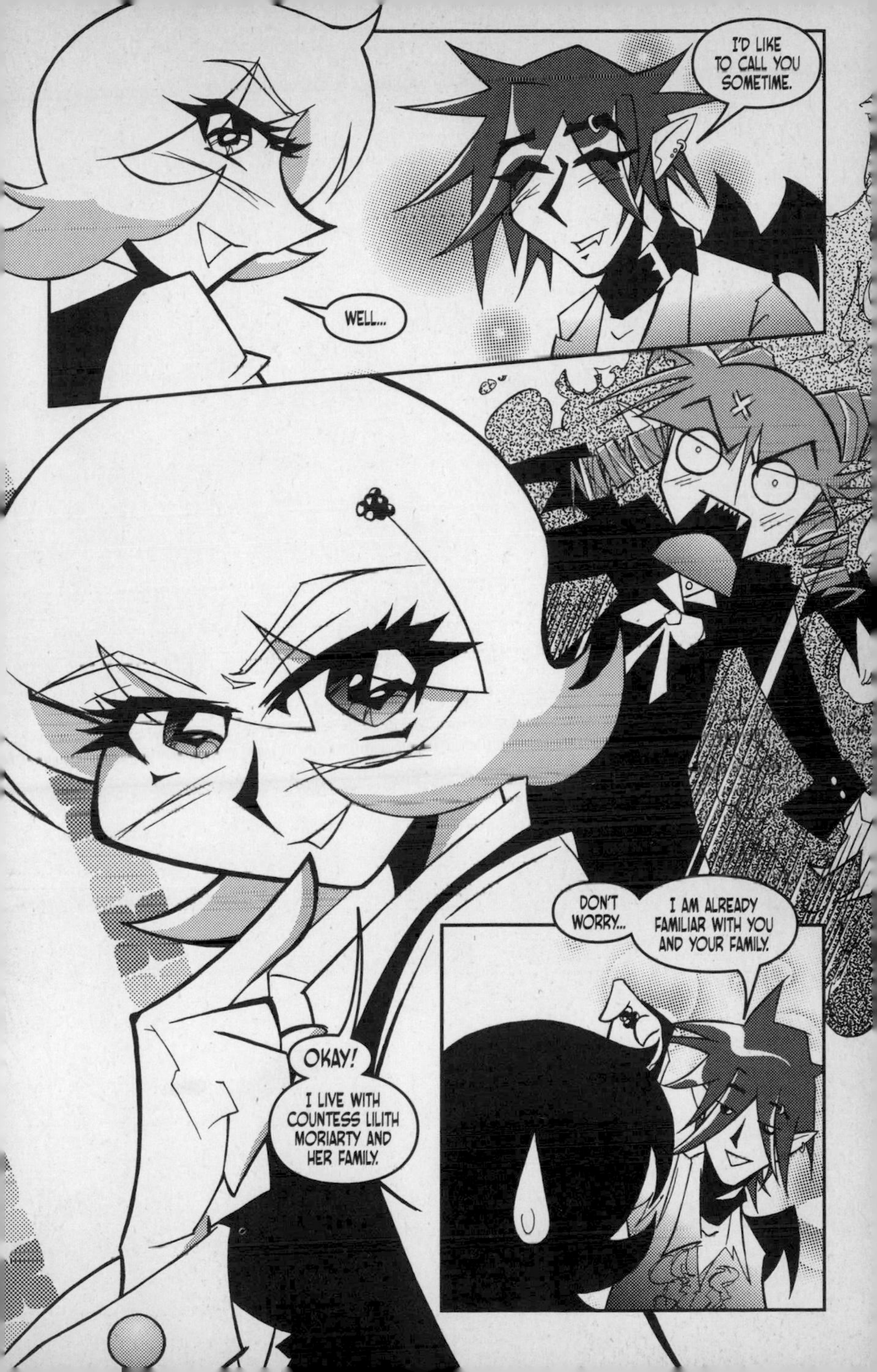
I'D LIKE TO CALL YOU SOMETIME.
WELL...
OKAY!
I LIVE WITH COUNTESS LILITH MORIARTY AND HER FAMILY.
DON'T WORRY...
I AM ALREADY FAMILIAR WITH YOU AND YOUR FAMILY.

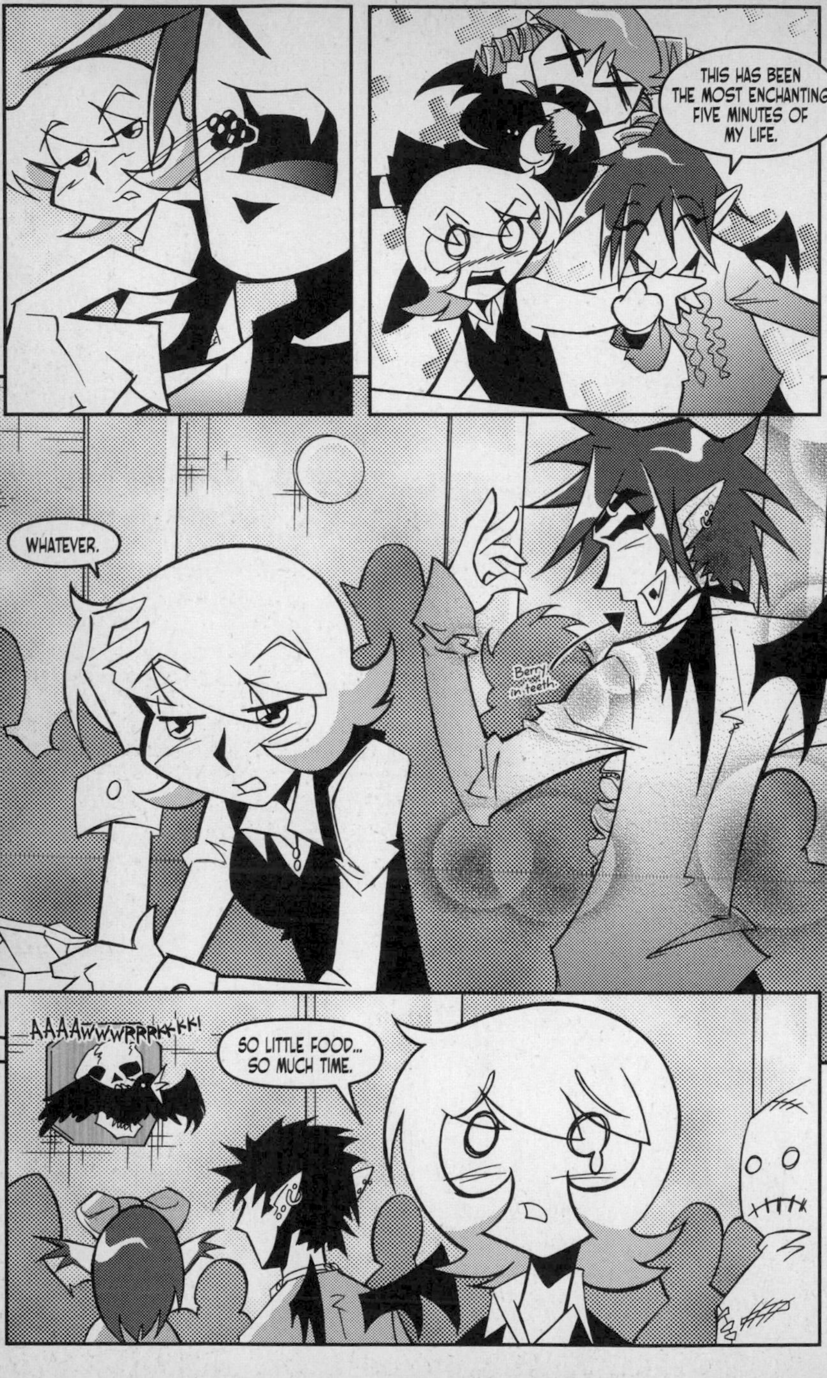
THIS HAS BEEN THE MOST ENCHANTING FIVE MINUTES OF MY LIFE.
Berry in teeth.
WHATEVER.
SO LITTLE FOOD... SO MUCH TIME.
AAAAWWWRRRKKK!

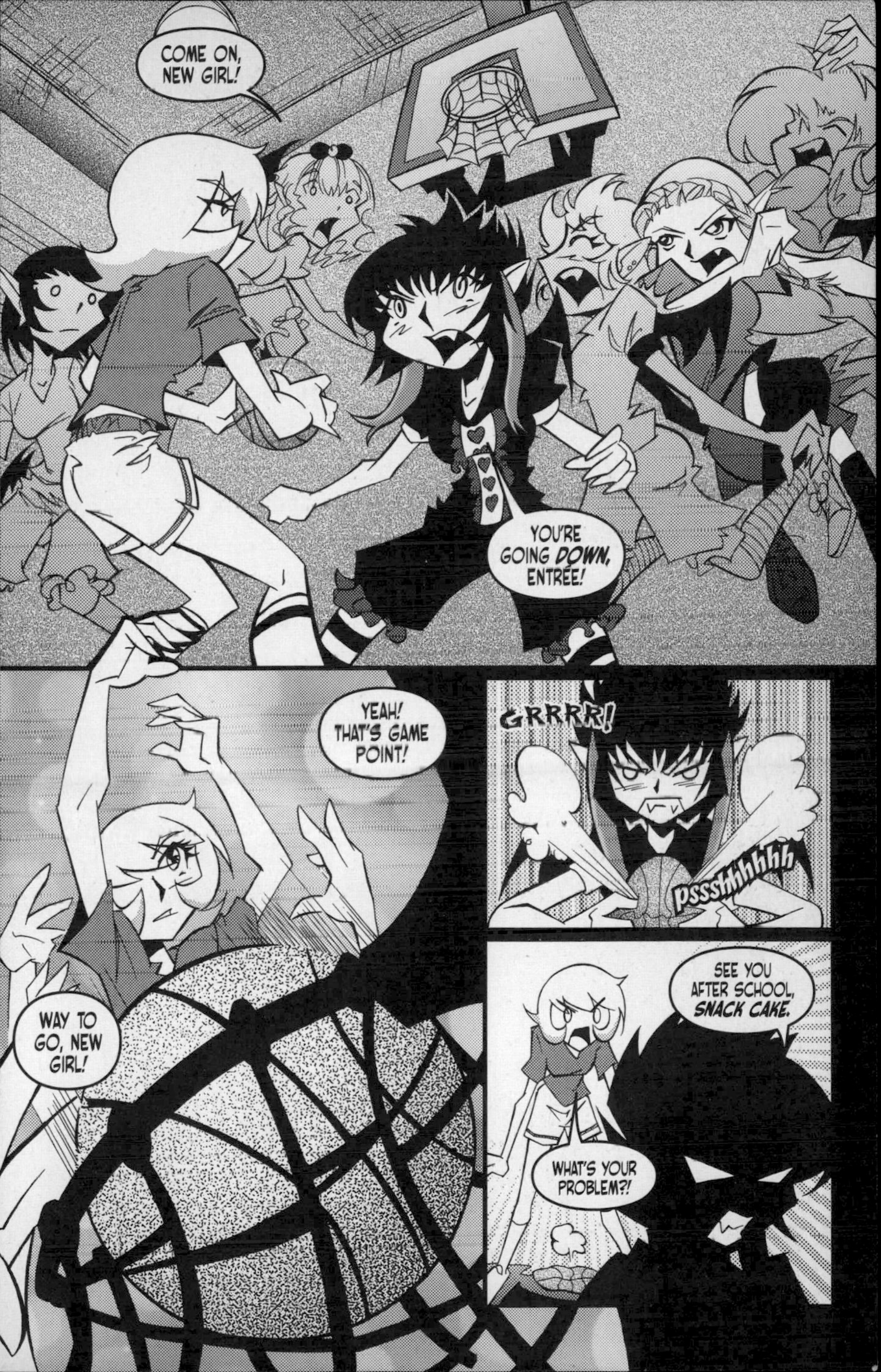
COME ON, NEW GIRL!
YOU'RE GOING *DOWN*, ENTRÉE!
YEAH! THAT'S GAME POINT!
WAY TO GO, NEW GIRL!
GRRRRR!
pssshhhhhh
SEE YOU AFTER SCHOOL, *SNACK CAKE.*
WHAT'S YOUR PROBLEM?!

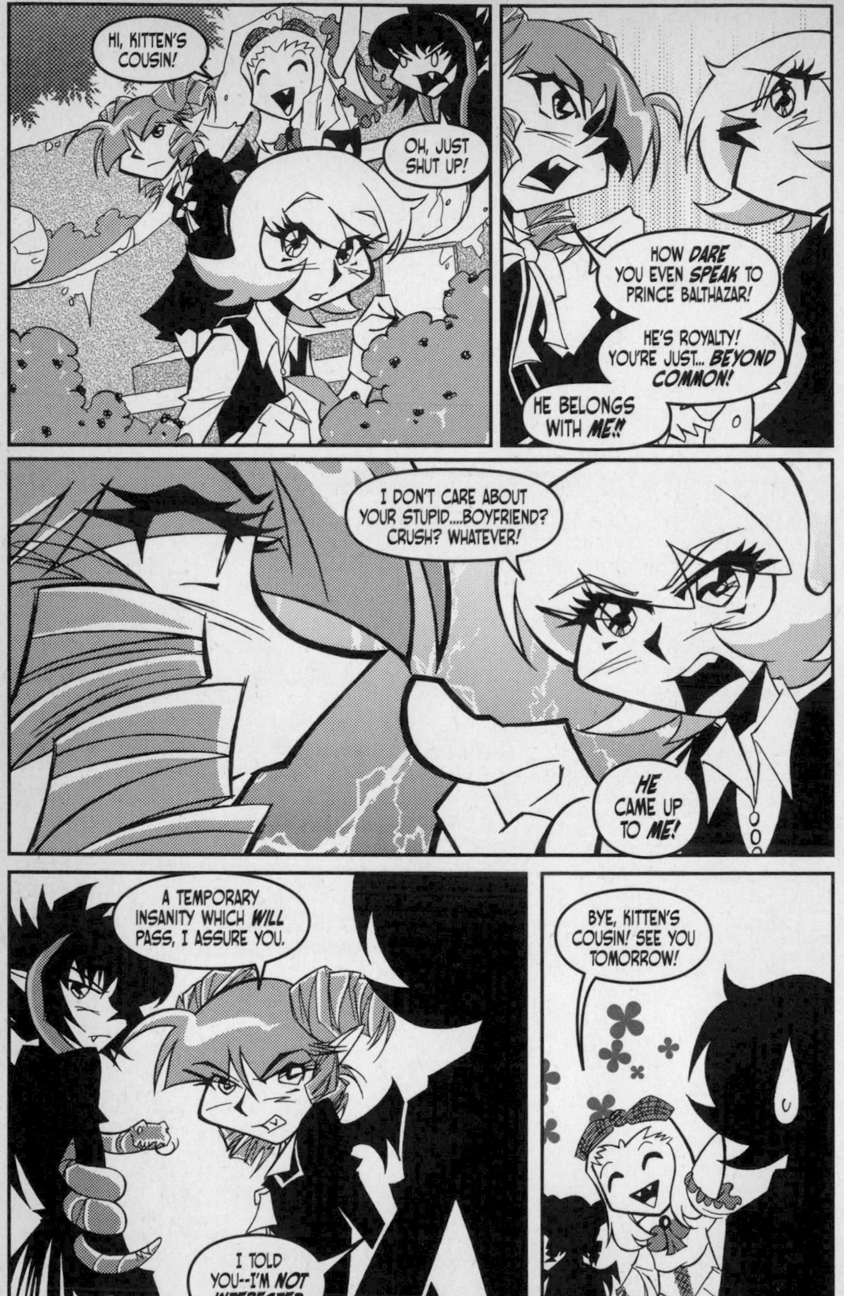
HI, KITTEN'S COUSIN!
OH, JUST SHUT UP!
HOW **DARE** YOU EVEN **SPEAK** TO PRINCE BALTHAZAR!
HE'S ROYALTY! YOU'RE JUST... **BEYOND COMMON!**
HE BELONGS WITH **ME!!**
I DON'T CARE ABOUT YOUR STUPID....BOYFRIEND? CRUSH? WHATEVER!
HE CAME UP TO **ME!**
A TEMPORARY INSANITY WHICH **WILL** PASS, I ASSURE YOU.
I TOLD YOU--I'M **NOT INTERESTED.**
BYE, KITTEN'S COUSIN! SEE YOU TOMORROW!

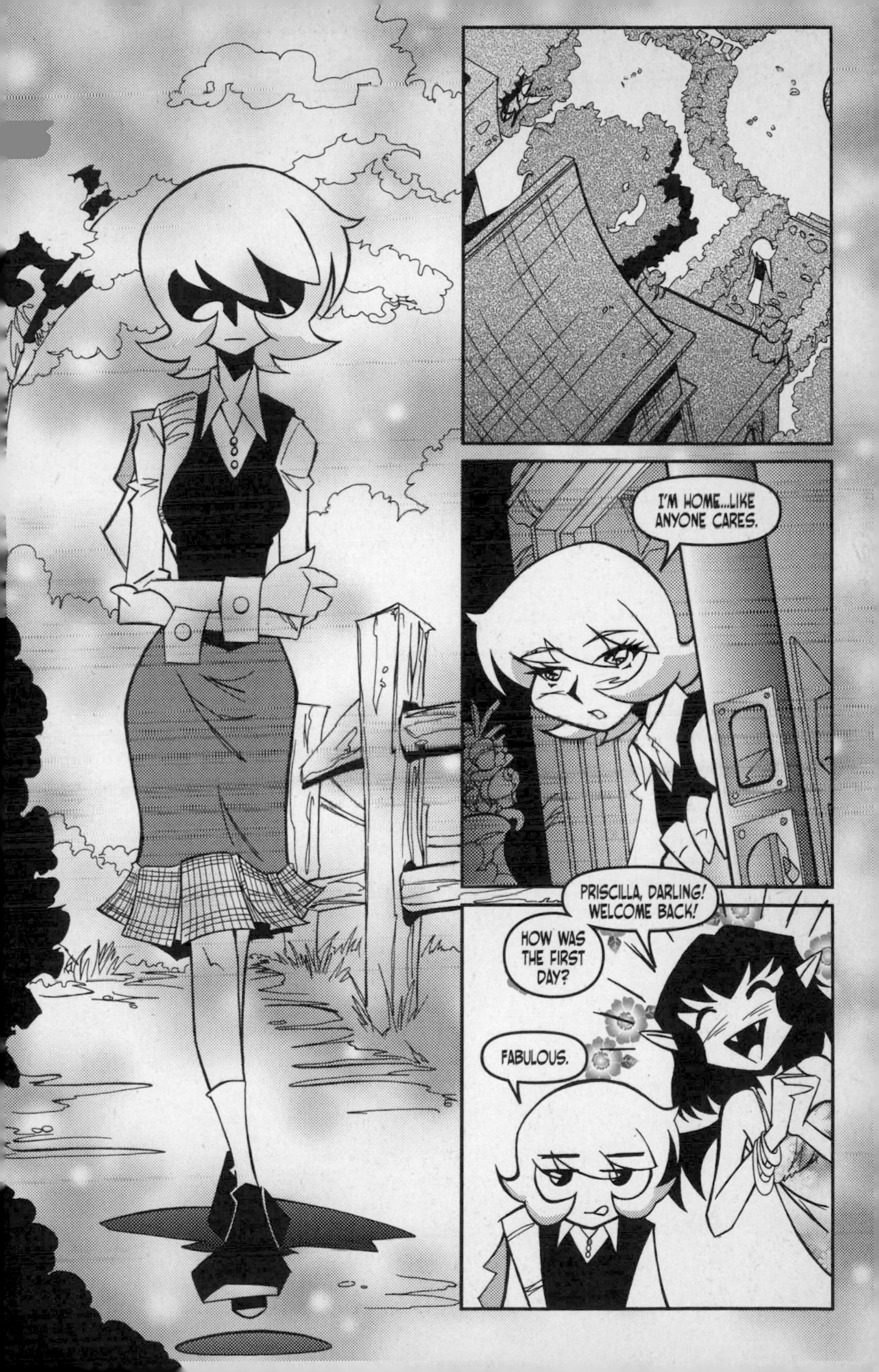
I'M HOME...LIKE ANYONE CARES.
PRISCILLA, DARLING! WELCOME BACK!
HOW WAS THE FIRST DAY?
FABULOUS.

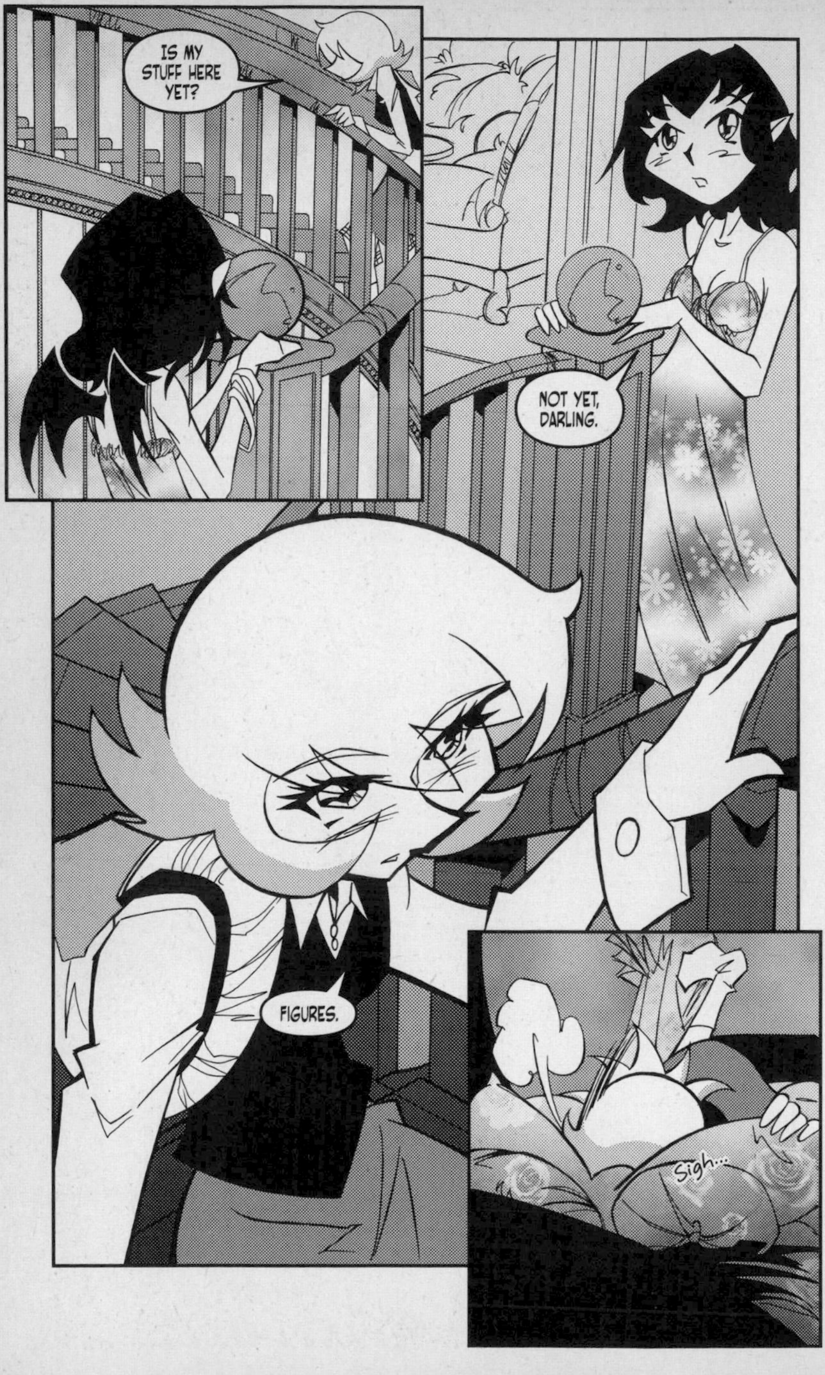
IS MY STUFF HERE YET?
NOT YET, DARLING.
FIGURES.
Sigh...

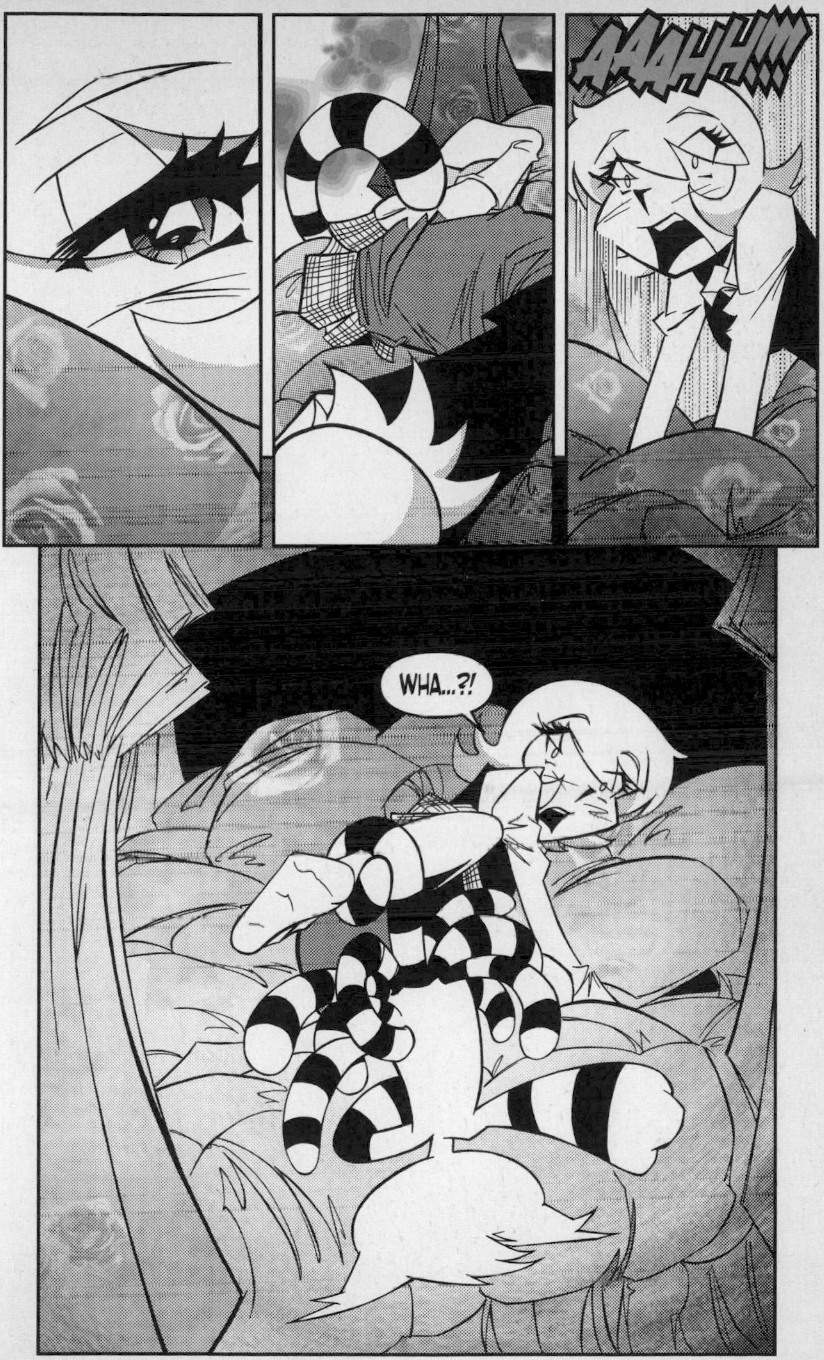
AAAHHH!!!
WHA...?!

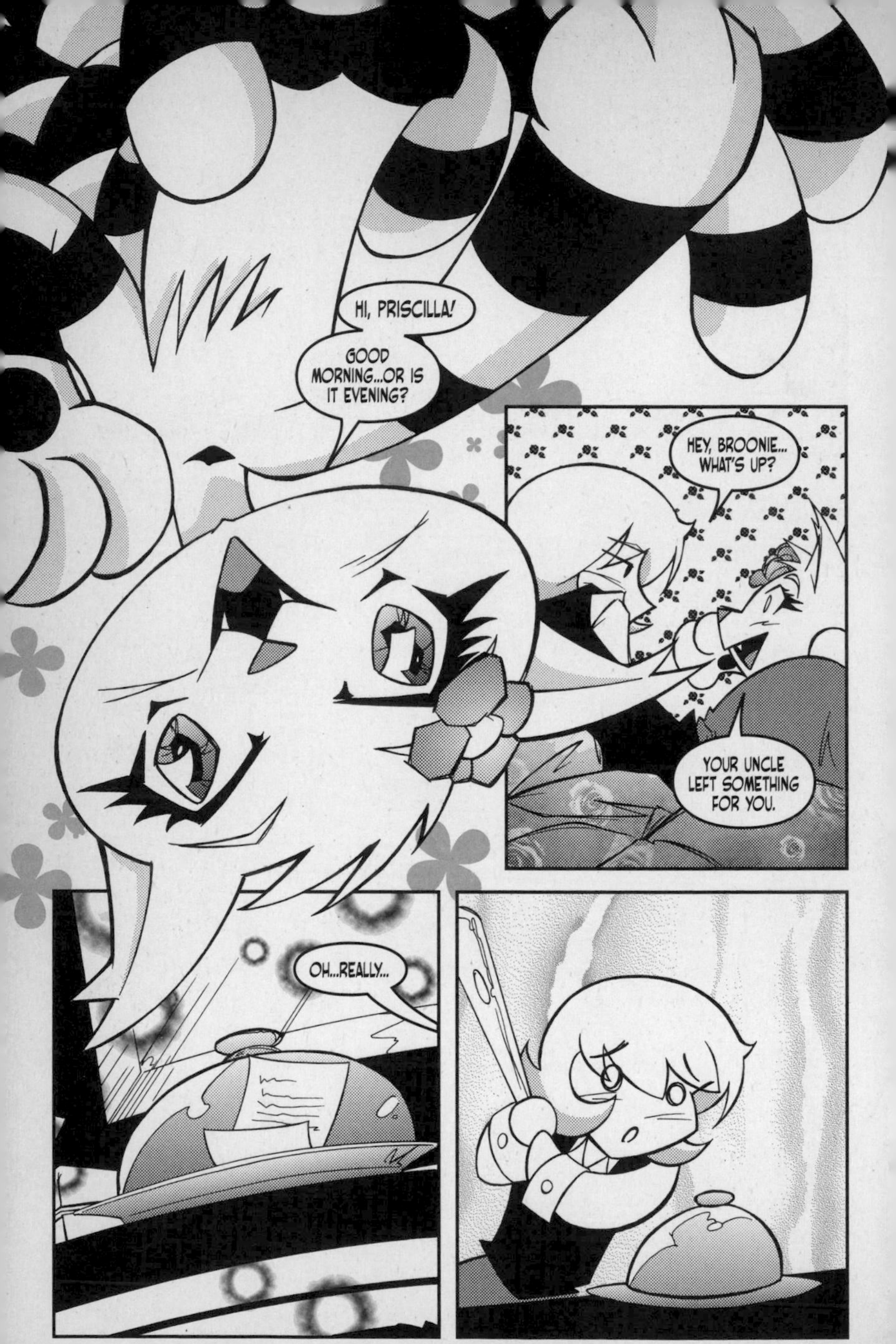
HI, PRISCILLA!
GOOD MORNING...OR IS IT EVENING?
HEY, BROONIE... WHAT'S UP?
YOUR UNCLE LEFT SOMETHING FOR YOU.
OH...REALLY...

Dear Priscilla
One time I heard about a recipe for a "sandwich" Popular with humans. I thought you might like one for an afternoon snack
Wolfgar
OH, WELL. IT'S STILL FOOD!
HOW WAS SCHOOL?
I ATE SOME DENIM LINT TODAY. *VERY* RARE.
YOU'RE NOT GONNA BELIEVE IT...
DO I SMELL BERRIES?

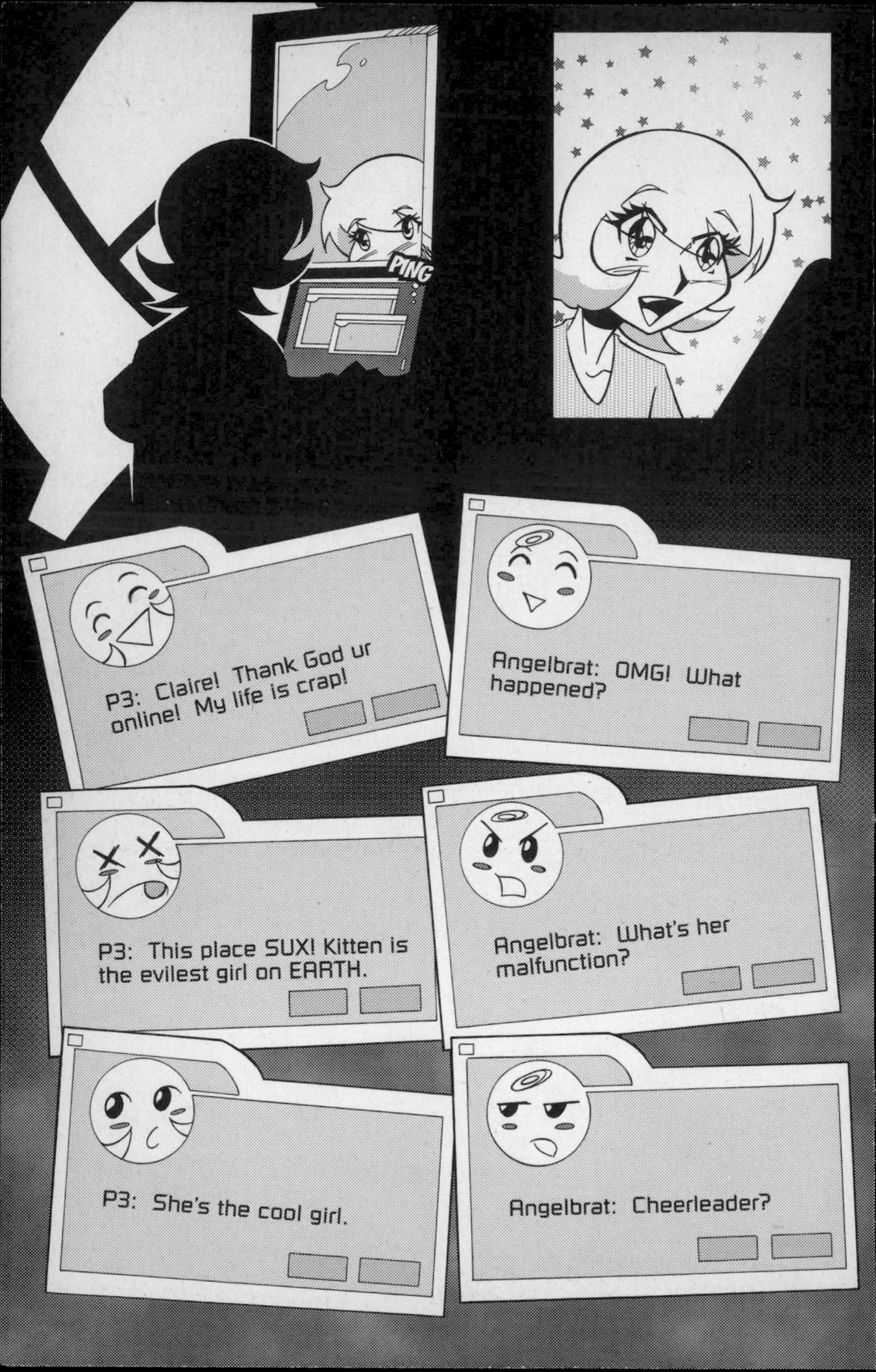
PING
P3: Claire! Thank God ur online! My life is crap!
Angelbrat: OMG! What happened?
P3: This place SUX! Kitten is the evilest girl on EARTH.
Angelbrat: What's her malfunction?
P3: She's the cool girl.
Angelbrat: Cheerleader?

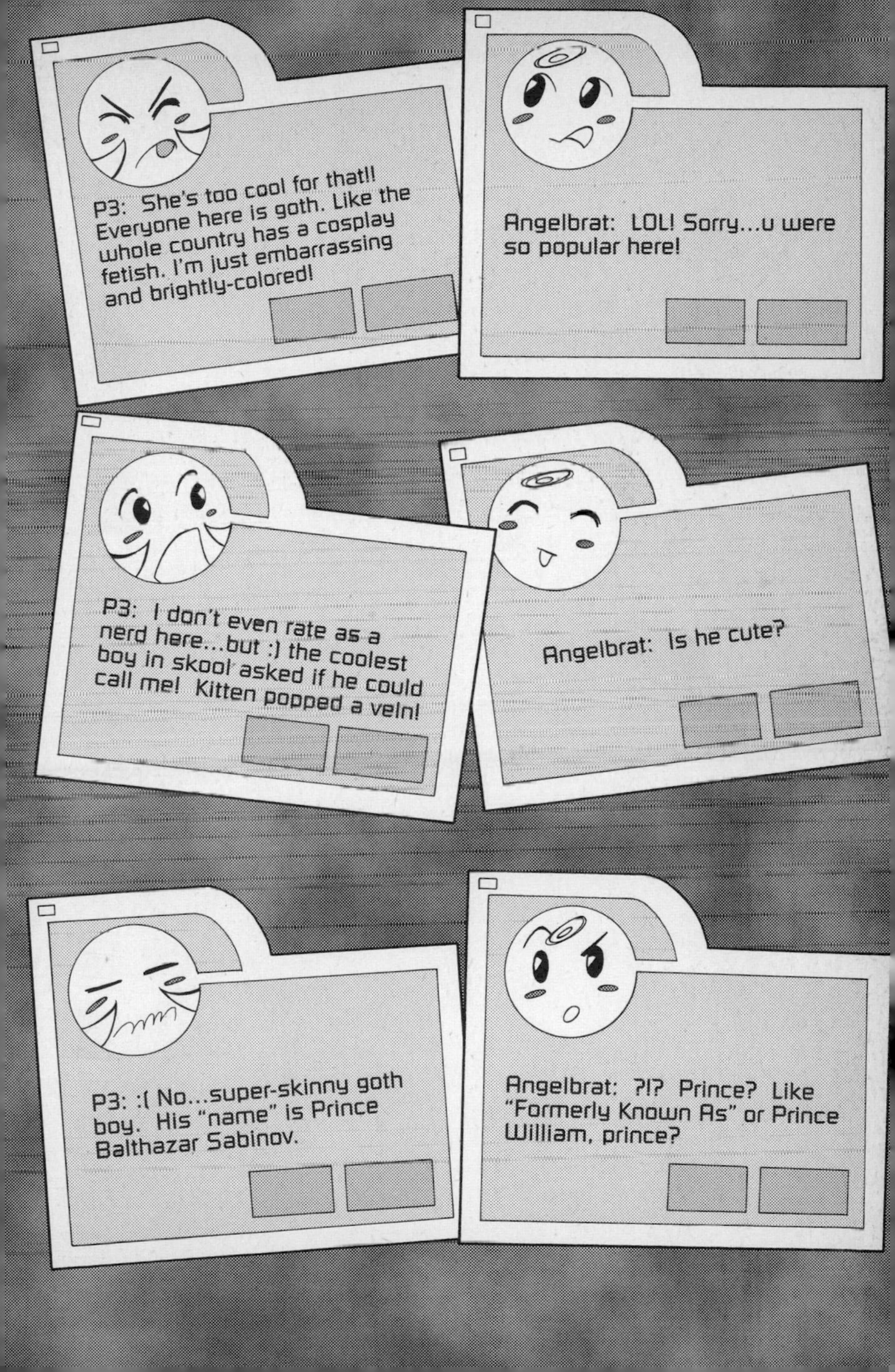
P3: She's too cool for that!! Everyone here is goth. Like the whole country has a cosplay fetish. I'm just embarrassing and brightly-colored!
Angelbrat: LOL! Sorry...u were so popular here!
P3: I don't even rate as a nerd here...but :) the coolest boy in skool asked if he could call me! Kitten popped a vein!
Angelbrat: Is he cute?
P3: :(No...super-skinny goth boy. His "name" is Prince Balthazar Sabinov.
Angelbrat: ?!? Prince? Like "Formerly Known As" or Prince William, prince?

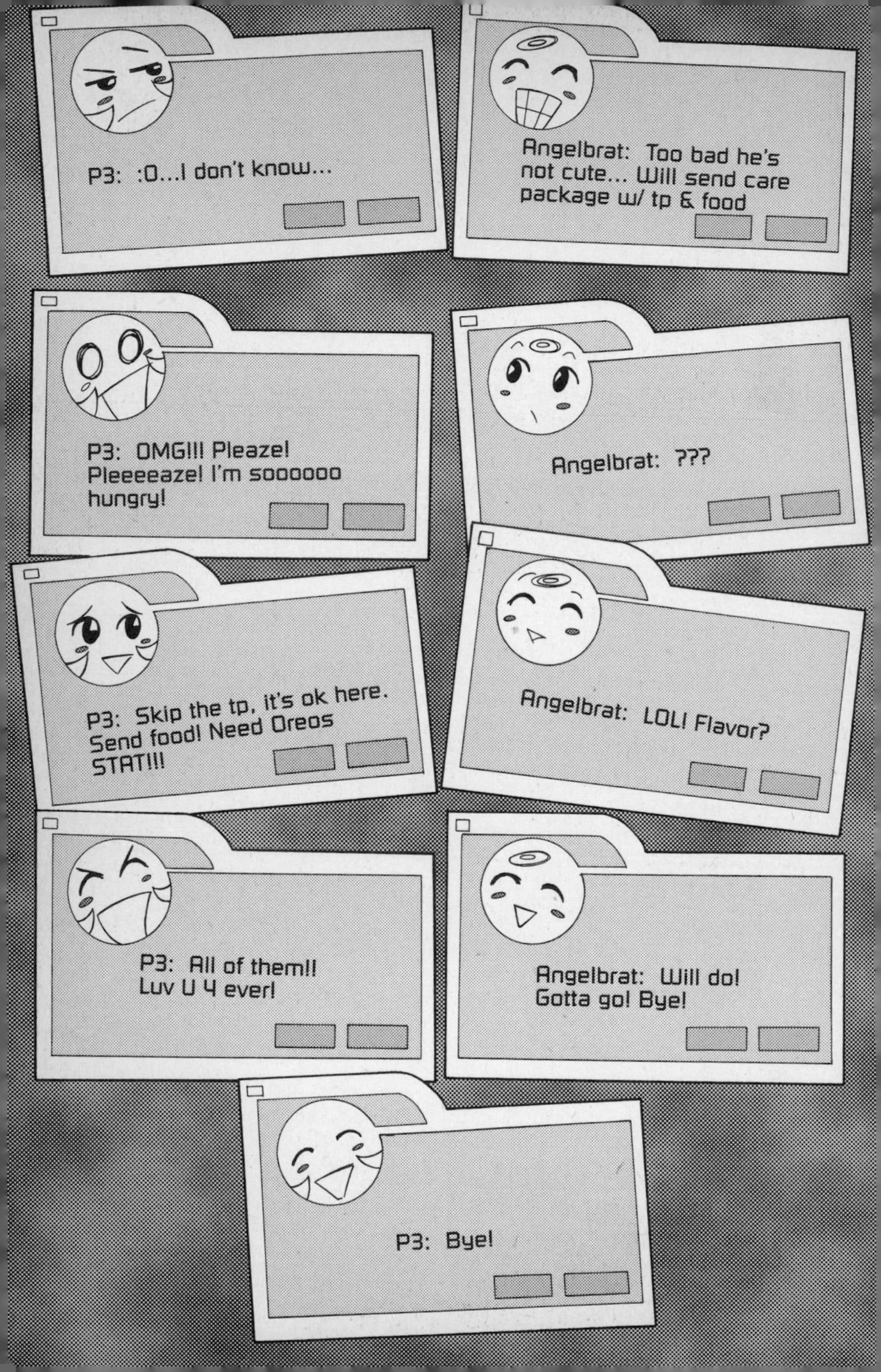
P3: :O...I don't know...
Angelbrat: Too bad he's not cute... Will send care package w/ tp & food
P3: OMG!!! Pleaze! Pleeeeaze! I'm soooooo hungry!
Angelbrat: ???
P3: Skip the tp, it's ok here. Send food! Need Oreos STAT!!!
Angelbrat: LOL! Flavor?
P3: All of them!! Luv U 4 ever!
Angelbrat: Will do! Gotta go! Bye!
P3: Bye!

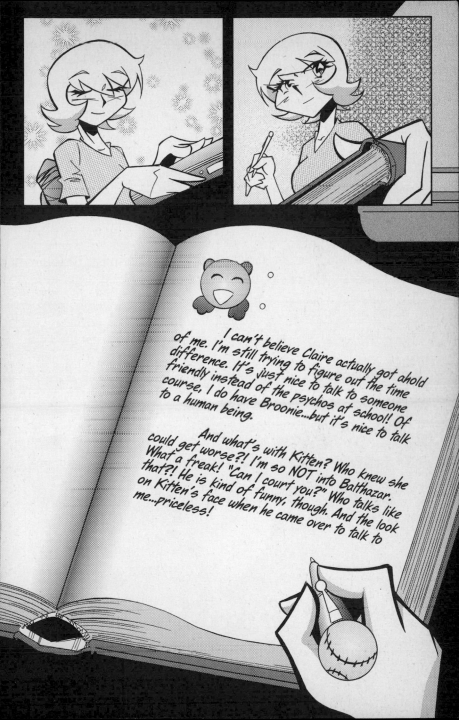

I can't believe Claire actually got ahold of me. I'm still trying to figure out the time difference. It's just nice to talk to someone friendly instead of the psychos at school! Of course, I do have Broonie...but it's nice to talk to a human being.

And what's with Kitten? Who knew she could get worse?! I'm so NOT into Balthazar. What a freak! "Can I court you?" Who talks like that?! He is kind of funny, though. And the look on Kitten's face when he came over to talk to me...priceless!

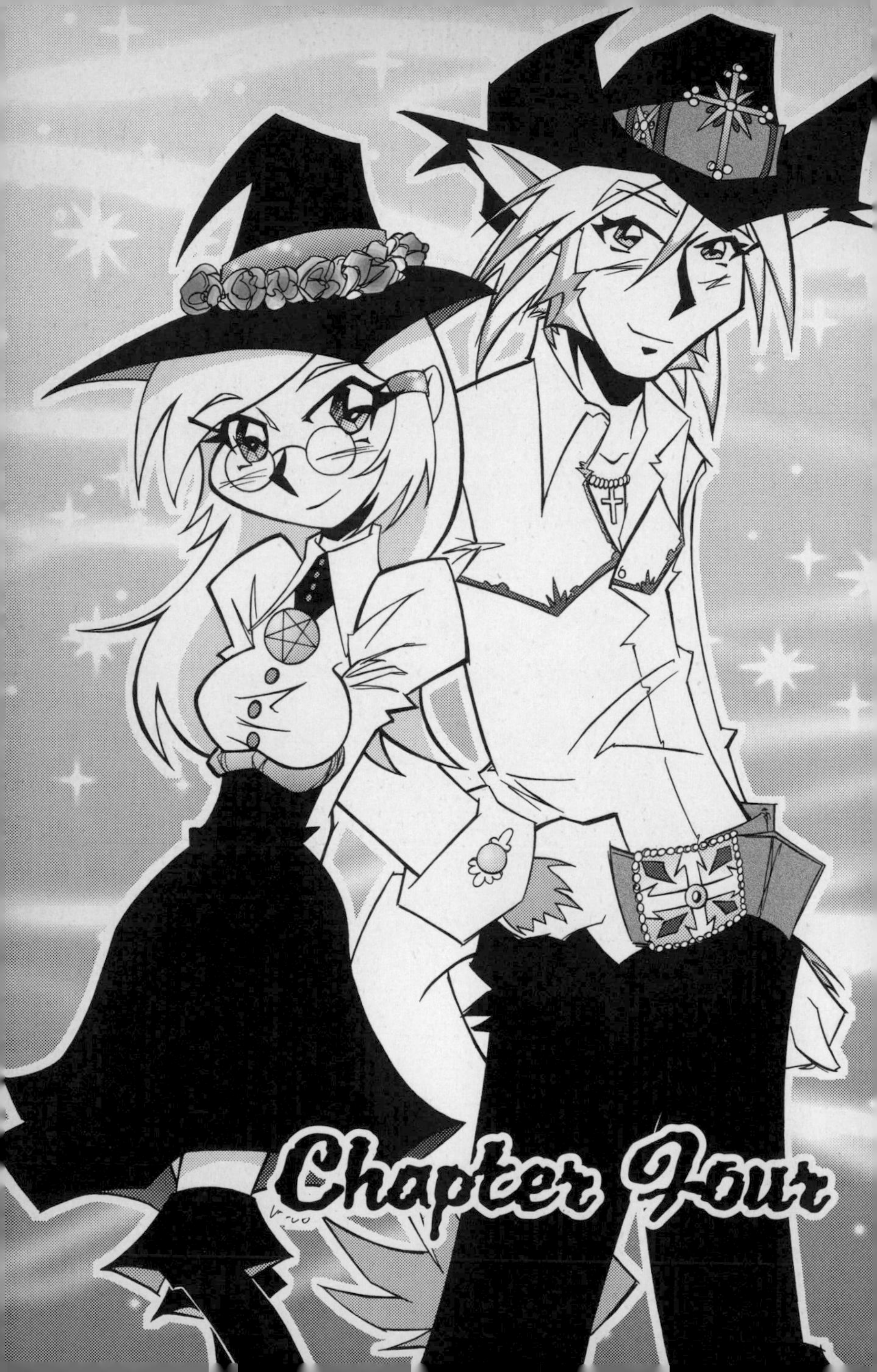
Chapter Four

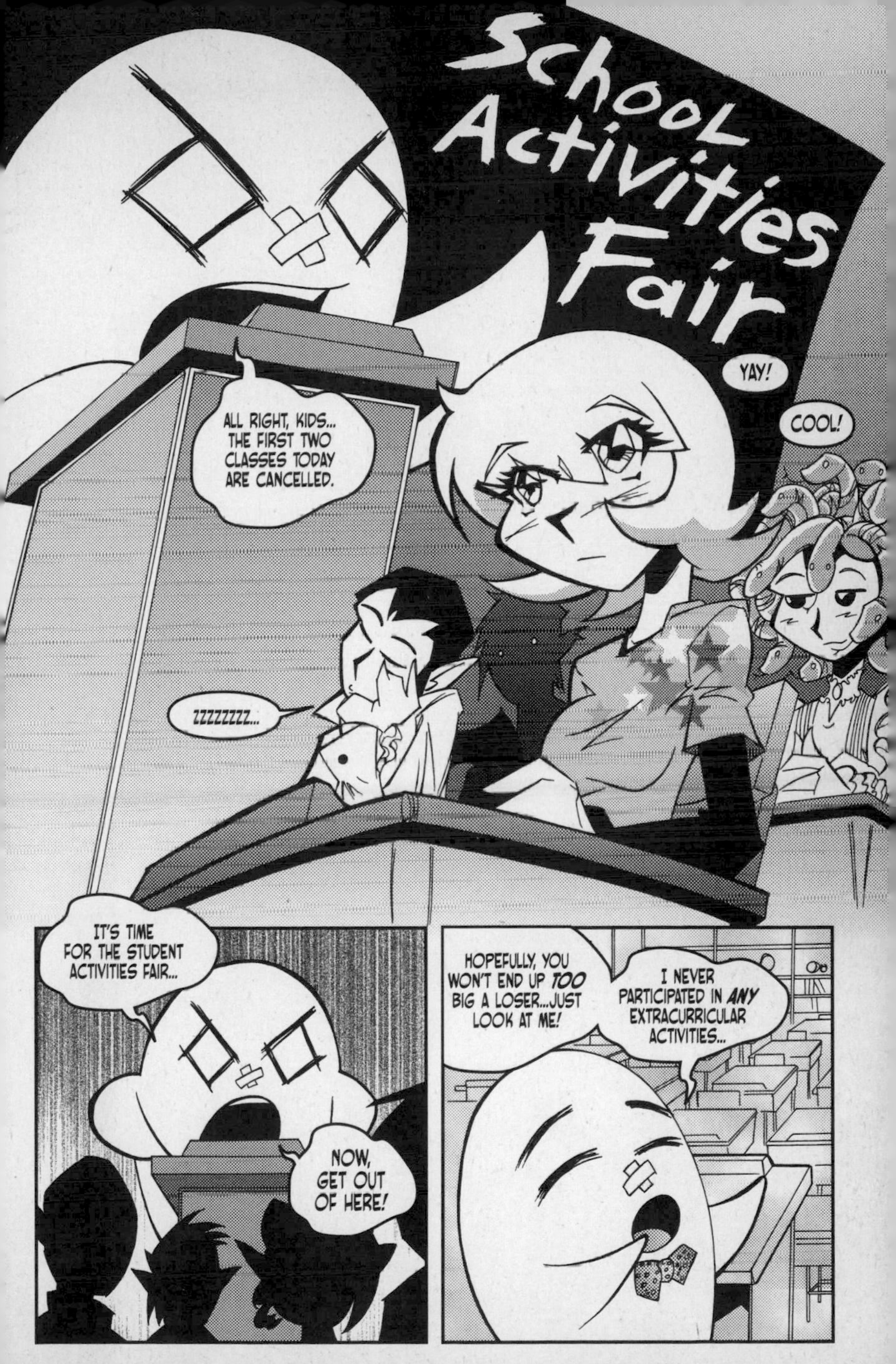
School Activities Fair
ALL RIGHT, KIDS... THE FIRST TWO CLASSES TODAY ARE CANCELLED.
YAY!
COOL!
ZZZZZZZZ...
IT'S TIME FOR THE STUDENT ACTIVITIES FAIR...
NOW, GET OUT OF HERE!
HOPEFULLY, YOU WON'T END UP *TOO* BIG A LOSER...JUST LOOK AT ME!
I NEVER PARTICIPATED IN *ANY* EXTRACURRICULAR ACTIVITIES...

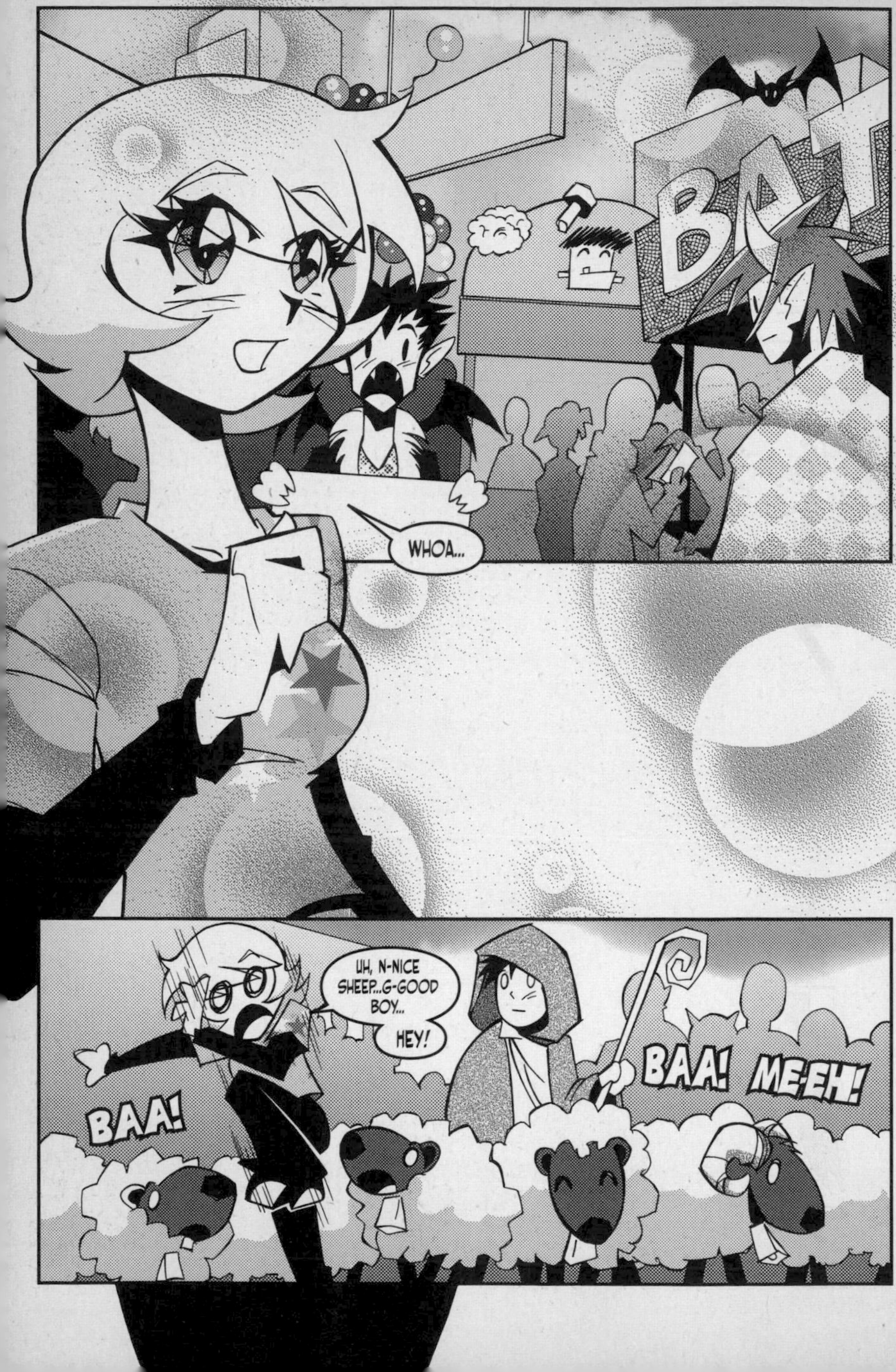
BAT
WHOA...
UH, N-NICE SHEEP...G-GOOD BOY...
HEY!
BAA!
BAA!
ME-EH!

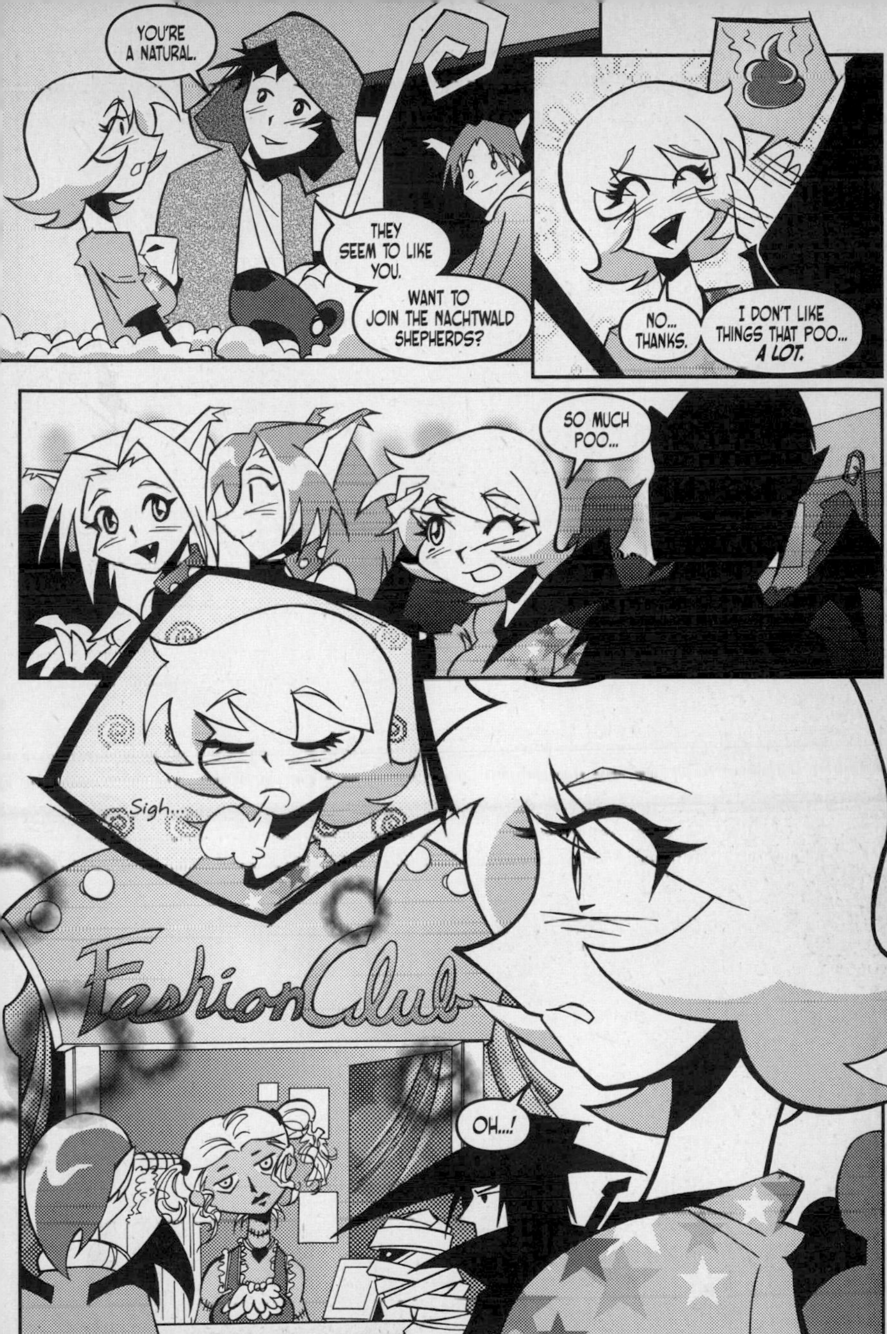
YOU'RE A NATURAL.
THEY SEEM TO LIKE YOU.
WANT TO JOIN THE NACHTWALD SHEPHERDS?
NO... THANKS.
I DON'T LIKE THINGS THAT POO... *A LOT.*
SO MUCH POO...
Sigh...
Fashion Club
OH...!

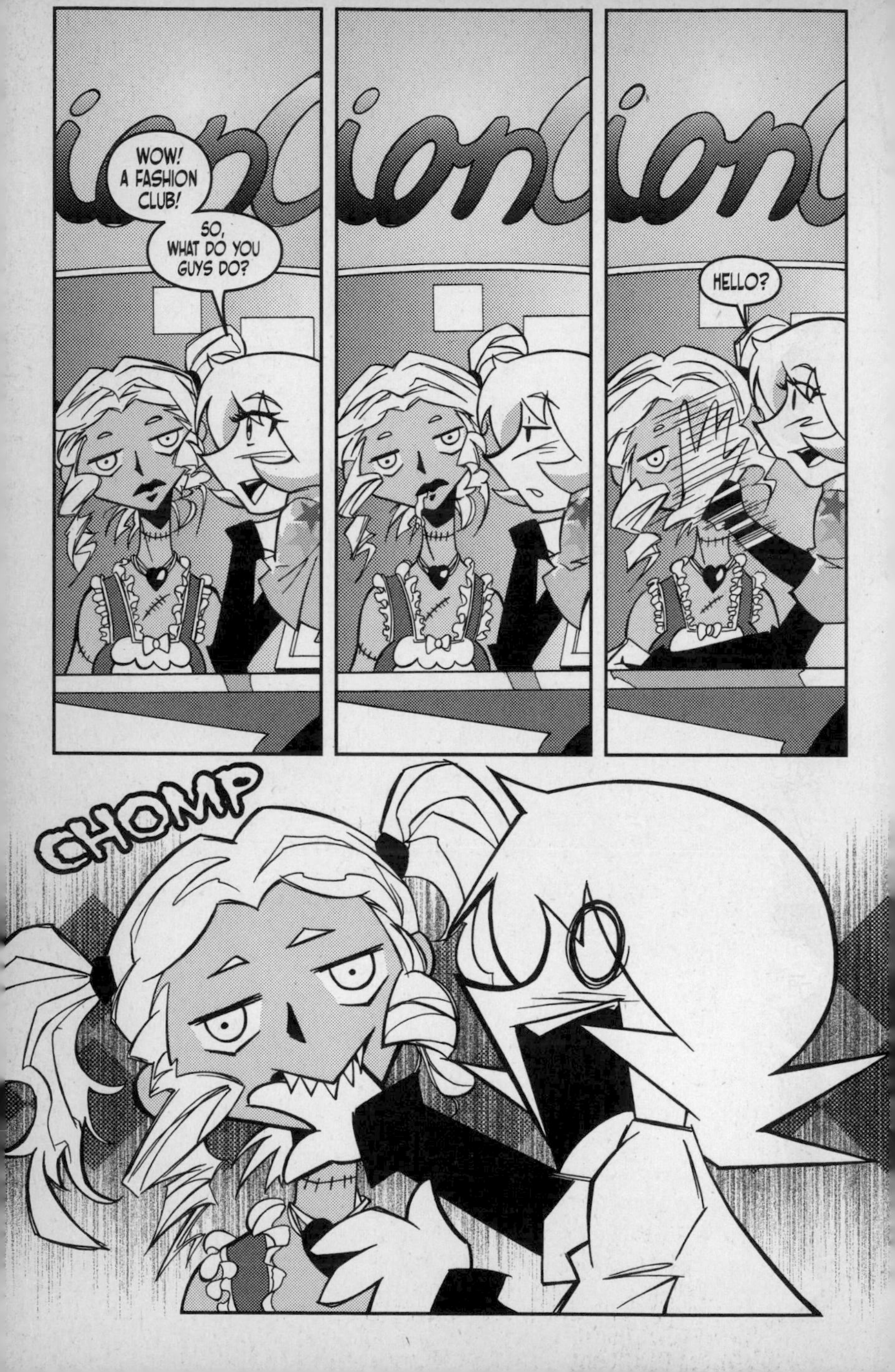
WOW! A FASHION CLUB!
SO, WHAT DO YOU GUYS DO?
HELLO?
CHOMP

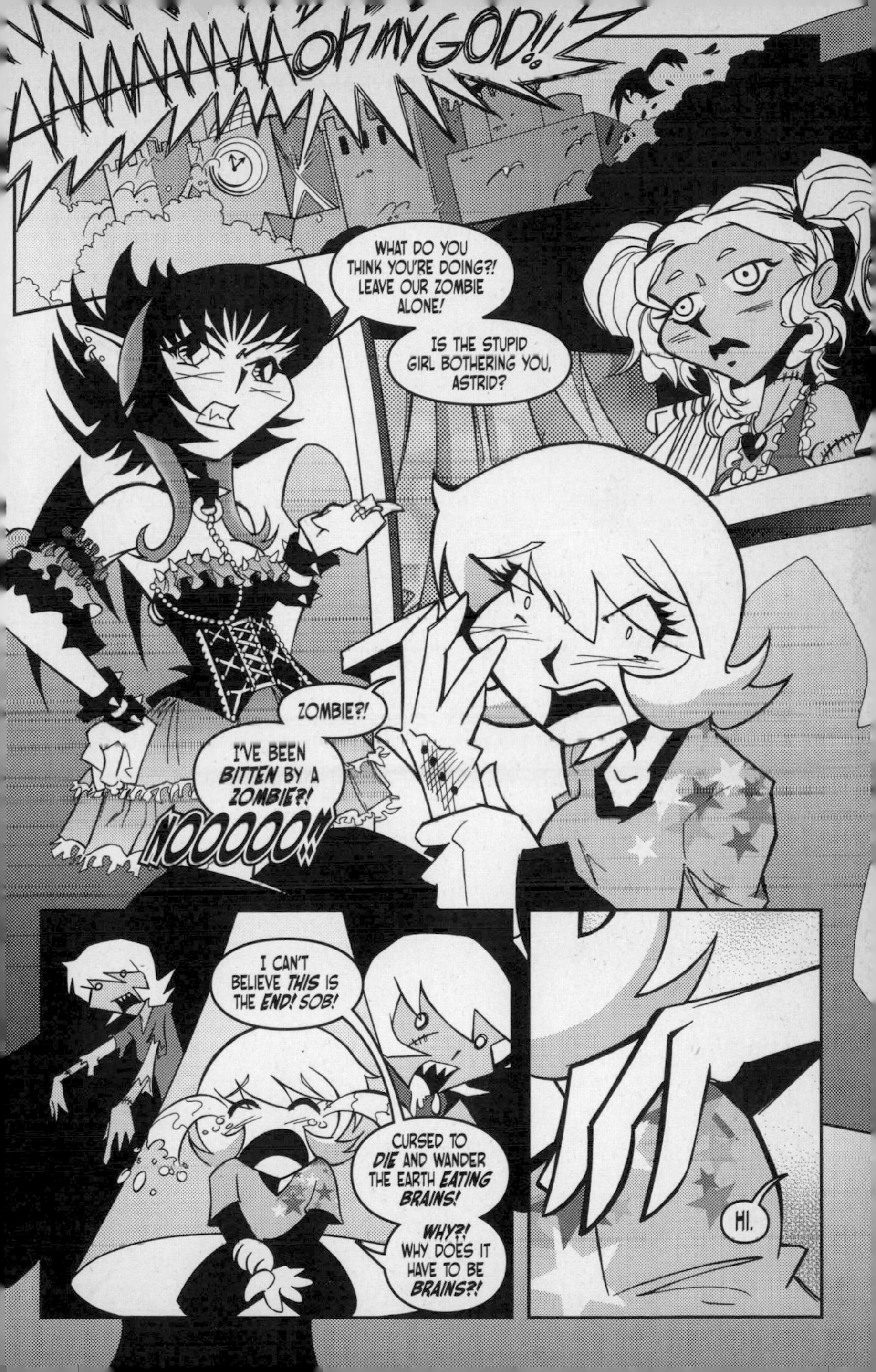
AAAAAAAAAAAAAAAAAAA oh my GOD!!
WHAT DO YOU THINK YOU'RE DOING?! LEAVE OUR ZOMBIE ALONE!
IS THE STUPID GIRL BOTHERING YOU, ASTRID?
ZOMBIE?!
I'VE BEEN *BITTEN* BY A *ZOMBIE?!*
NOOOOO!!
I CAN'T BELIEVE *THIS* IS THE *END!* SOB!
CURSED TO *DIE* AND WANDER THE EARTH *EATING BRAINS!*
WHY?! WHY DOES IT HAVE TO BE *BRAINS?!*
HI.

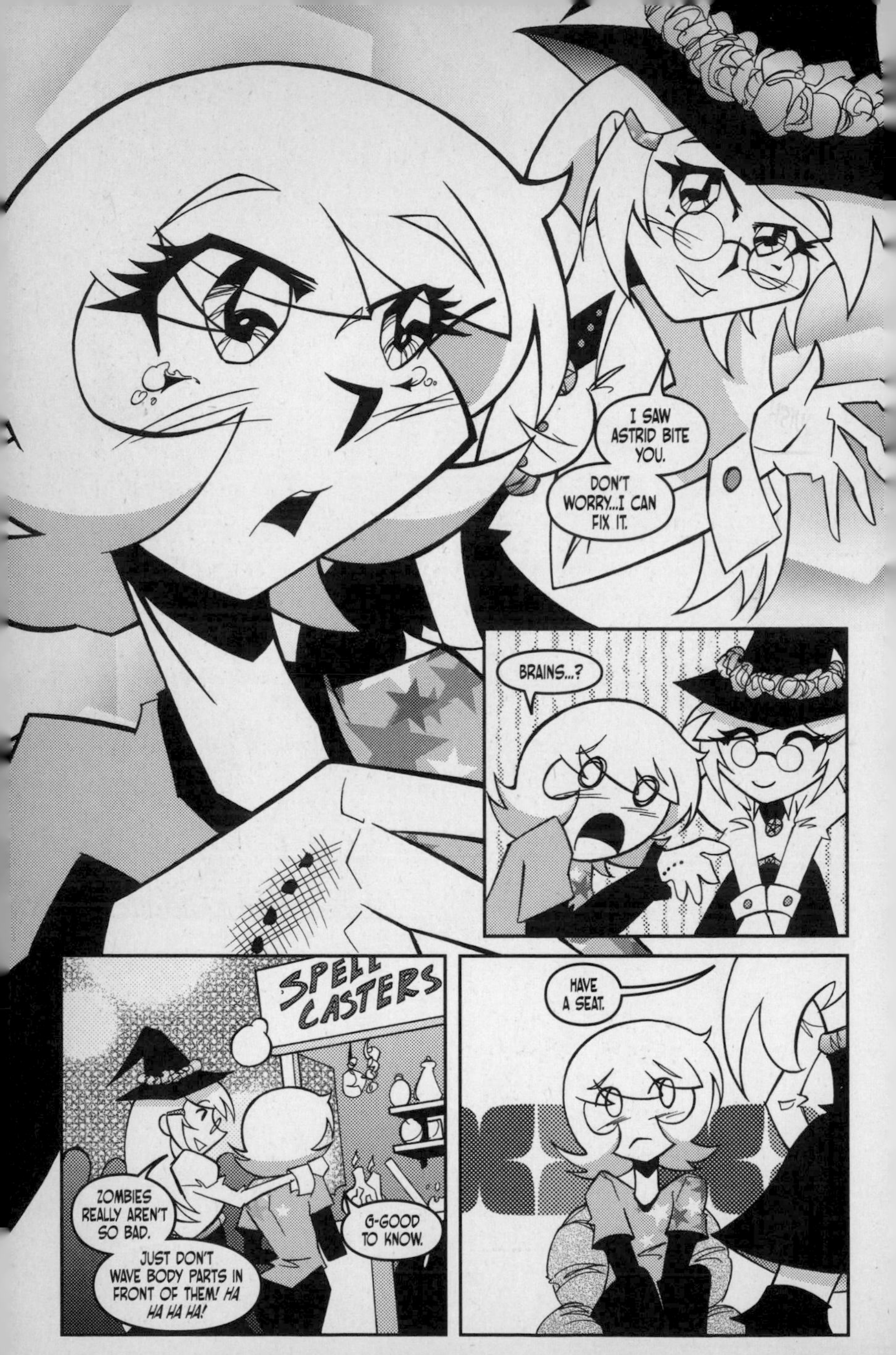
I SAW ASTRID BITE YOU.
DON'T WORRY...I CAN FIX IT.
BRAINS...?
SPELL CASTERS
ZOMBIES REALLY AREN'T SO BAD.
JUST DON'T WAVE BODY PARTS IN FRONT OF THEM! HA HA HA HA!
G-GOOD TO KNOW.
HAVE A SEAT.

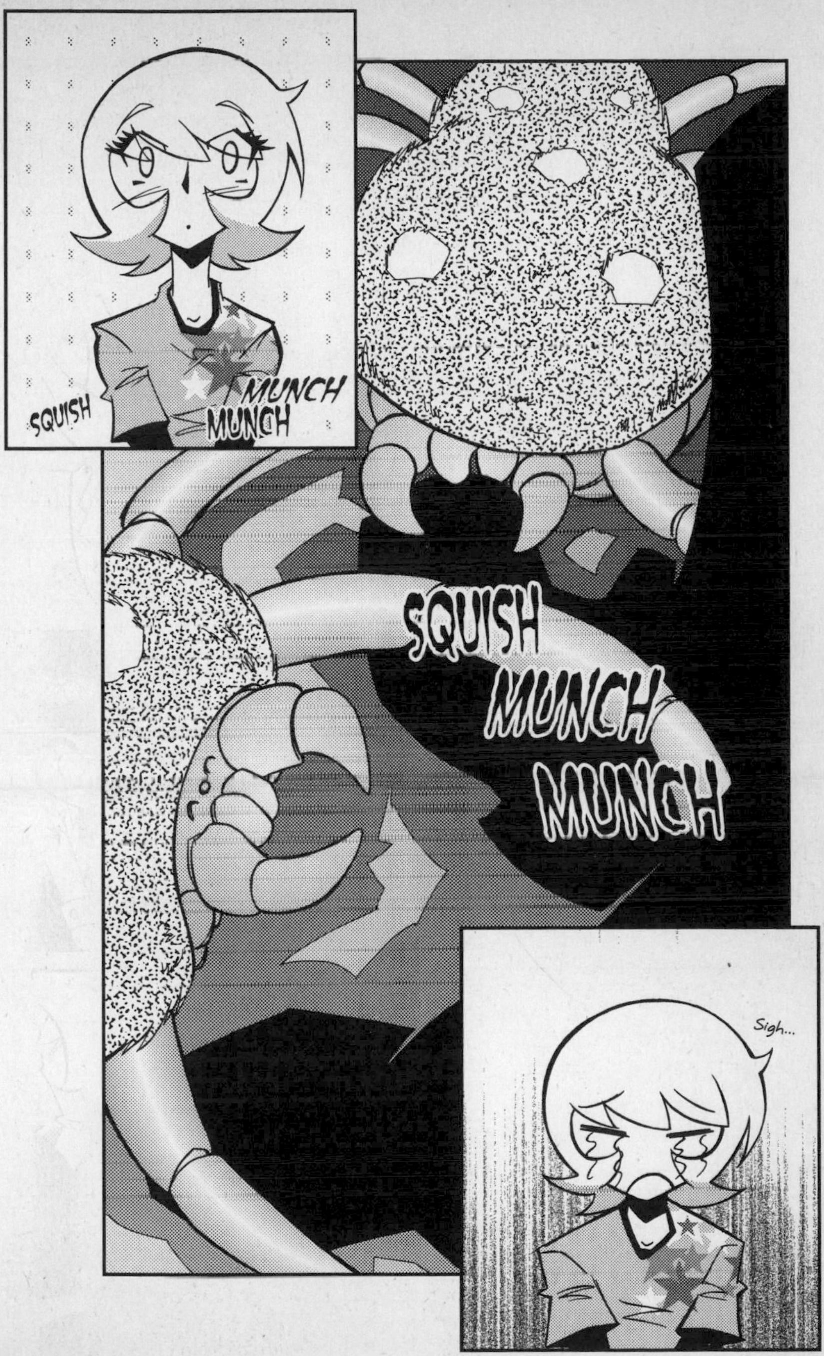
SQUISH
MUNCH
MUNCH
SQUISH
MUNCH
MUNCH
Sigh...

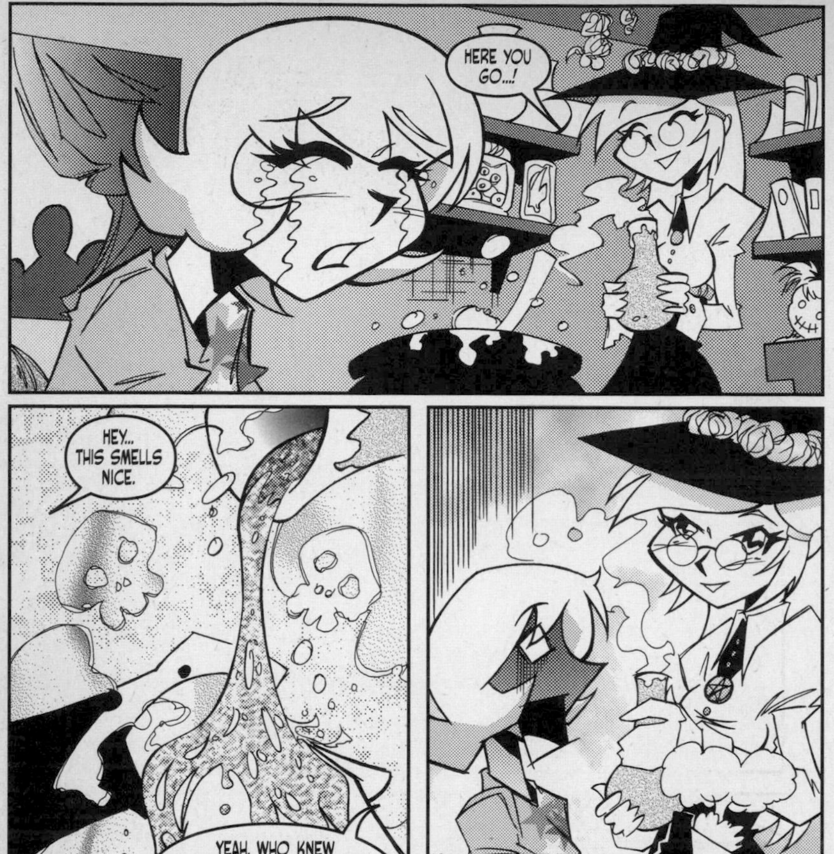
HERE YOU GO...!
HEY... THIS SMELLS NICE.
YEAH. WHO KNEW TONGUE OF TOAD, EYE OF NEWT, BEAR URINE, BRATWURST AND TOFU COULD SMELL SO GOOD, HUH?

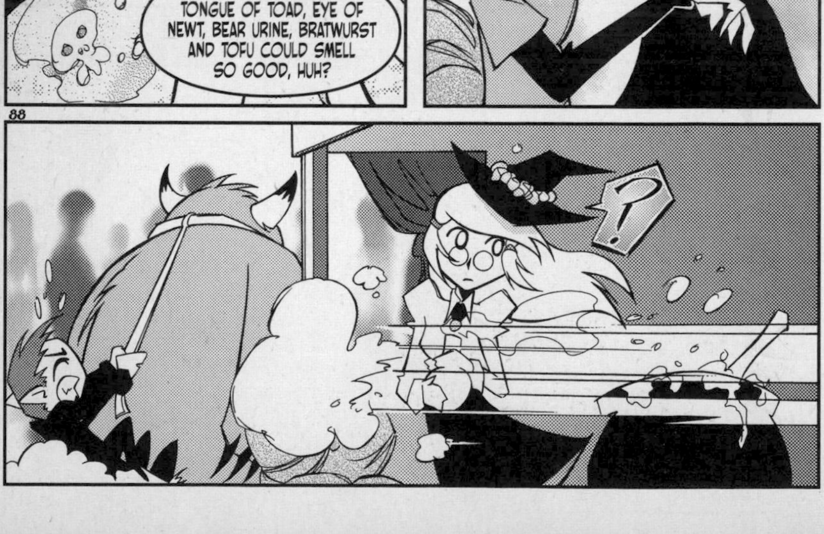
?!

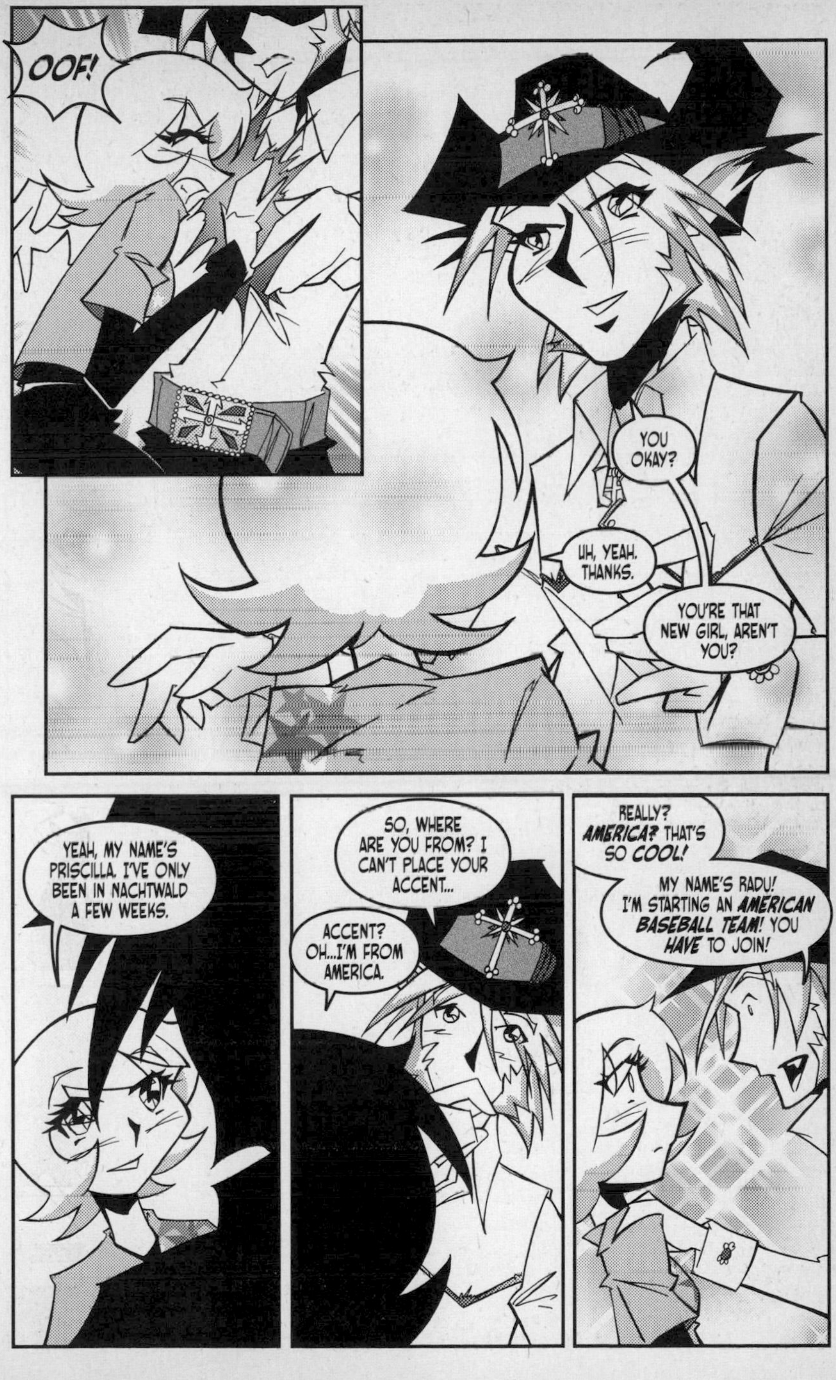
OOF!
YOU OKAY?
UH, YEAH. THANKS.
YOU'RE THAT NEW GIRL, AREN'T YOU?
YEAH, MY NAME'S PRISCILLA. I'VE ONLY BEEN IN NACHTWALD A FEW WEEKS.
SO, WHERE ARE YOU FROM? I CAN'T PLACE YOUR ACCENT...
ACCENT? OH...I'M FROM AMERICA.
REALLY? AMERICA? THAT'S SO COOL!
MY NAME'S RADU! I'M STARTING AN AMERICAN BASEBALL TEAM! YOU HAVE TO JOIN!

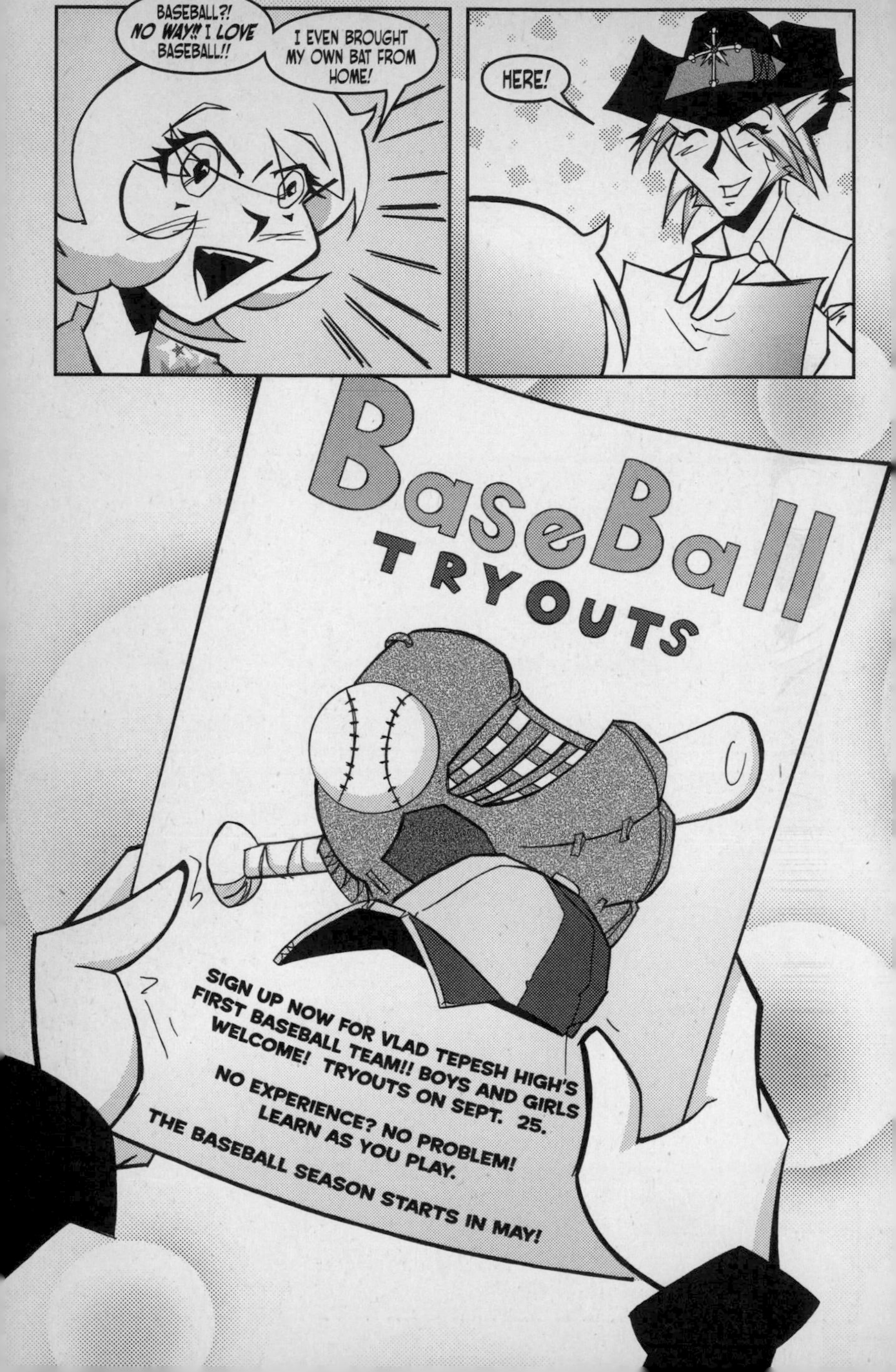

BASEBALL?! NO WAY!! I LOVE BASEBALL!!
I EVEN BROUGHT MY OWN BAT FROM HOME!
HERE!
BaseBall TRYOUTS
SIGN UP NOW FOR VLAD TEPESH HIGH'S FIRST BASEBALL TEAM!! BOYS AND GIRLS WELCOME! TRYOUTS ON SEPT. 25.
NO EXPERIENCE? NO PROBLEM! LEARN AS YOU PLAY.
THE BASEBALL SEASON STARTS IN MAY!

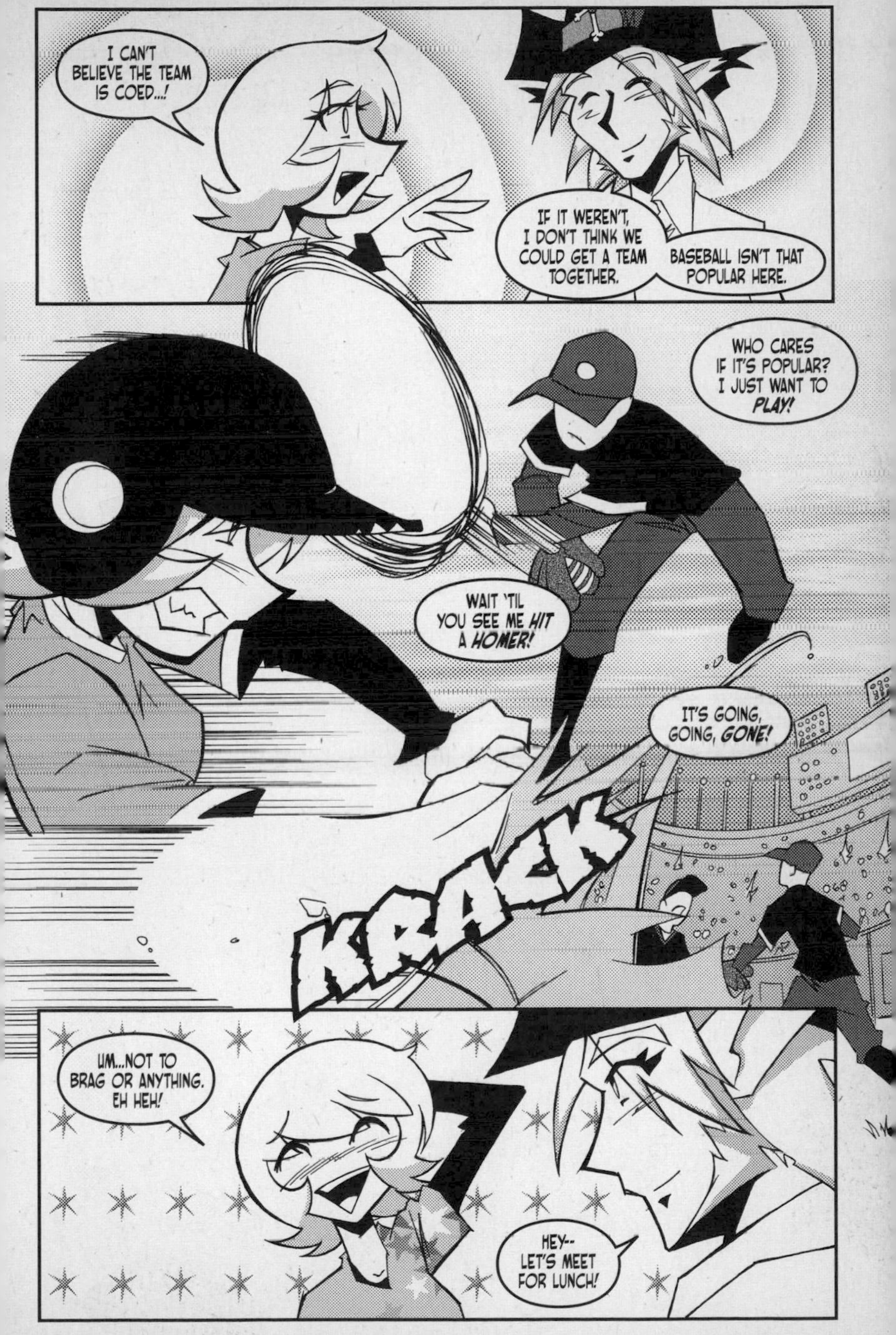
I CAN'T BELIEVE THE TEAM IS COED...!
IF IT WEREN'T, I DON'T THINK WE COULD GET A TEAM TOGETHER.
BASEBALL ISN'T THAT POPULAR HERE.
WHO CARES IF IT'S POPULAR? I JUST WANT TO PLAY!
WAIT 'TIL YOU SEE ME HIT A HOMER!
IT'S GOING, GOING, GONE!
KRACK
UM...NOT TO BRAG OR ANYTHING. EH HEH!
HEY-- LET'S MEET FOR LUNCH!

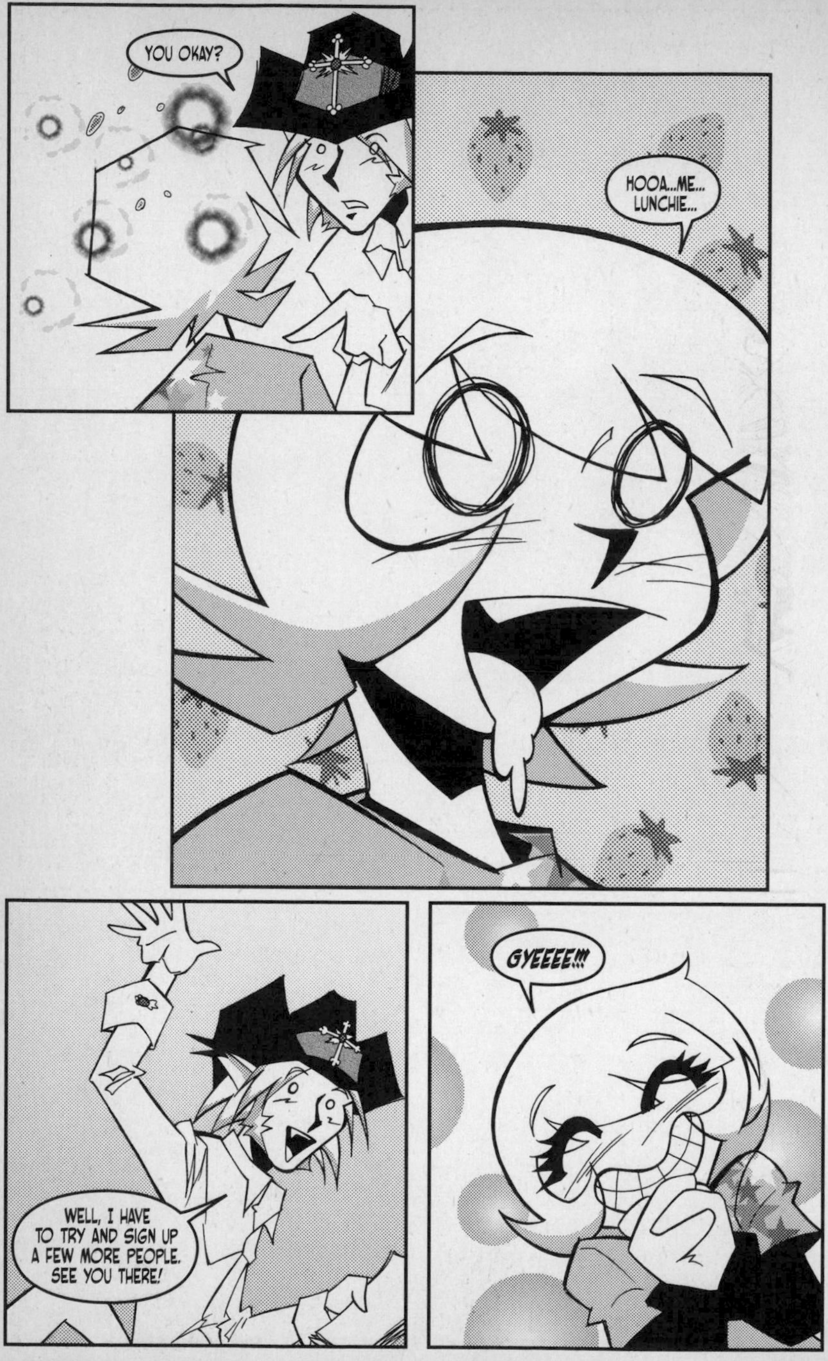
YOU OKAY?
HOOA...ME... LUNCHIE...
WELL, I HAVE TO TRY AND SIGN UP A FEW MORE PEOPLE. SEE YOU THERE!
GYEEEE!!!

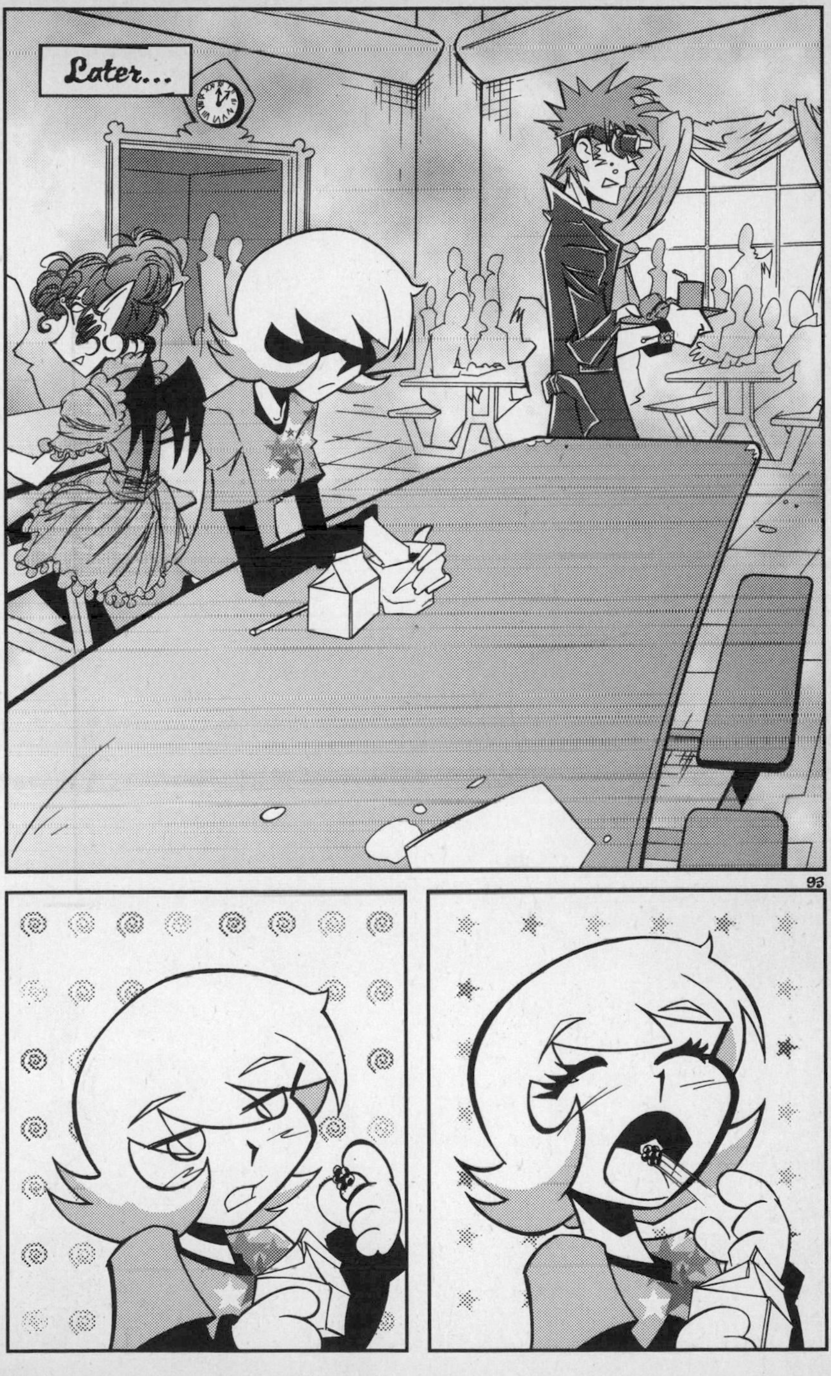
Later...

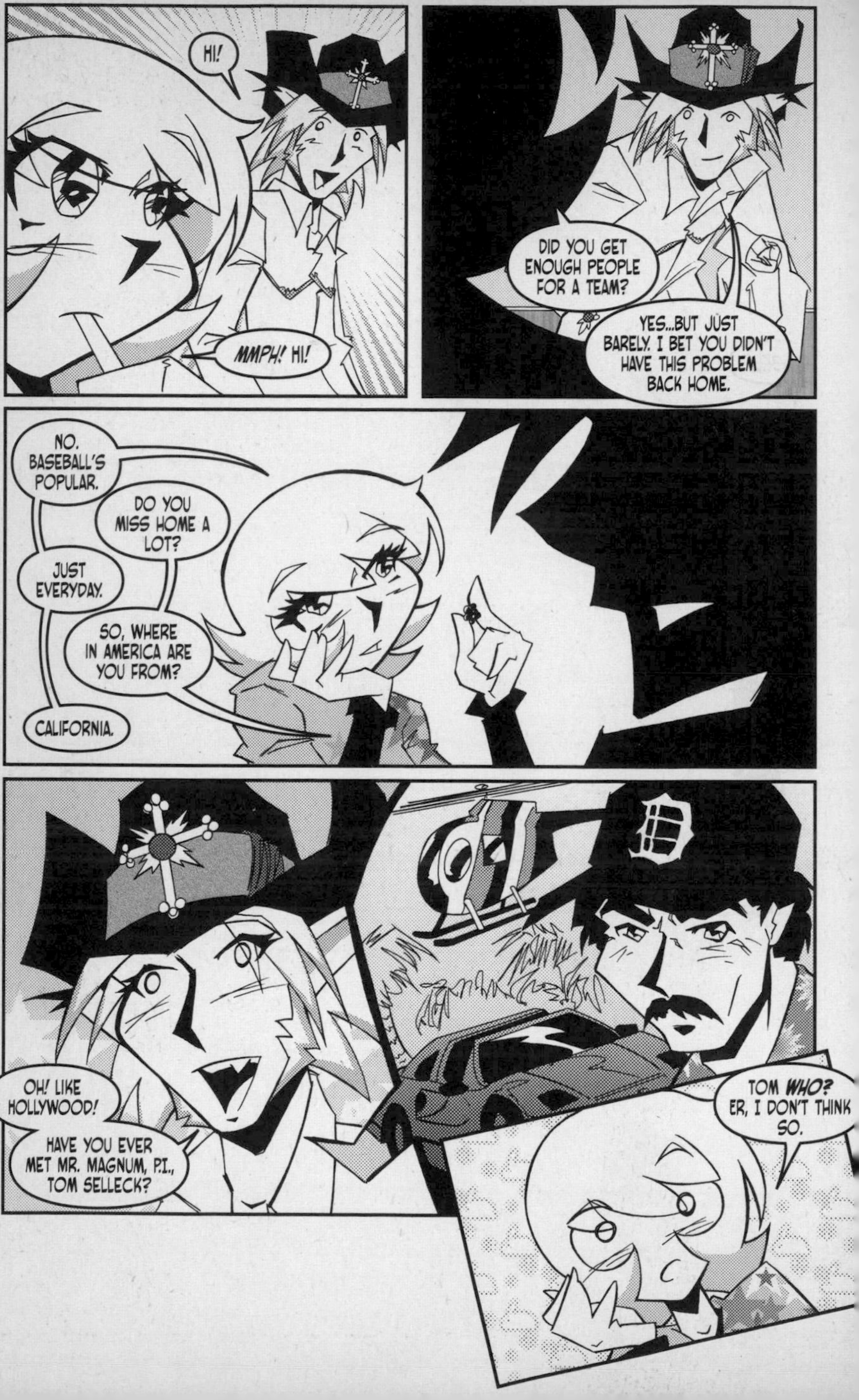
HI!
MMPH! HI!
DID YOU GET ENOUGH PEOPLE FOR A TEAM?
YES...BUT JUST BARELY. I BET YOU DIDN'T HAVE THIS PROBLEM BACK HOME.
NO. BASEBALL'S POPULAR.
DO YOU MISS HOME A LOT?
JUST EVERYDAY.
SO, WHERE IN AMERICA ARE YOU FROM?
CALIFORNIA.
OH! LIKE HOLLYWOOD!
HAVE YOU EVER MET MR. MAGNUM, P.I., TOM SELLECK?
TOM WHO? ER, I DON'T THINK SO.

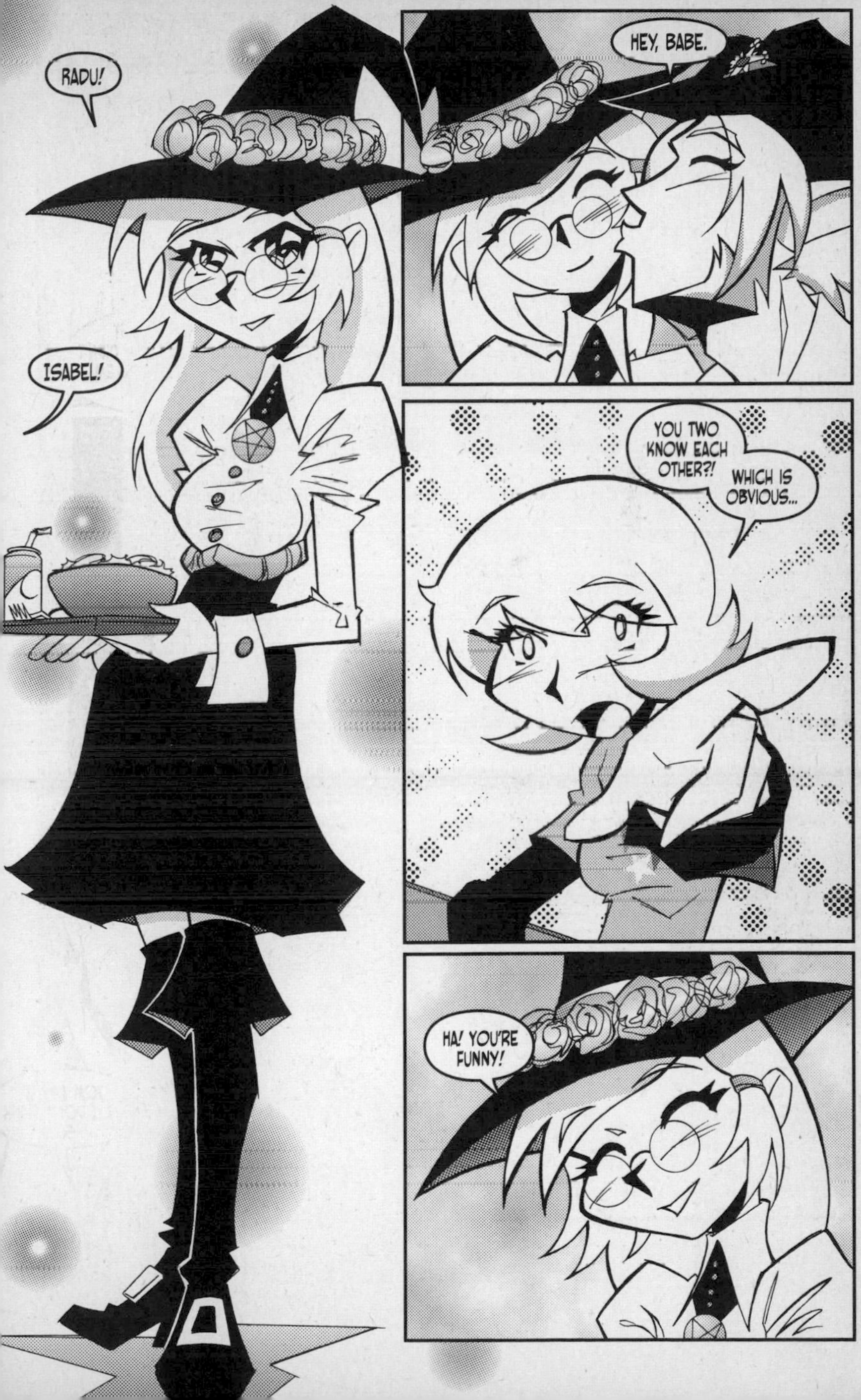
RADU!
ISABEL!
HEY, BABE.
YOU TWO KNOW EACH OTHER?!
WHICH IS OBVIOUS...
HA! YOU'RE FUNNY!

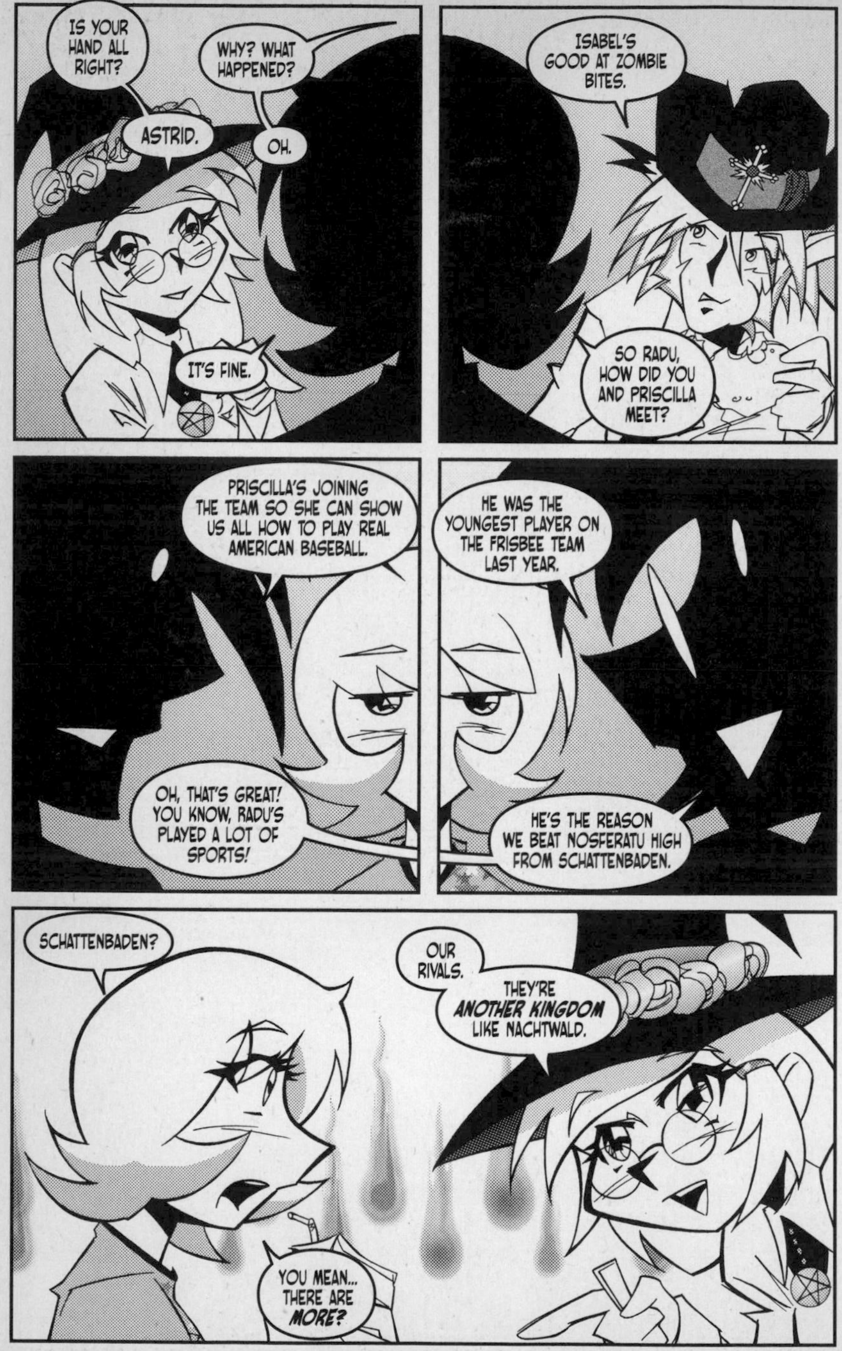
IS YOUR HAND ALL RIGHT?
WHY? WHAT HAPPENED?
ASTRID.
OH.
IT'S FINE.
ISABEL'S GOOD AT ZOMBIE BITES.
SO RADU, HOW DID YOU AND PRISCILLA MEET?
PRISCILLA'S JOINING THE TEAM SO SHE CAN SHOW US ALL HOW TO PLAY REAL AMERICAN BASEBALL.
OH, THAT'S GREAT! YOU KNOW, RADU'S PLAYED A LOT OF SPORTS!
HE WAS THE YOUNGEST PLAYER ON THE FRISBEE TEAM LAST YEAR.
HE'S THE REASON WE BEAT NOSFERATU HIGH FROM SCHATTENBADEN.
SCHATTENBADEN?
OUR RIVALS.
THEY'RE ***ANOTHER KINGDOM*** LIKE NACHTWALD.
YOU MEAN... THERE ARE ***MORE?***

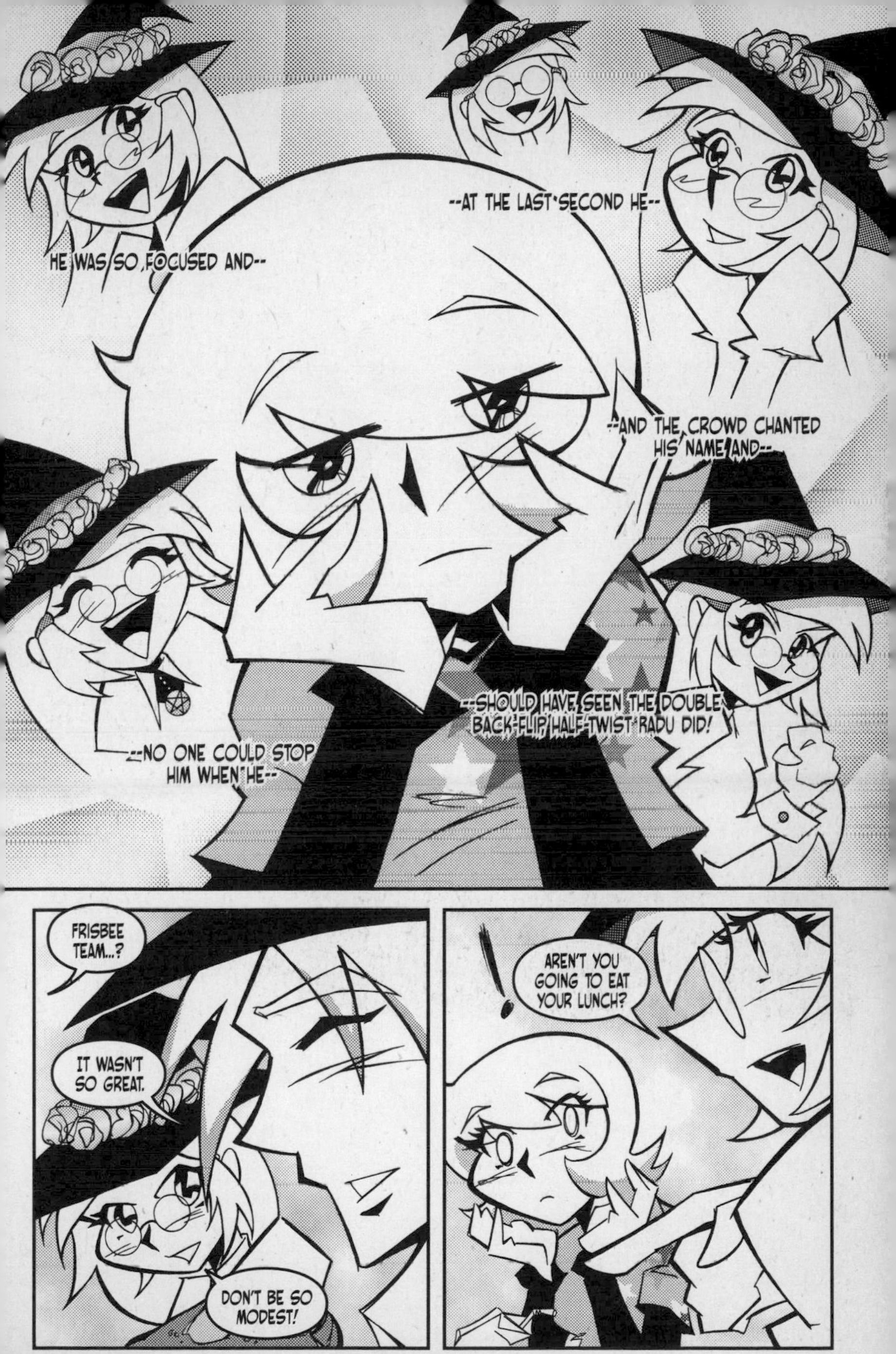
HE WAS SO FOCUSED AND--
--AT THE LAST SECOND HE--
--AND THE CROWD CHANTED HIS NAME AND--
--NO ONE COULD STOP HIM WHEN HE--
--SHOULD HAVE SEEN THE DOUBLE BACK-FLIP HALF-TWIST RADU DID!
FRISBEE TEAM...?
IT WASN'T SO GREAT.
DON'T BE SO MODEST!
!
AREN'T YOU GOING TO EAT YOUR LUNCH?

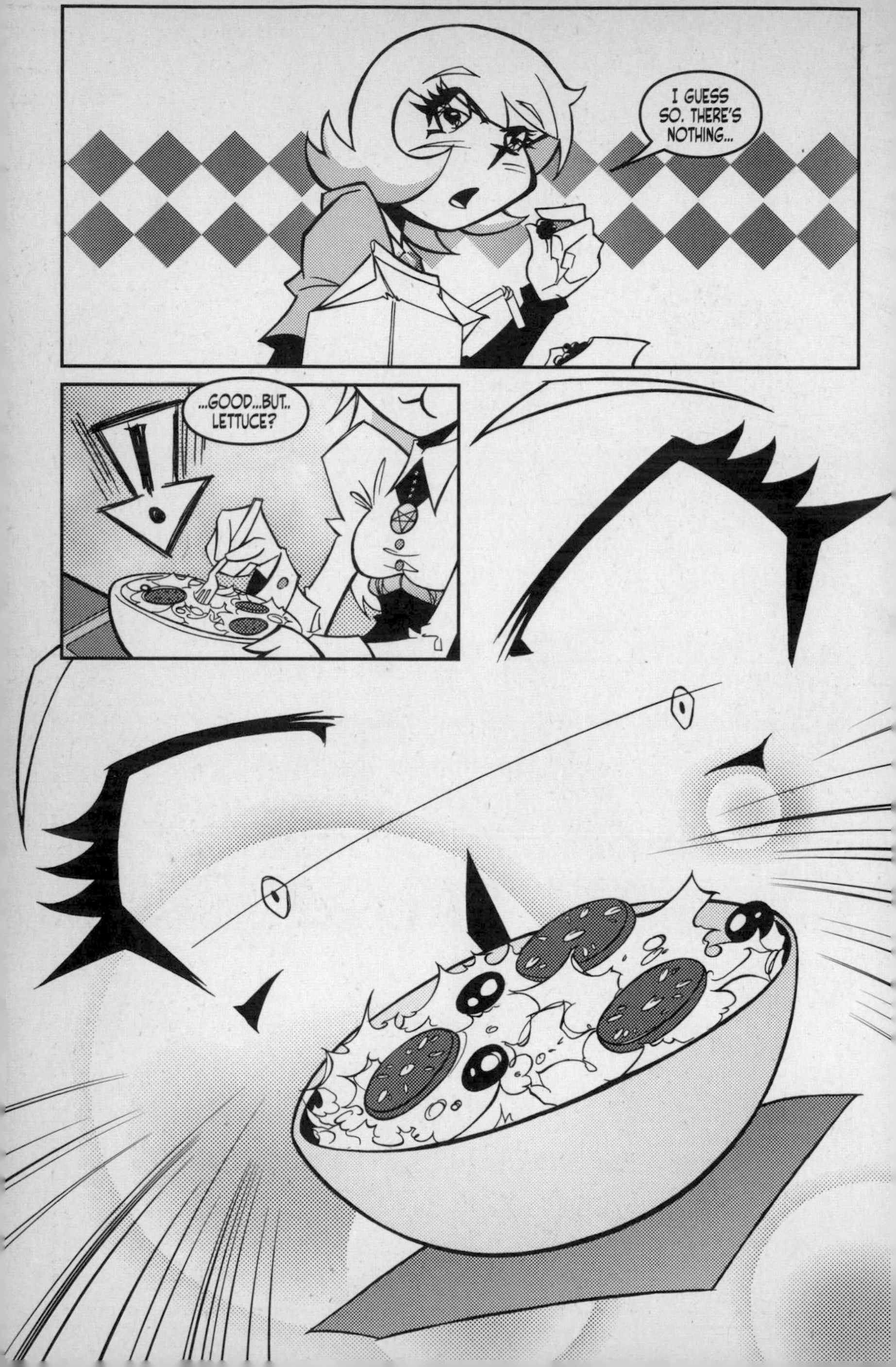
I GUESS SO. THERE'S NOTHING...
...GOOD...BUT.. LETTUCE?

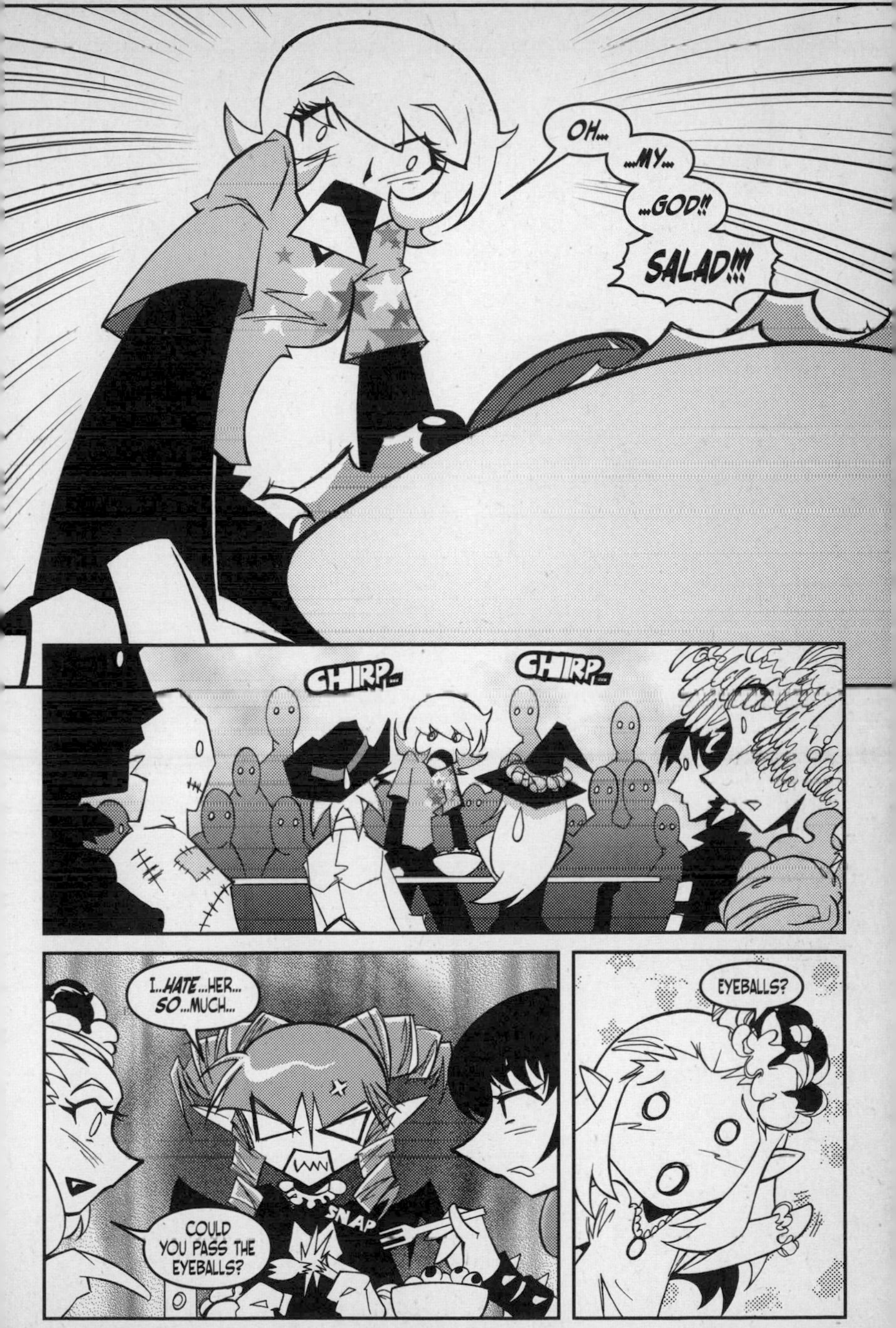
OH...
...MY...
...GOD!!
SALAD!!!
CHIRP...
CHIRP...
I...HATE...HER... SO...MUCH...
COULD YOU PASS THE EYEBALLS?
SNAP
EYEBALLS?

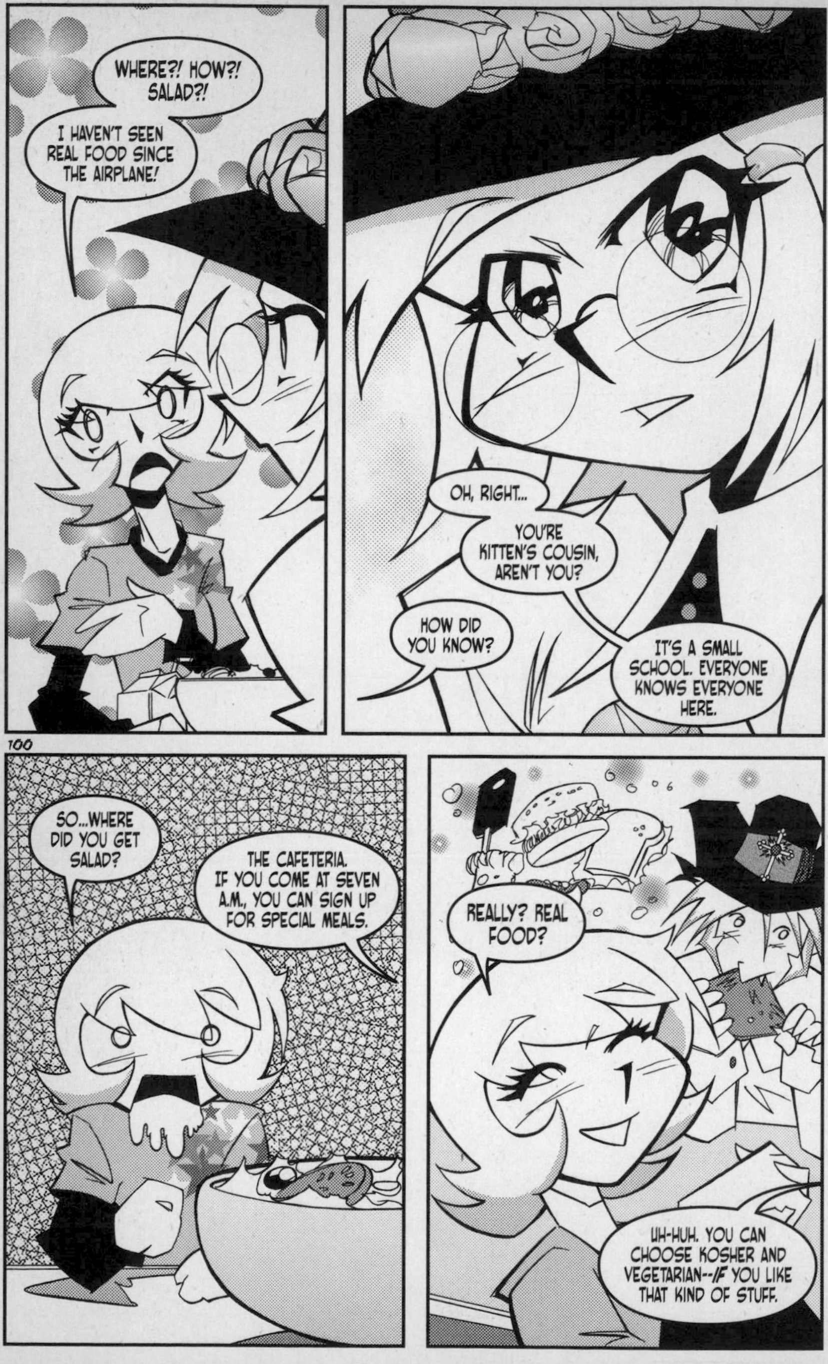
WHERE?! HOW?! SALAD?!
I HAVEN'T SEEN REAL FOOD SINCE THE AIRPLANE!
OH, RIGHT...
YOU'RE KITTEN'S COUSIN, AREN'T YOU?
HOW DID YOU KNOW?
IT'S A SMALL SCHOOL. EVERYONE KNOWS EVERYONE HERE.
SO...WHERE DID YOU GET SALAD?
THE CAFETERIA. IF YOU COME AT SEVEN A.M., YOU CAN SIGN UP FOR SPECIAL MEALS.
REALLY? REAL FOOD?
UH-HUH. YOU CAN CHOOSE KOSHER AND VEGETARIAN--IF YOU LIKE THAT KIND OF STUFF.

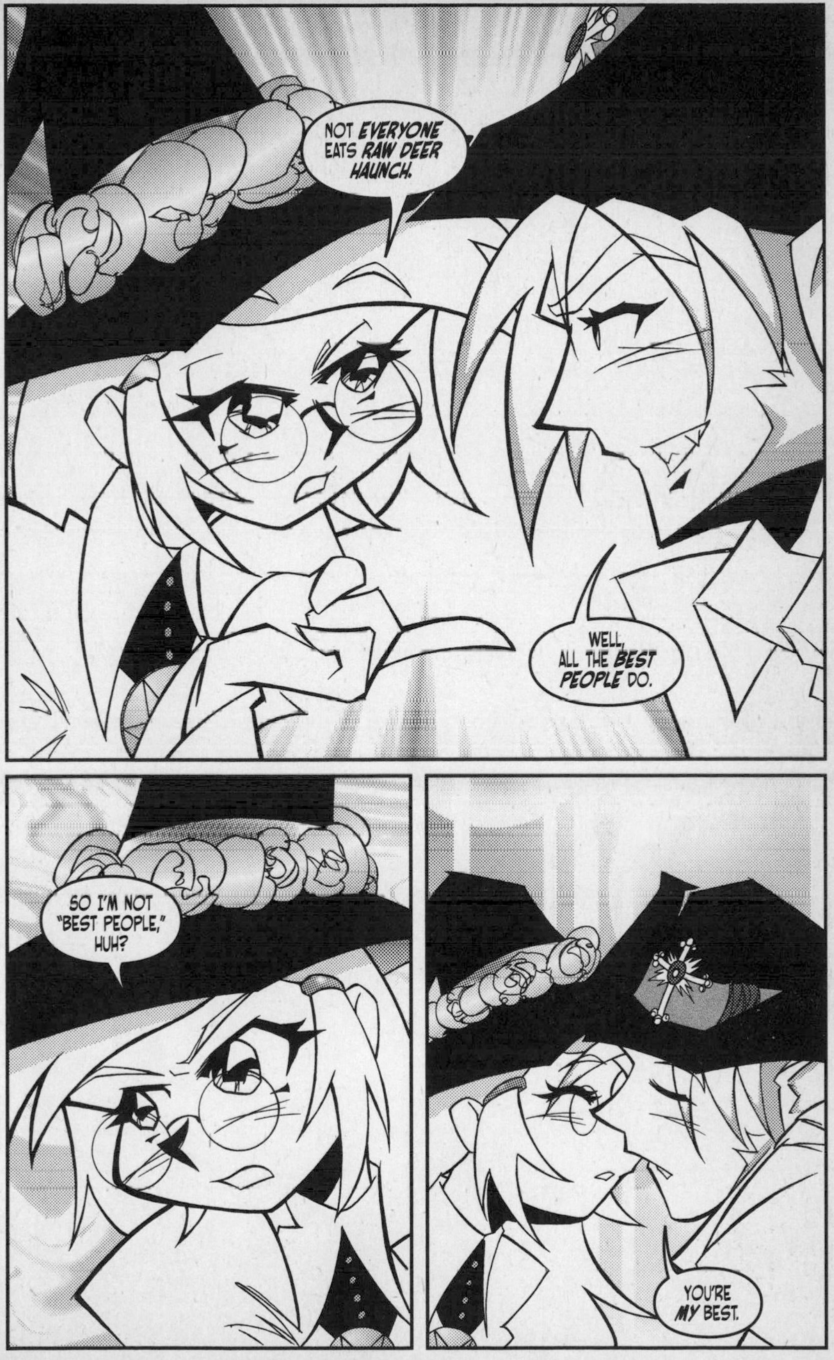
NOT EVERYONE EATS RAW DEER HAUNCH.
WELL, ALL THE BEST PEOPLE DO.
SO I'M NOT "BEST PEOPLE," HUH?
YOU'RE MY BEST.

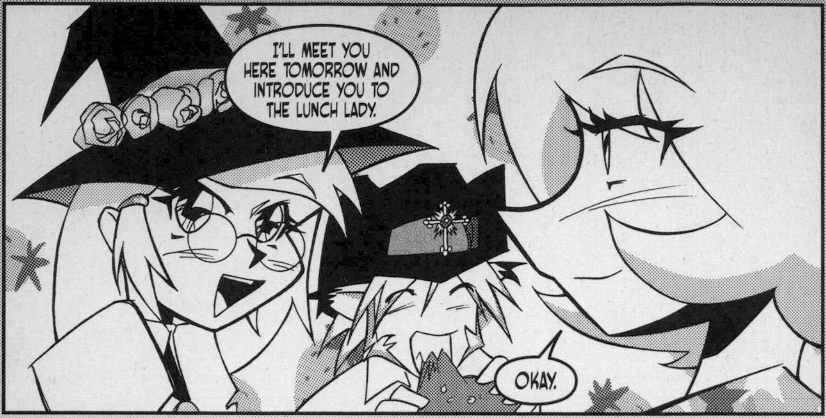
I'LL MEET YOU HERE TOMORROW AND INTRODUCE YOU TO THE LUNCH LADY.
OKAY.

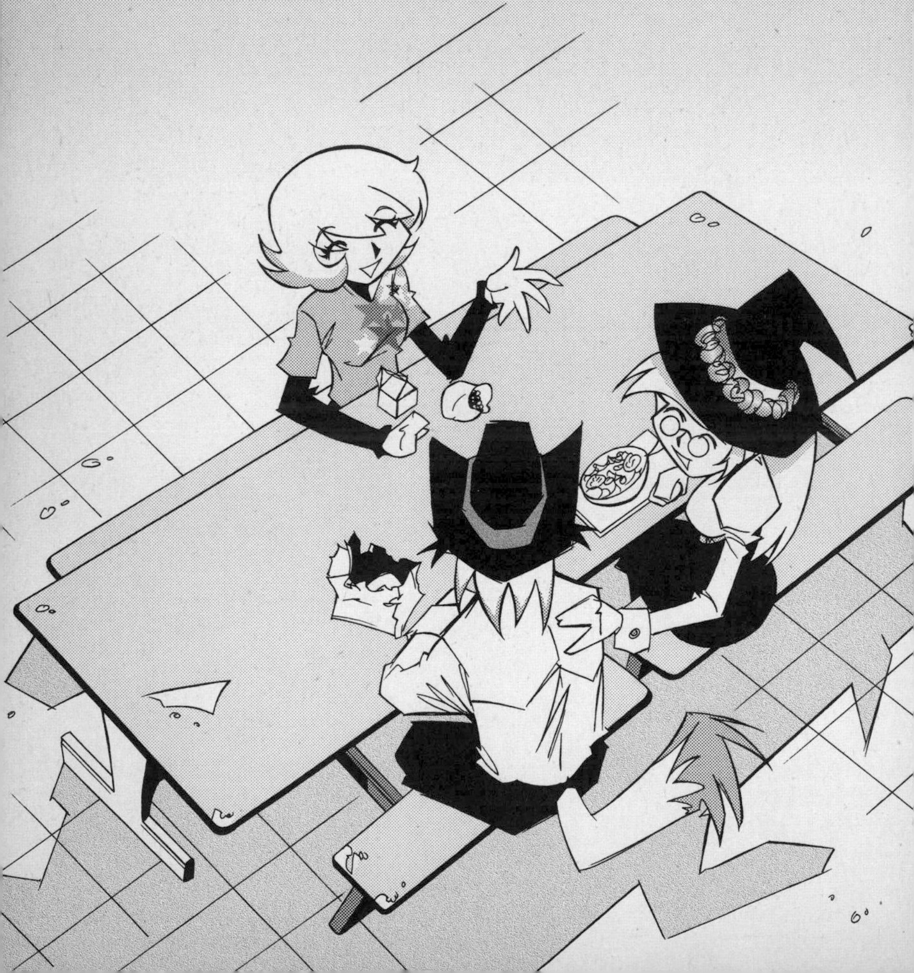

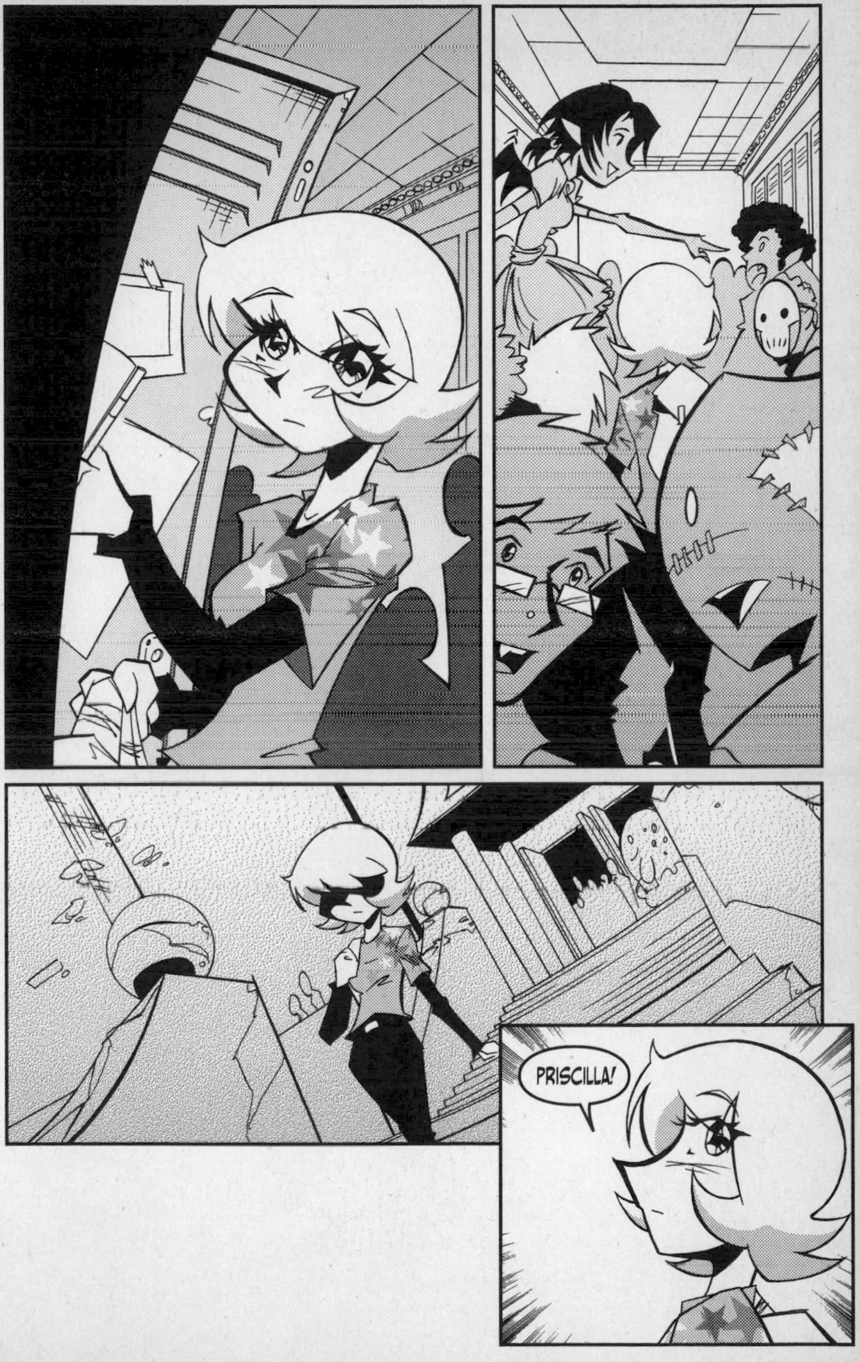
PRISCILLA!

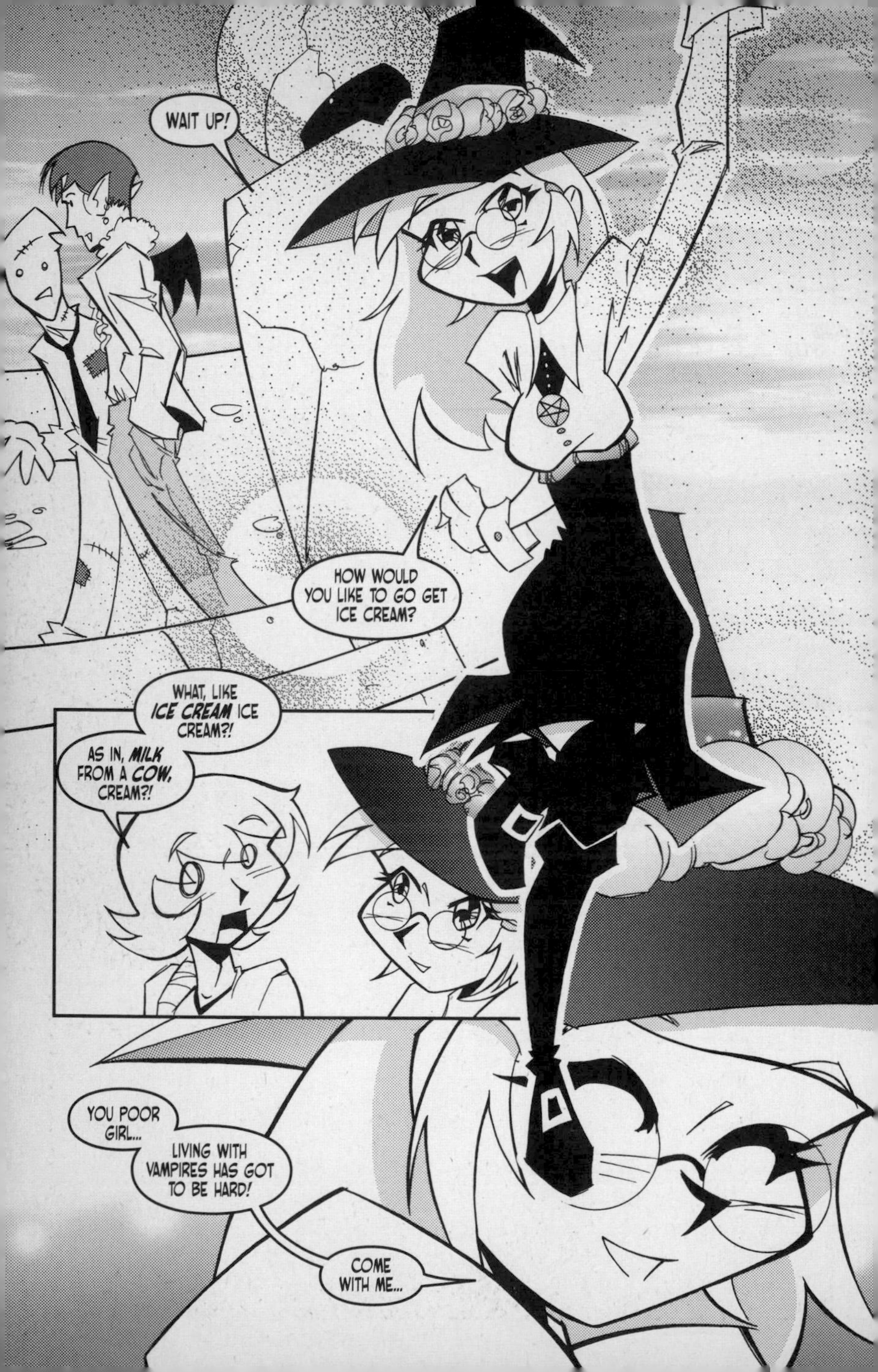
WAIT UP!
HOW WOULD YOU LIKE TO GO GET ICE CREAM?
WHAT, LIKE *ICE CREAM* ICE CREAM?!
AS IN, *MILK* FROM A *COW,* CREAM?!
YOU POOR GIRL...
LIVING WITH VAMPIRES HAS GOT TO BE HARD!
COME WITH ME...

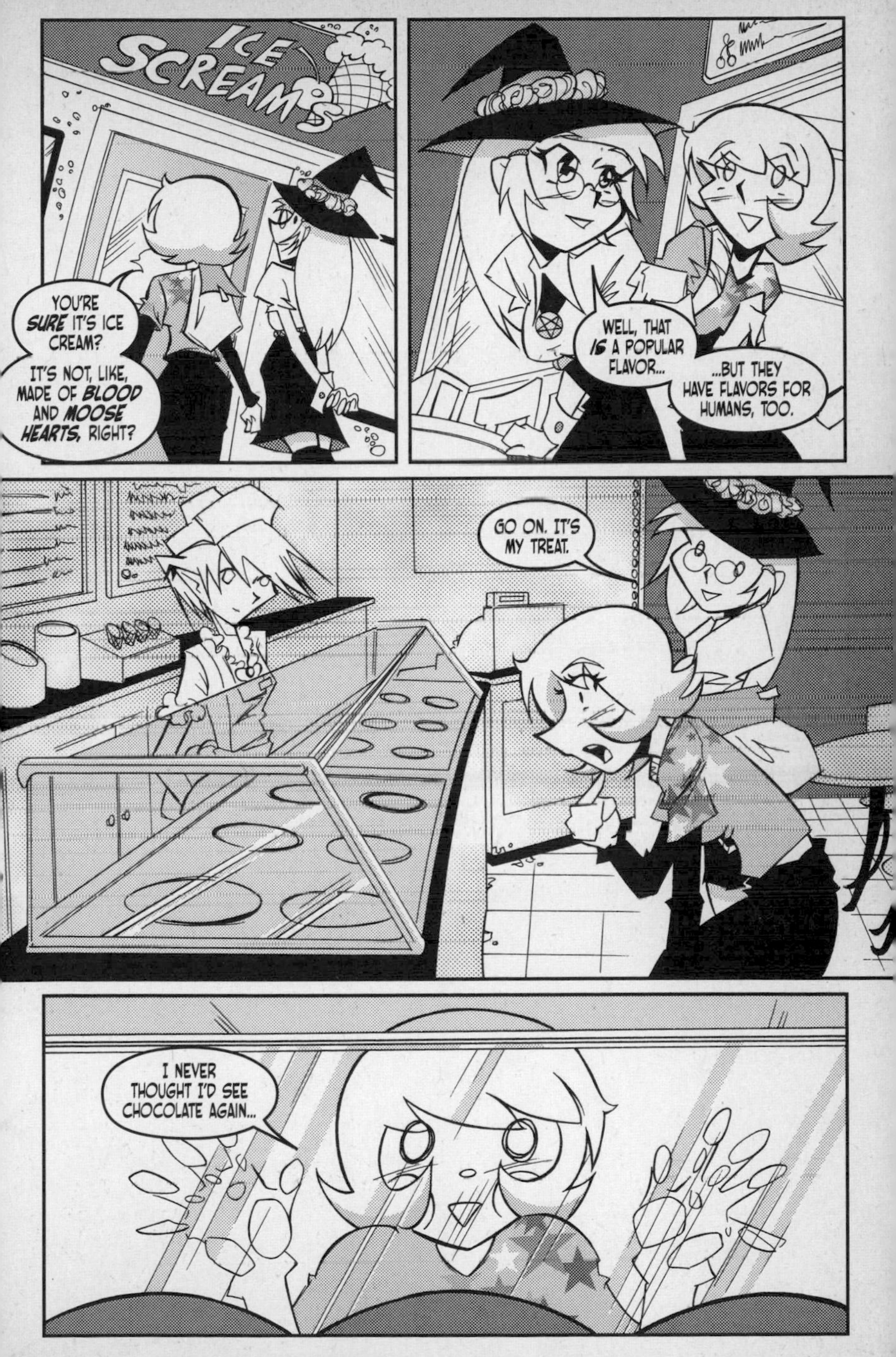
ICE SCREAMS
YOU'RE *SURE* IT'S ICE CREAM?
IT'S NOT, LIKE, MADE OF *BLOOD* AND *MOOSE HEARTS,* RIGHT?
WELL, THAT *IS* A POPULAR FLAVOR...
...BUT THEY HAVE FLAVORS FOR HUMANS, TOO.
GO ON. IT'S MY TREAT.
I NEVER THOUGHT I'D SEE CHOCOLATE AGAIN...

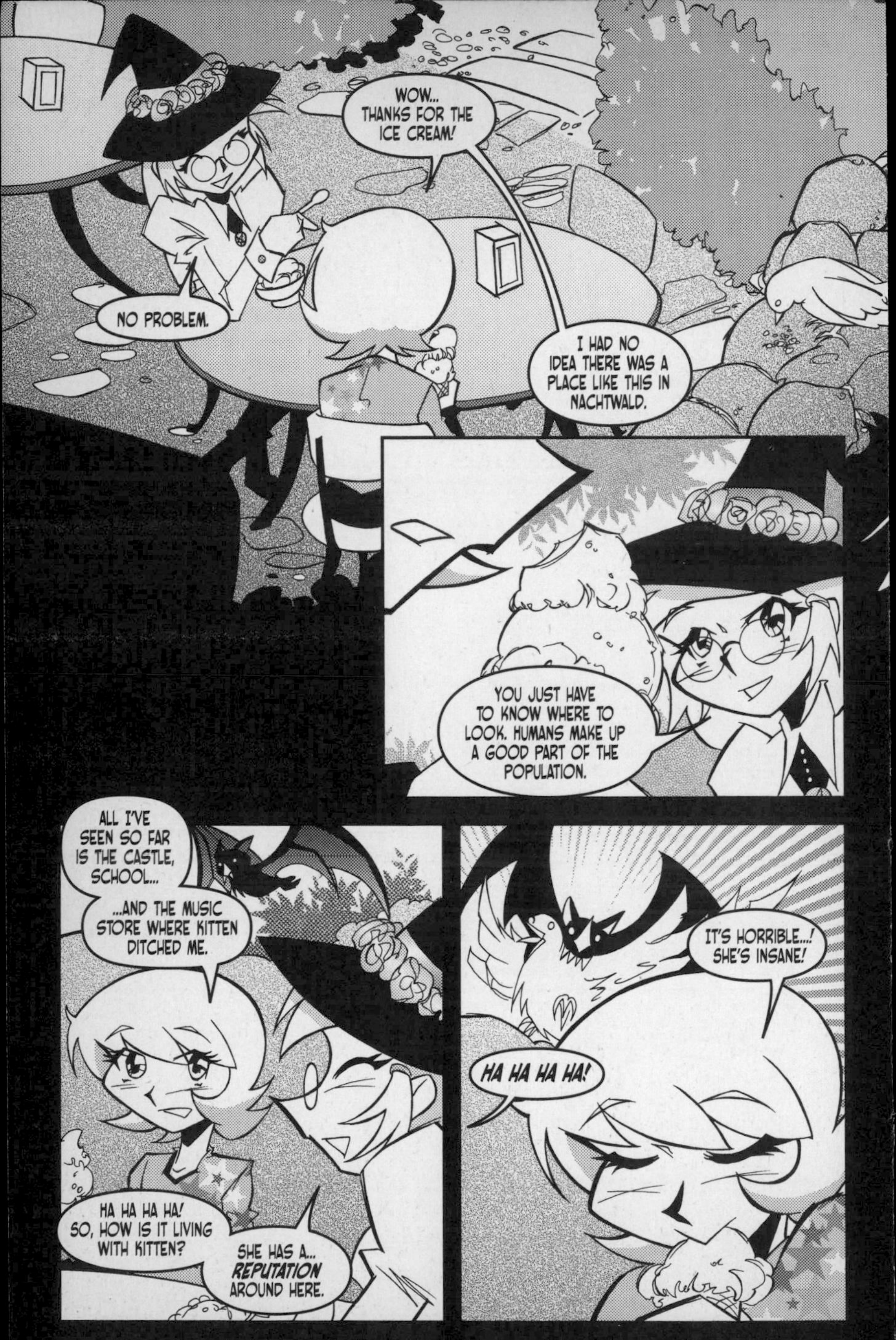
WOW... THANKS FOR THE ICE CREAM!
NO PROBLEM.
I HAD NO IDEA THERE WAS A PLACE LIKE THIS IN NACHTWALD.
YOU JUST HAVE TO KNOW WHERE TO LOOK. HUMANS MAKE UP A GOOD PART OF THE POPULATION.
ALL I'VE SEEN SO FAR IS THE CASTLE, SCHOOL...
...AND THE MUSIC STORE WHERE KITTEN DITCHED ME.
HA HA HA HA! SO, HOW IS IT LIVING WITH KITTEN?
SHE HAS A... *REPUTATION* AROUND HERE.
IT'S HORRIBLE...! SHE'S INSANE!
HA HA HA HA!

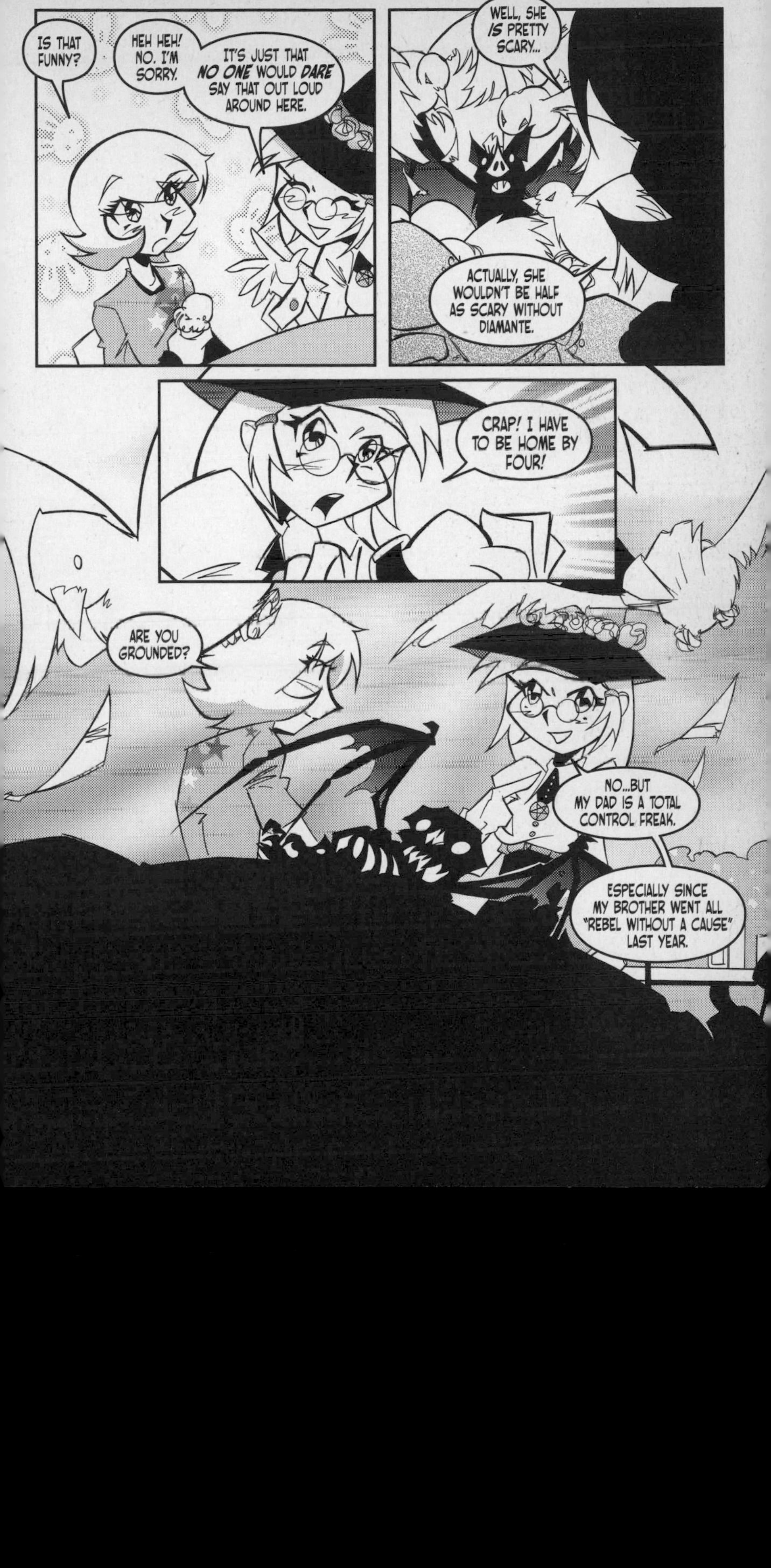
IS THAT FUNNY?
HEH HEH! NO. I'M SORRY.
IT'S JUST THAT NO ONE WOULD DARE SAY THAT OUT LOUD AROUND HERE.
WELL, SHE IS PRETTY SCARY...
ACTUALLY, SHE WOULDN'T BE HALF AS SCARY WITHOUT DIAMANTE.
CRAP! I HAVE TO BE HOME BY FOUR!
ARE YOU GROUNDED?
NO...BUT MY DAD IS A TOTAL CONTROL FREAK.
ESPECIALLY SINCE MY BROTHER WENT ALL "REBEL WITHOUT A CAUSE" LAST YEAR.

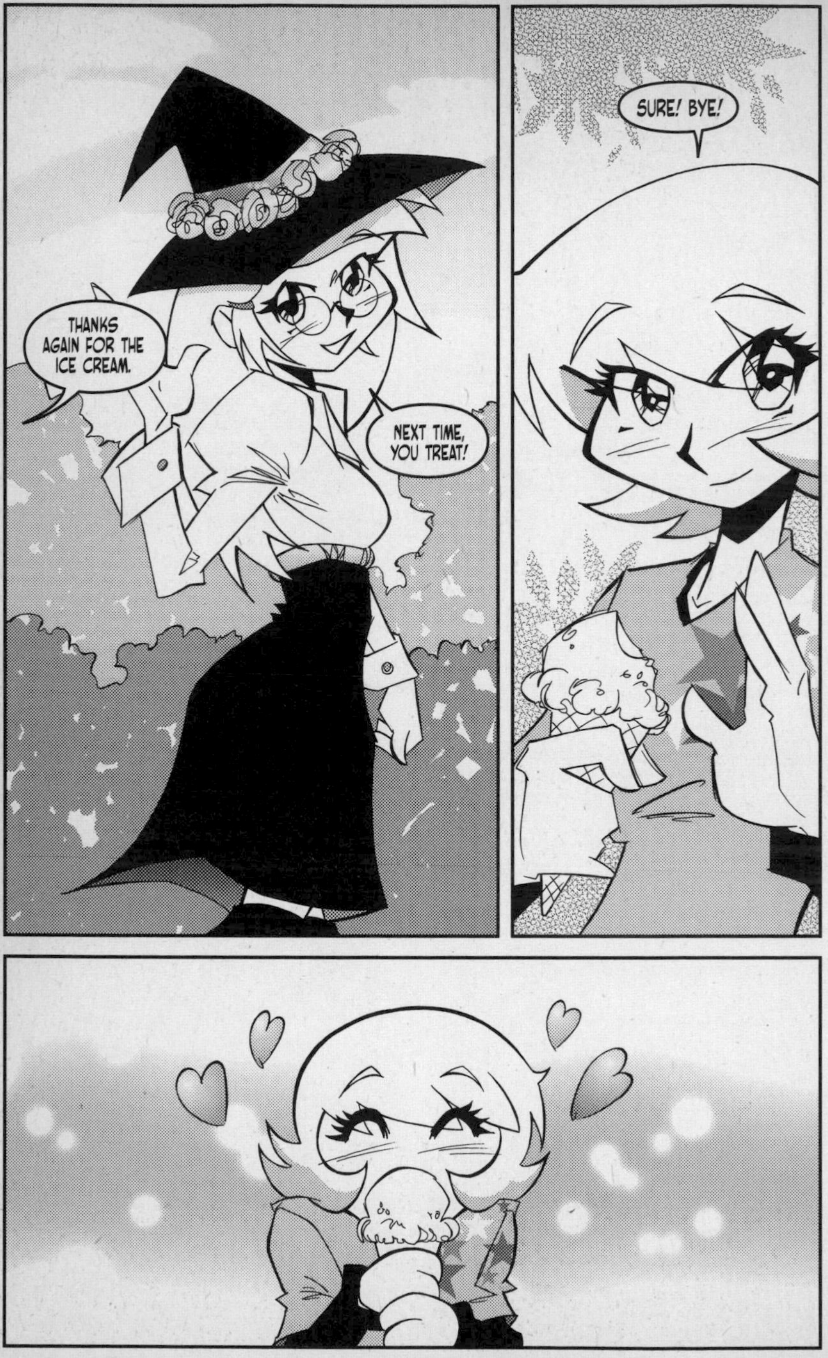
THANKS AGAIN FOR THE ICE CREAM.
NEXT TIME, YOU TREAT!
SURE! BYE!

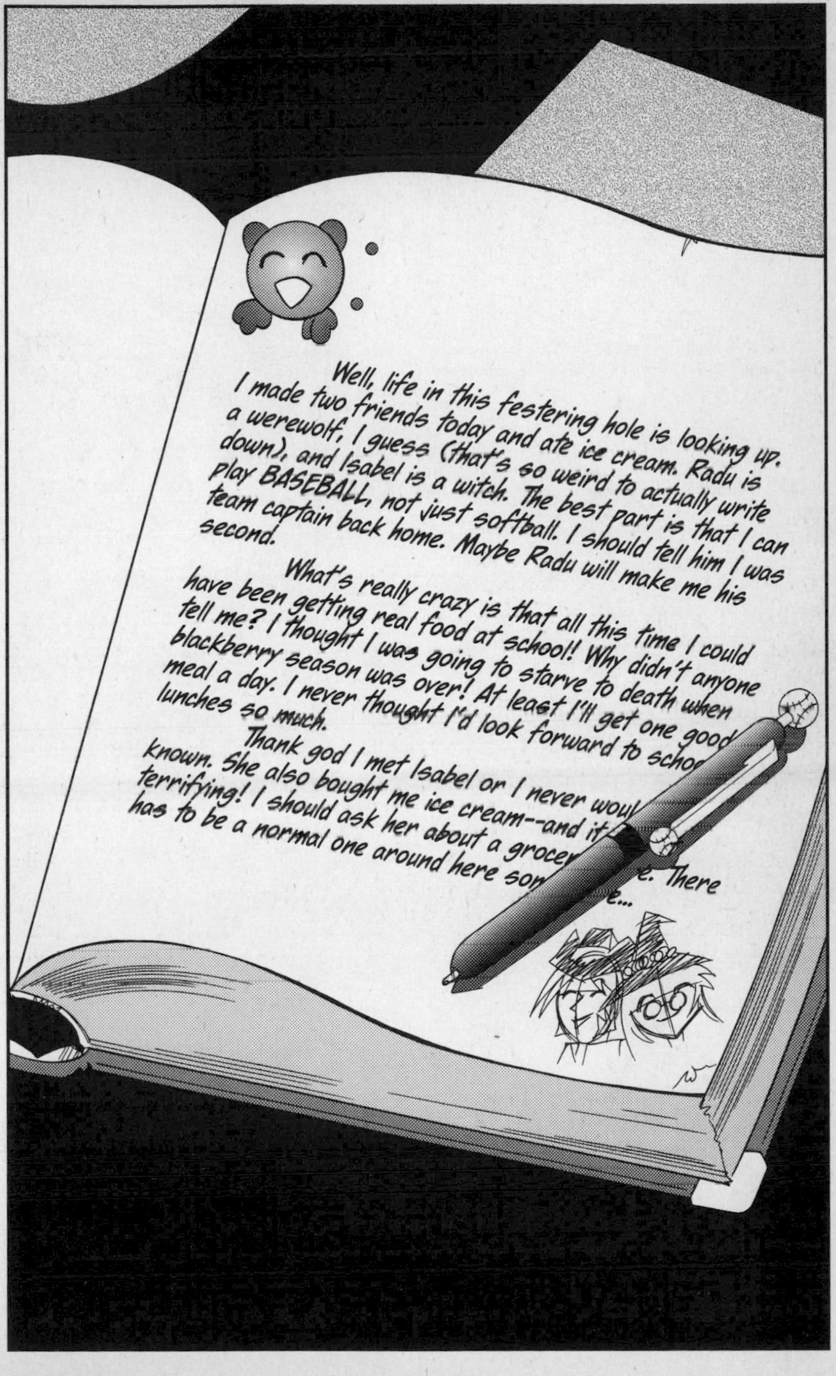

Well, life in this festering hole is looking up.
I made two friends today and ate ice cream. Radu is
a werewolf, I guess (that's so weird to actually write
down), and Isabel is a witch. The best part is that I can
play BASEBALL, not just softball. I should tell him I was
team captain back home. Maybe Radu will make me his
second.
What's really crazy is that all this time I could
have been getting real food at school! Why didn't anyone
tell me? I thought I was going to starve to death when
blackberry season was over! At least I'll get one good
meal a day. I never thought I'd look forward to scho
lunches so much.
Thank god I met Isabel or I never woul
known. She also bought me ice cream--and it
terrifying! I should ask her about a grocer e. There
has to be a normal one around here som e...

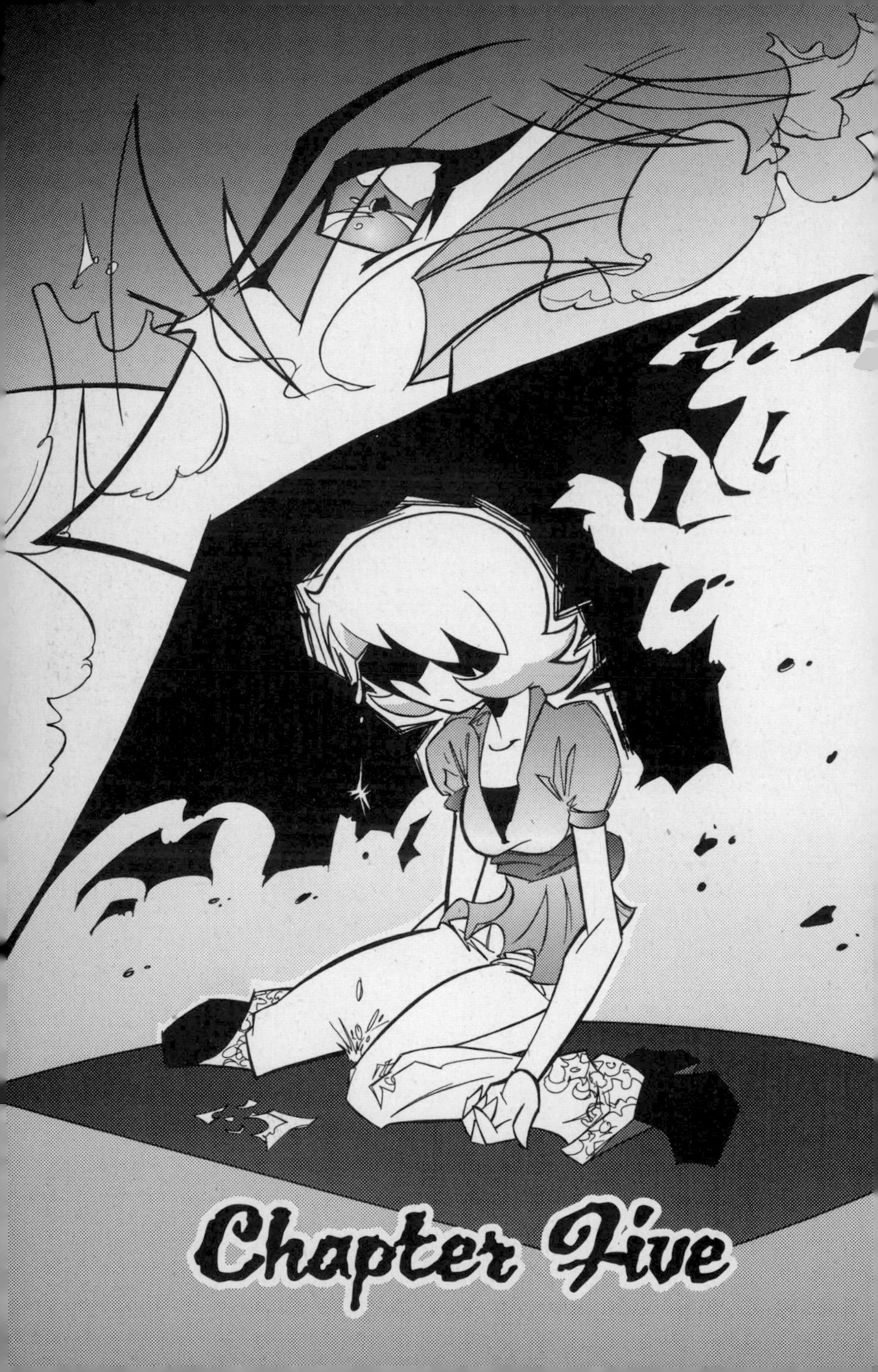
Chapter Five

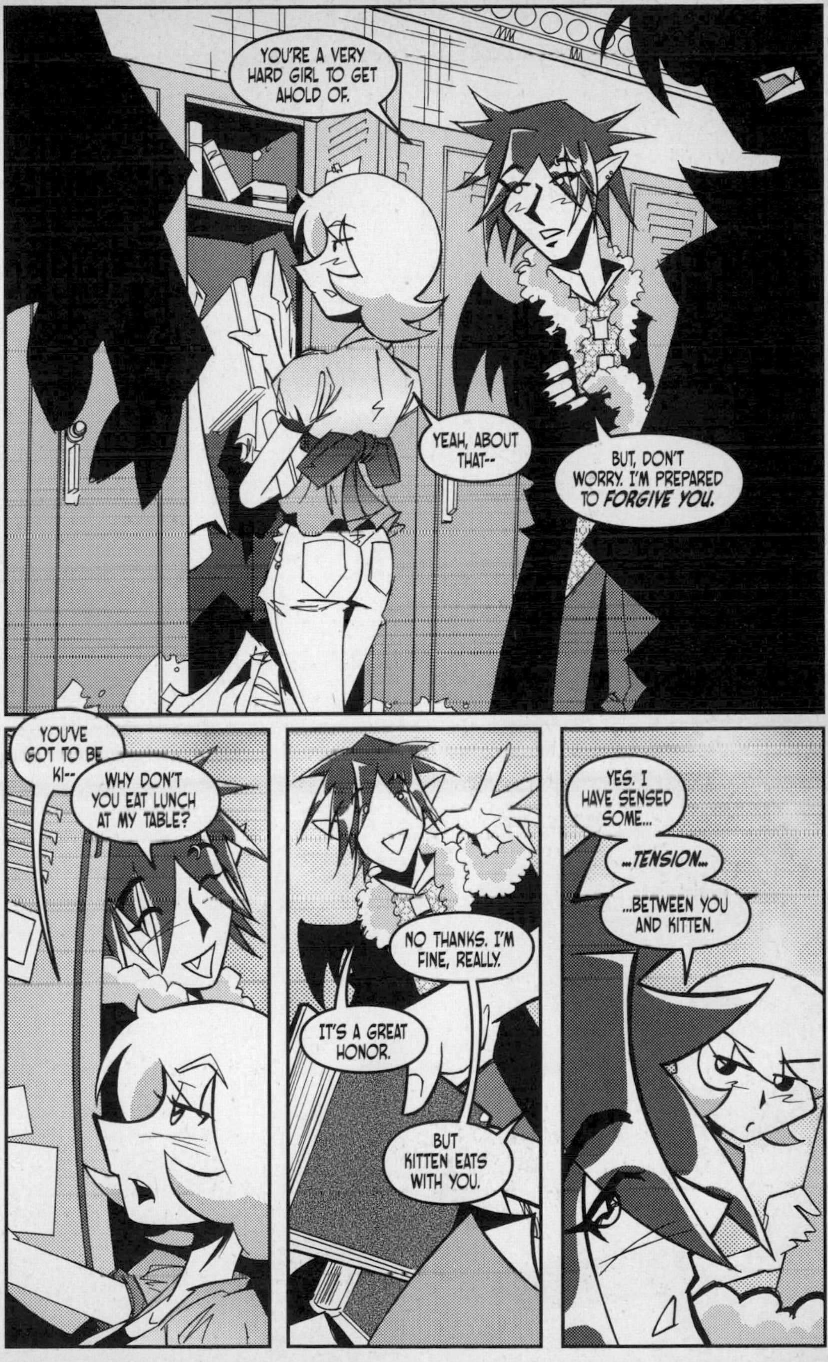
YOU'RE A VERY HARD GIRL TO GET AHOLD OF.
YEAH, ABOUT THAT--
BUT, DON'T WORRY. I'M PREPARED TO *FORGIVE YOU.*
YOU'VE GOT TO BE KI--
WHY DON'T YOU EAT LUNCH AT MY TABLE?
NO THANKS. I'M FINE, REALLY.
IT'S A GREAT HONOR.
BUT KITTEN EATS WITH YOU.
YES. I HAVE SENSED SOME...
...*TENSION*...
...BETWEEN YOU AND KITTEN.

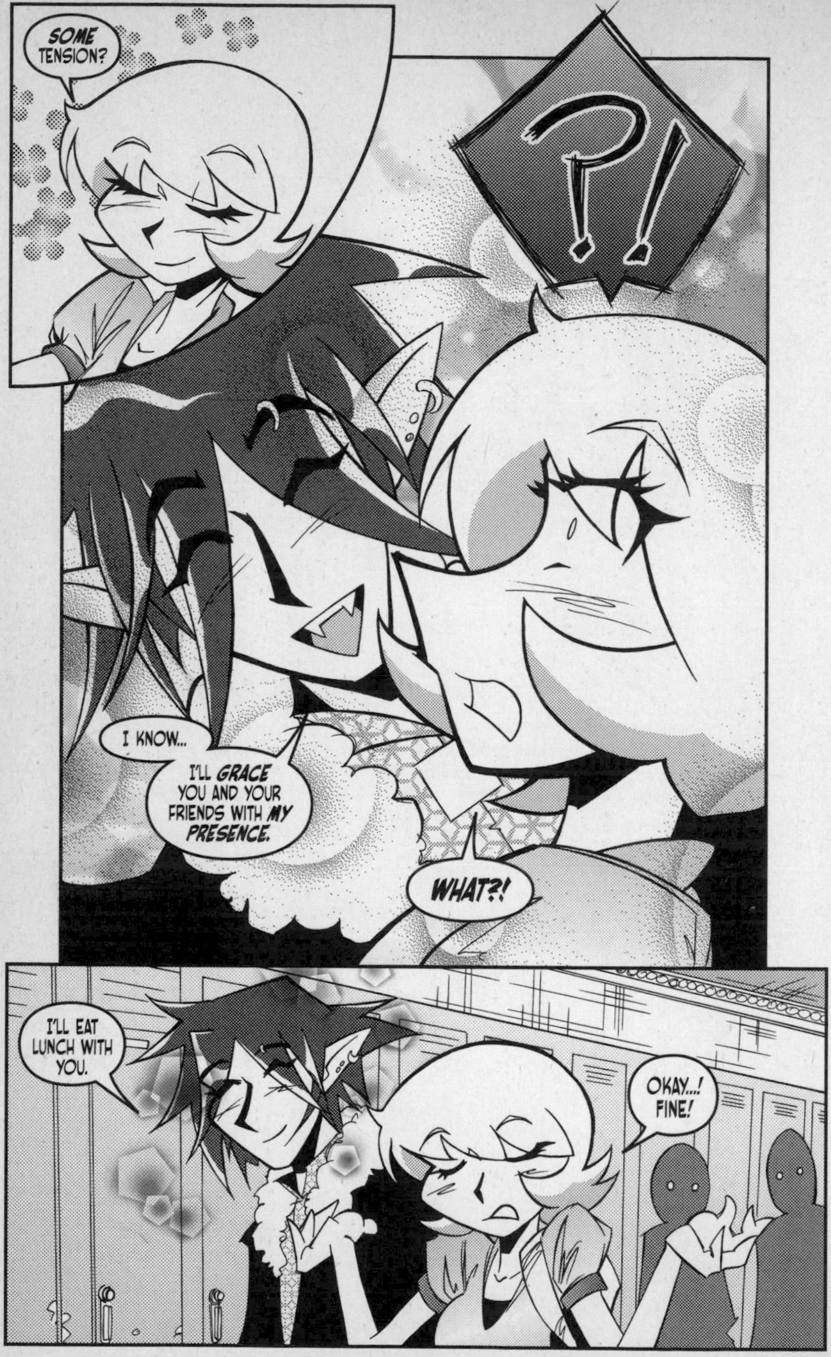
SOME TENSION?
?!
I KNOW...
I'LL GRACE YOU AND YOUR FRIENDS WITH MY PRESENCE.
WHAT?!
I'LL EAT LUNCH WITH YOU.
OKAY...! FINE!

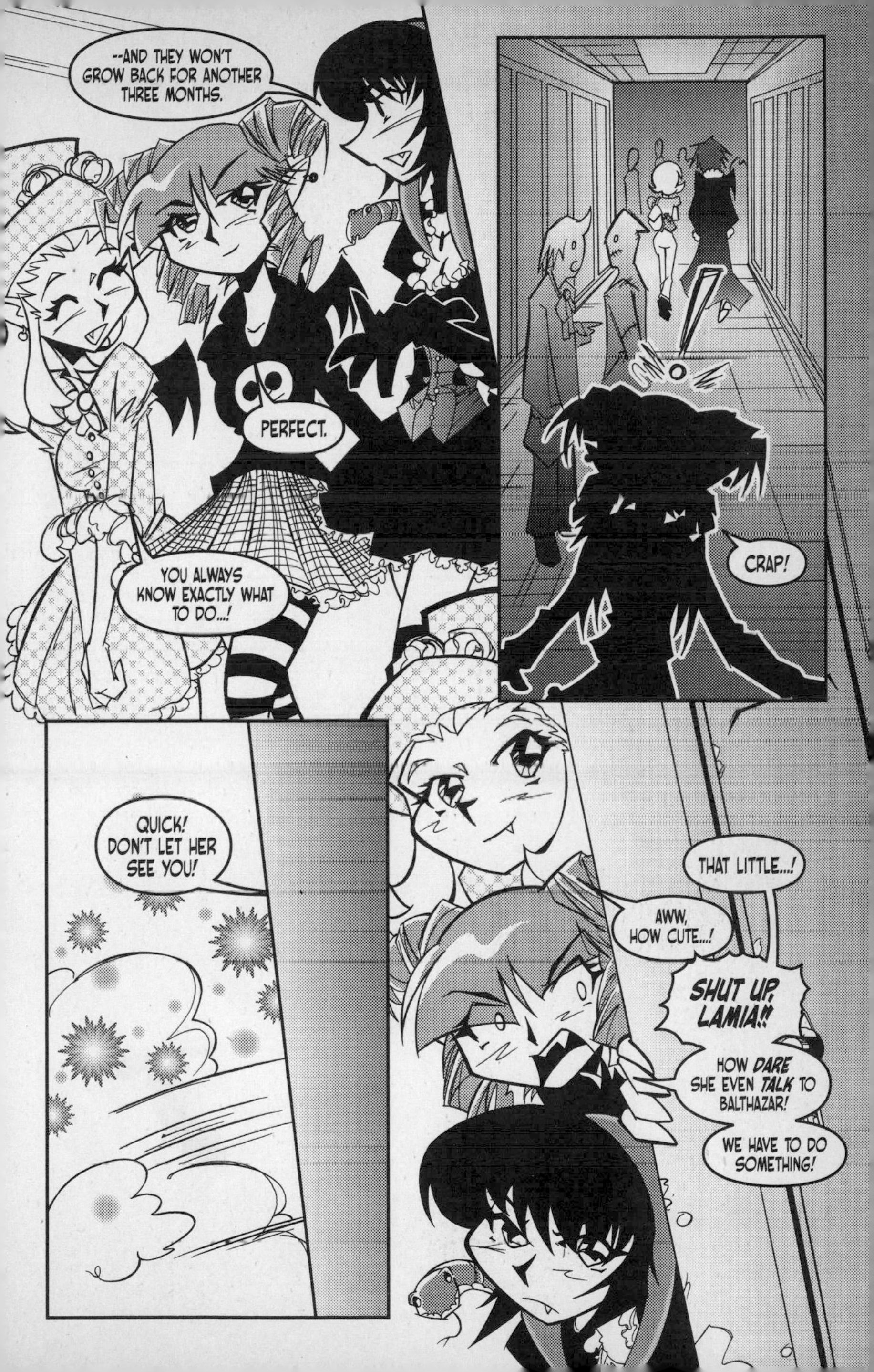
--AND THEY WON'T GROW BACK FOR ANOTHER THREE MONTHS.
PERFECT.
YOU ALWAYS KNOW EXACTLY WHAT TO DO...!
CRAP!
QUICK! DON'T LET HER SEE YOU!
THAT LITTLE...!
AWW, HOW CUTE...!
SHUT UP, LAMIA!!
HOW *DARE* SHE EVEN *TALK* TO BALTHAZAR!
WE HAVE TO DO SOMETHING!

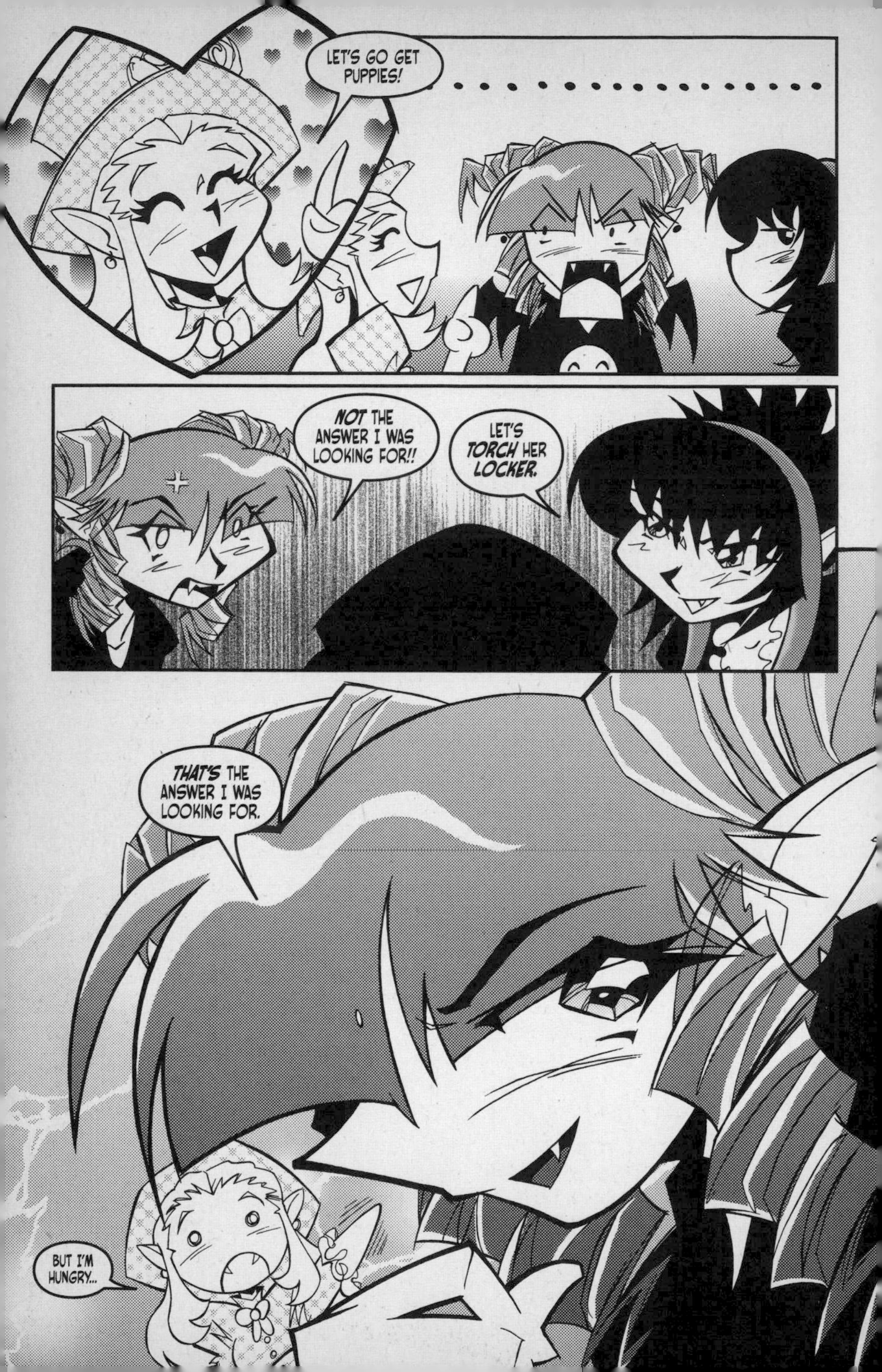

LET'S GO GET PUPPIES!
NOT THE ANSWER I WAS LOOKING FOR!!
LET'S *TORCH* HER *LOCKER.*
THAT'S THE ANSWER I WAS LOOKING FOR.
BUT I'M HUNGRY...

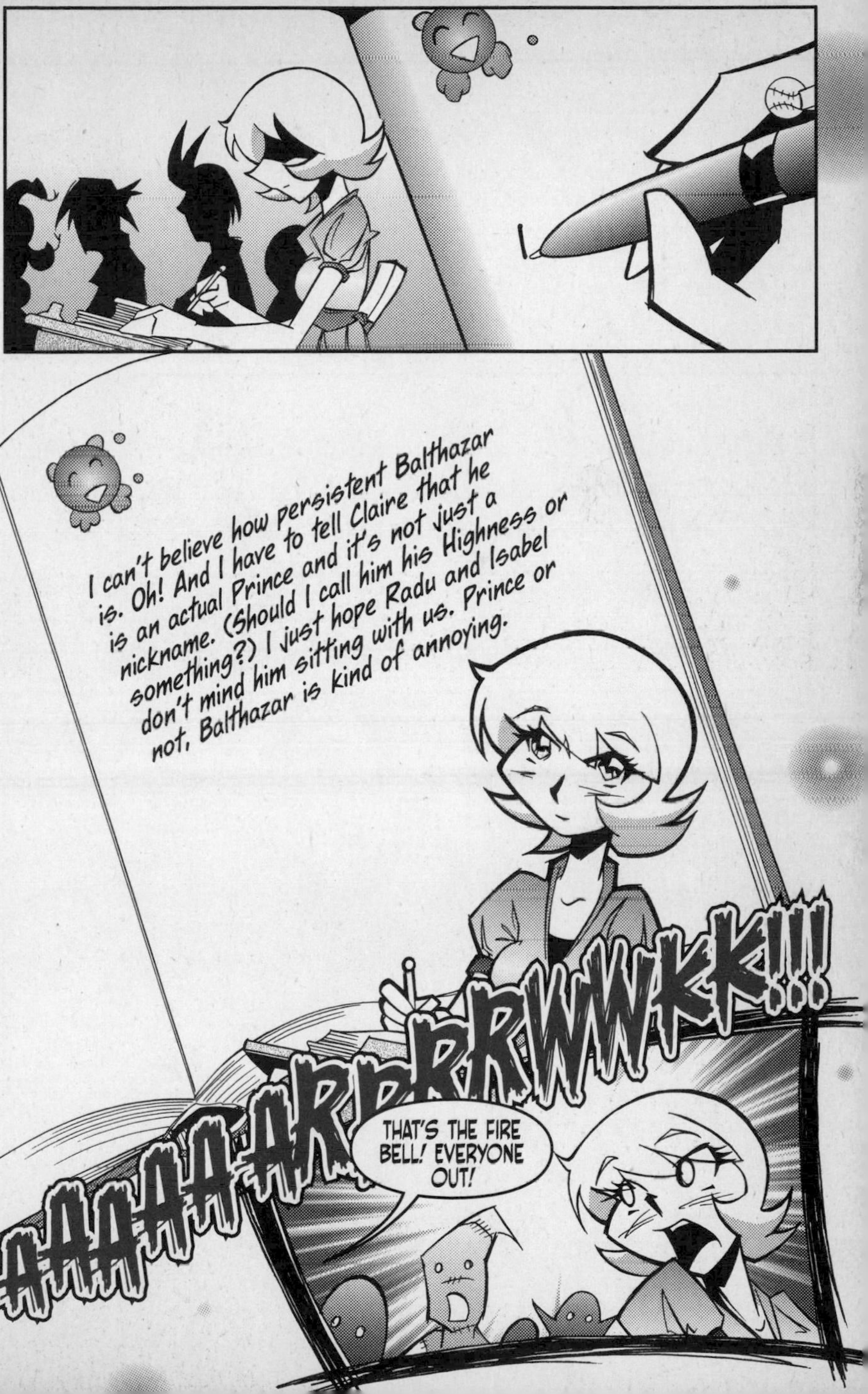
I can't believe how persistent Balthazar is. Oh! And I have to tell Claire that he is an actual Prince and it's not just a nickname. (Should I call him his Highness or something?) I just hope Radu and Isabel don't mind him sitting with us. Prince or not, Balthazar is kind of annoying.
AAAAAARRRRWWKK!!!
THAT'S THE FIRE BELL! EVERYONE OUT!

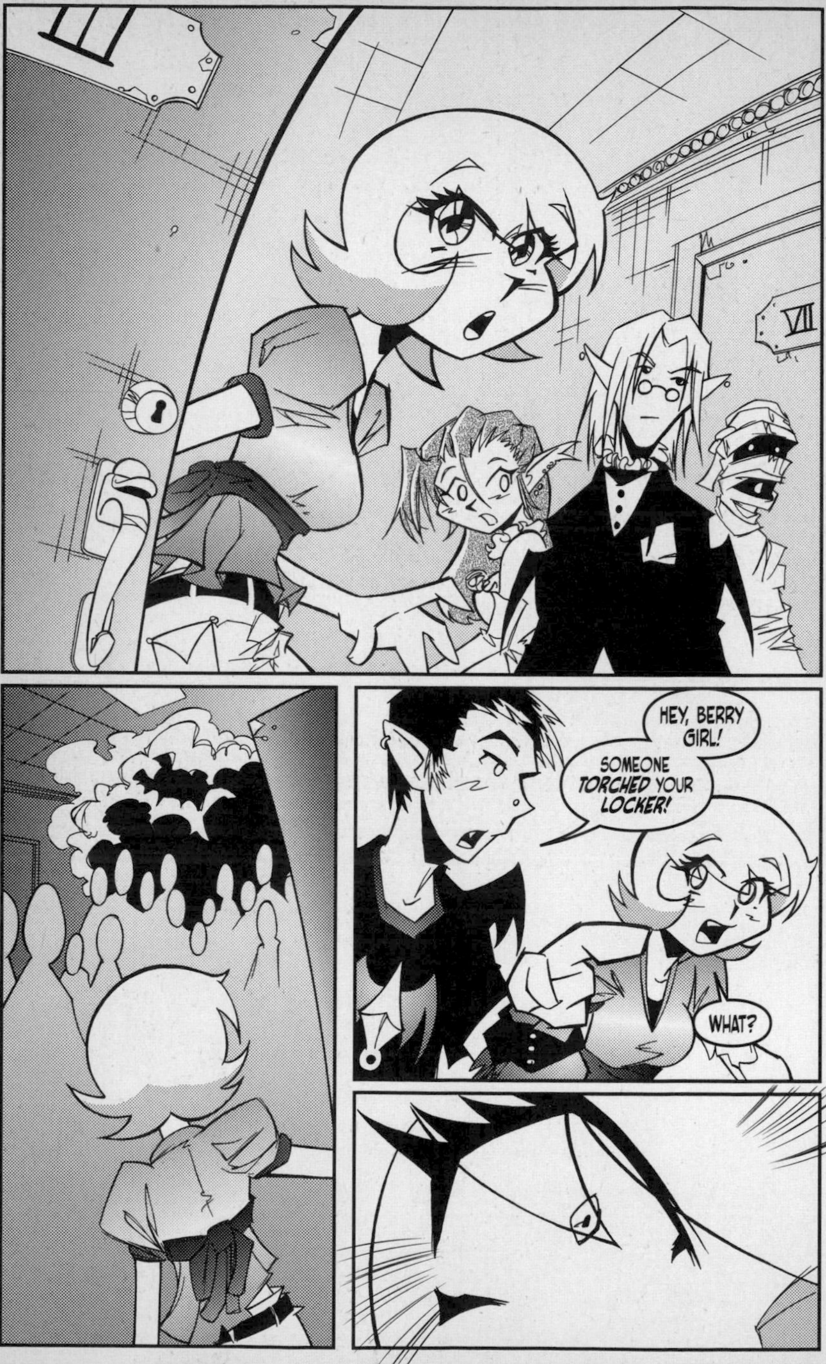
III
VII
HEY, BERRY GIRL!
SOMEONE *TORCHED* YOUR *LOCKER!*
WHAT?

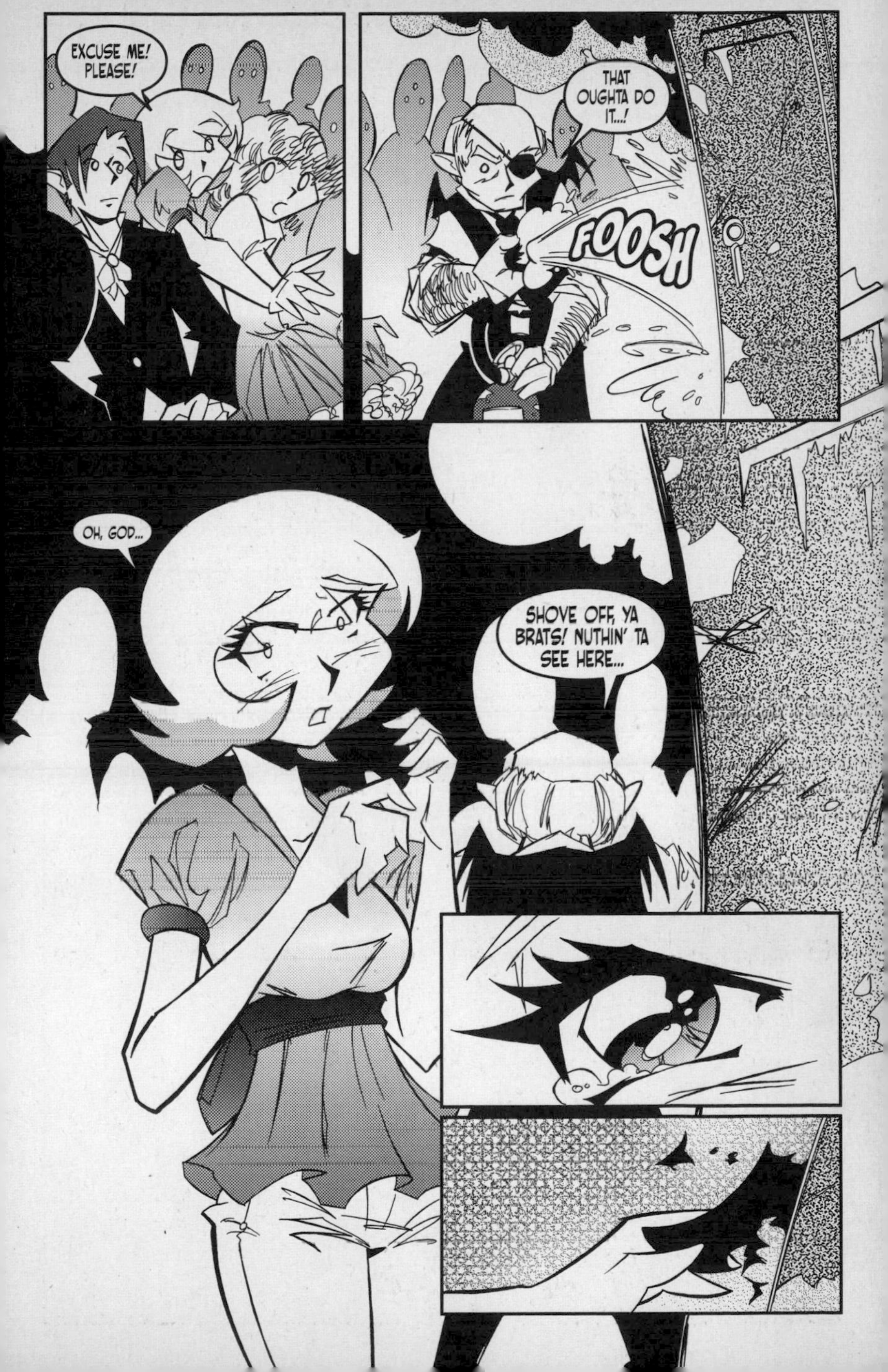
EXCUSE ME! PLEASE!
THAT OUGHTA DO IT...!
FOOSH
OH, GOD...
SHOVE OFF, YA BRATS! NUTHIN' TA SEE HERE...

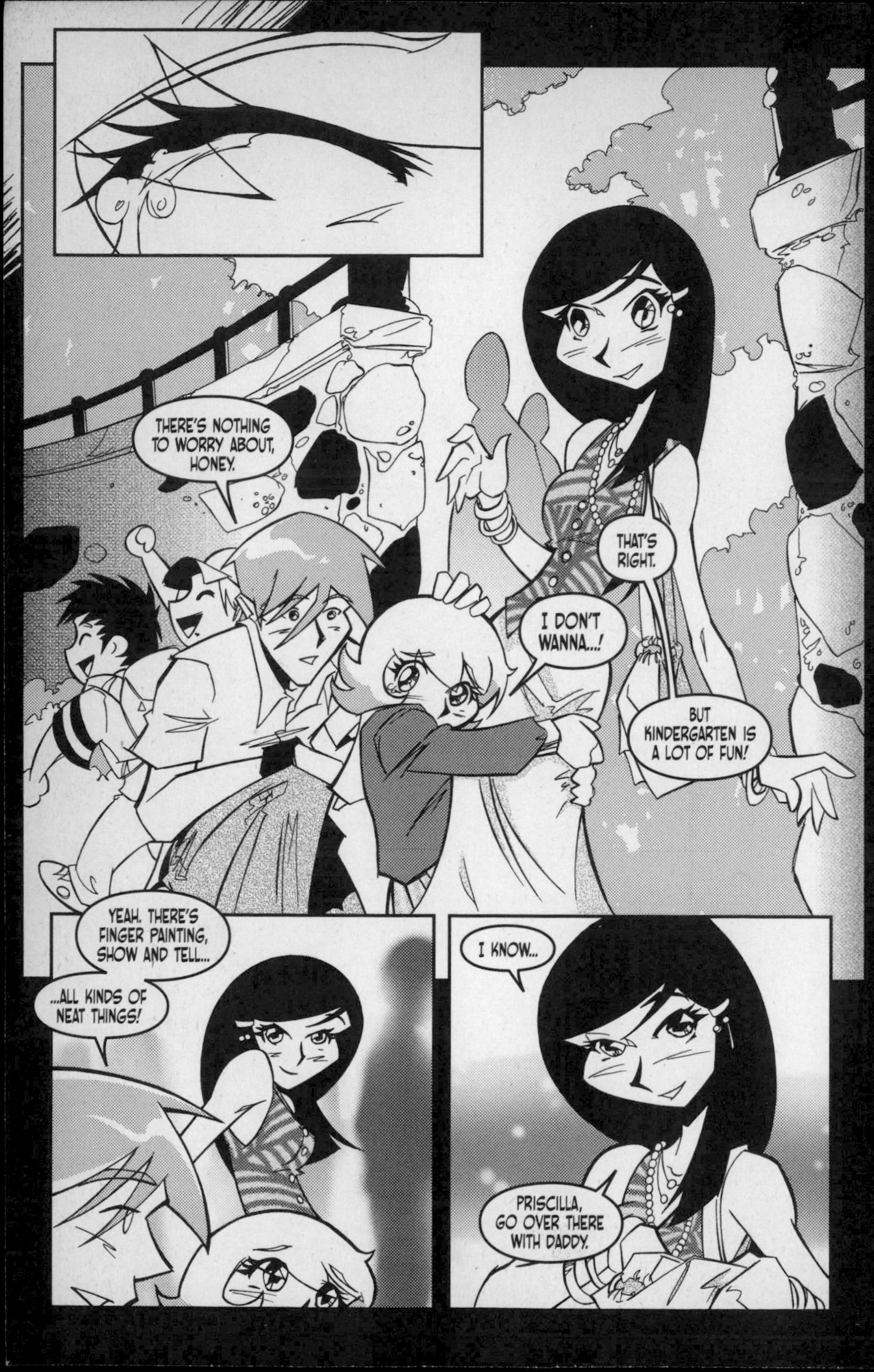

THERE'S NOTHING TO WORRY ABOUT, HONEY.
THAT'S RIGHT.
I DON'T WANNA...!
BUT KINDERGARTEN IS A LOT OF FUN!
YEAH. THERE'S FINGER PAINTING, SHOW AND TELL...
...ALL KINDS OF NEAT THINGS!
I KNOW...
PRISCILLA, GO OVER THERE WITH DADDY.

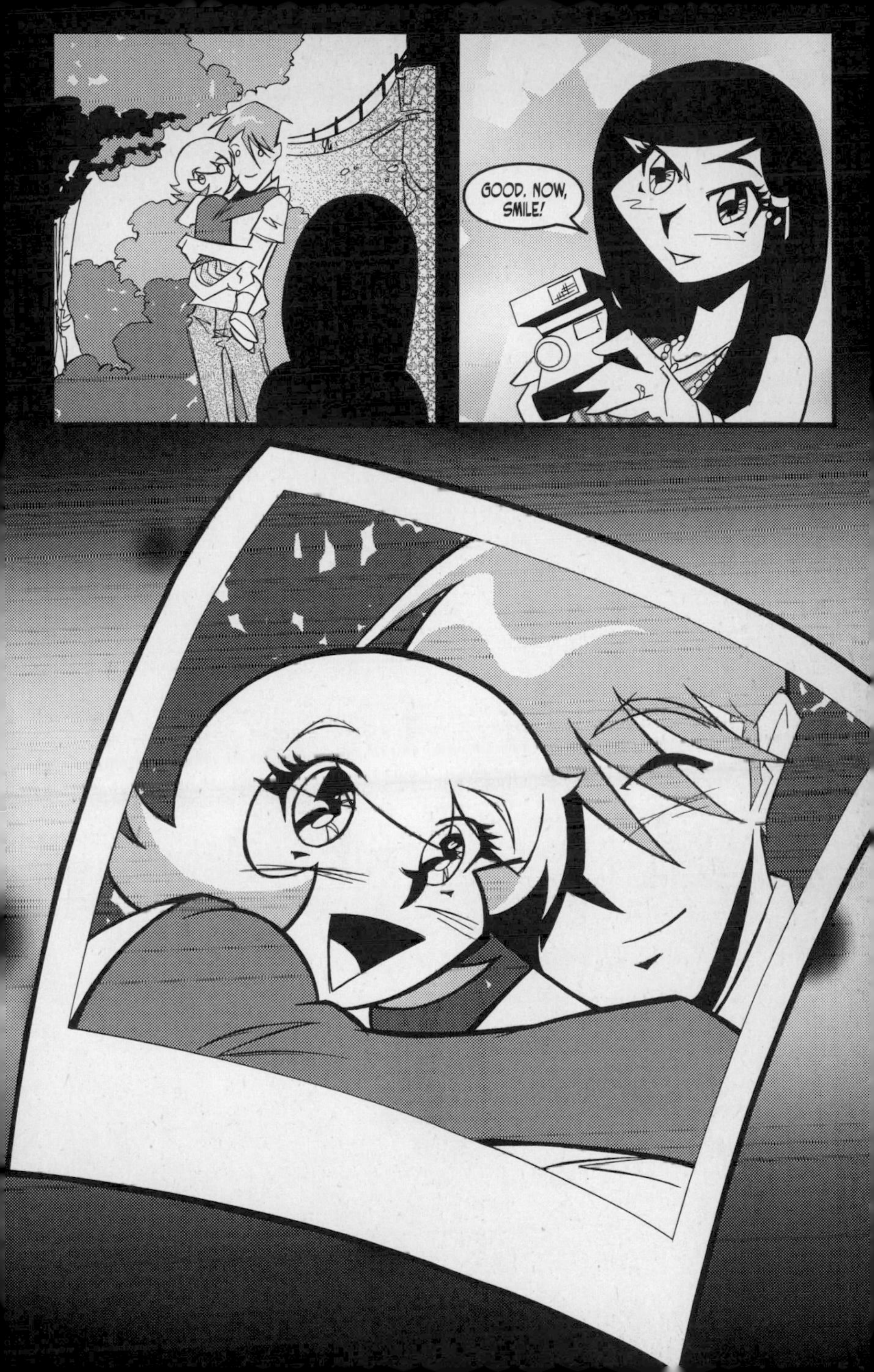
GOOD. NOW, SMILE!

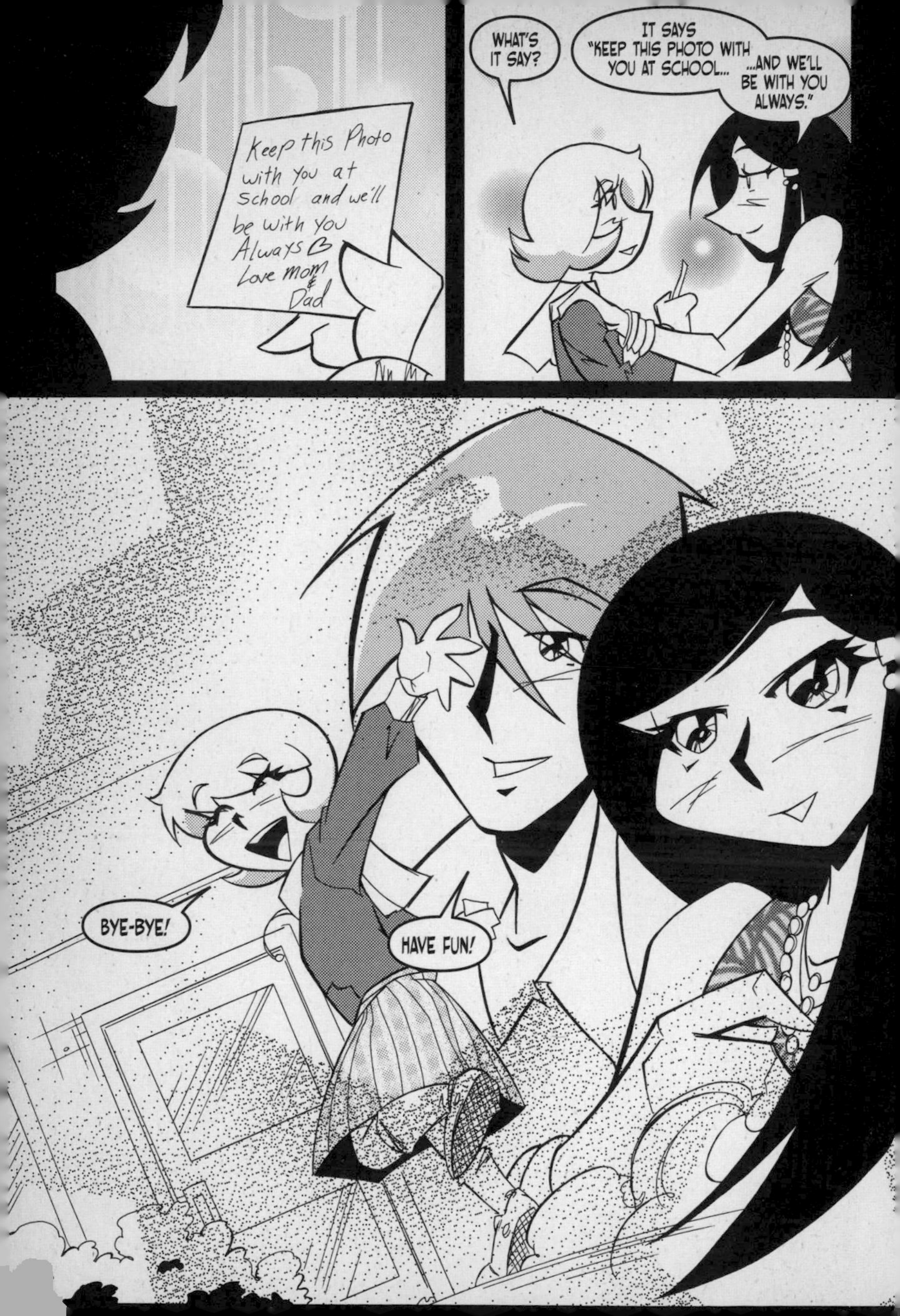
Keep this Photo with you at school and we'll be with you Always Love mom & Dad
WHAT'S IT SAY?
IT SAYS "KEEP THIS PHOTO WITH YOU AT SCHOOL...
...AND WE'LL BE WITH YOU ALWAYS."
BYE-BYE!
HAVE FUN!

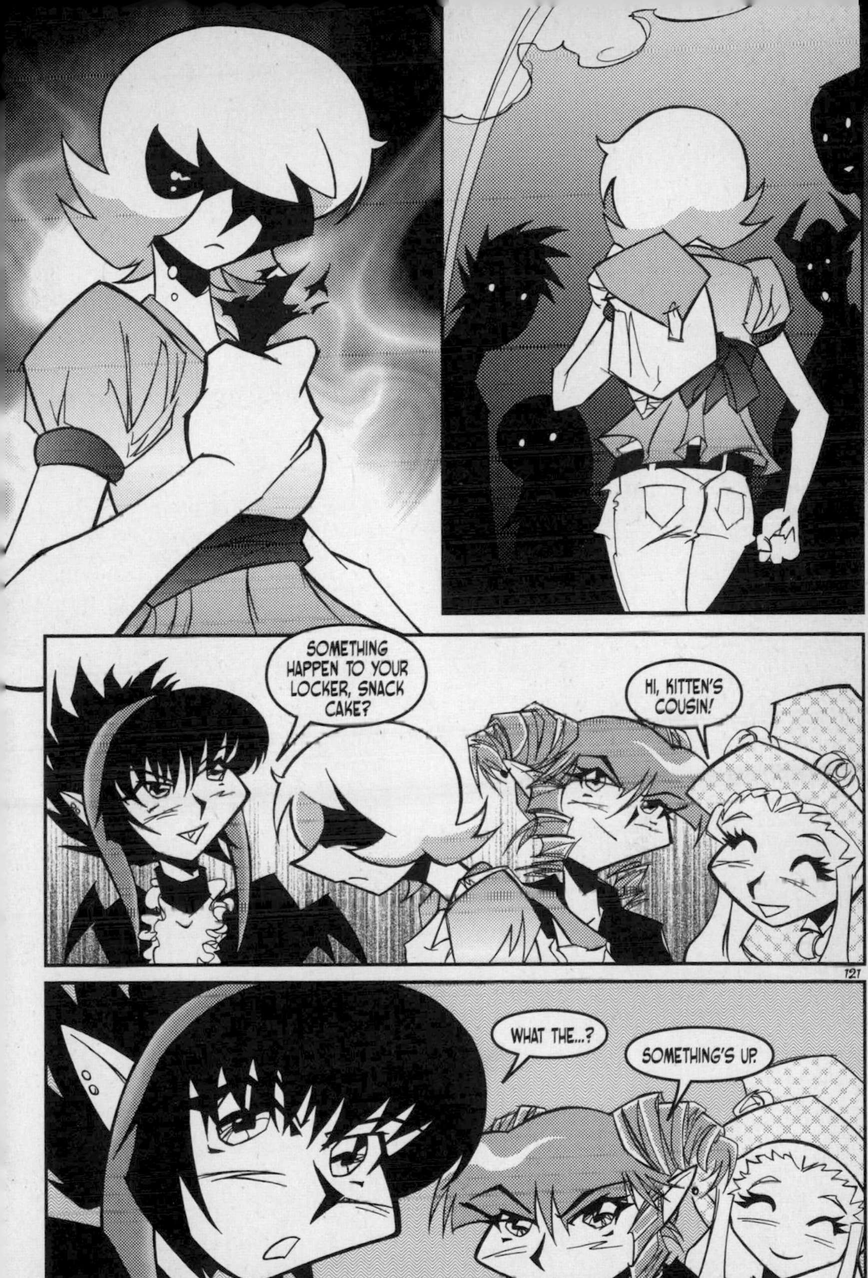
SOMETHING HAPPEN TO YOUR LOCKER, SNACK CAKE?
HI, KITTEN'S COUSIN!
WHAT THE...?
SOMETHING'S UP.

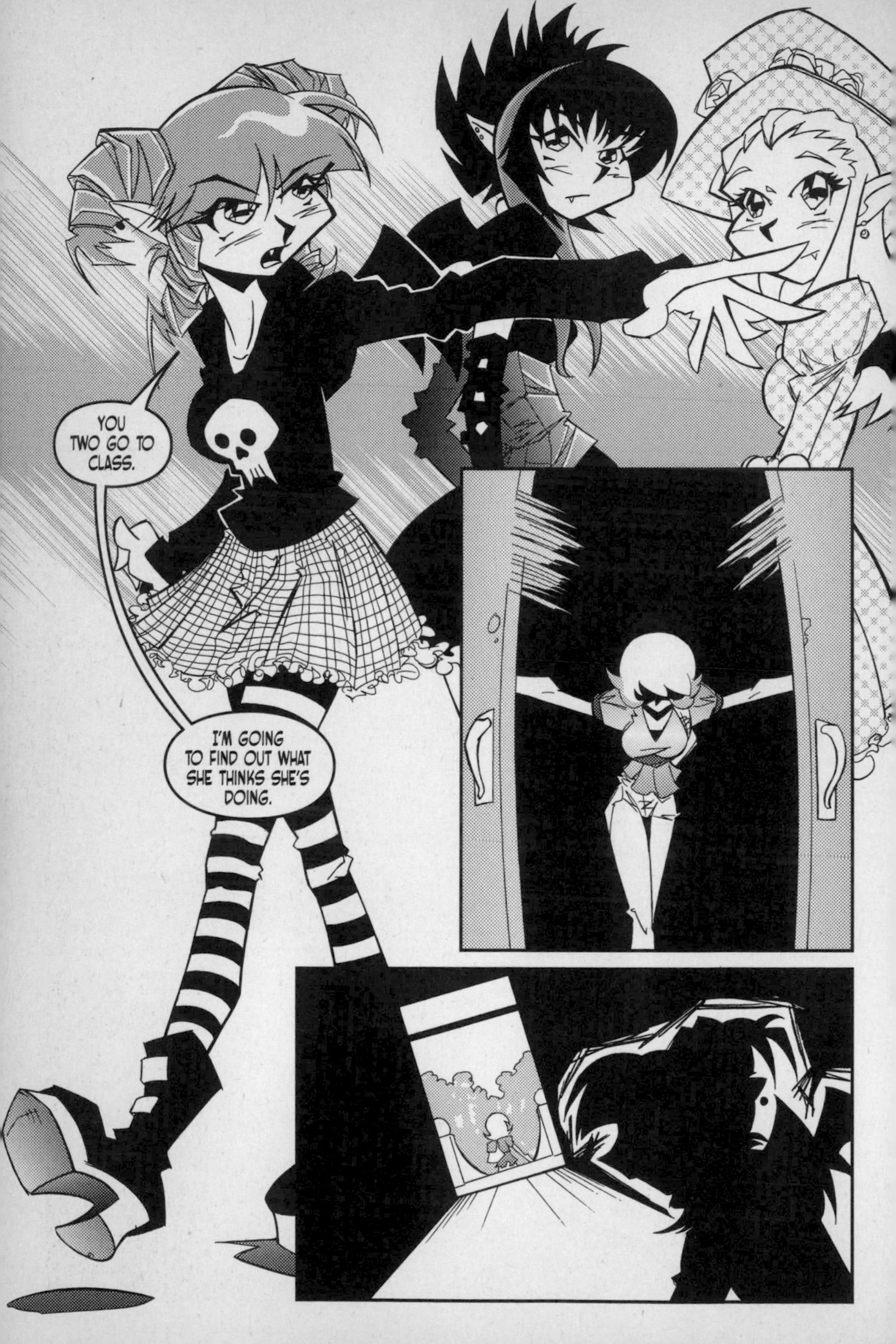
YOU TWO GO TO CLASS.
I'M GOING TO FIND OUT WHAT SHE THINKS SHE'S DOING.

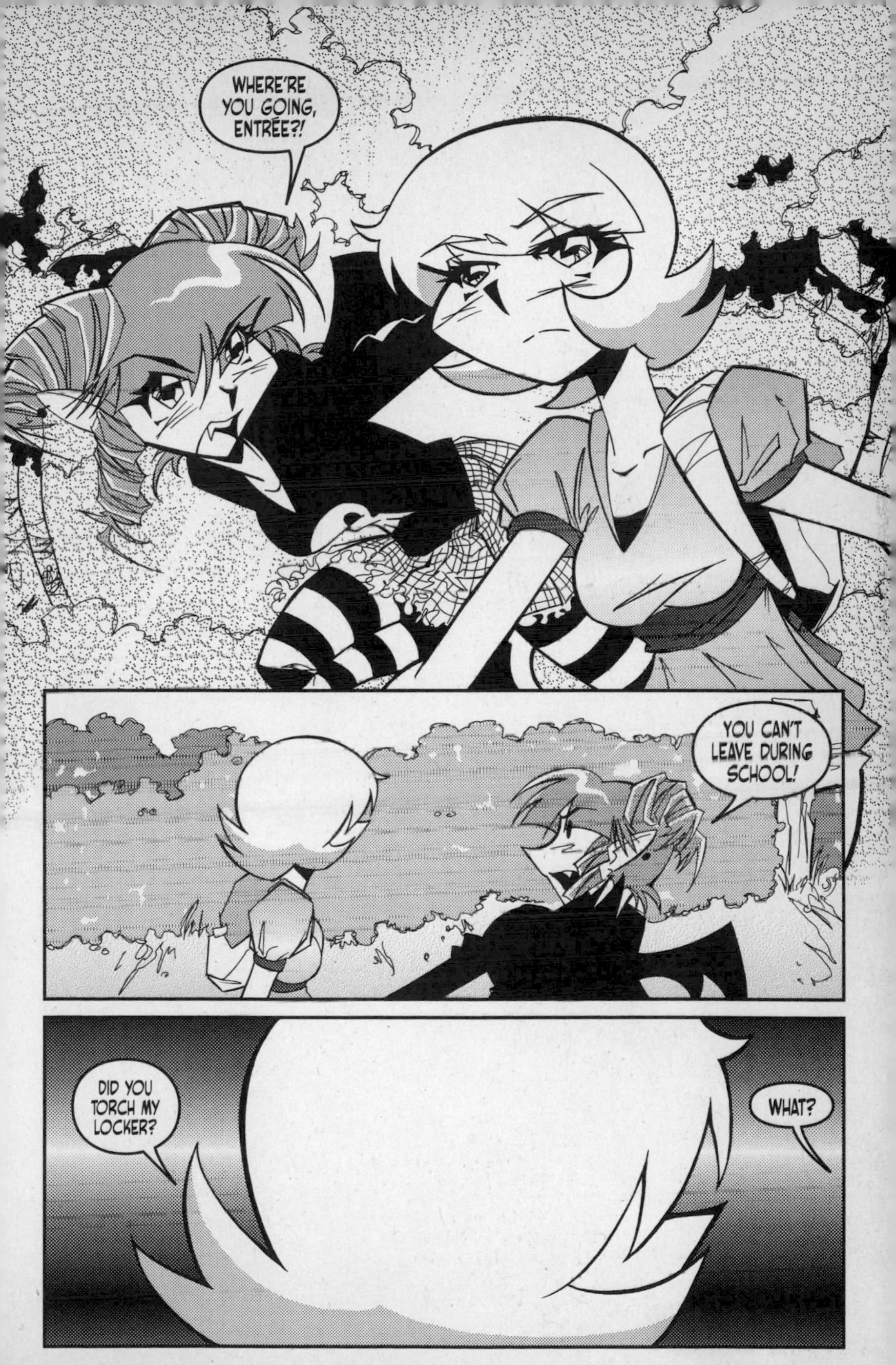
WHERE'RE YOU GOING, ENTRÉE?!
YOU CAN'T LEAVE DURING SCHOOL!
DID YOU TORCH MY LOCKER?
WHAT?

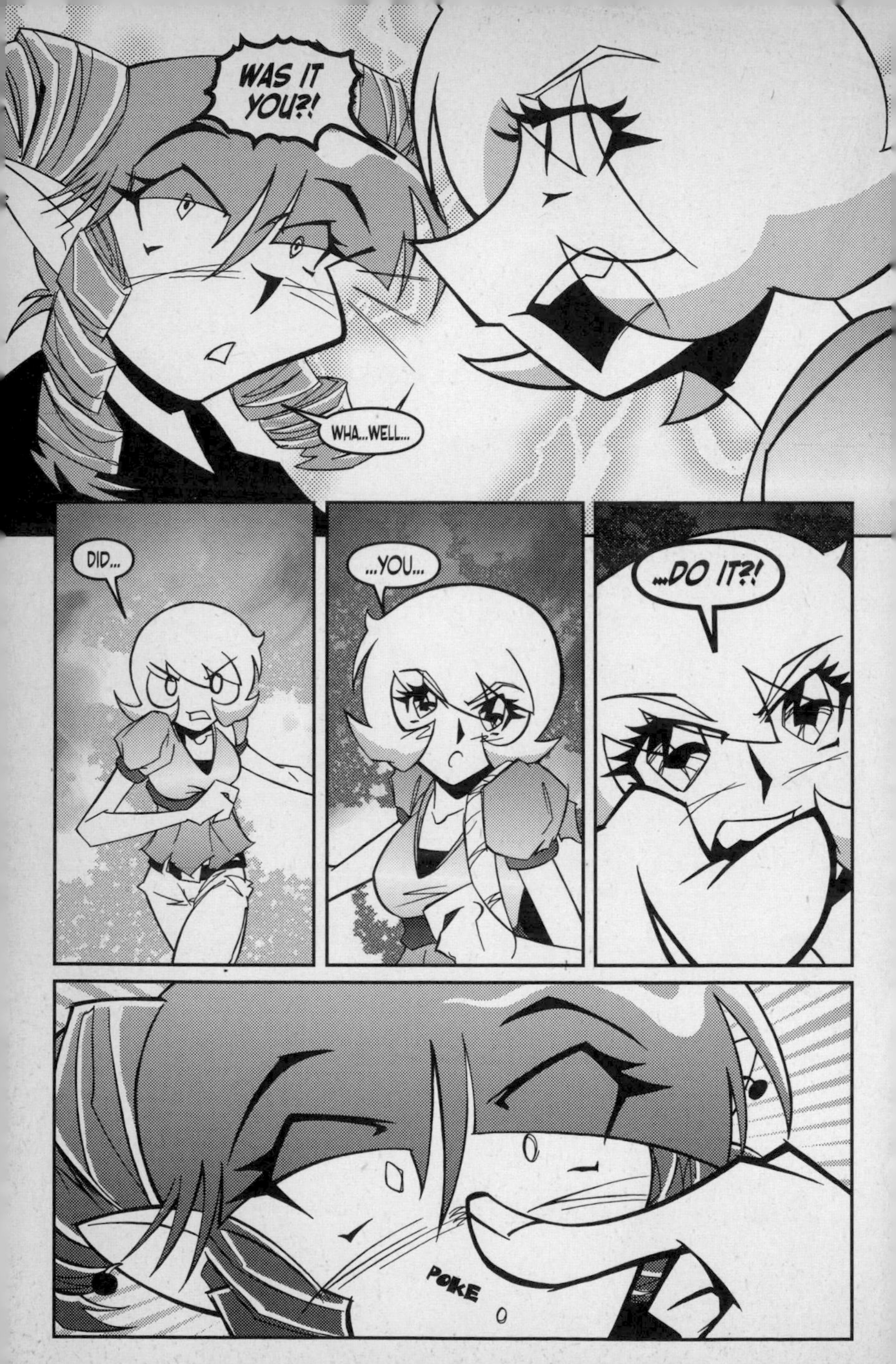
WAS IT YOU?!
WHA...WELL...
DID...
...YOU...
...DO IT?!
POKE

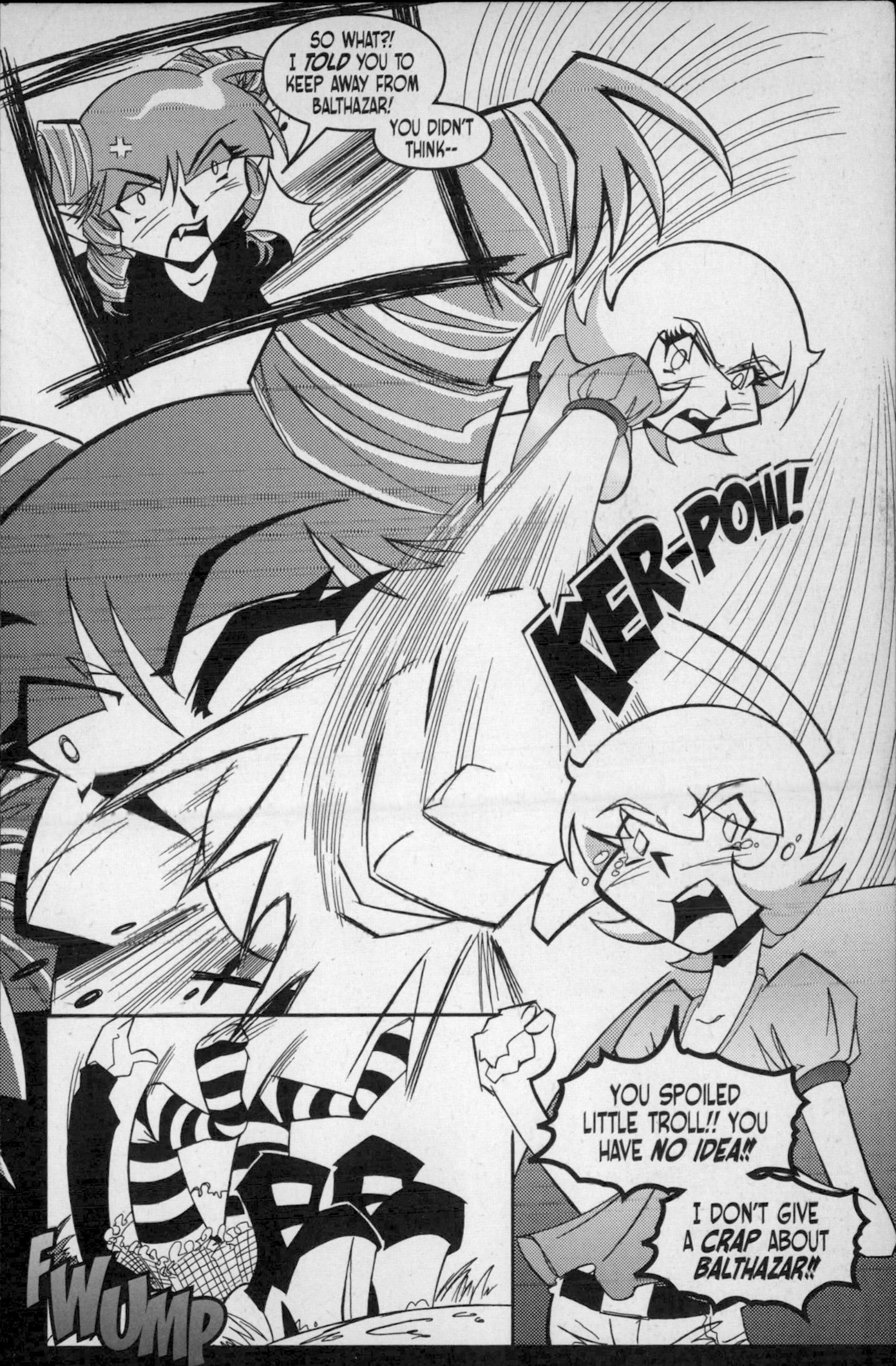
SO WHAT?! I TOLD YOU TO KEEP AWAY FROM BALTHAZAR!
YOU DIDN'T THINK--
KER-POW!
YOU SPOILED LITTLE TROLL!! YOU HAVE NO IDEA!!
I DON'T GIVE A CRAP ABOUT BALTHAZAR!!
FWUMP

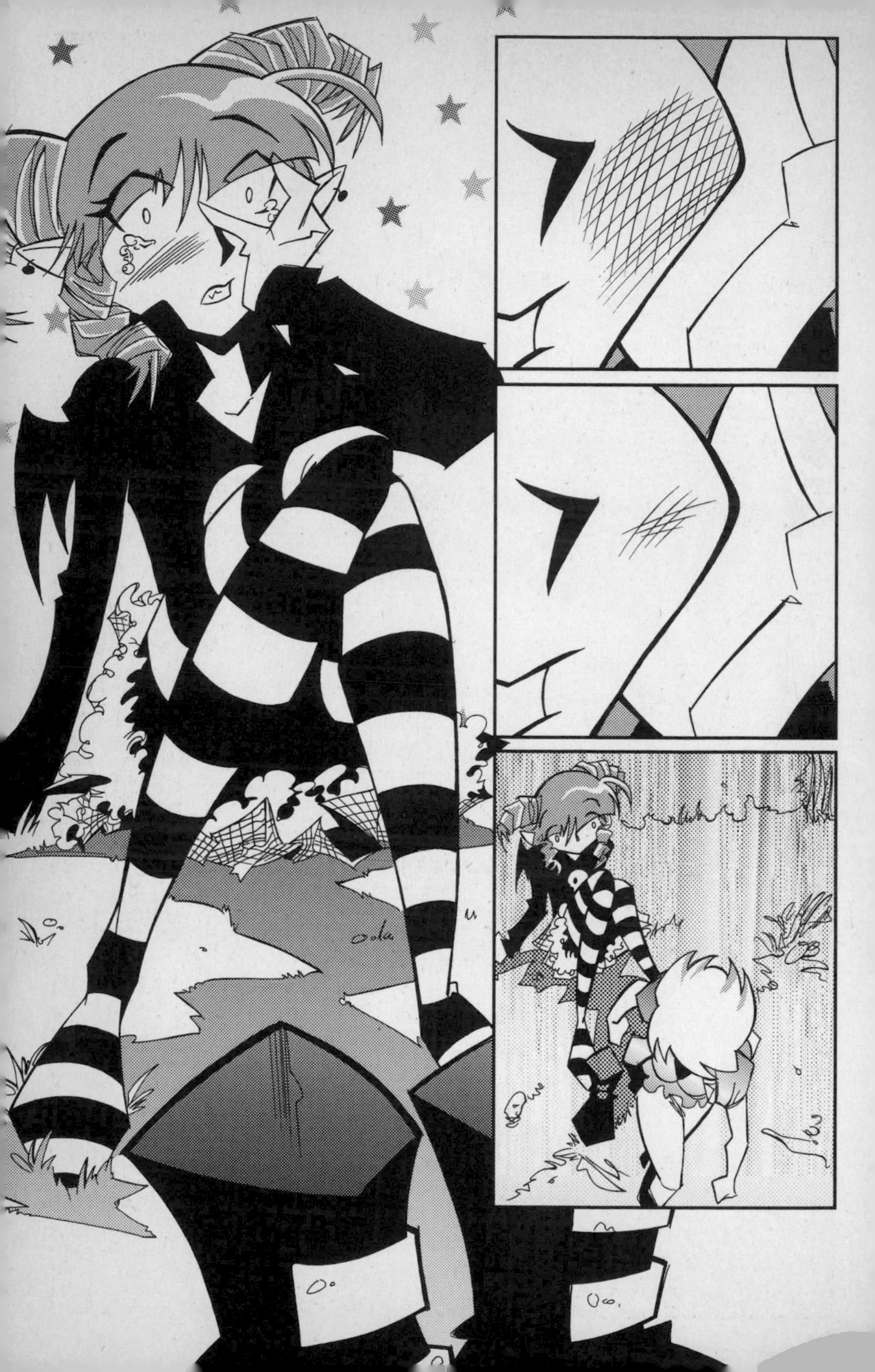

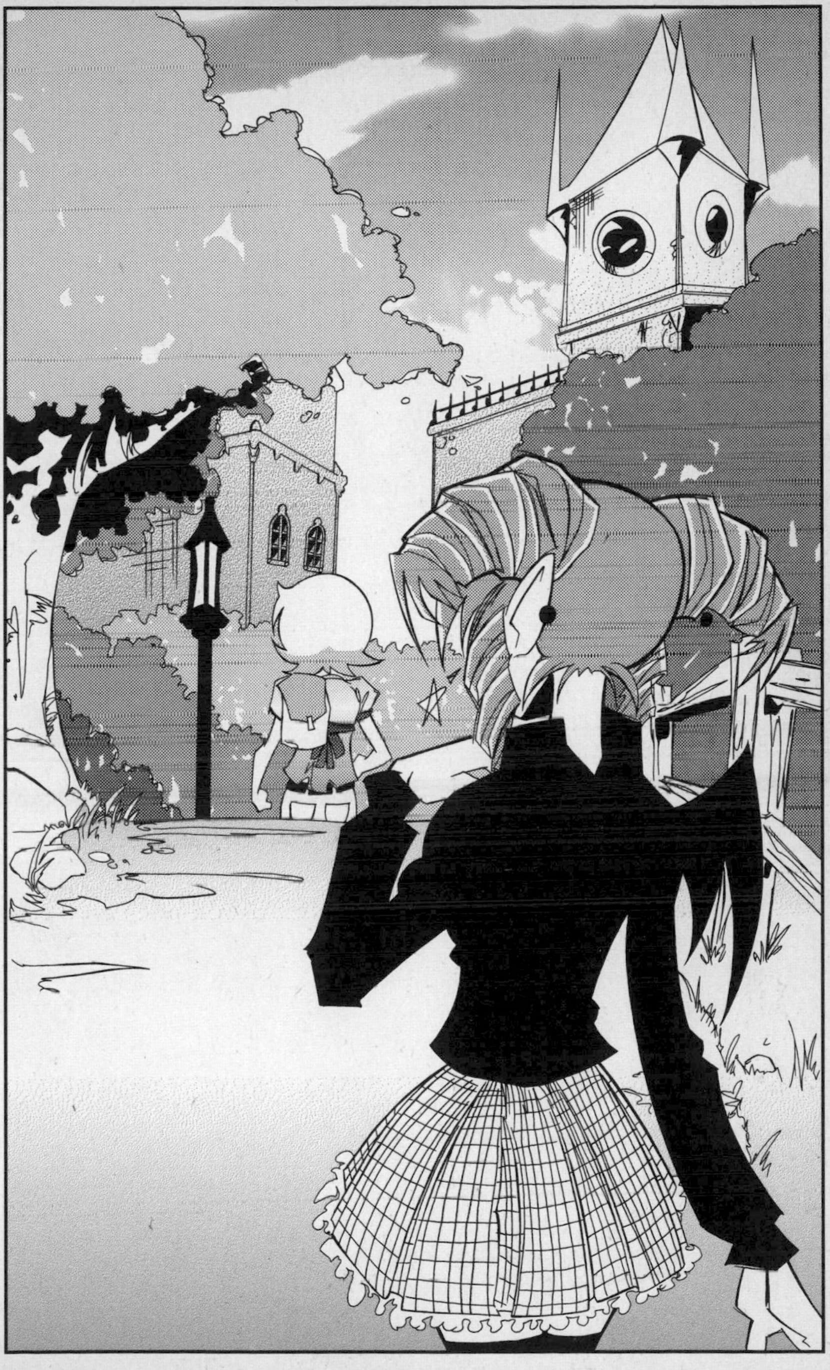

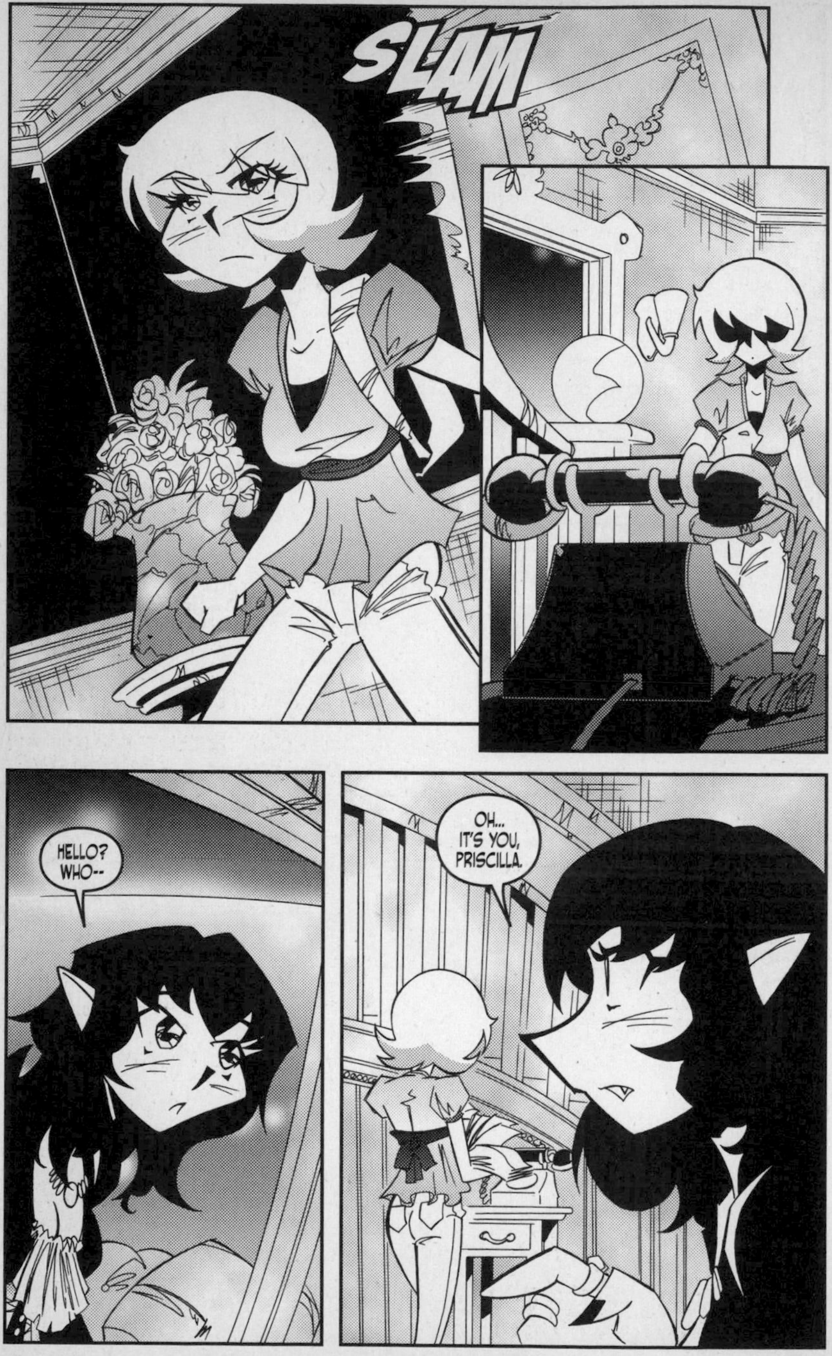
SLAM
HELLO? WHO--
OH... IT'S YOU, PRISCILLA.

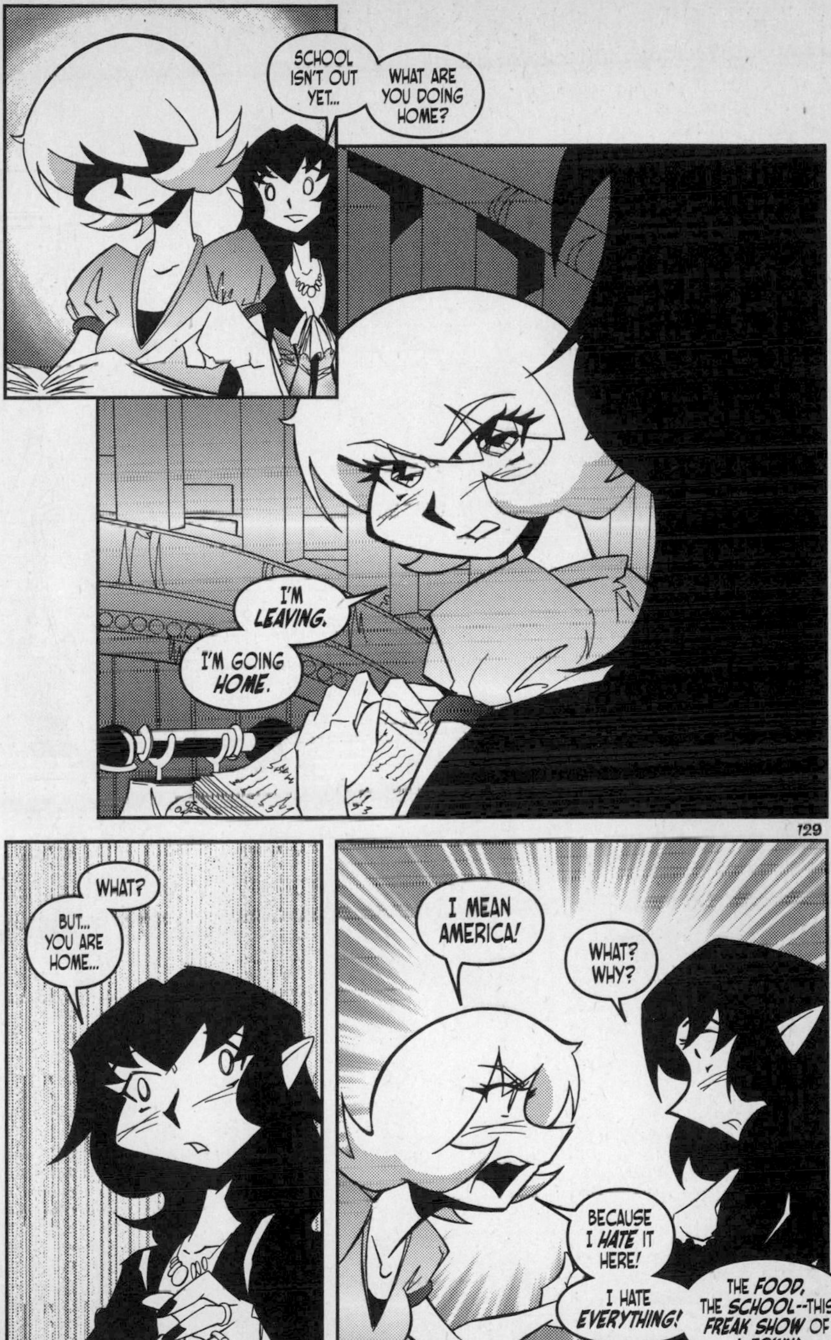
SCHOOL ISN'T OUT YET...
WHAT ARE YOU DOING HOME?
I'M LEAVING.
I'M GOING HOME.
WHAT?
BUT... YOU ARE HOME...
I MEAN AMERICA!
WHAT? WHY?
BECAUSE I HATE IT HERE!
I HATE EVERYTHING!
THE FOOD, THE SCHOOL--THIS FREAK SHOW OF A TOWN!

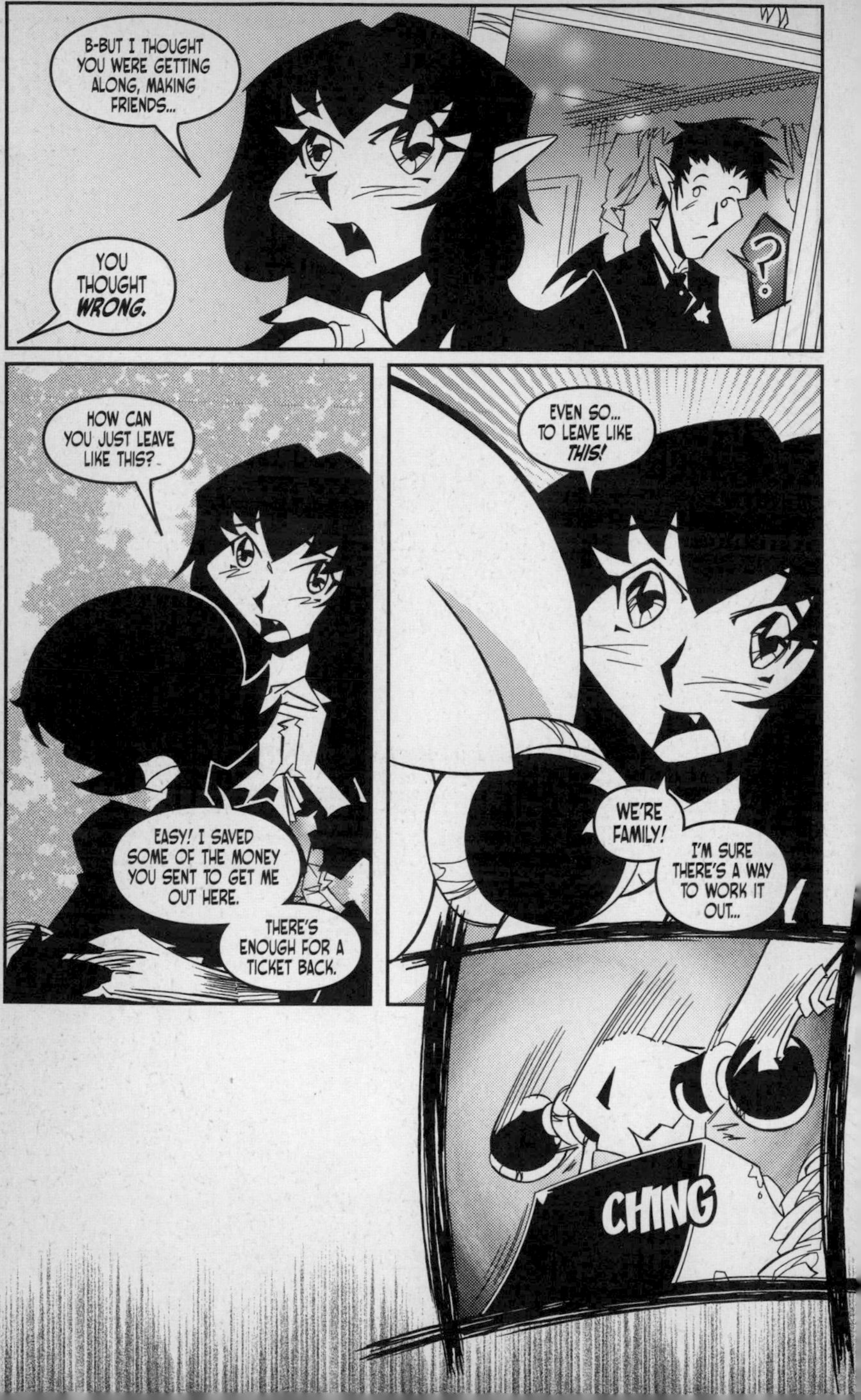
B-BUT I THOUGHT YOU WERE GETTING ALONG, MAKING FRIENDS...
YOU THOUGHT ***WRONG.***
?
HOW CAN YOU JUST LEAVE LIKE THIS?
EASY! I SAVED SOME OF THE MONEY YOU SENT TO GET ME OUT HERE.
THERE'S ENOUGH FOR A TICKET BACK.
EVEN SO... TO LEAVE LIKE ***THIS!***
WE'RE FAMILY!
I'M SURE THERE'S A WAY TO WORK IT OUT...
CHING

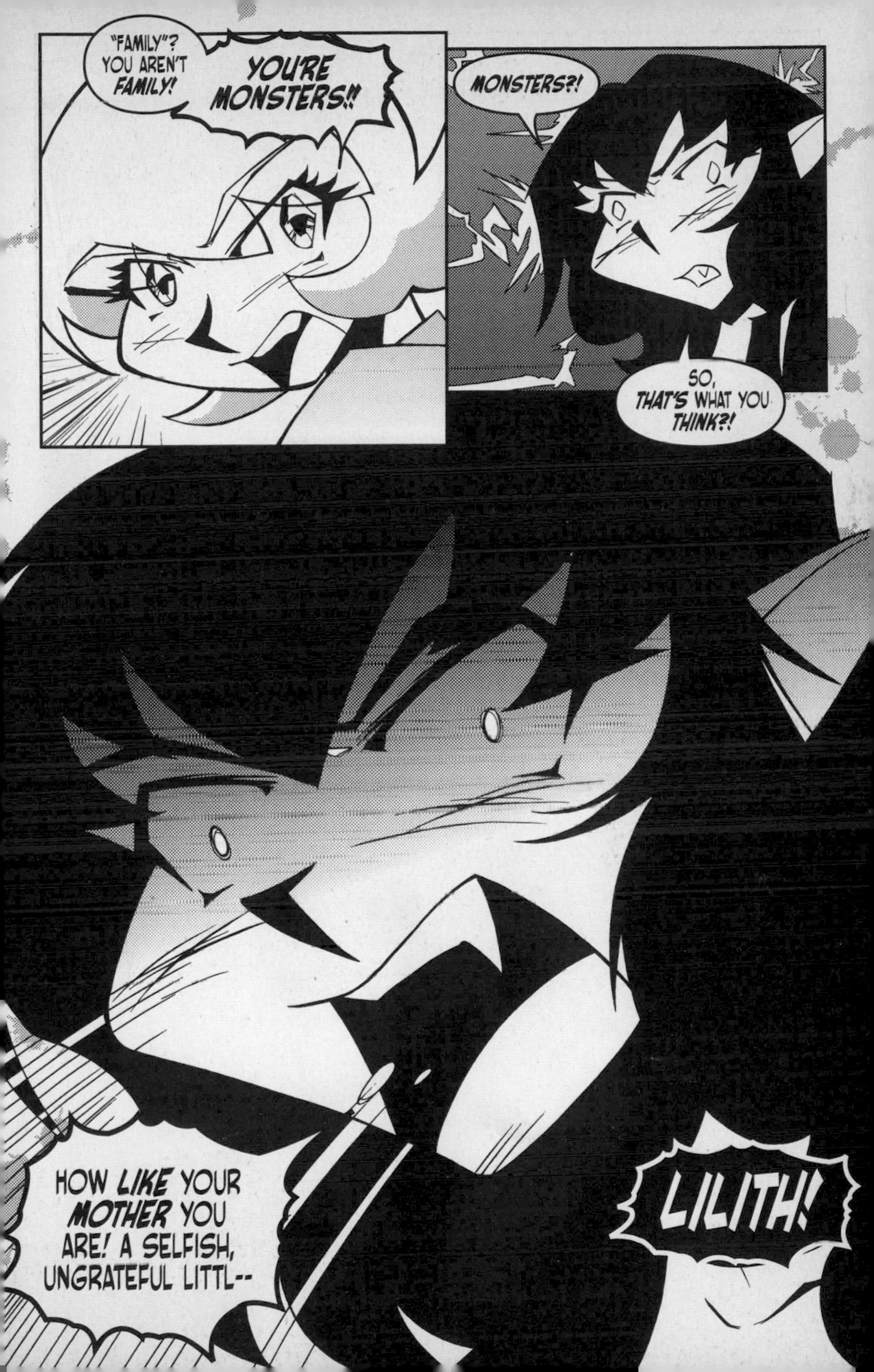
"FAMILY"? YOU AREN'T FAMILY!
YOU'RE MONSTERS!!
MONSTERS?!
SO, THAT'S WHAT YOU THINK?!
HOW LIKE YOUR MOTHER YOU ARE! A SELFISH, UNGRATEFUL LITTL--
LILITH!

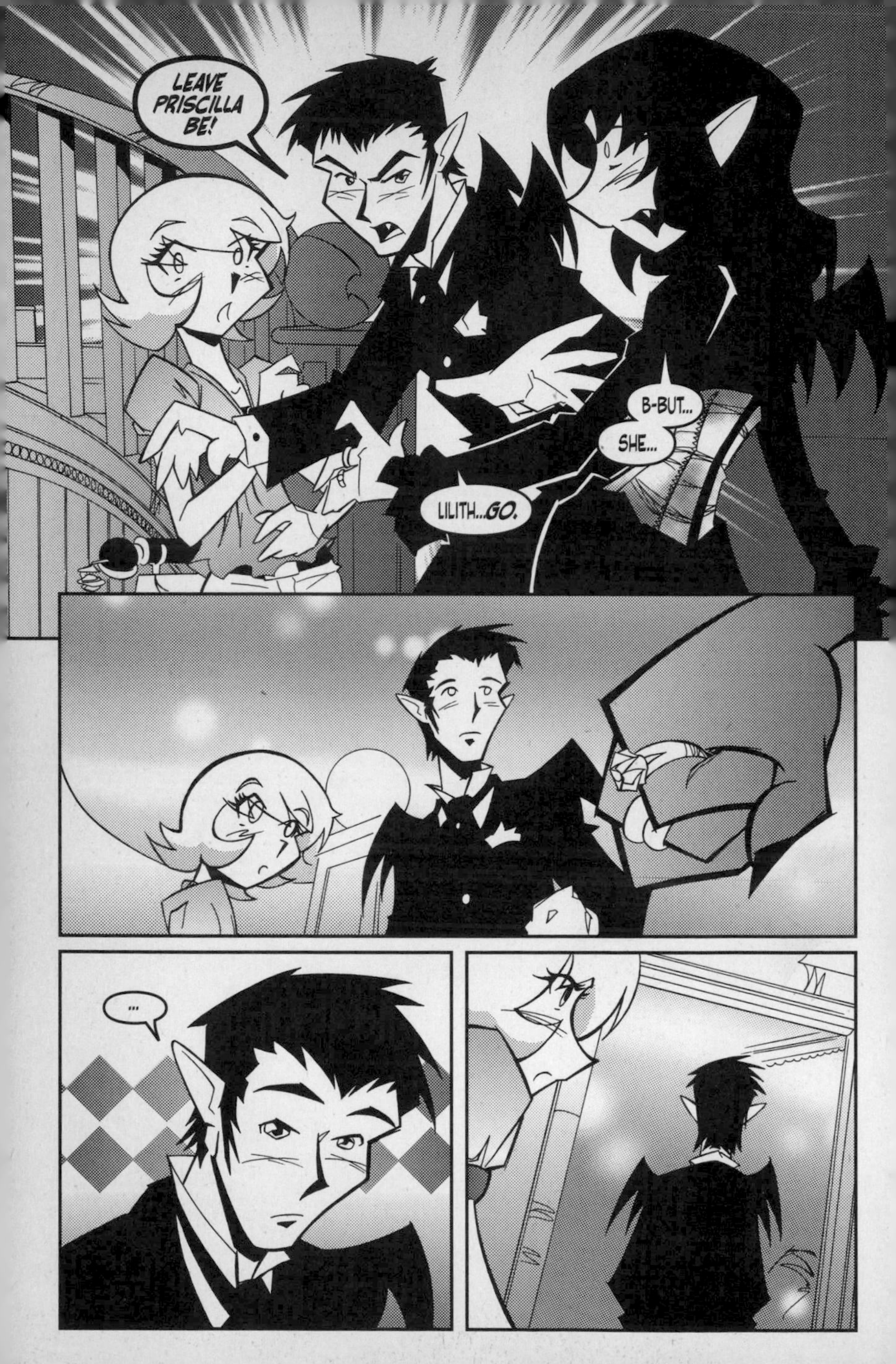
LEAVE PRISCILLA BE!
B-BUT...
SHE...
LILITH...GO.
...

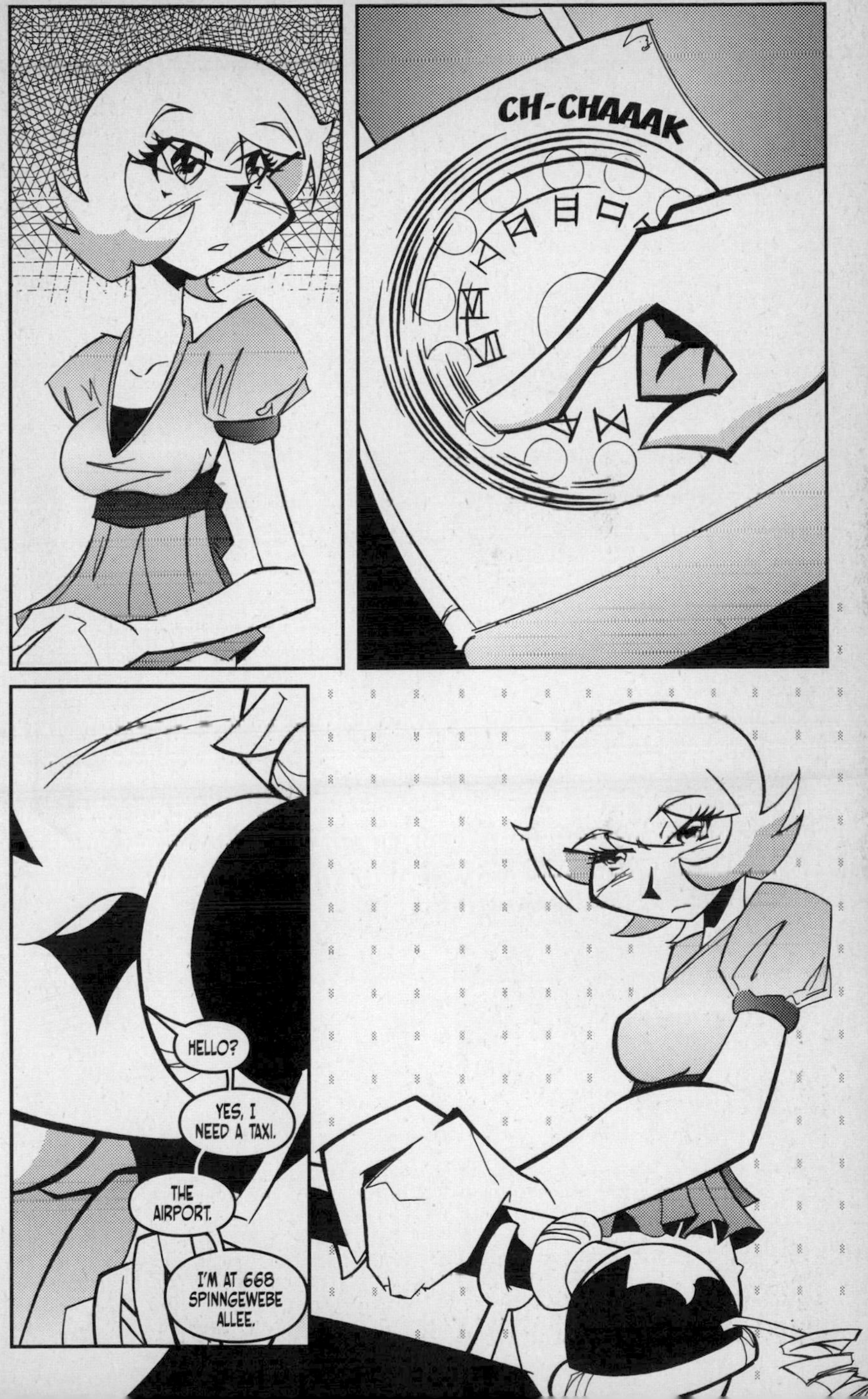
CH-CHAAAK
HELLO?
YES, I NEED A TAXI.
THE AIRPORT.
I'M AT 668 SPINNGEWEBE ALLEE.

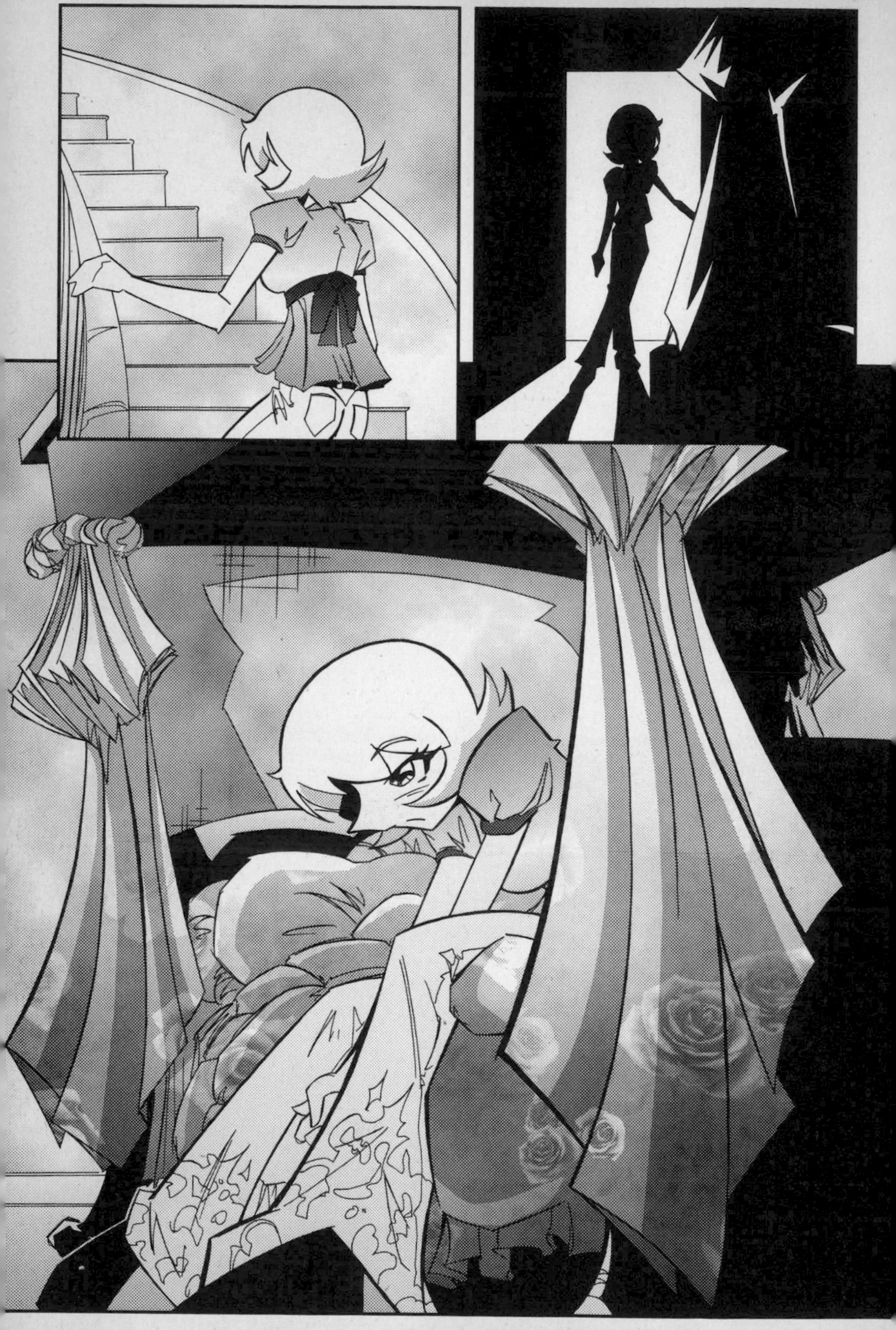

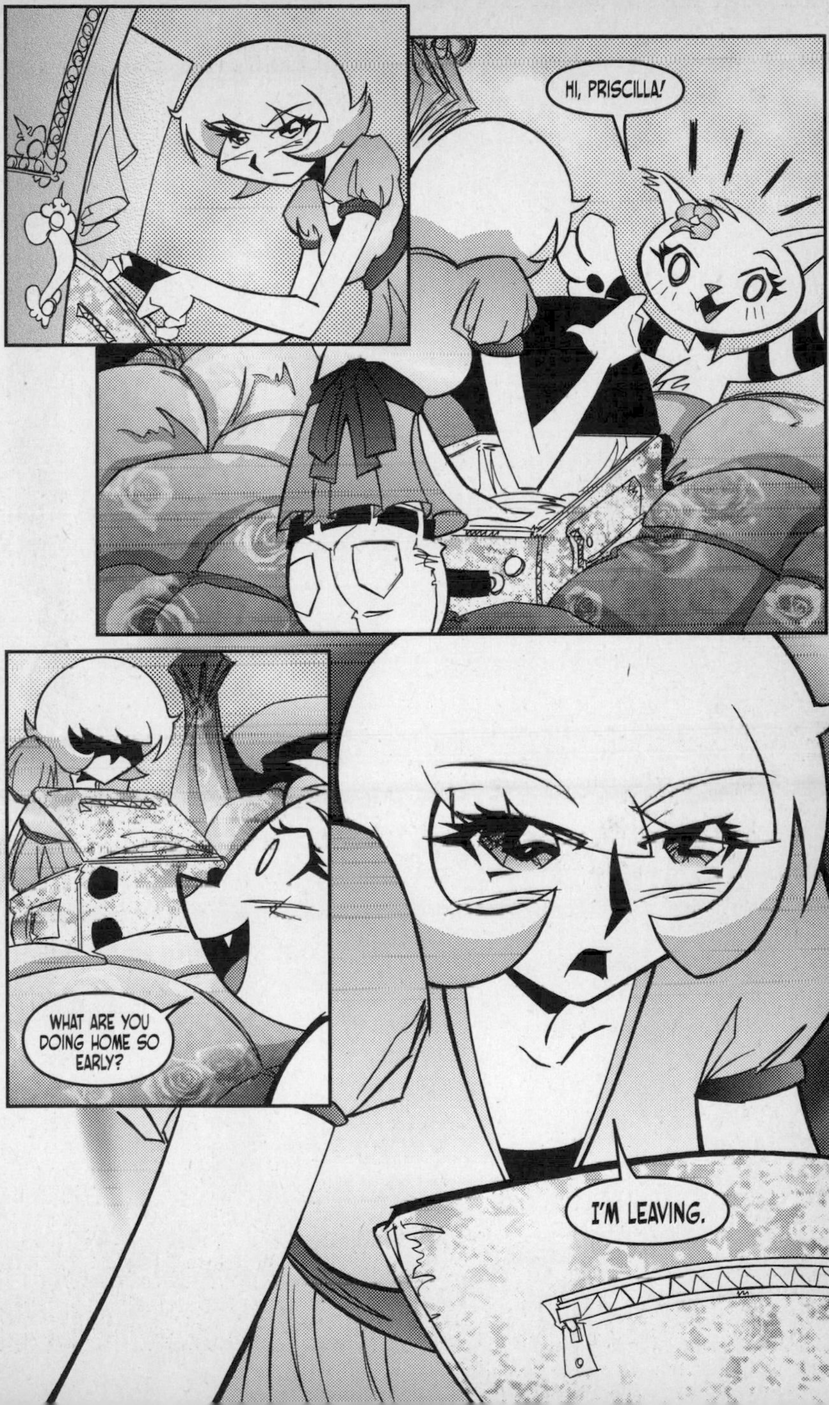
HI, PRISCILLA!
WHAT ARE YOU DOING HOME SO EARLY?
I'M LEAVING.

Chapter Six

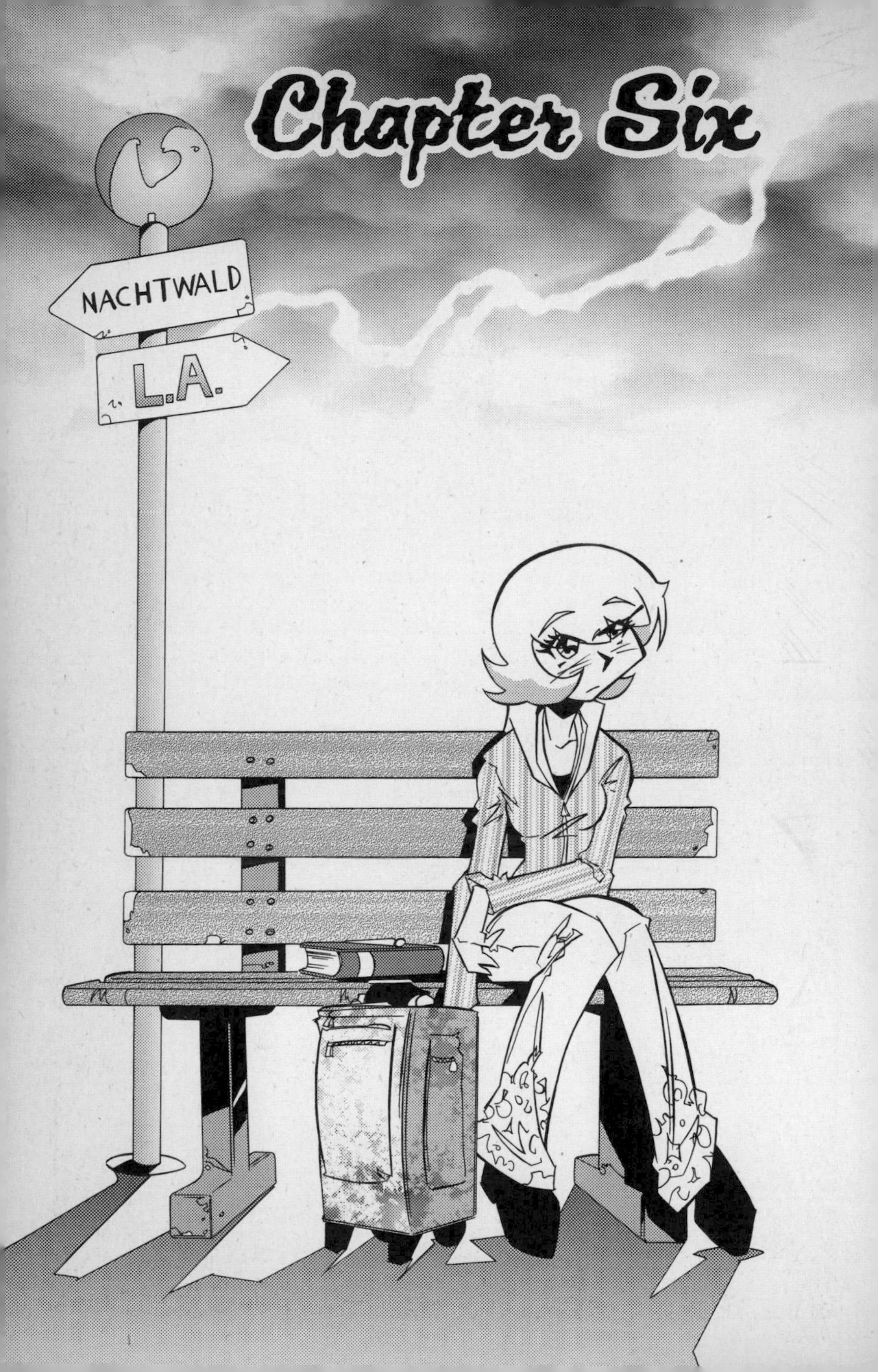
NACHTWALD
L.A.

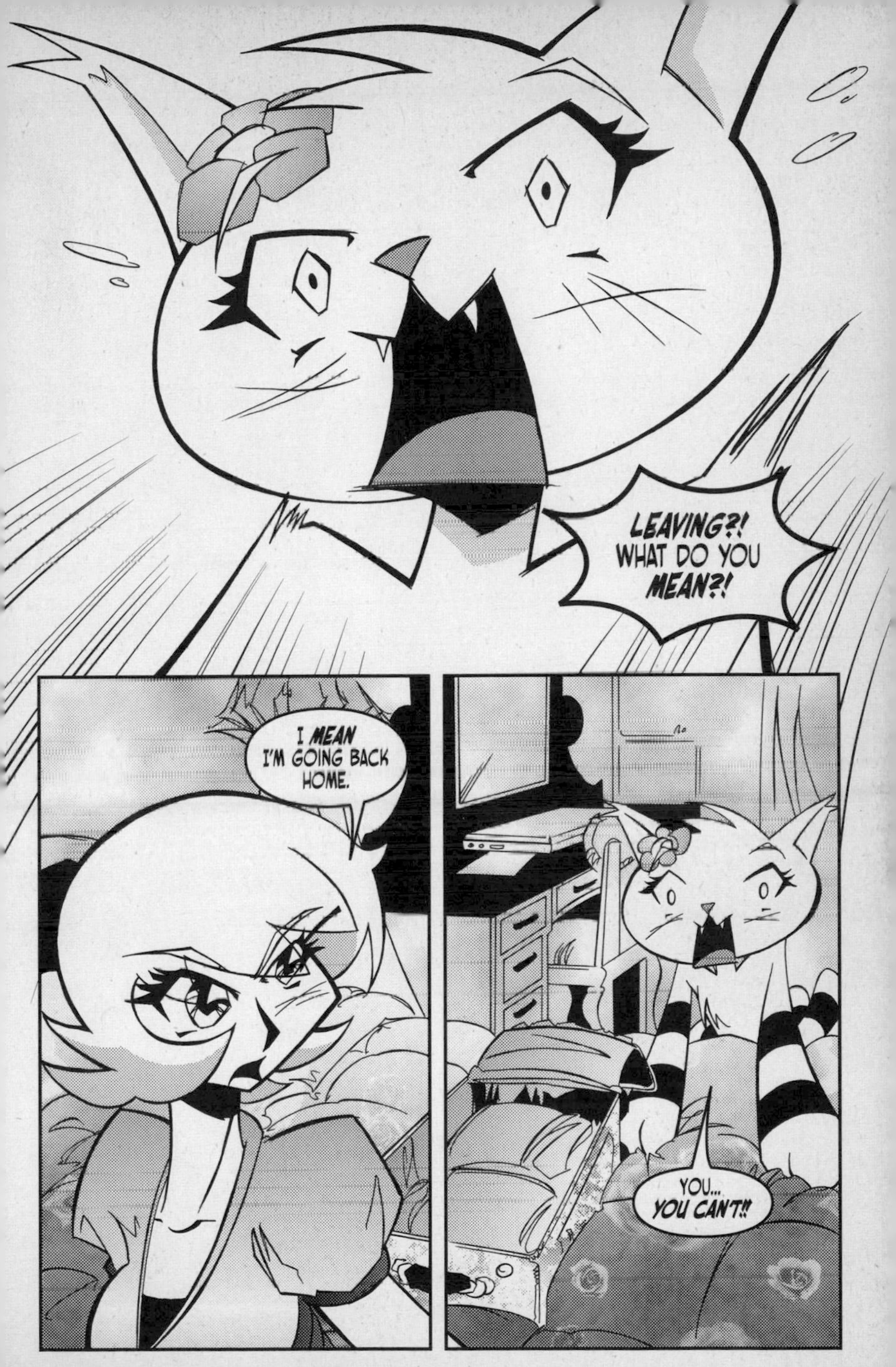
LEAVING?! WHAT DO YOU MEAN?!
I MEAN I'M GOING BACK HOME.
YOU... YOU CAN'T!!

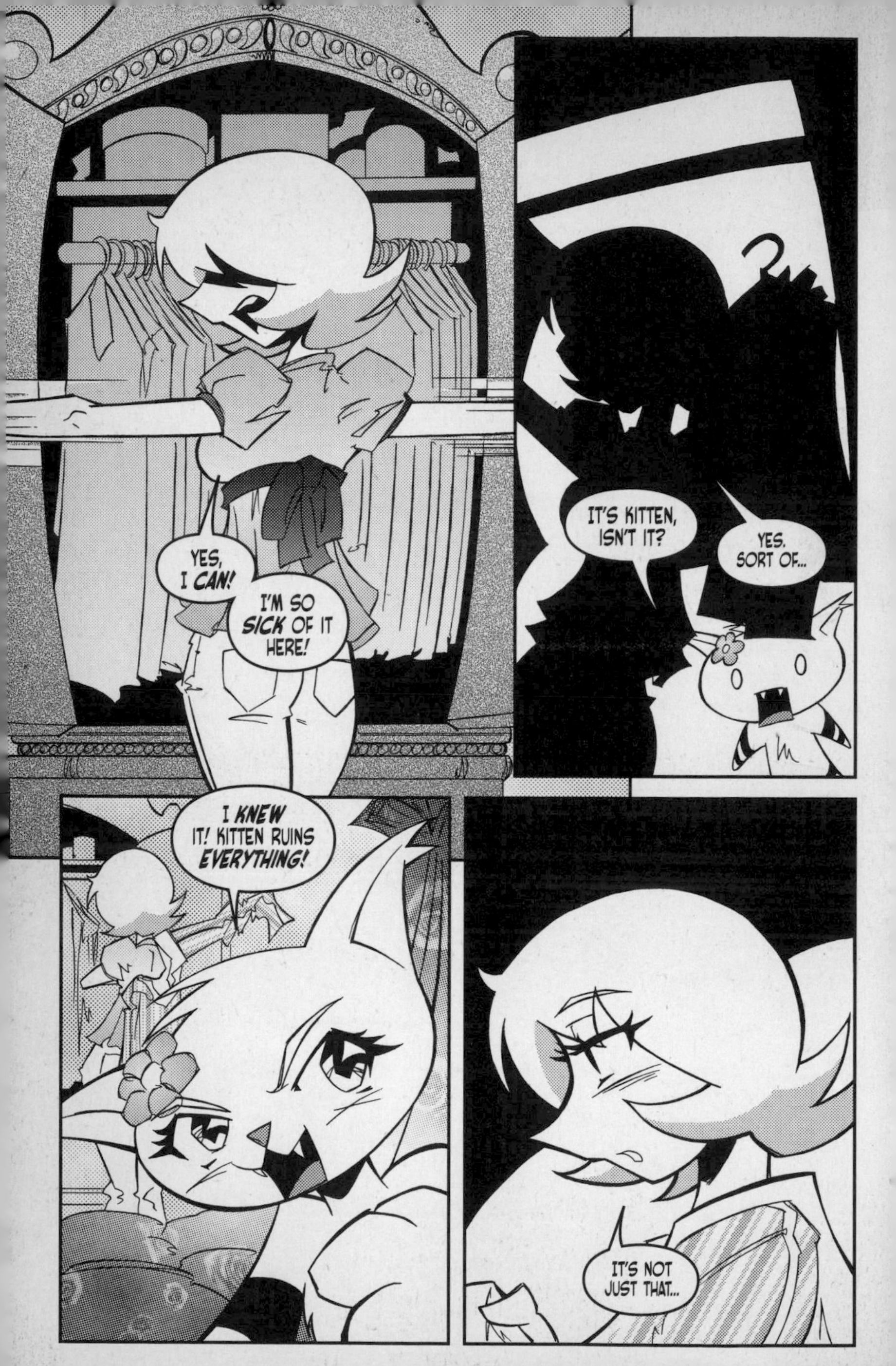
YES, I *CAN!*
I'M SO *SICK* OF IT HERE!
IT'S KITTEN, ISN'T IT?
YES. SORT OF...
I *KNEW* IT! KITTEN RUINS *EVERYTHING!*
IT'S NOT JUST THAT...

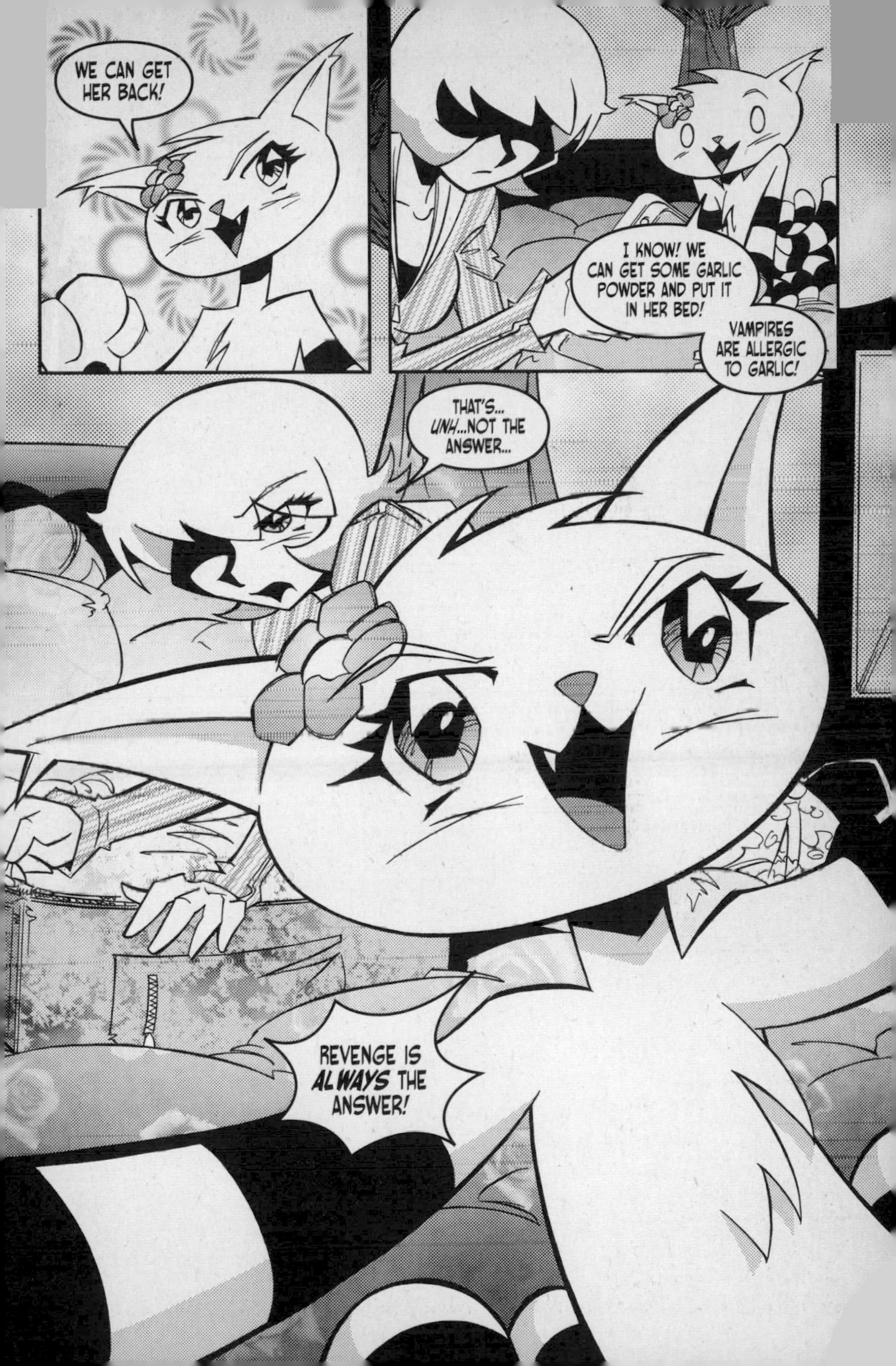
WE CAN GET HER BACK!
I KNOW! WE CAN GET SOME GARLIC POWDER AND PUT IT IN HER BED!
VAMPIRES ARE ALLERGIC TO GARLIC!
THAT'S... *UNH*...NOT THE ANSWER...
REVENGE IS ***ALWAYS*** THE ANSWER!

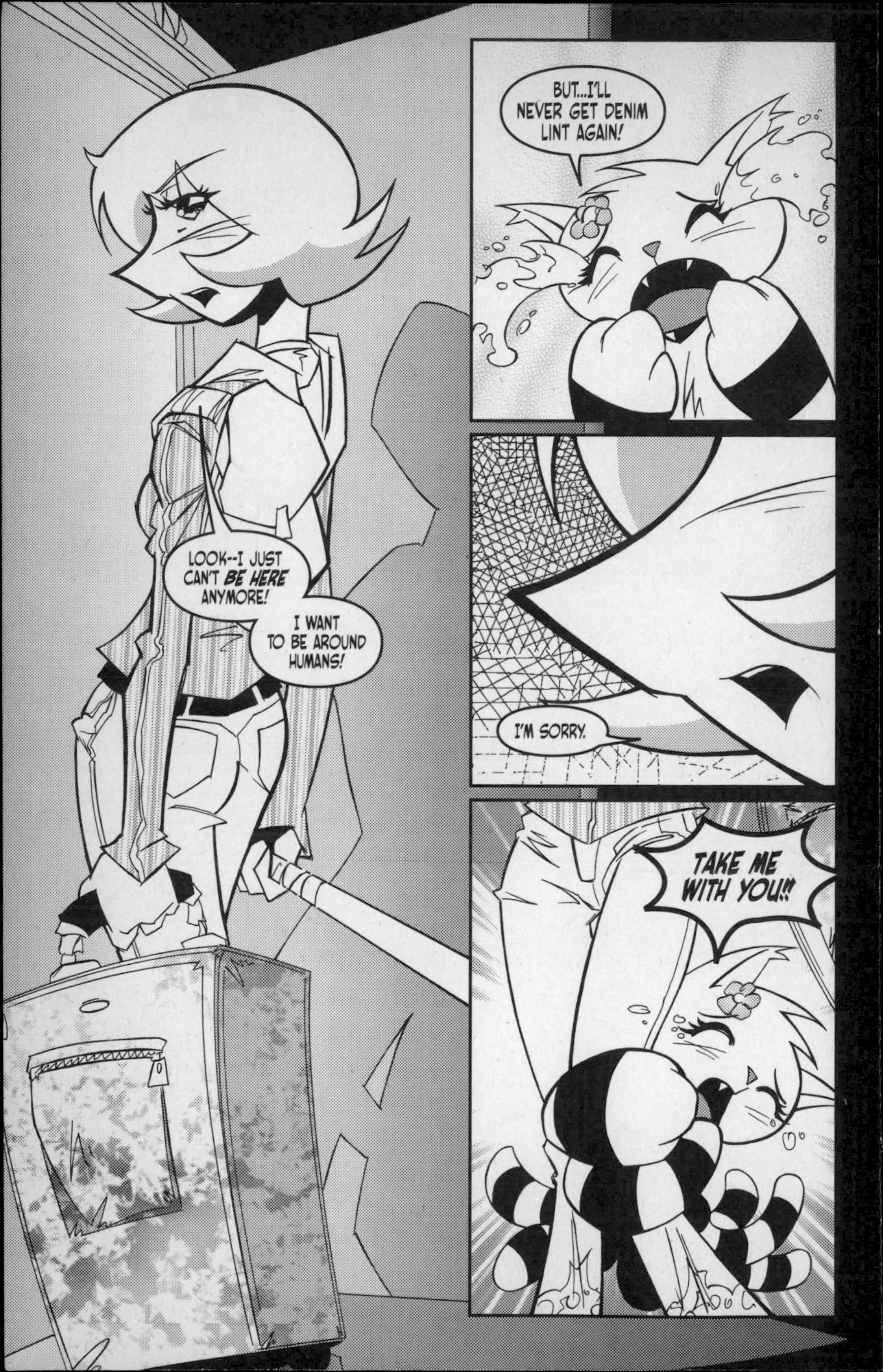
LOOK--I JUST CAN'T *BE HERE* ANYMORE!
I WANT TO BE AROUND HUMANS!
BUT...I'LL NEVER GET DENIM LINT AGAIN!
I'M SORRY.
TAKE ME WITH YOU!!

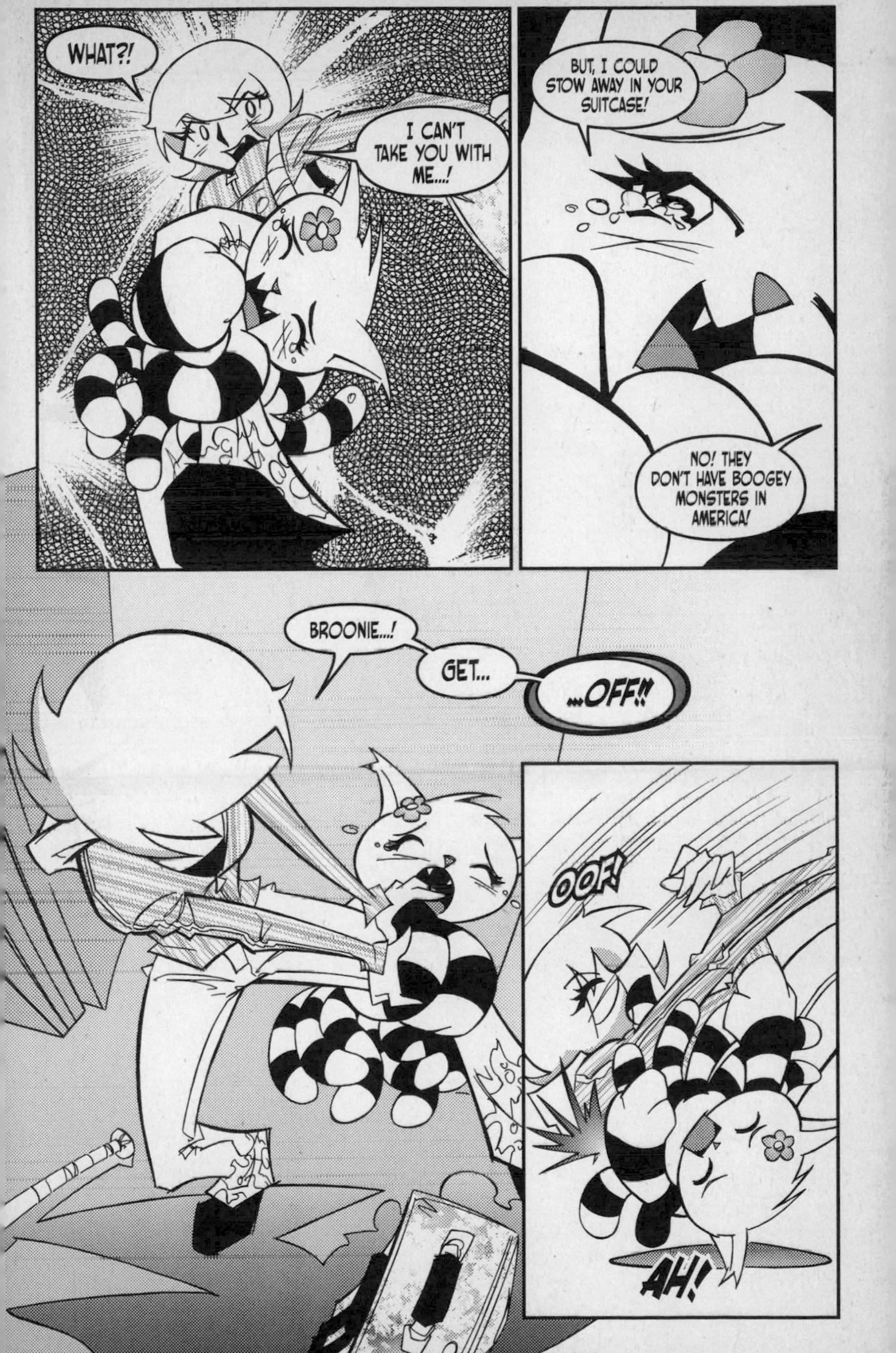
WHAT?!
I CAN'T TAKE YOU WITH ME...!
BUT, I COULD STOW AWAY IN YOUR SUITCASE!
NO! THEY DON'T HAVE BOOGEY MONSTERS IN AMERICA!
BROONIE...!
GET...
...OFF!!
OOF!
AH!

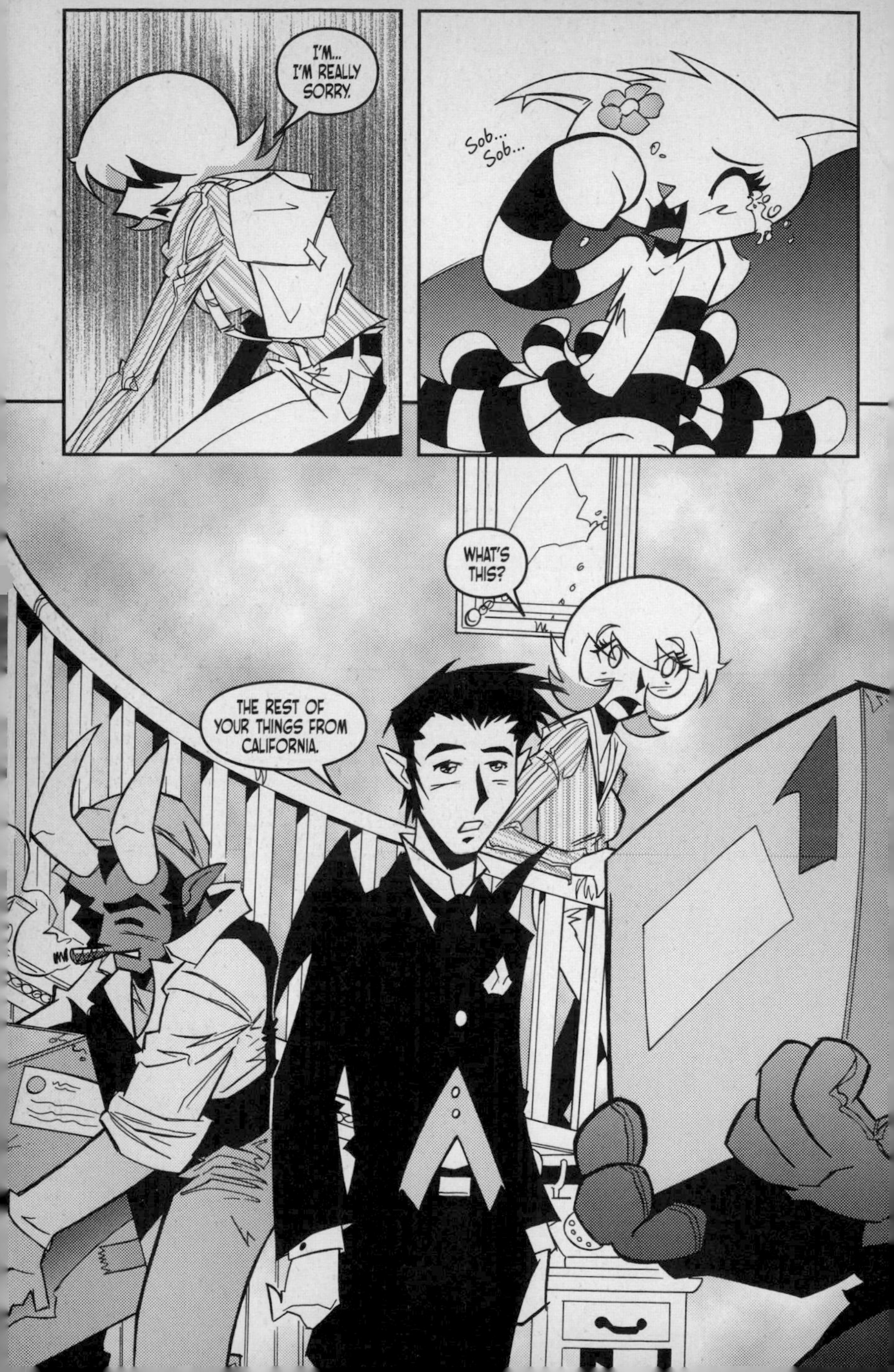
I'M... I'M REALLY SORRY.
Sob... Sob...
WHAT'S THIS?
THE REST OF YOUR THINGS FROM CALIFORNIA.

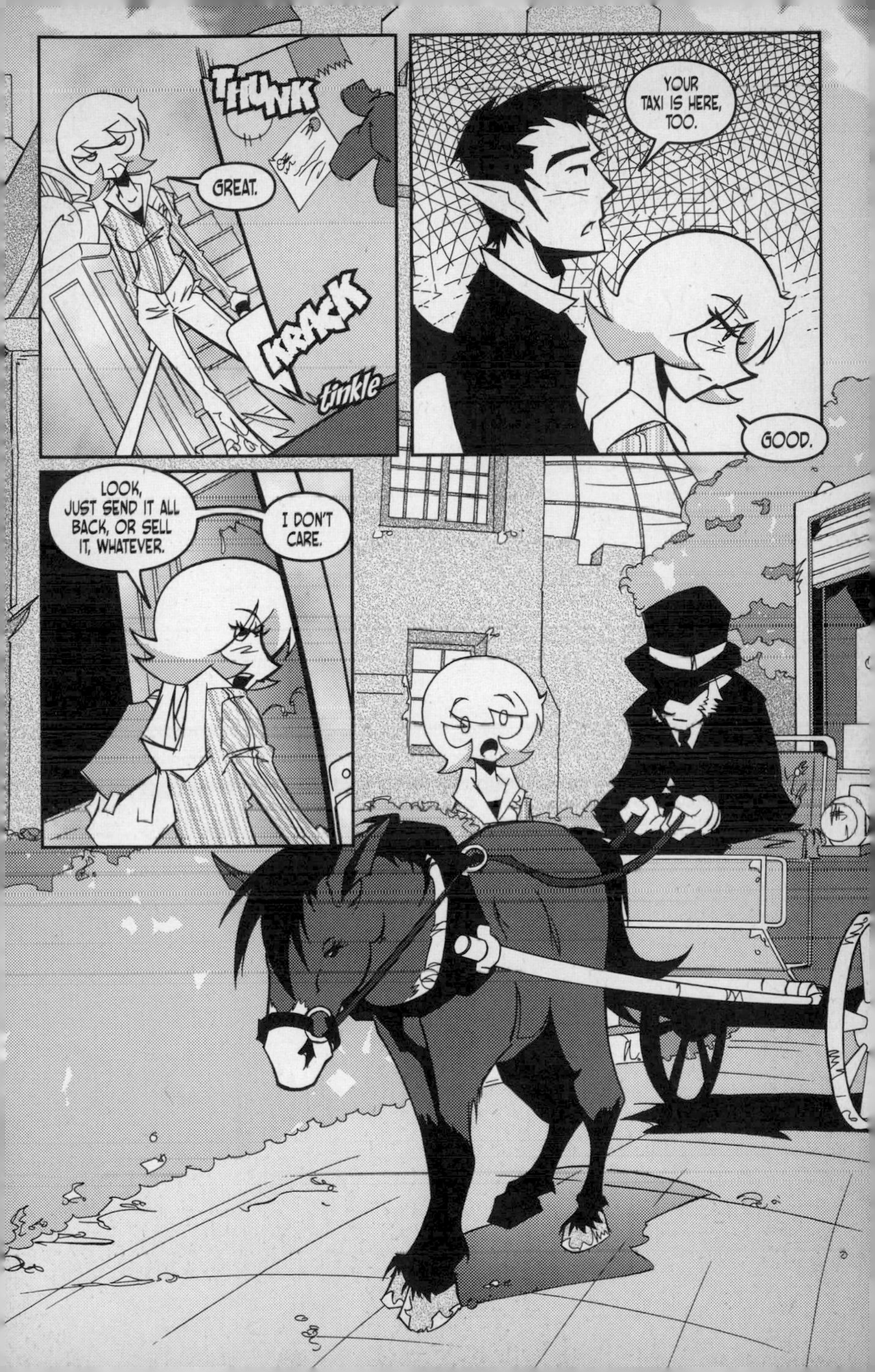
THUNK
GREAT.
KRAKK
tinkle
YOUR TAXI IS HERE, TOO.
GOOD.
LOOK, JUST SEND IT ALL BACK, OR SELL IT, WHATEVER.
I DON'T CARE.

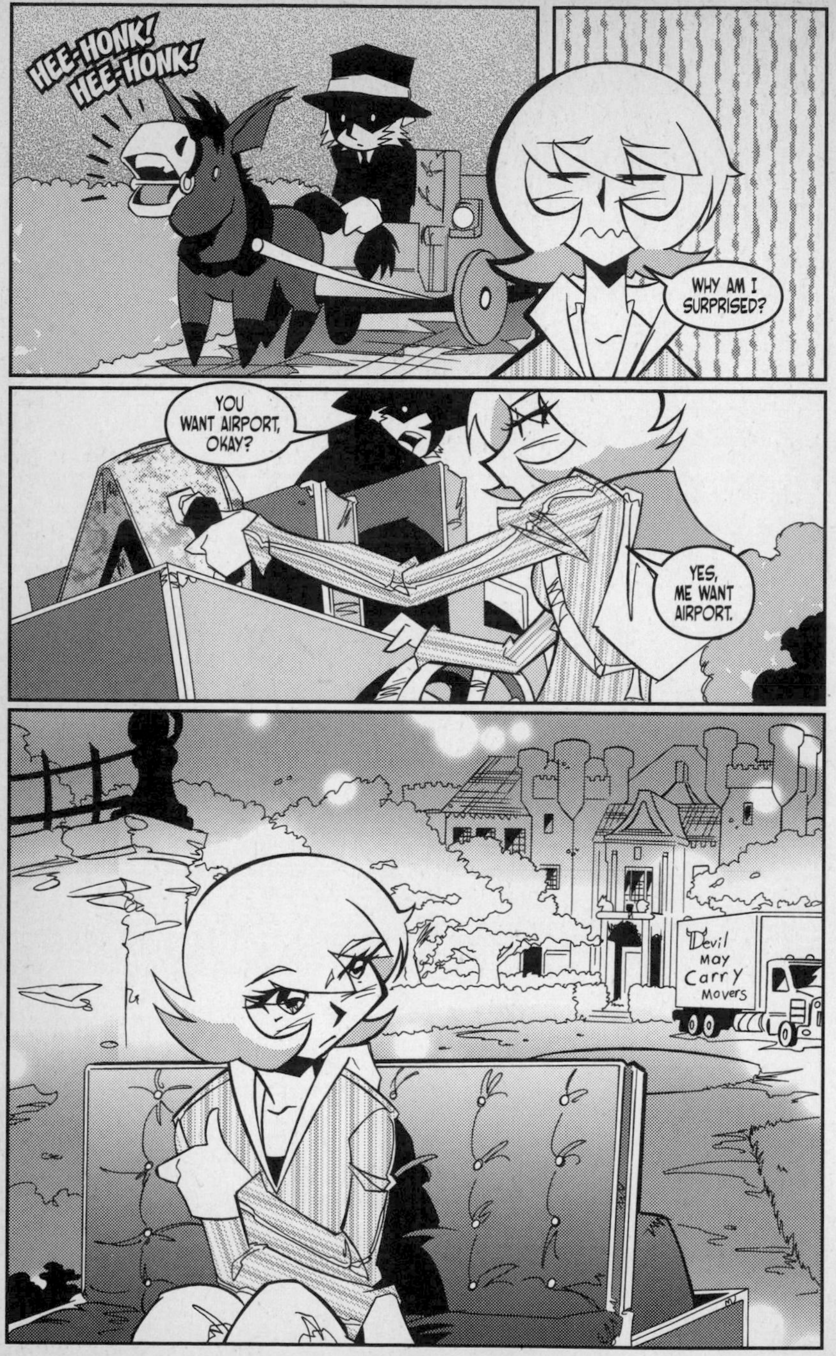
HEE-HONK! HEE-HONK!
WHY AM I SURPRISED?
YOU WANT AIRPORT, OKAY?
YES, ME WANT AIRPORT.
Devil May Carry Movers

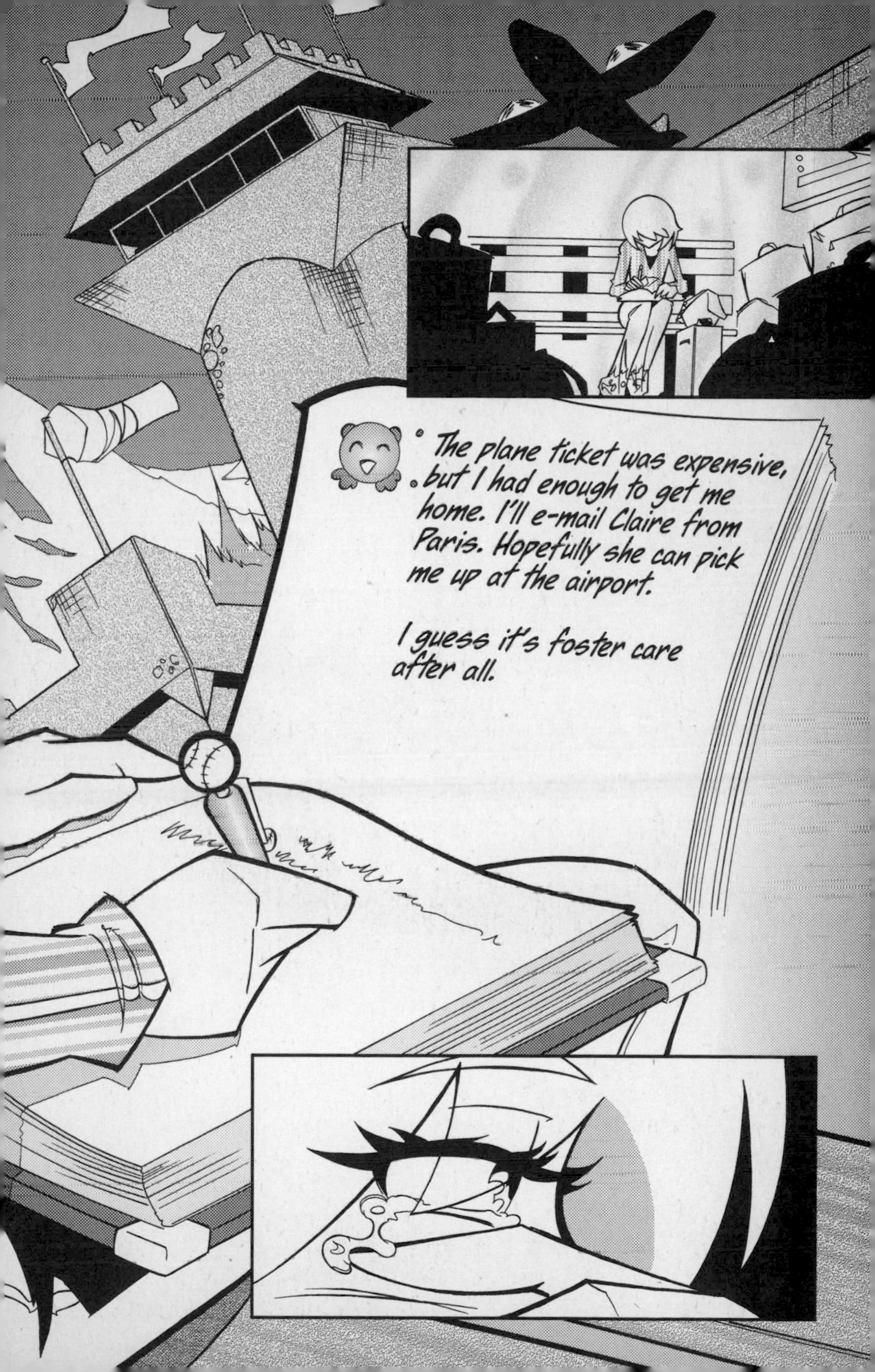
The plane ticket was expensive, but I had enough to get me home. I'll e-mail Claire from Paris. Hopefully she can pick me up at the airport.
I guess it's foster care after all.

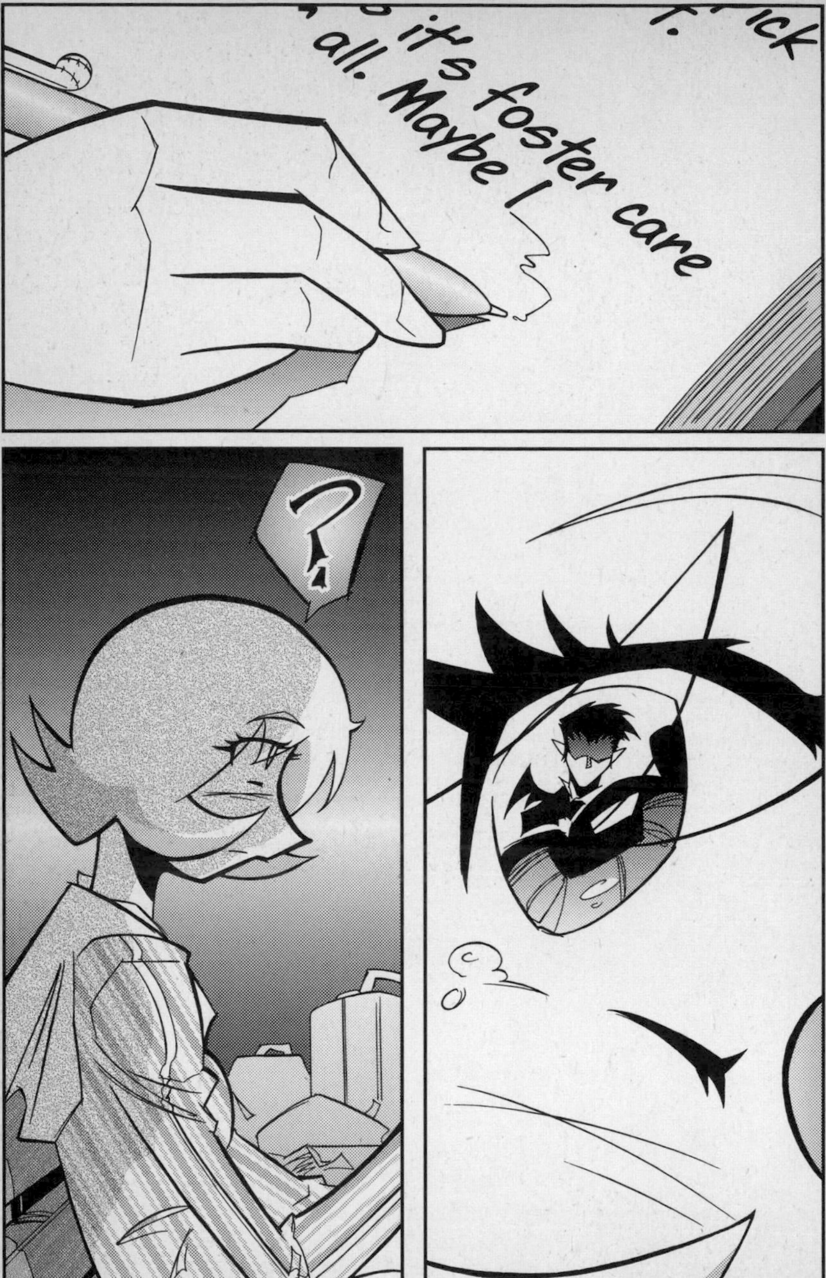
it's foster care
all. Maybe I
?!

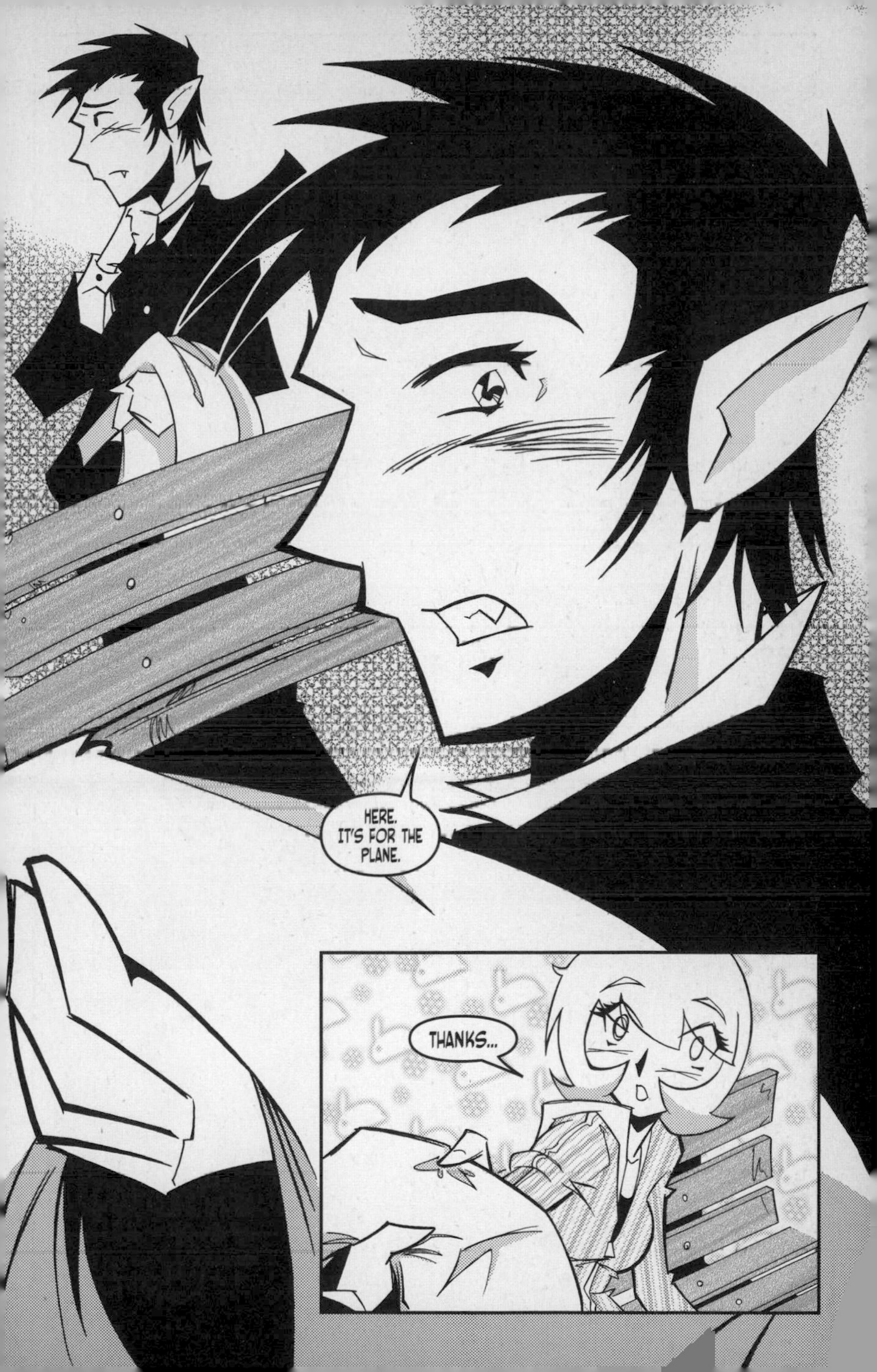
HERE. IT'S FOR THE PLANE.
THANKS...

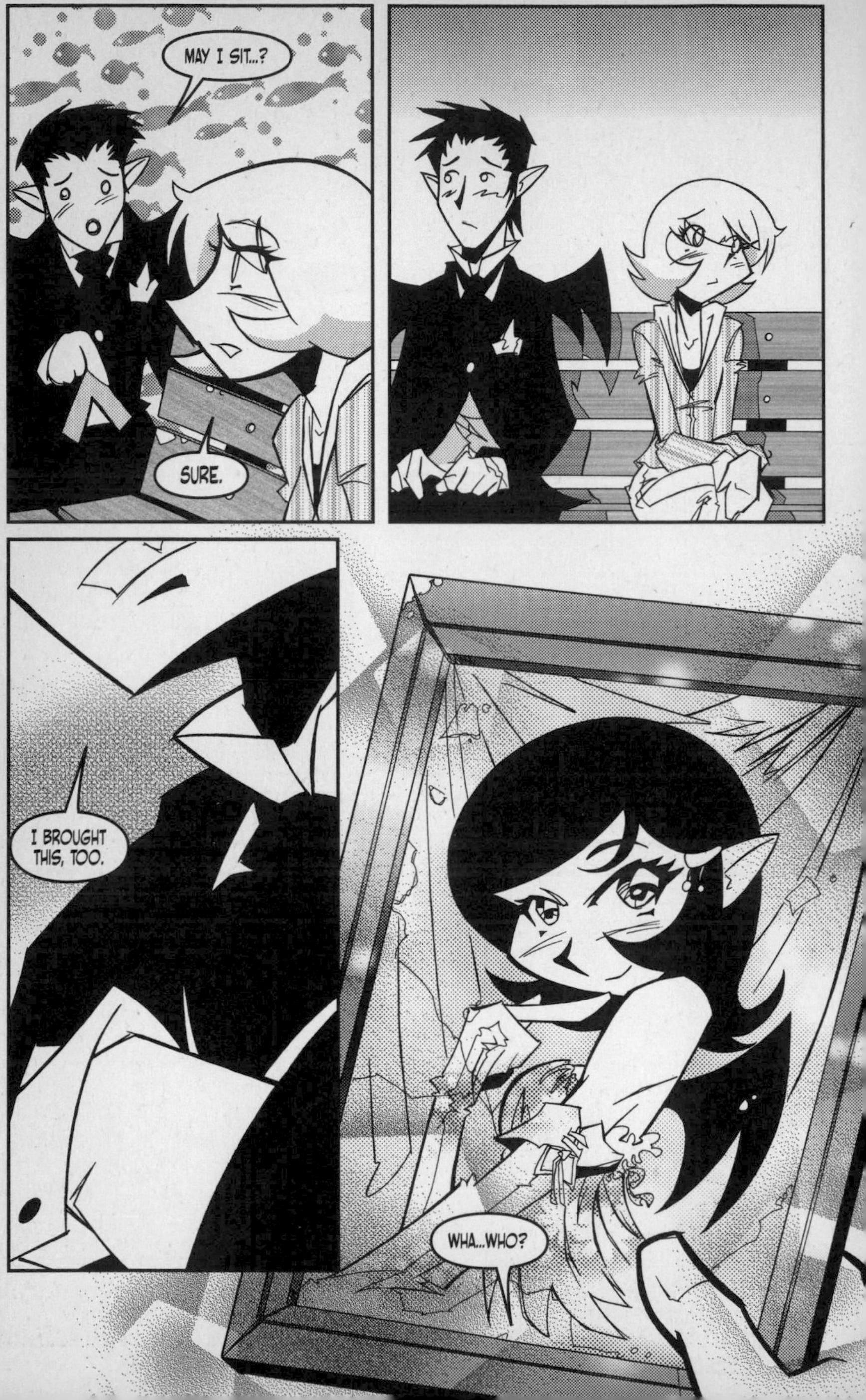
MAY I SIT...?
SURE.
I BROUGHT THIS, TOO.
WHA...WHO?

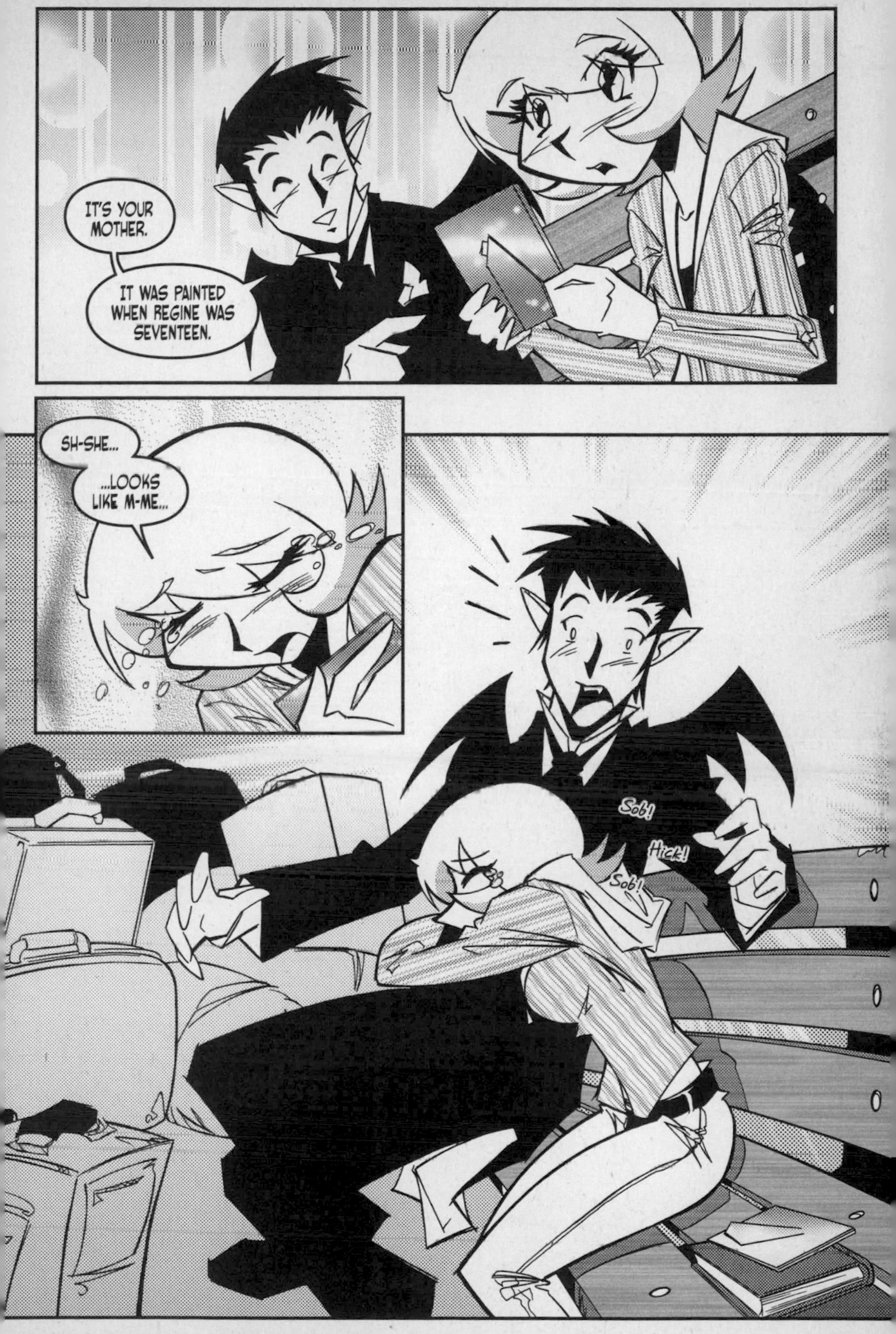
IT'S YOUR MOTHER.
IT WAS PAINTED WHEN REGINE WAS SEVENTEEN.
SH-SHE...
...LOOKS LIKE M-ME...
Sob!
Hick!
Sob!

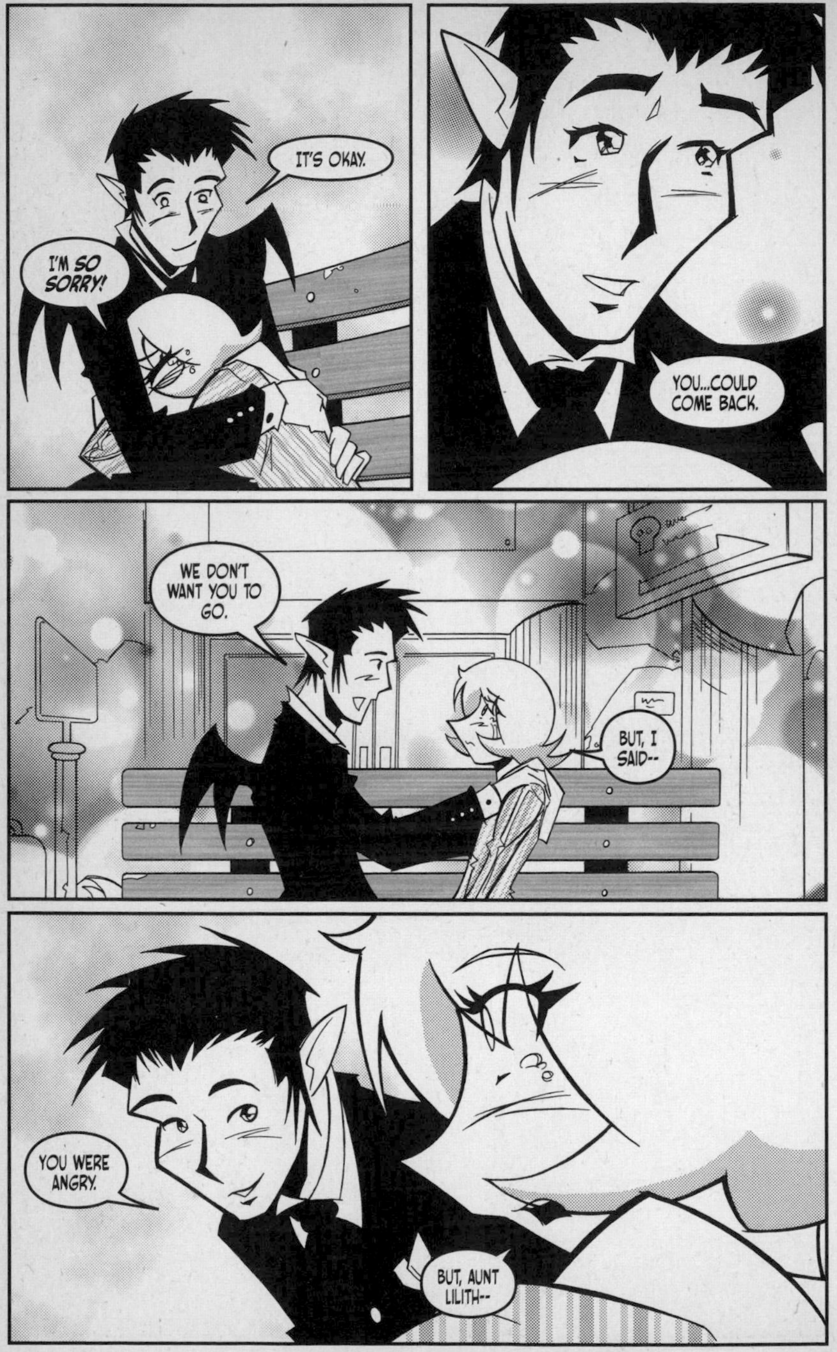

I'M SO SORRY!
IT'S OKAY.
YOU...COULD COME BACK.
WE DON'T WANT YOU TO GO.
BUT, I SAID--
YOU WERE ANGRY.
BUT, AUNT LILITH--

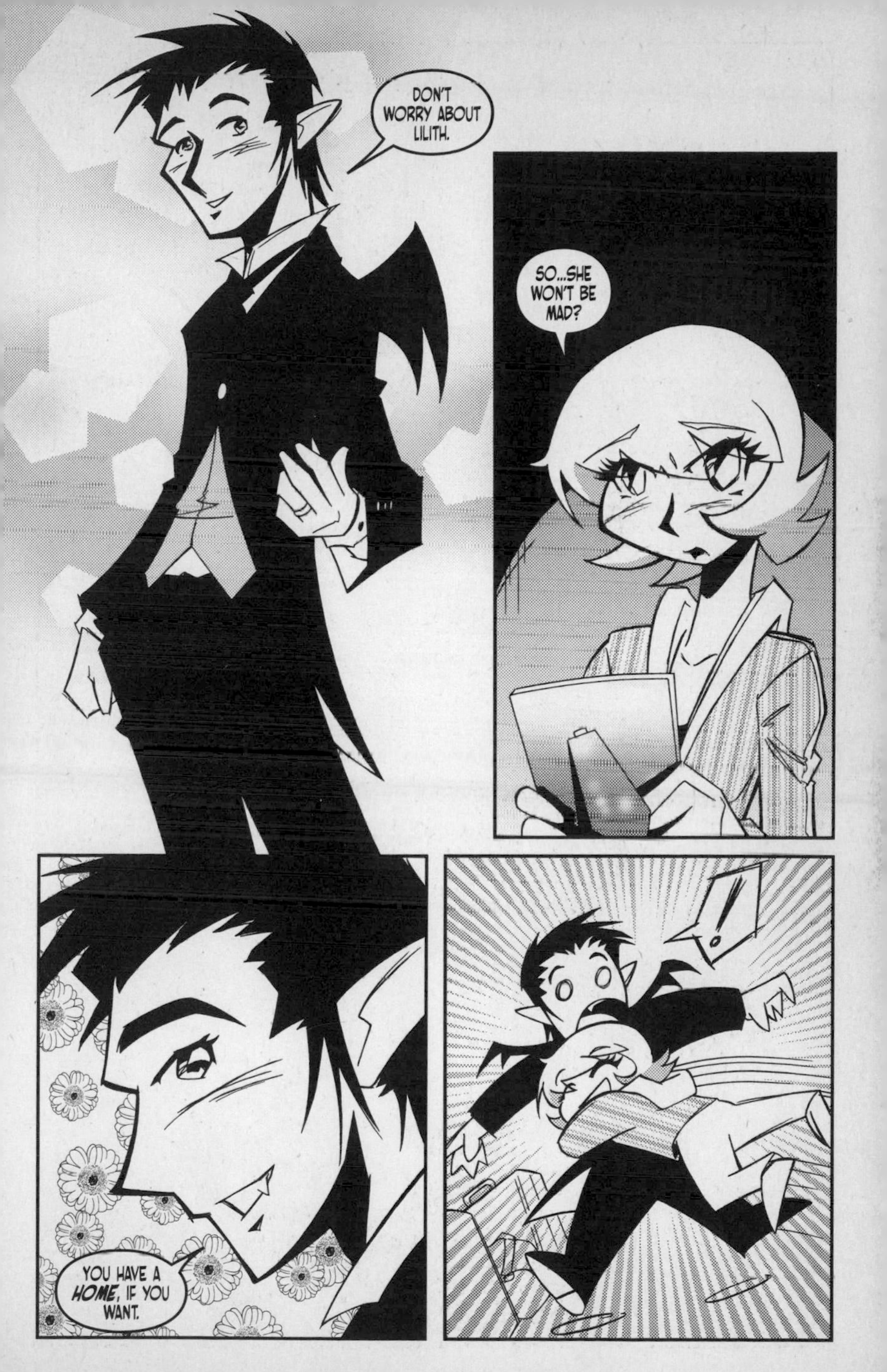
DON'T WORRY ABOUT LILITH.
SO...SHE WON'T BE MAD?
YOU HAVE A *HOME*, IF YOU WANT.
!

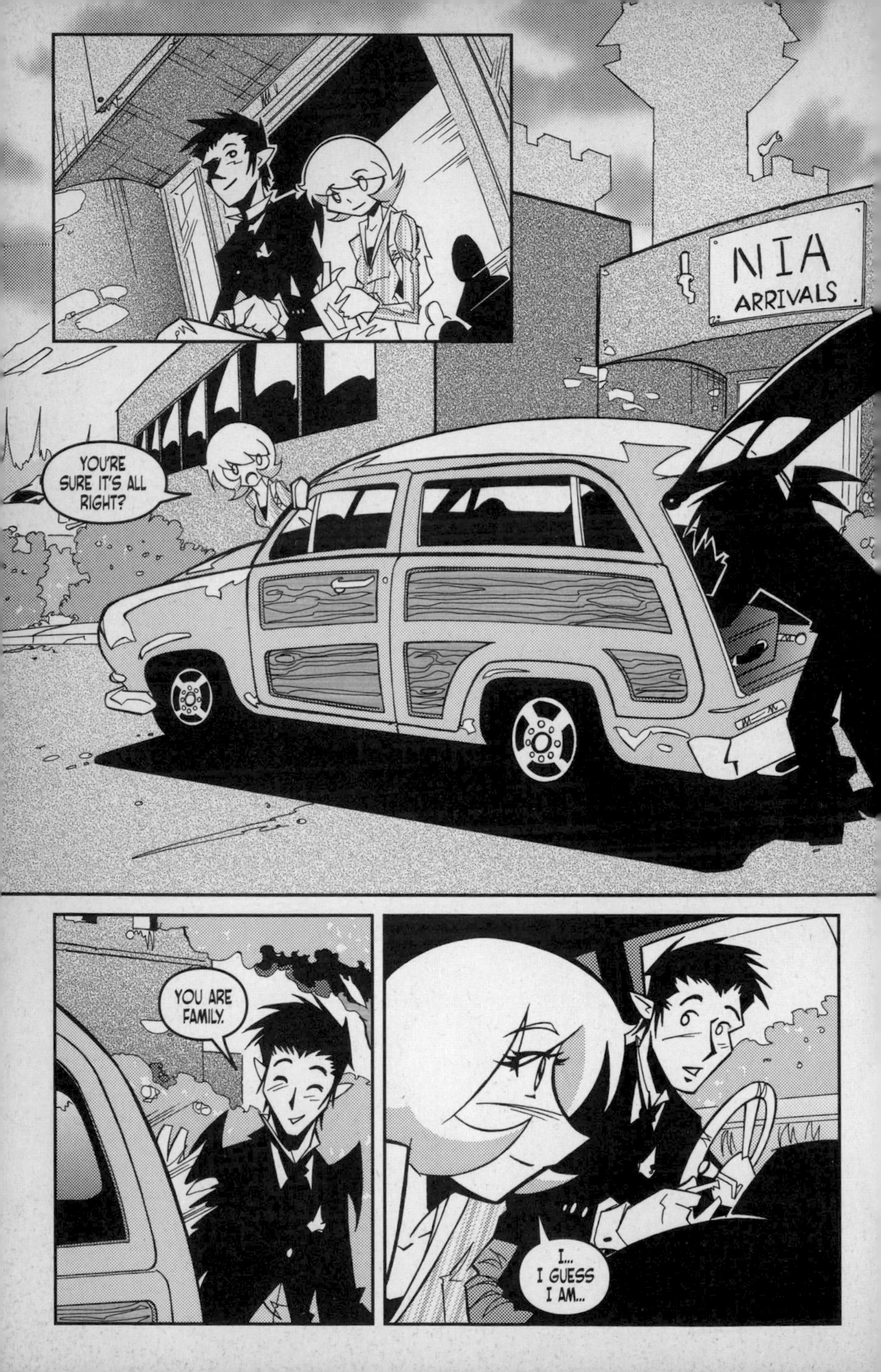
NIA
ARRIVALS
YOU'RE SURE IT'S ALL RIGHT?
YOU ARE FAMILY.
I... I GUESS I AM...

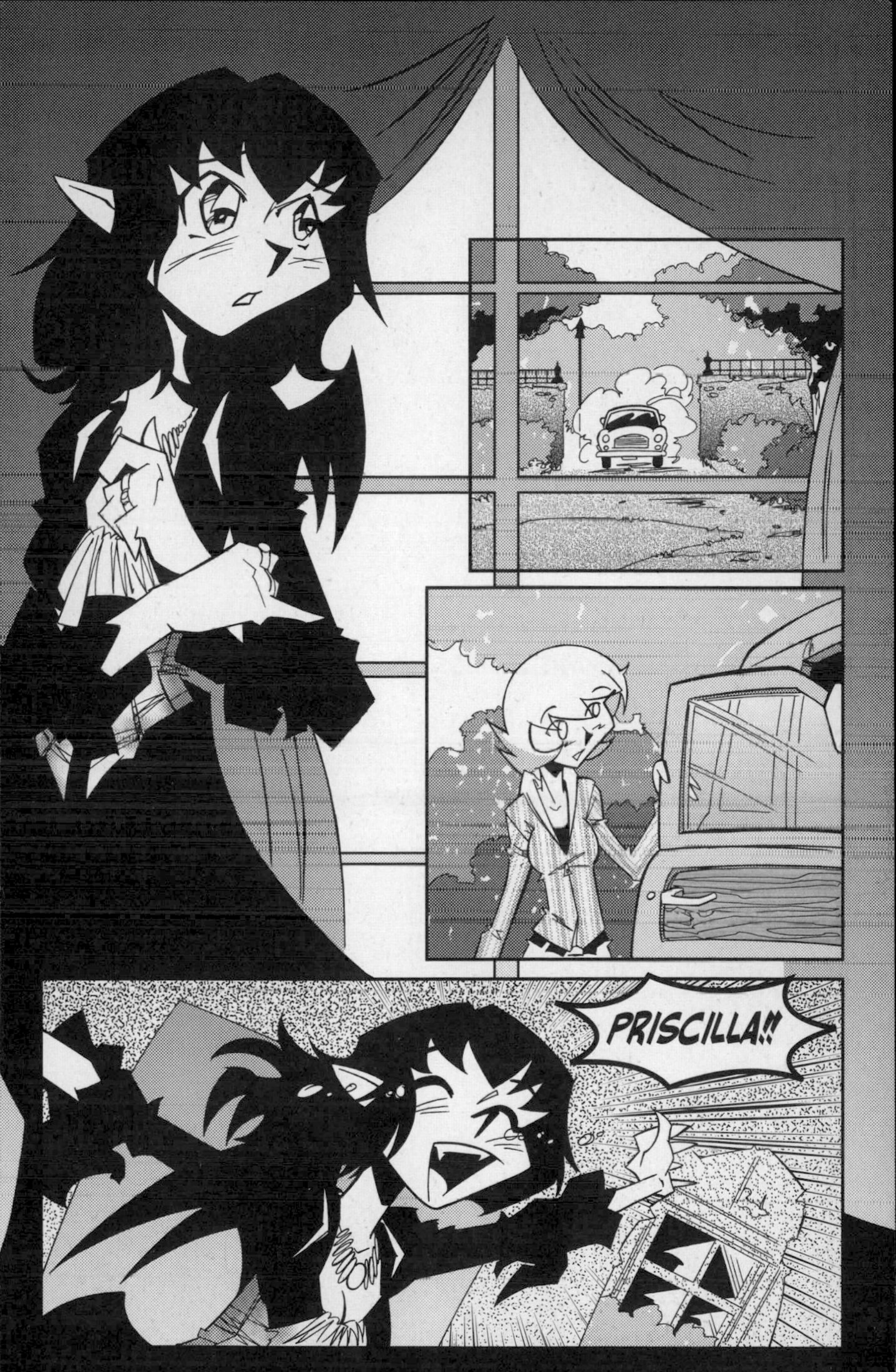
PRISCILLA!!

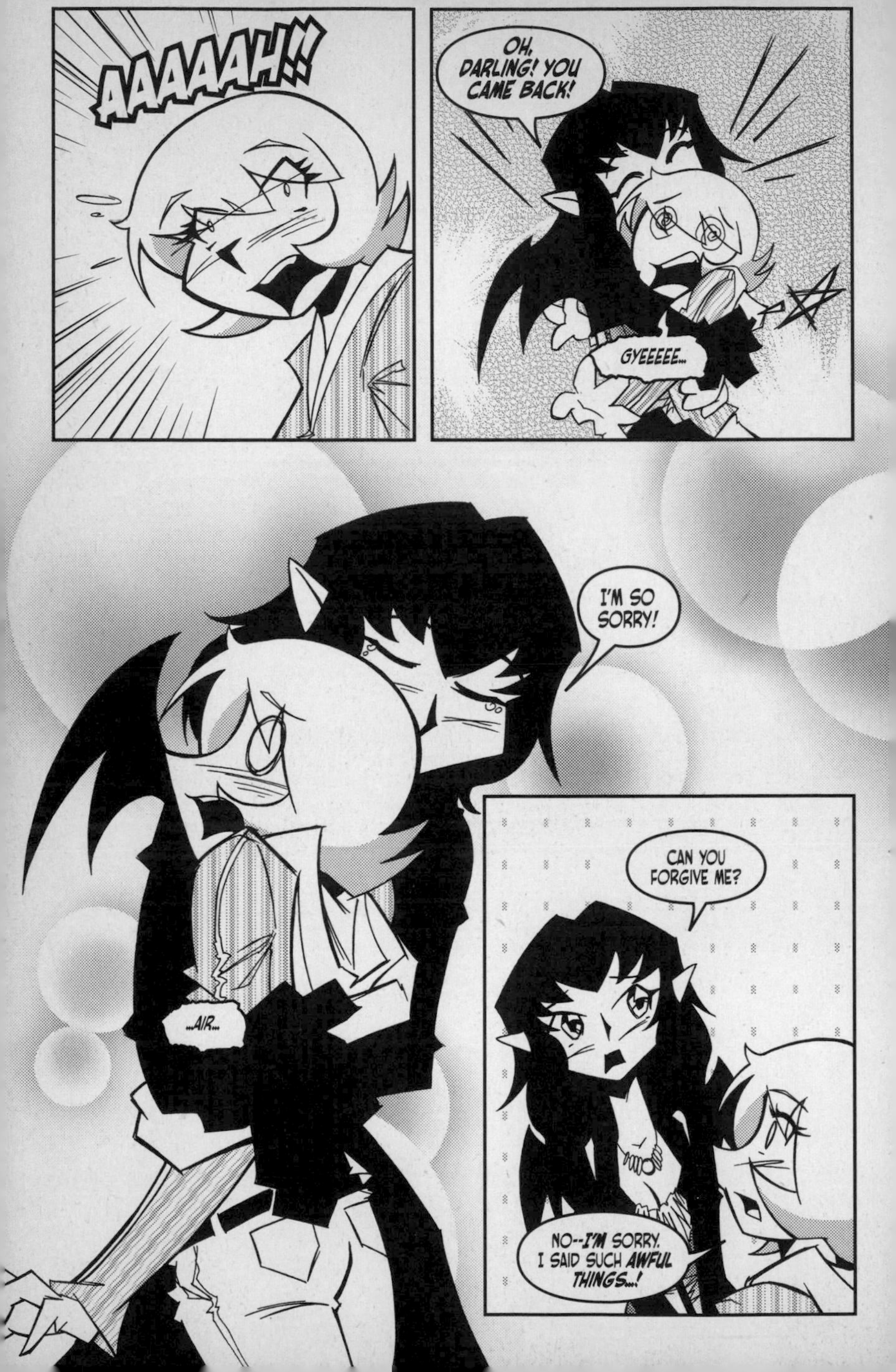
AAAAAH!!
OH, DARLING! YOU CAME BACK!
GYEEEEE...
I'M SO SORRY!
...AIR...
CAN YOU FORGIVE ME?
NO--I'M SORRY. I SAID SUCH AWFUL THINGS...!

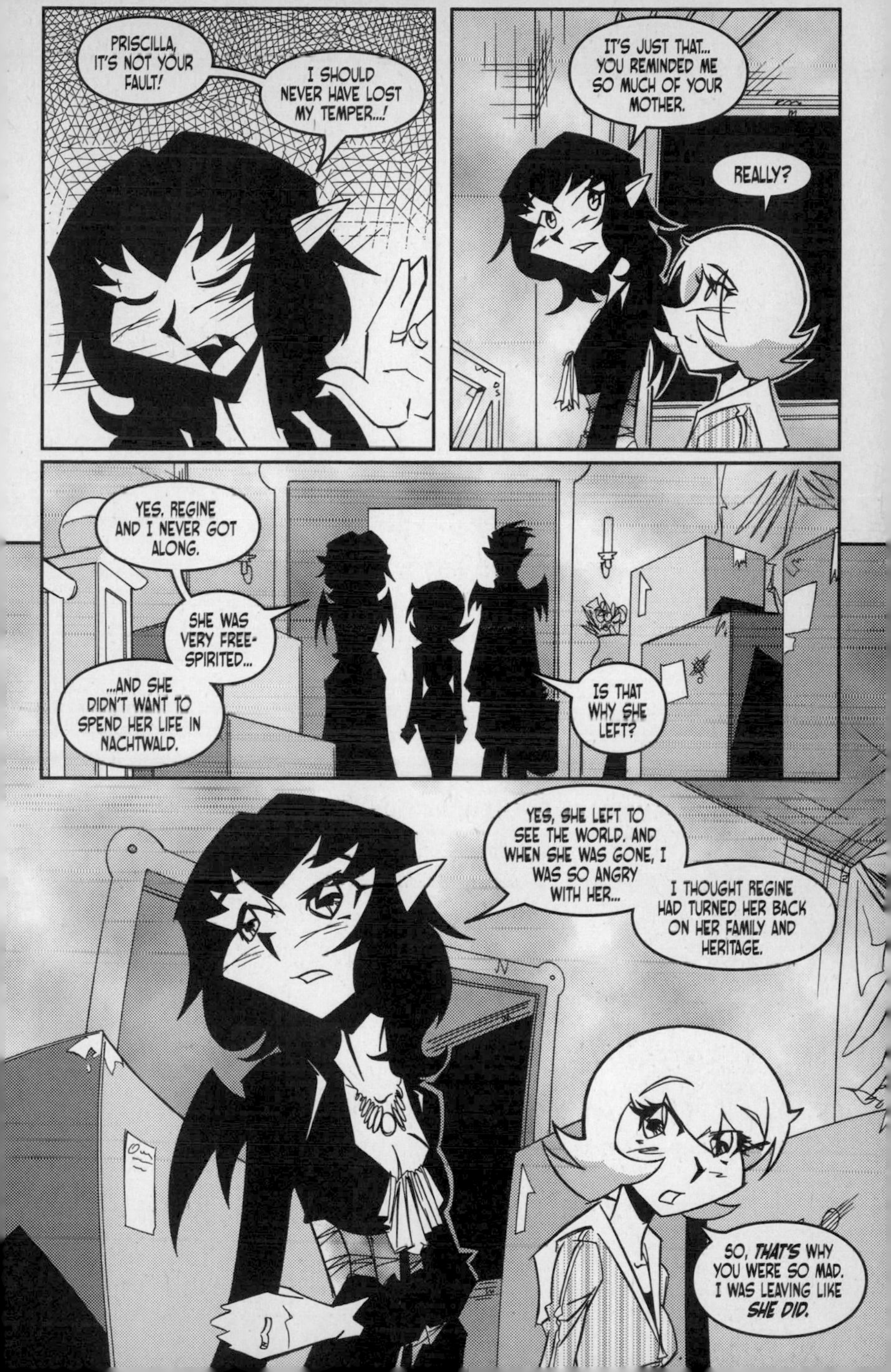
PRISCILLA, IT'S NOT YOUR FAULT!
I SHOULD NEVER HAVE LOST MY TEMPER...!
IT'S JUST THAT... YOU REMINDED ME SO MUCH OF YOUR MOTHER.
REALLY?
YES. REGINE AND I NEVER GOT ALONG.
SHE WAS VERY FREE-SPIRITED...
...AND SHE DIDN'T WANT TO SPEND HER LIFE IN NACHTWALD.
IS THAT WHY SHE LEFT?
YES, SHE LEFT TO SEE THE WORLD. AND WHEN SHE WAS GONE, I WAS SO ANGRY WITH HER...
I THOUGHT REGINE HAD TURNED HER BACK ON HER FAMILY AND HERITAGE.
SO, *THAT'S* WHY YOU WERE SO MAD. I WAS LEAVING LIKE ***SHE DID.***

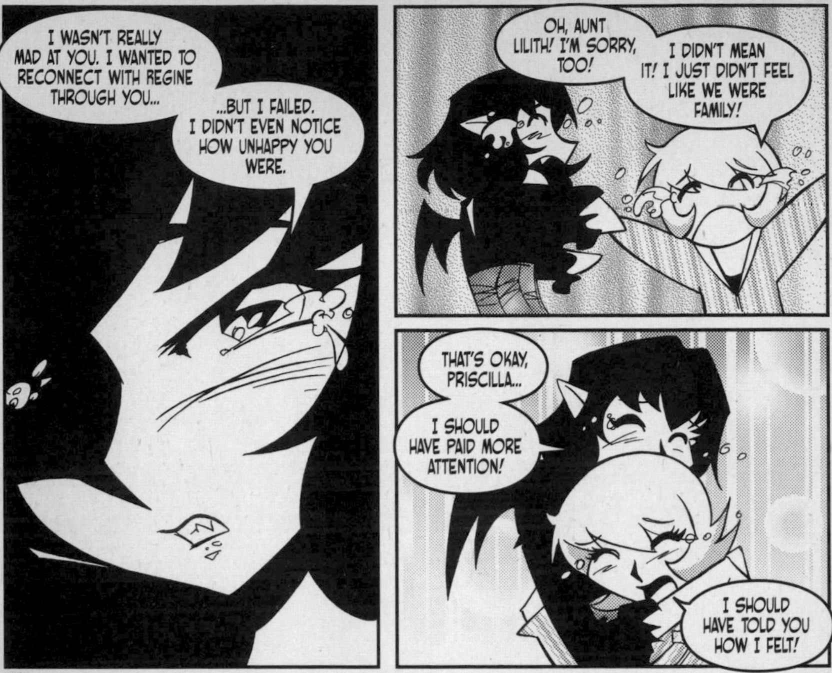
I WASN'T REALLY MAD AT YOU. I WANTED TO RECONNECT WITH REGINE THROUGH YOU...
...BUT I FAILED. I DIDN'T EVEN NOTICE HOW UNHAPPY YOU WERE.
OH, AUNT LILITH! I'M SORRY, TOO!
I DIDN'T MEAN IT! I JUST DIDN'T FEEL LIKE WE WERE FAMILY!
THAT'S OKAY, PRISCILLA...
I SHOULD HAVE PAID MORE ATTENTION!
I SHOULD HAVE TOLD YOU HOW I FELT!

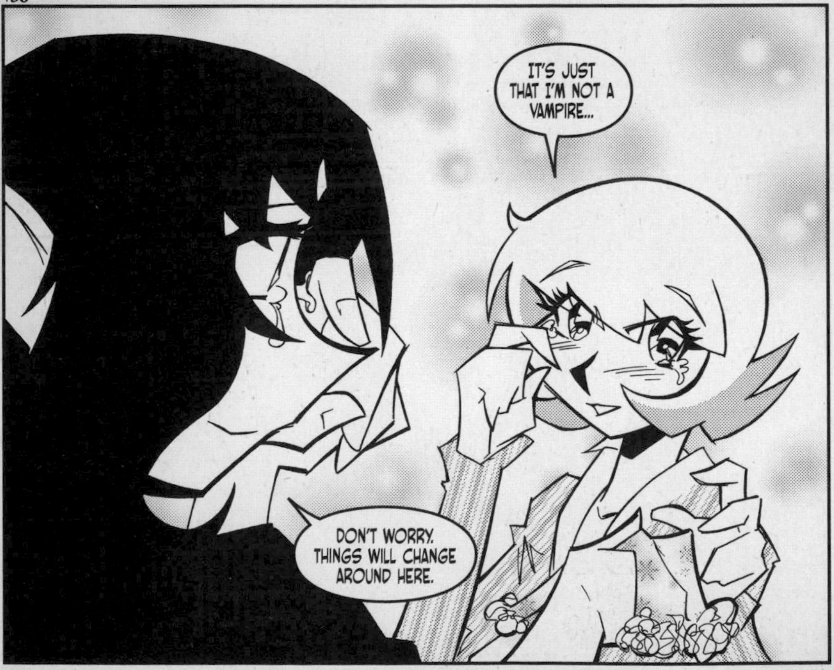
IT'S JUST THAT I'M NOT A VAMPIRE...
DON'T WORRY. THINGS WILL CHANGE AROUND HERE.

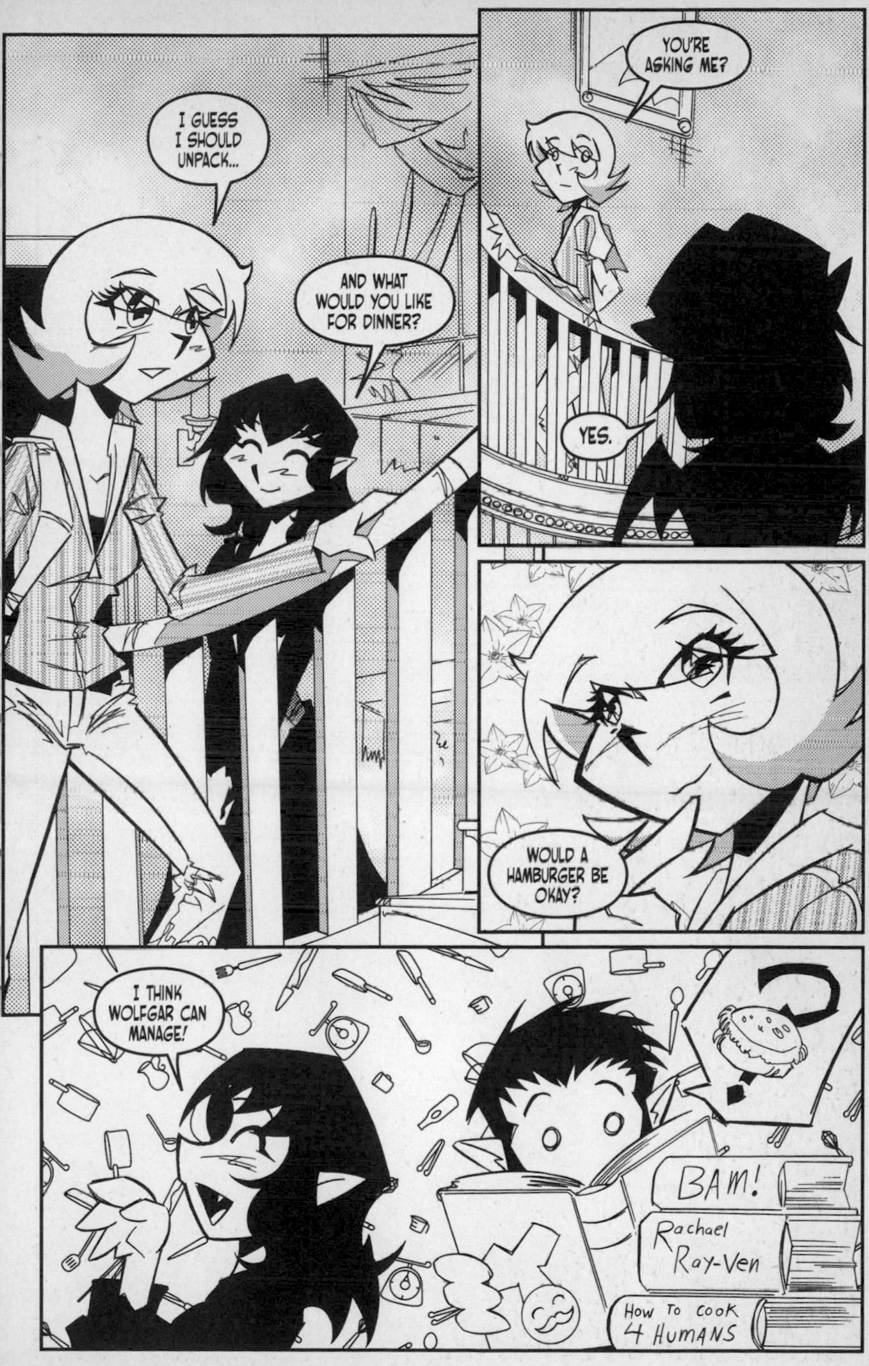
I GUESS I SHOULD UNPACK...
AND WHAT WOULD YOU LIKE FOR DINNER?
YOU'RE ASKING ME?
YES.
WOULD A HAMBURGER BE OKAY?
I THINK WOLFGAR CAN MANAGE!
BAM!
Rachael Ray-Ven
How To Cook 4 HUMANS

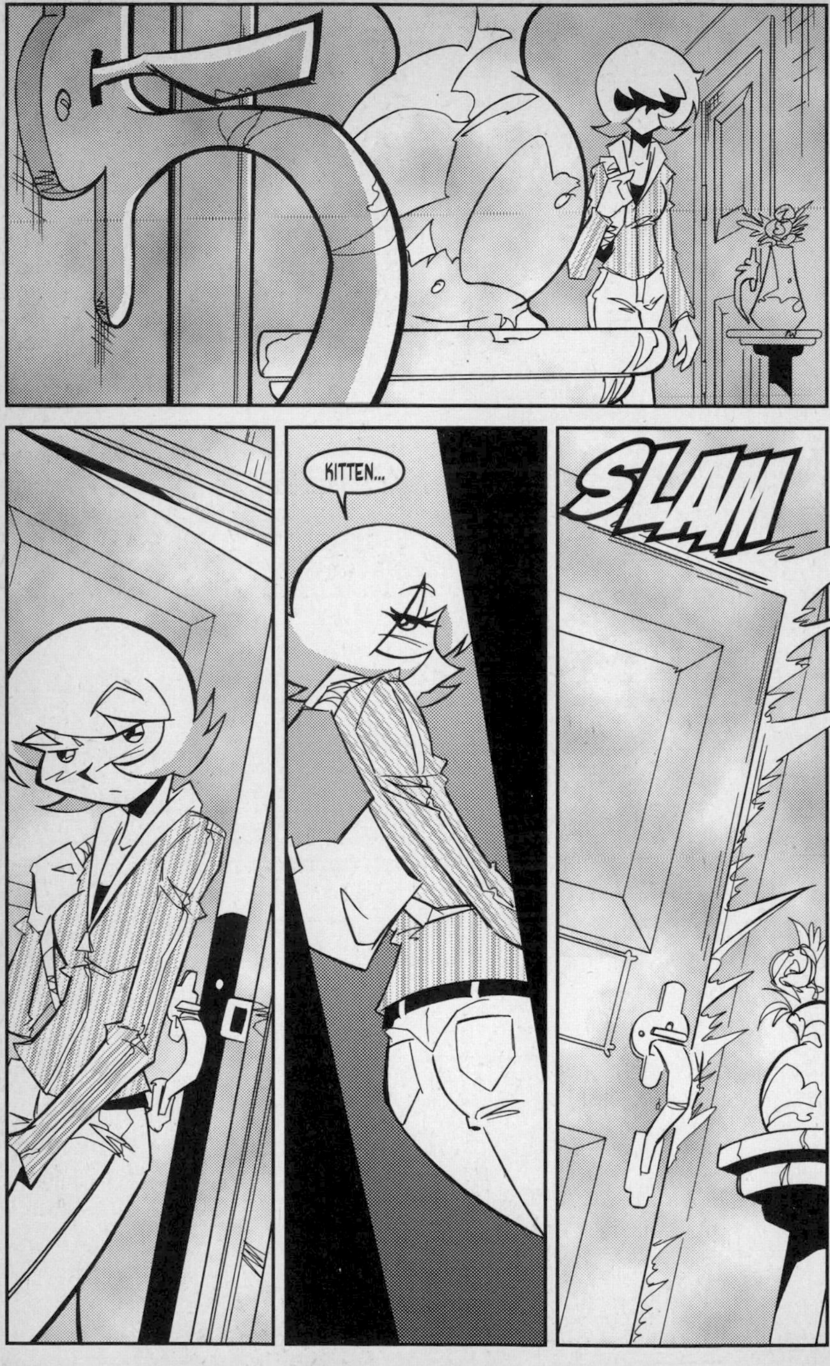
KITTEN...
SLAM

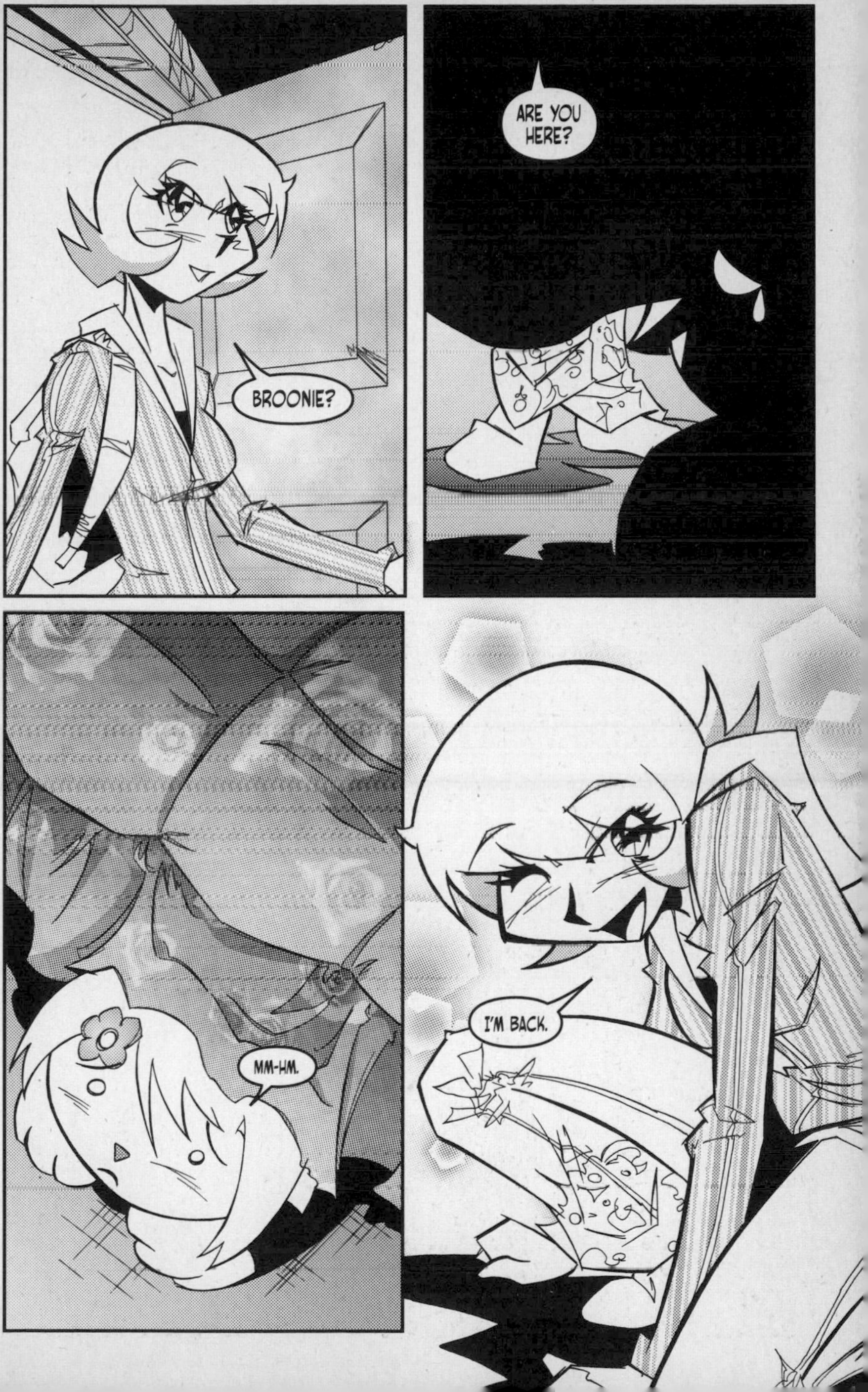
BROONIE?
ARE YOU HERE?
MM-HM.
I'M BACK.

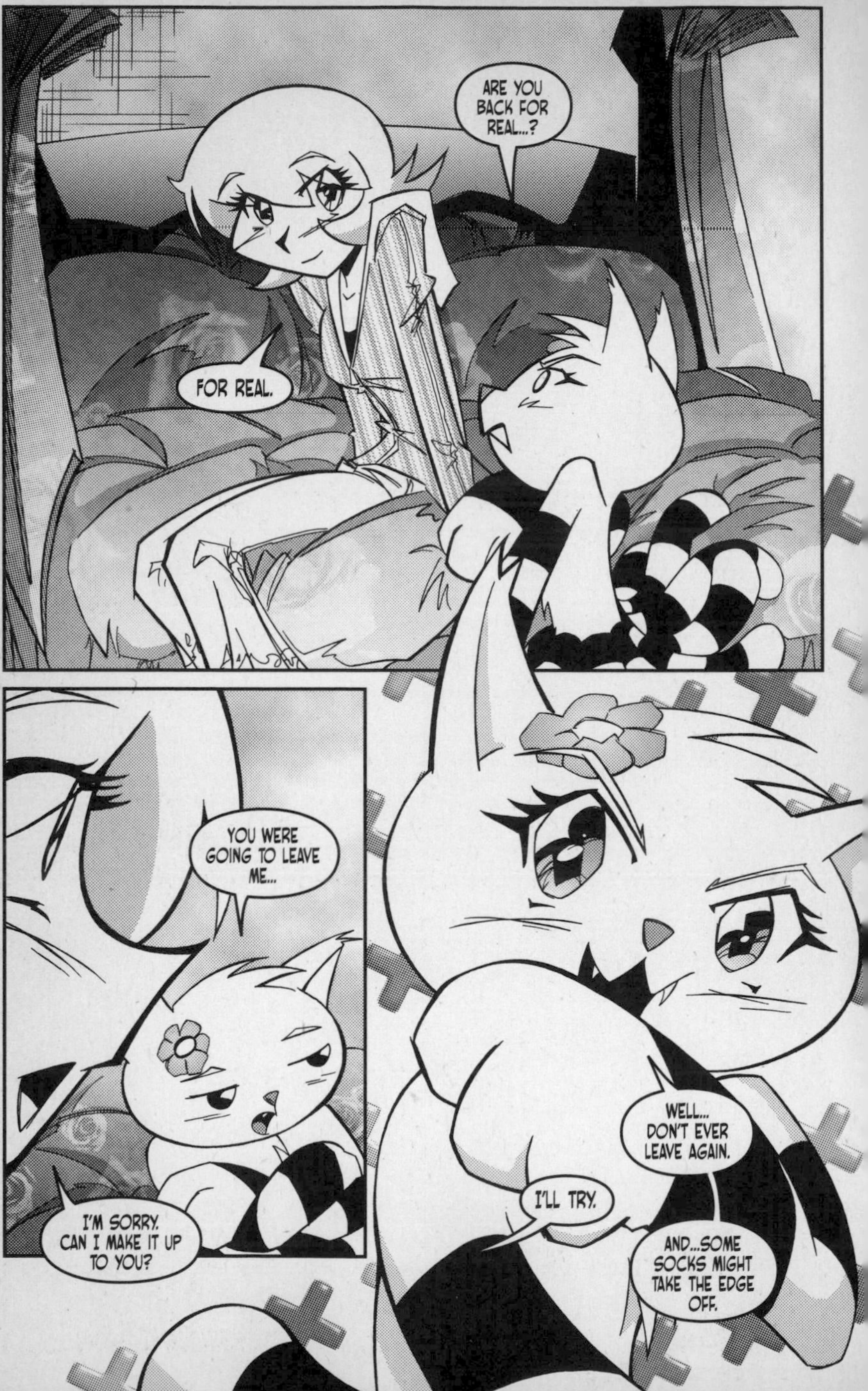
ARE YOU BACK FOR REAL...?
FOR REAL.
YOU WERE GOING TO LEAVE ME...
I'M SORRY. CAN I MAKE IT UP TO YOU?
WELL... DON'T EVER LEAVE AGAIN.
I'LL TRY.
AND...SOME SOCKS MIGHT TAKE THE EDGE OFF.

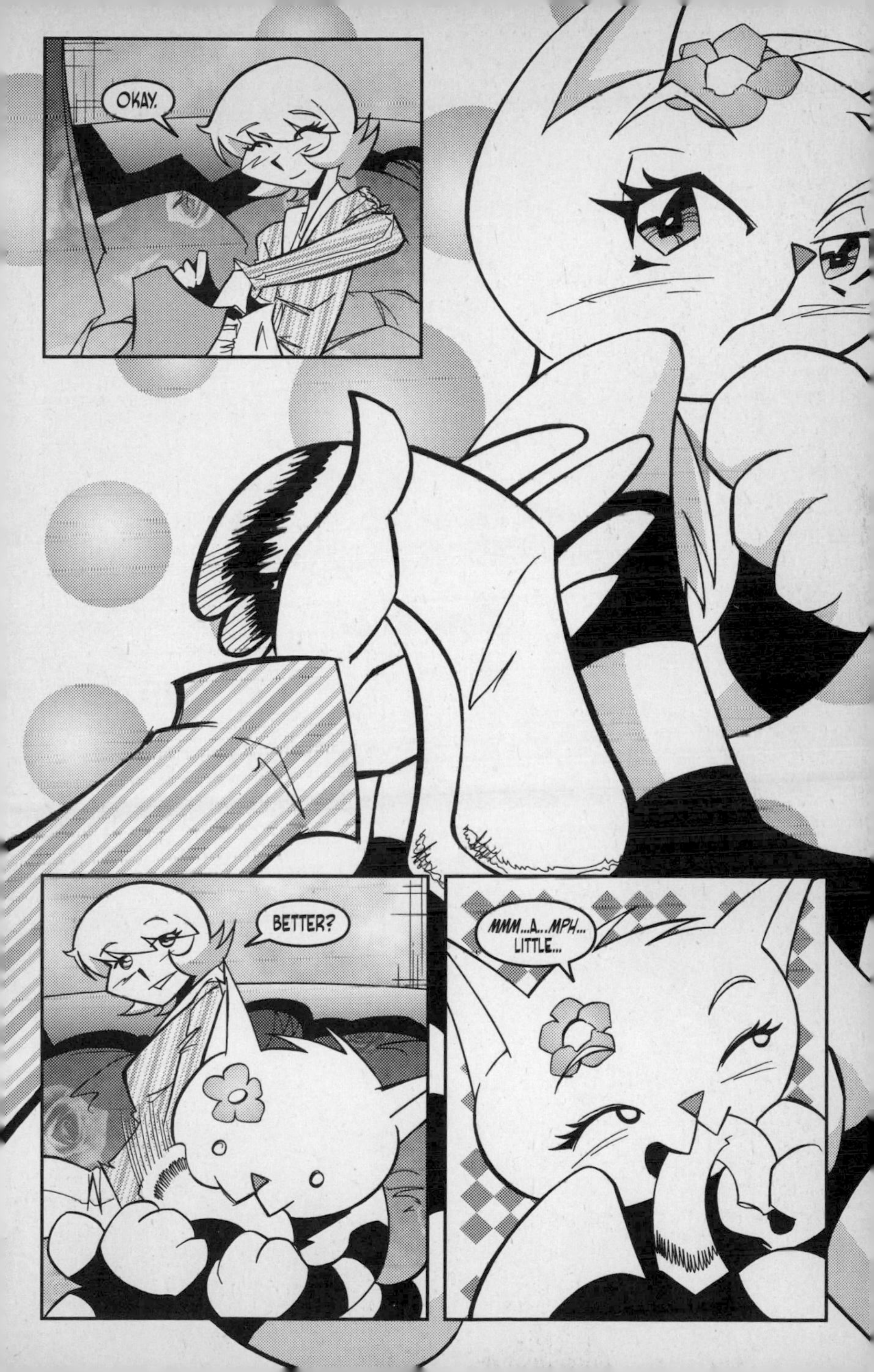
OKAY.
BETTER?
MMM...A...MPH...
LITTLE...

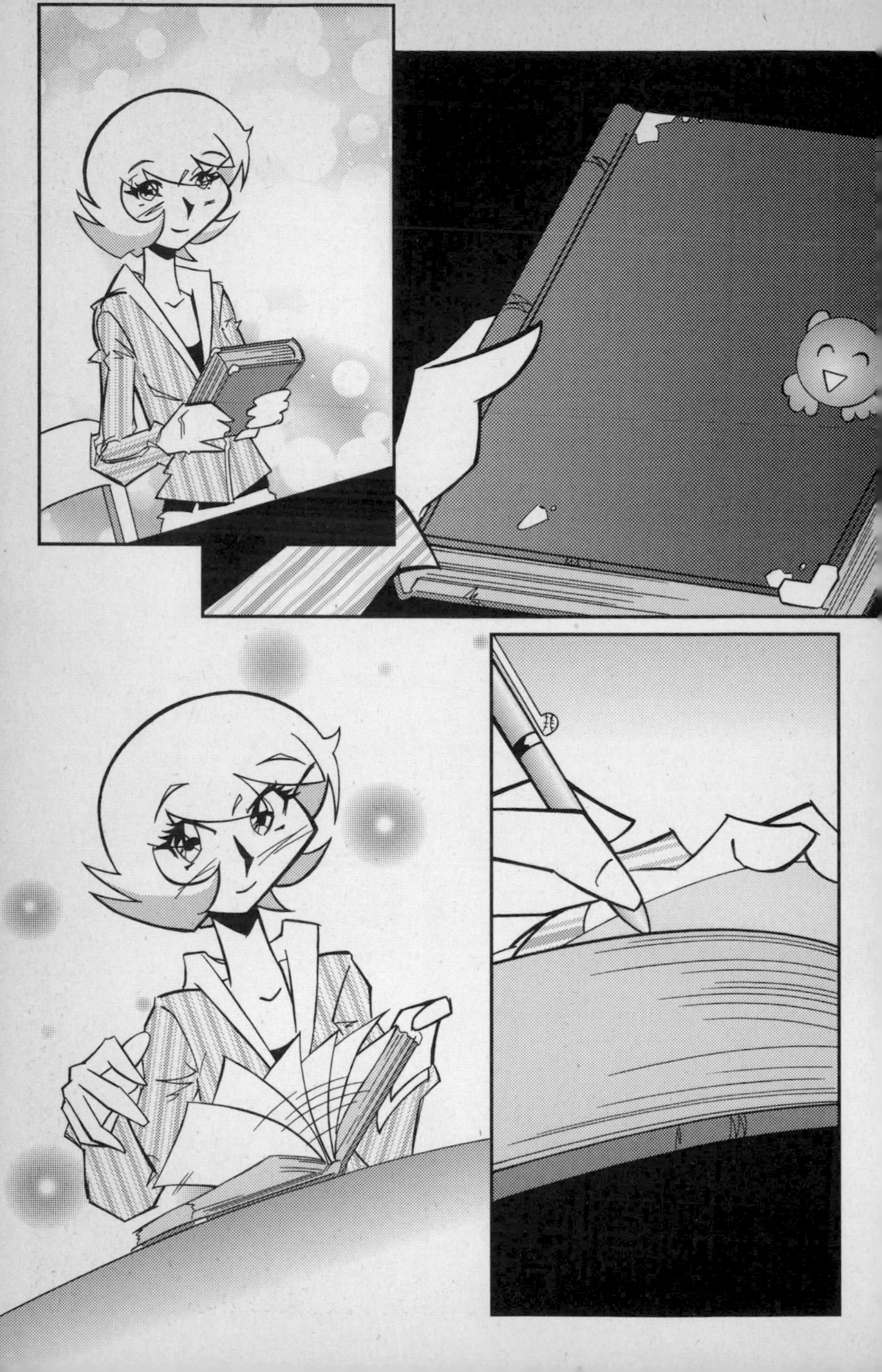

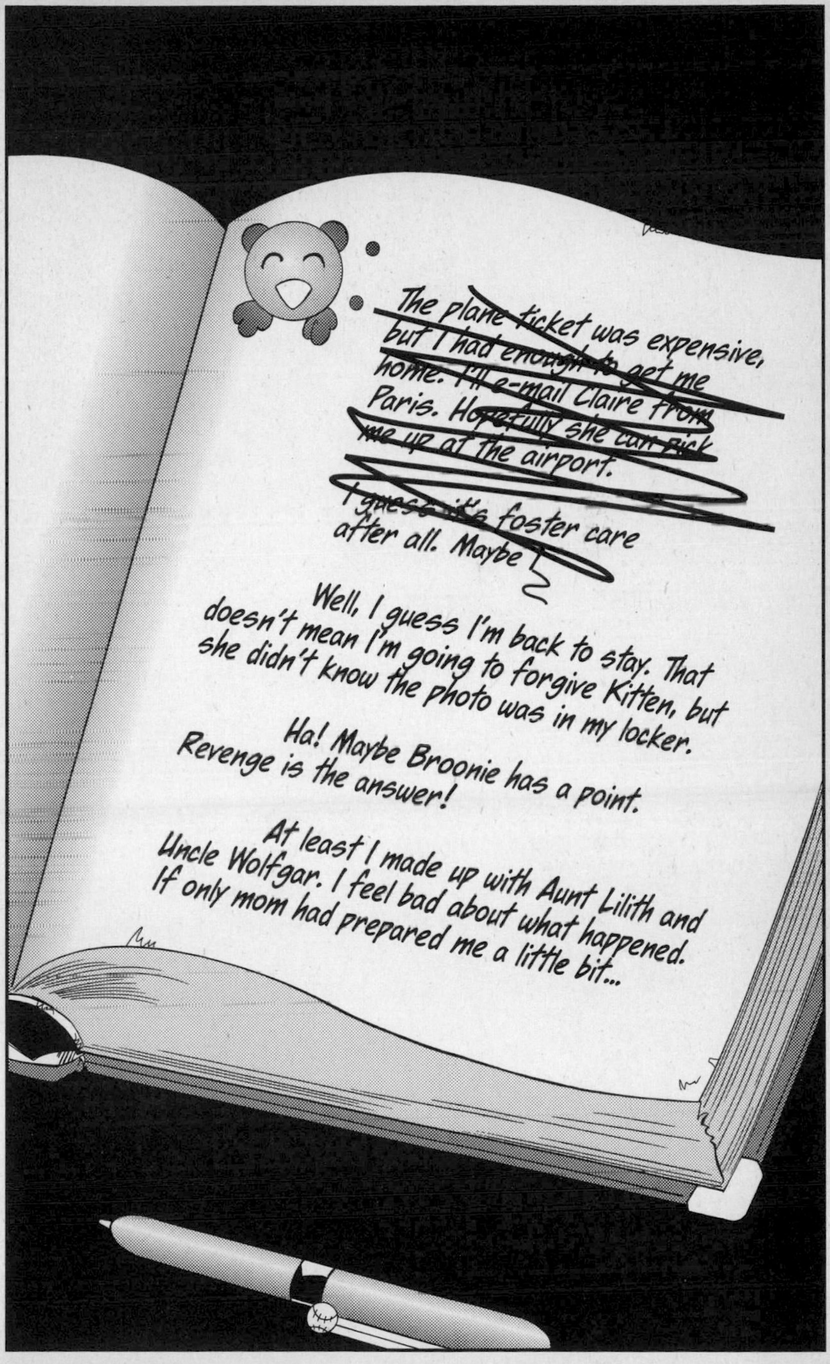
The plane ticket was expensive, but I had enough to get me home. I'll e-mail Claire from Paris. Hopefully she can pick me up at the airport.
I guess it's foster care after all. Maybe
Well, I guess I'm back to stay. That doesn't mean I'm going to forgive Kitten, but she didn't know the photo was in my locker.
Ha! Maybe Broonie has a point. Revenge is the answer!
At least I made up with Aunt Lilith and Uncle Wolfgar. I feel bad about what happened. If only mom had prepared me a little bit...

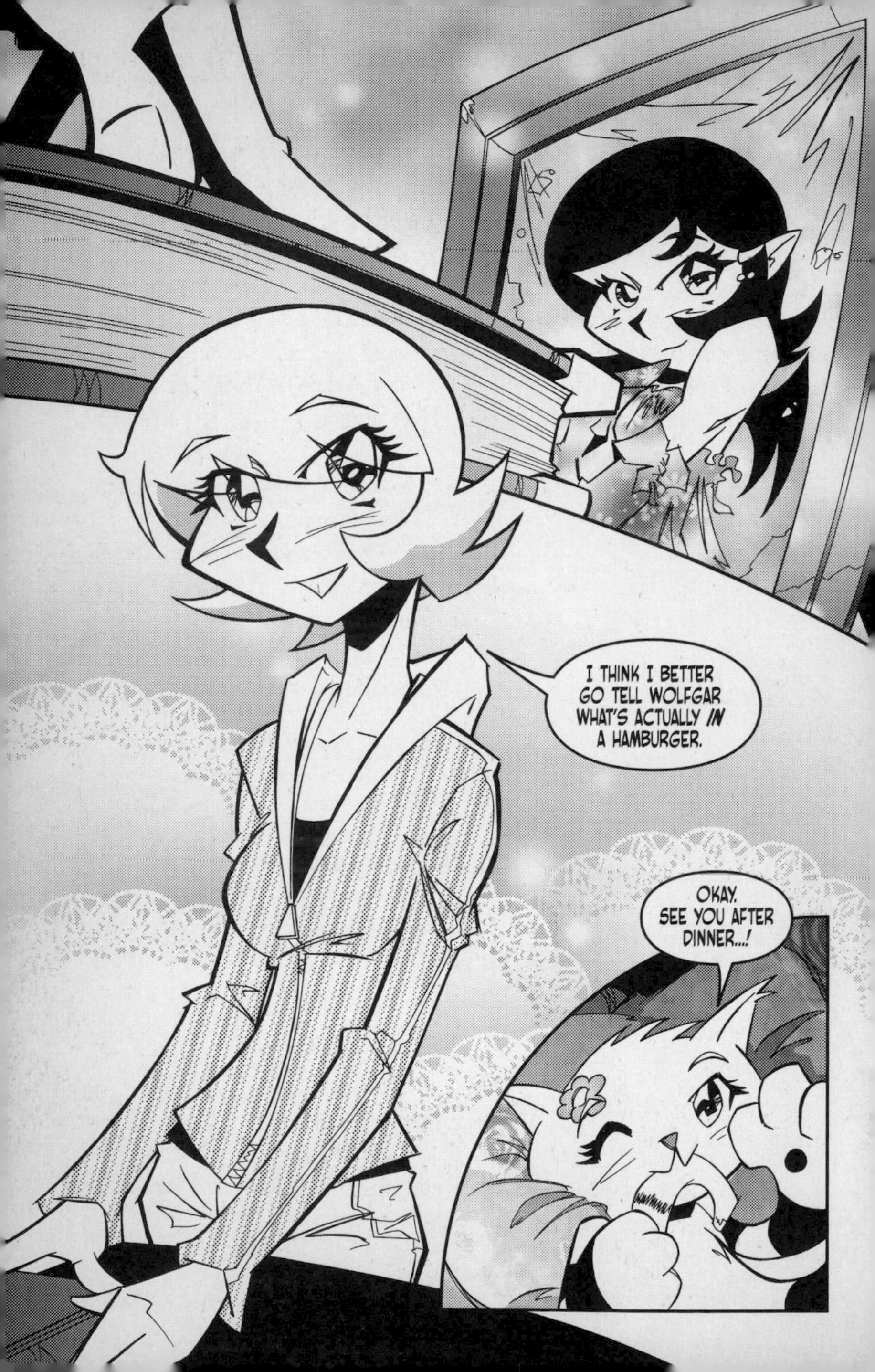
I THINK I BETTER GO TELL WOLFGAR WHAT'S ACTUALLY *IN* A HAMBURGER.
OKAY. SEE YOU AFTER DINNER...!

In the Next Vulgar Volume of

DARK MOON DIARY

In her new town, Priscilla has been attacked by her lunch, bitten by a zombie and befriended by a boogey monster---and that's just in the first week! And even though Priscilla has reconciled with her Aunt and Uncle, she's still on Kitten's "To Maim" list.

So when Priscilla and Balthazar go out on their first date, Kitten sees red---and comes up with a dastardly plan that may drive the final nail in Priscilla's coffin! And if Priscilla thought Kitten was bad, wait until she meets her cranky vampiric grandparents. Not only do they suck blood...they just plain suck!

So don't be a stupid entrée---pick up volume 2!

I drew it! →

←Fancey

Phtoshop is my friend

Hello! OMG! OMG! OMG! I'm so happy to be writing this, my first omake! (Well, second, if you count the afterword in *Avigon: Gods and Demons.*) I've always wanted to write one ever since I started reading manga. The authors always sound so gracious and happy.

So, first, thank you for buying the book! YAY! I really hope you enjoyed it. Please come back for volume two!

Second, thanks to all my friends, family and everyone who supported me through all the bad times and good times.

I'm all over the web (I don't have just one site), so I'd love to hear from you guys! You can find me at spiderliing666. deviantart.com, Chehime.etsy.com and spiderling.livejournal.com. I know, I have too many, but I'm hopeless at updating a "real" website. Oh! I also have a Cafe Press store I never update...

My wish for the future: To find more artists to work with and write more manga. And to draw more. I'd like to do that, too.

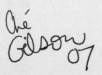

Ché Gilson 07

PRISCILLA

THIS IS WHAT I CALL "JURASSIC PRISCILLA." HER CHARACTER DESIGN CHANGED A LOT DURING THE TWO YEARS DMD WAS IN PRE-PRODUCTION.

WHEN I DREW THIS, I WAS OBSESSED WITH KATSUYA TERADA. I LOVED (AND STILL DO) HIS LAYERED, CRISSCROSSING HAIRDOS.

STILL, I'M REALLY PLEASED WITH HOW SHE TURNED OUT IN THE BOOK.

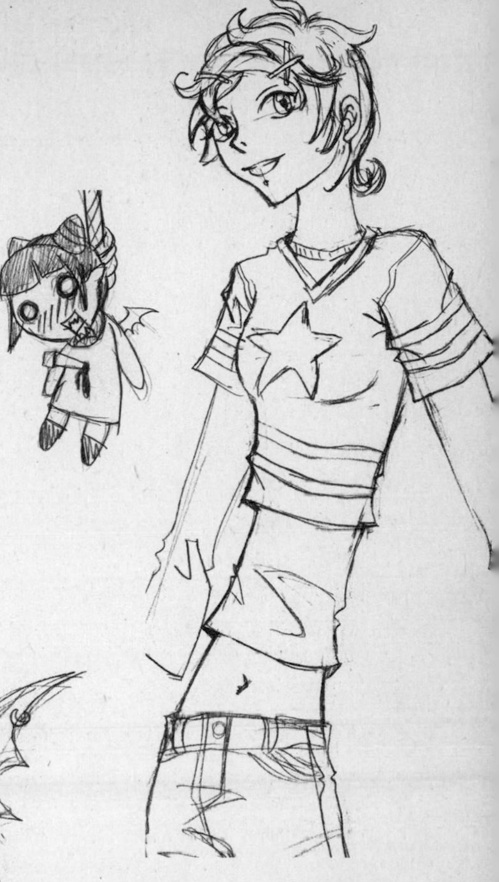

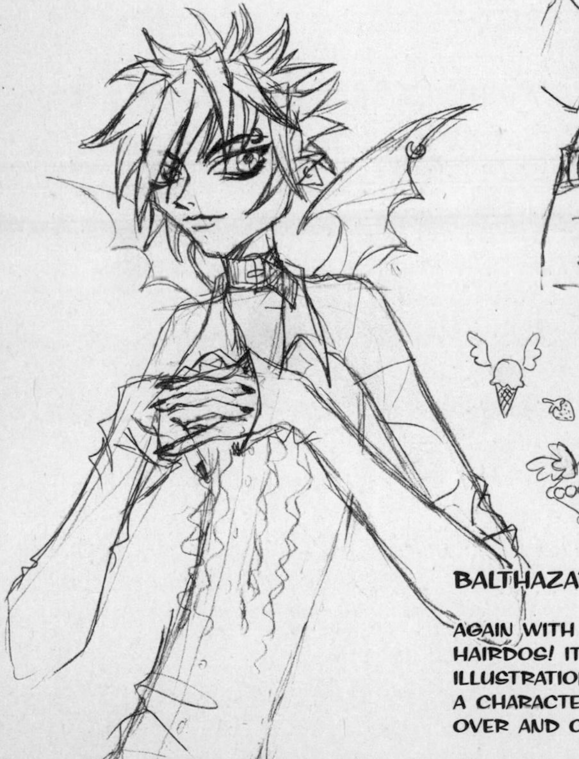

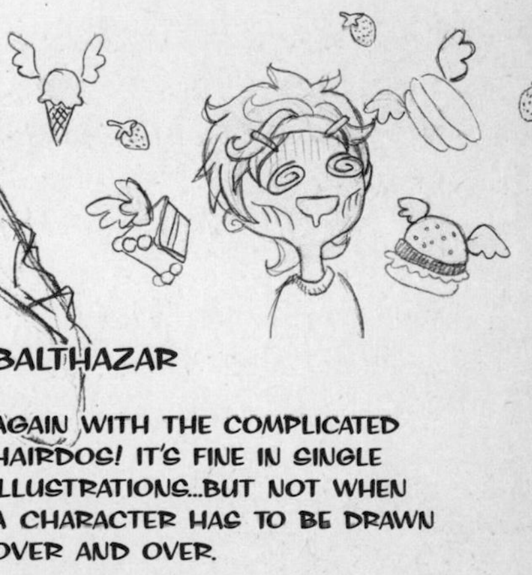

BALTHAZAR

AGAIN WITH THE COMPLICATED HAIRDOS! IT'S FINE IN SINGLE ILLUSTRATIONS...BUT NOT WHEN A CHARACTER HAS TO BE DRAWN OVER AND OVER.

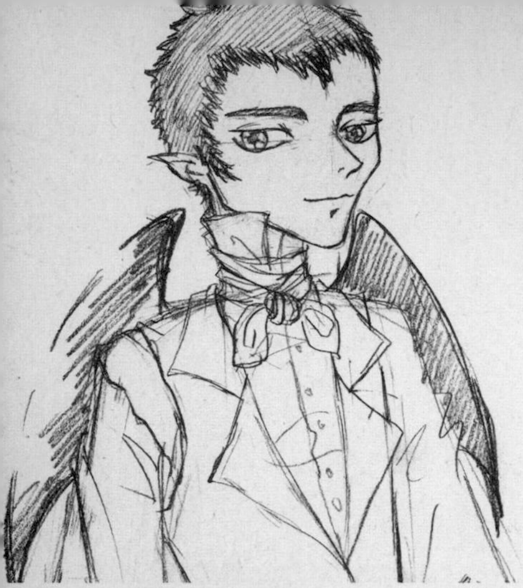

LILITH/WOLFGAR

I HATE GENERIC PARENTS, SO I WANTED TO GIVE KITTEN FUN, GOTH PARENTS. I ALSO HAD TO STAY AWAY FROM ADDAMS FAMILY/ MUNSTERS TERRITORY. I THINK THEY TURNED OUT WELL.

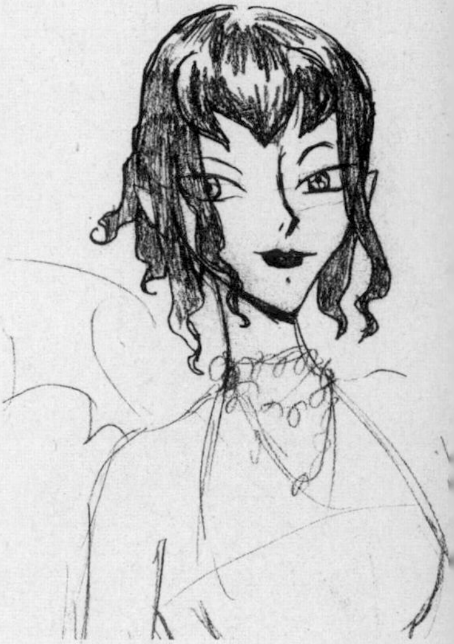

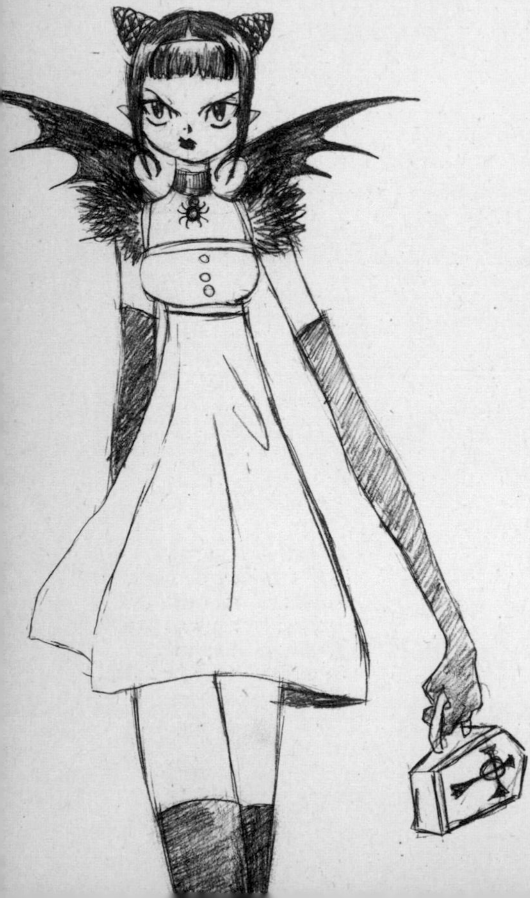

KITTEN

BASICALLY, EVERYTHING ABOUT HER CHANGED... BUT THE BUN/CAT EAR HAIRSTYLE STAYED THE SAME. IT HAD TO!

DIAMANTE

VILLAINS ARE ALWAYS THE BEST CHARACTERS, SO I WANTED TO GIVE KITTEN SOME INTERESTING HENCHMEN. BASICALLY, I WANTED CHARACTERS THAT WOULD BE FUN WITH OR WITHOUT KITTEN. AT ONE POINT I EVEN THOUGHT OF A NAME FOR HER PET SNAKE, BUT I DIDN'T WRITE IT DOWN, SO I FORGOT. FEEL FREE TO WRITE IN WITH YOUR SUGGESTIONS!

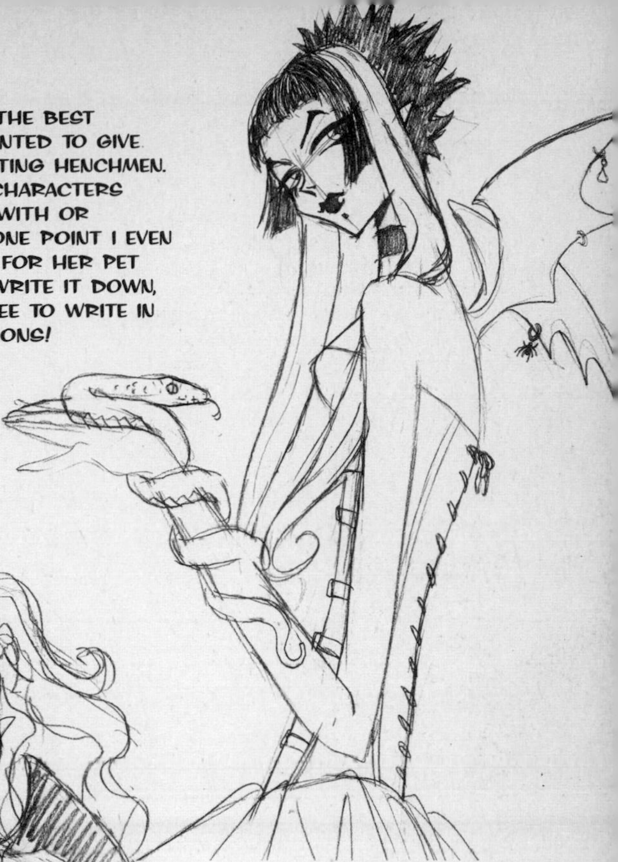

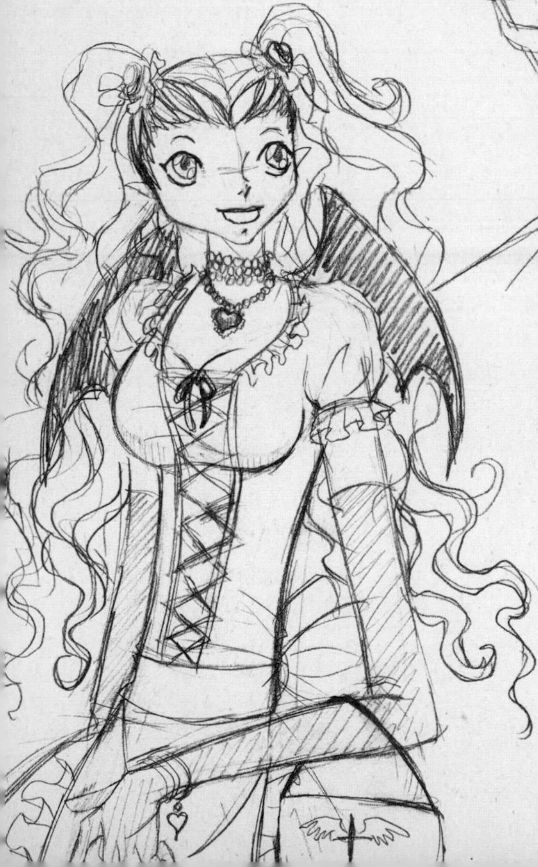

LAMIA

I LOVE GOTHIC LOLITA FASHION, SO I WANTED AT LEAST ONE CHARACTER DRESSED IN LOLITA CLOTHES. THIS HAD TO BE LAMIA.

BROONIE

AT FIRST I WAS LAZY AND NAMED THE BOOGEY MONSTER BOOGIE. LUCKILY THOUGH, I CAN'T STAND TO BE LAZY--SO I CAME UP WITH A BETTER NAME.

BROONIE IS A CHARACTER THAT REALLY HASN'T CHANGED MUCH FROM THE MOMENT I CONCEIVED HER. I TRIED REALLY HARD TO THINK OF SOMETHING ELSE FOR THE BOOGEY MONSTER, MAINLY BECAUSE I THOUGHT MY IDEA WAS STUPID...BUT EVENTUALLY I CAVED AND JUST DREW HER.

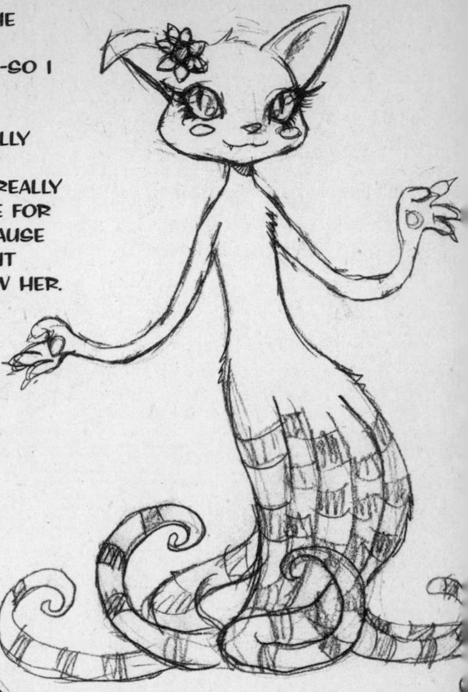

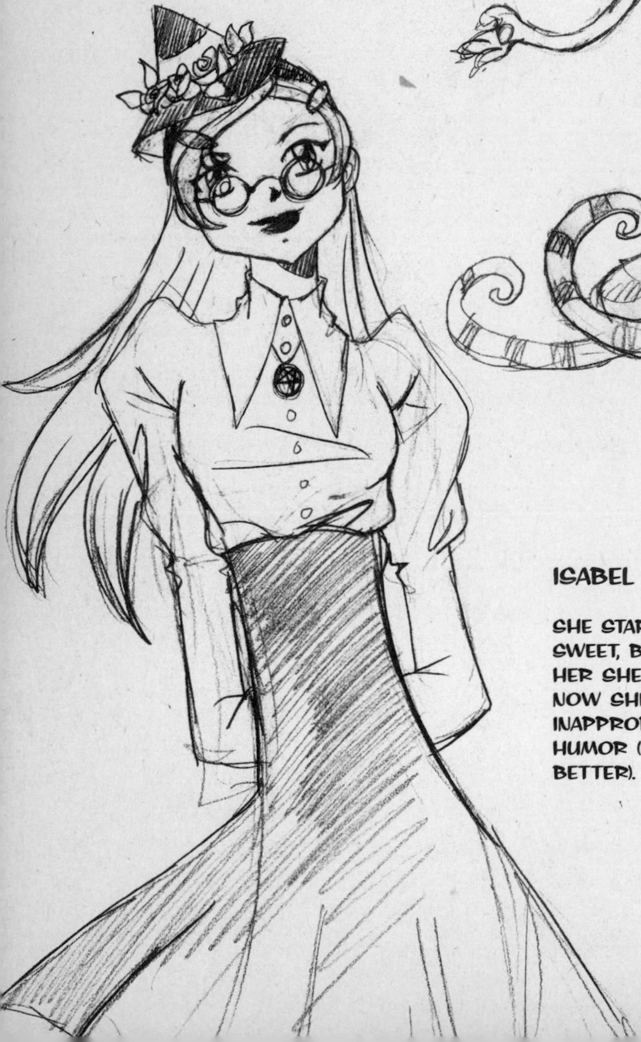

ISABEL

SHE STARTED OUT REALLY SWEET, BUT AS I WROTE HER SHE TURNED GOOFY. NOW SHE HAS A REALLY INAPPROPRIATE SENSE OF HUMOR (WHICH I LIKE BETTER).

First off, I would like to dedicate this book to my mom and dad. It's pretty much my mother's fault for getting me into comics when she bought me Ghost Rider issue 20, as well as my dad's, who would pick up the new issues at the comic shop for me (the nearest shop was two hours away).

I would also like to thank Che (for the great story), Mara (for the wonderful inks and tones), Troy and the rest of Tokyopop for giving an Alaskan artist the chance to work in comics. Here's hoping for the start of a long career.

I don't like to draw self-portraits, so I'm going to let my ferrets, "Optimus" and "Prime," represent me here.

Brett Uher, 6/19/2007

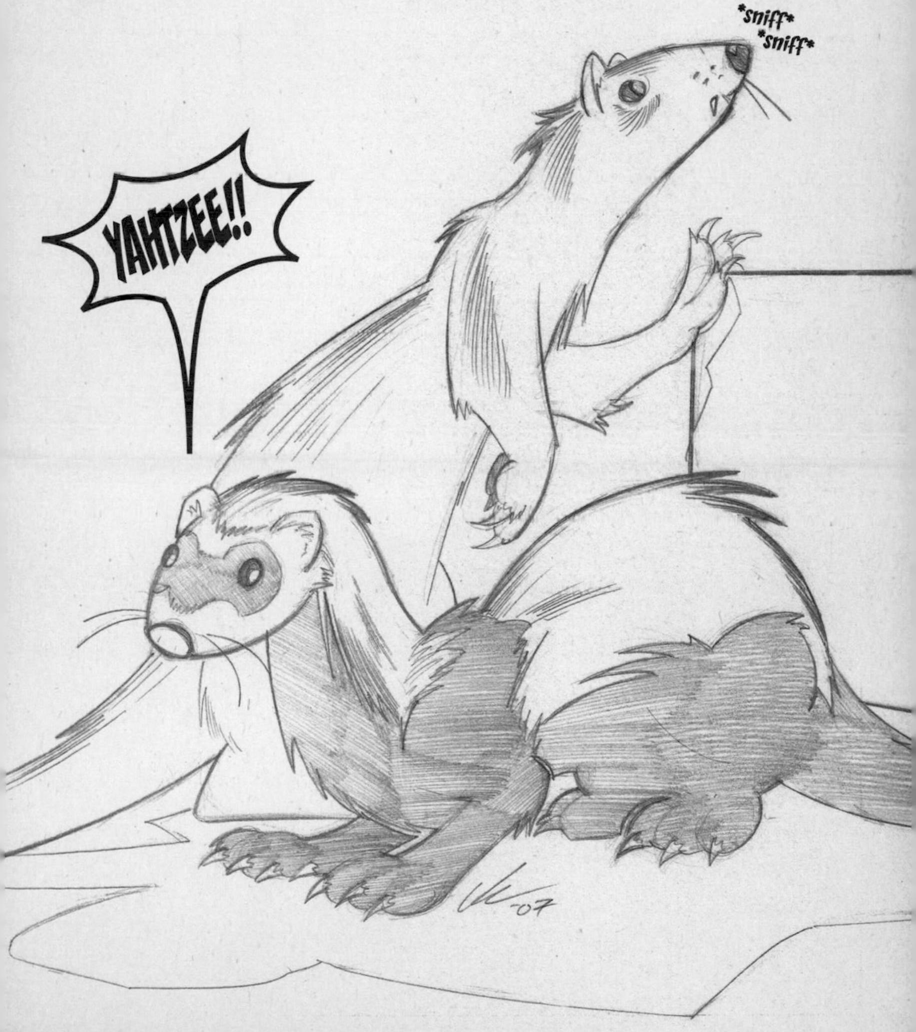
sniff
sniff
YAHTZEE!!

IN THE NEXT ACTION-PACKED VOLUME OF DARK MOON DIARY!!!

PRISCILLA, FUELED BY LACK OF NORMAL FOOD AND HATRED OF ALL THINGS KITTEN, GOES ON A CRAZED ZOMBIE-KILLING SPREE!!

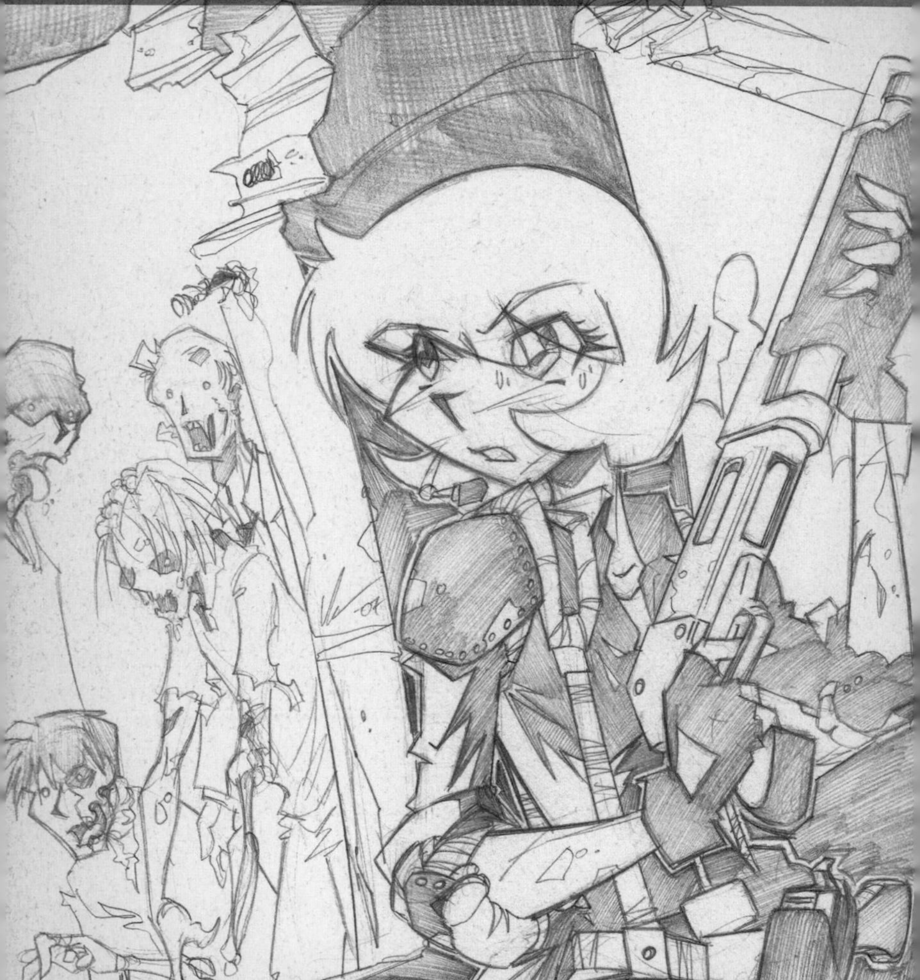

Uh...yeeeah. Not so much.

But wouldn't it be kinda cool if Pris went all "Claire Redfield"? Well, that was the very thing Che wondered when she asked Brett for a cool "Priscilla fighting zombies" pin-up.

Hmm... Maybe I can still convince Che to slip this scene into volume 2...

--Editor

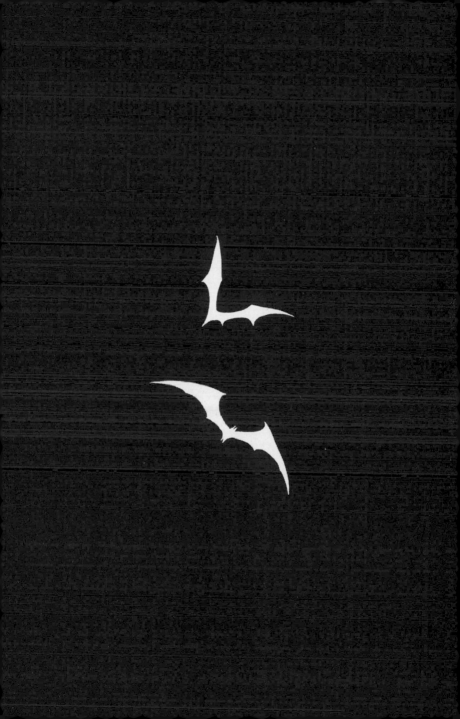

TOKYOPOP®

Shojo your Mojo sampler

Dramacon

VOLUME 3

If you are a fan of *Dramacon*, then here's a treat for you! Hot off the presses comes this preview of volume 3, not due in stores until December 2007! Christie is riding high as she greets her loyal fan following, but will she have the guts to finally ask Matt out?

T TEEN AGE 13+ ROMANCE COMEDY

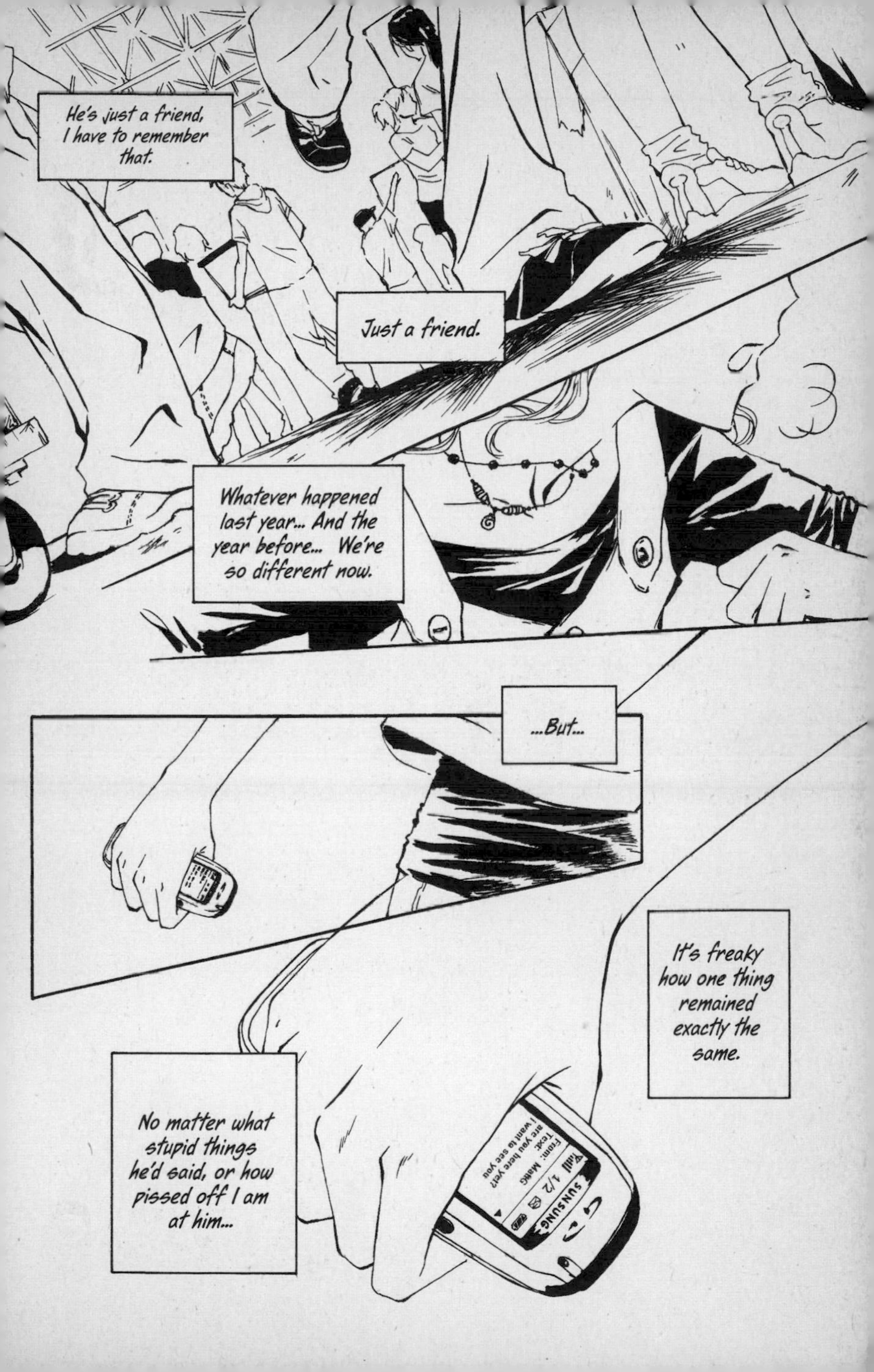

He's just a friend, I have to remember that.
Just a friend.
Whatever happened last year... And the year before... We're so different now.
...But...
It's freaky how one thing remained exactly the same.
No matter what stupid things he'd said, or how pissed off I am at him...
SUNSUNG
1/2
From: MattG
Text: are you here yet?
i want to see you

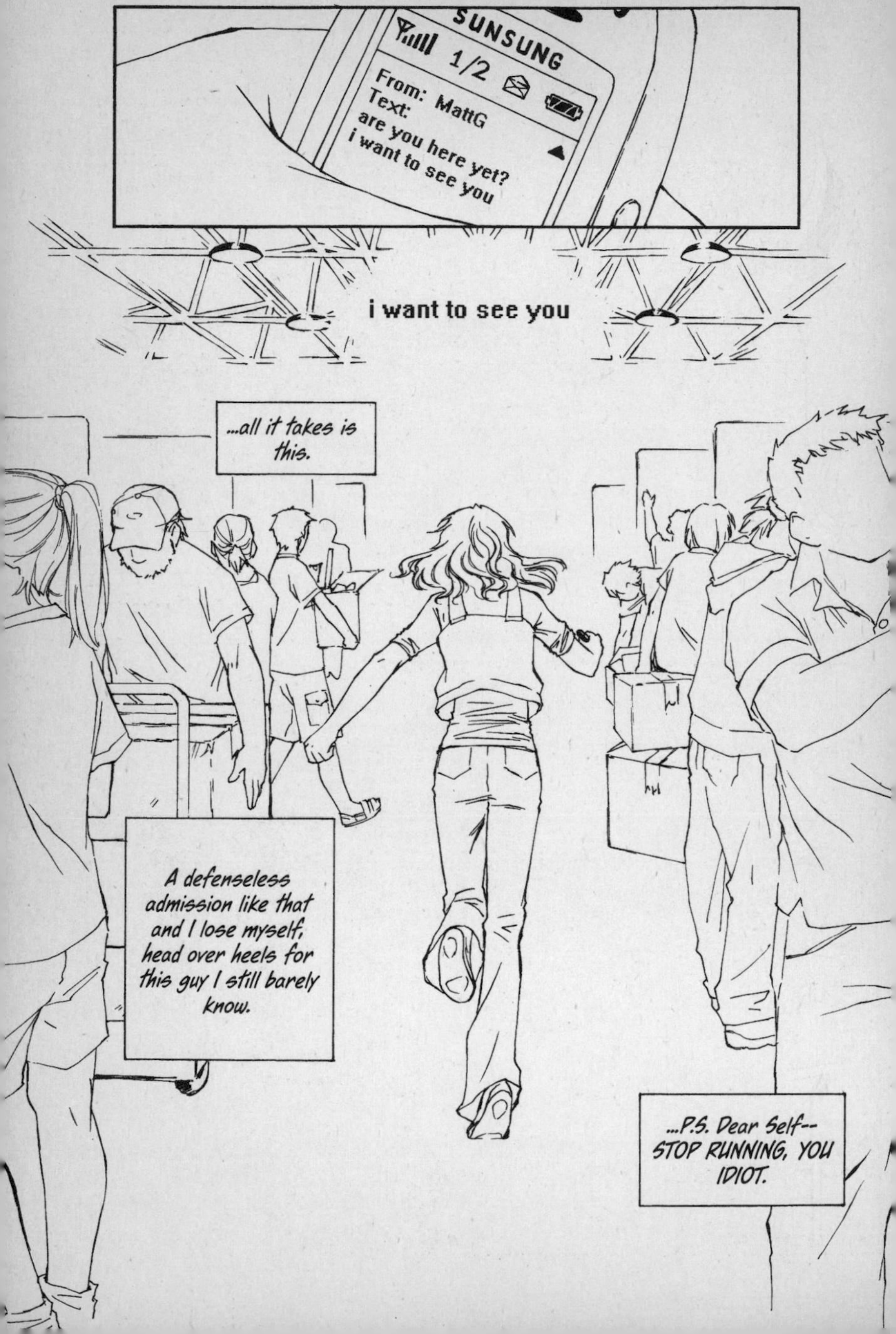
SUNSUNG
1/2
From: MattG
Text:
are you here yet?
i want to see you
i want to see you
...all it takes is this.
A defenseless admission like that and I lose myself, head over heels for this guy I still barely know.
...P.S. Dear Self--STOP RUNNING, YOU IDIOT.

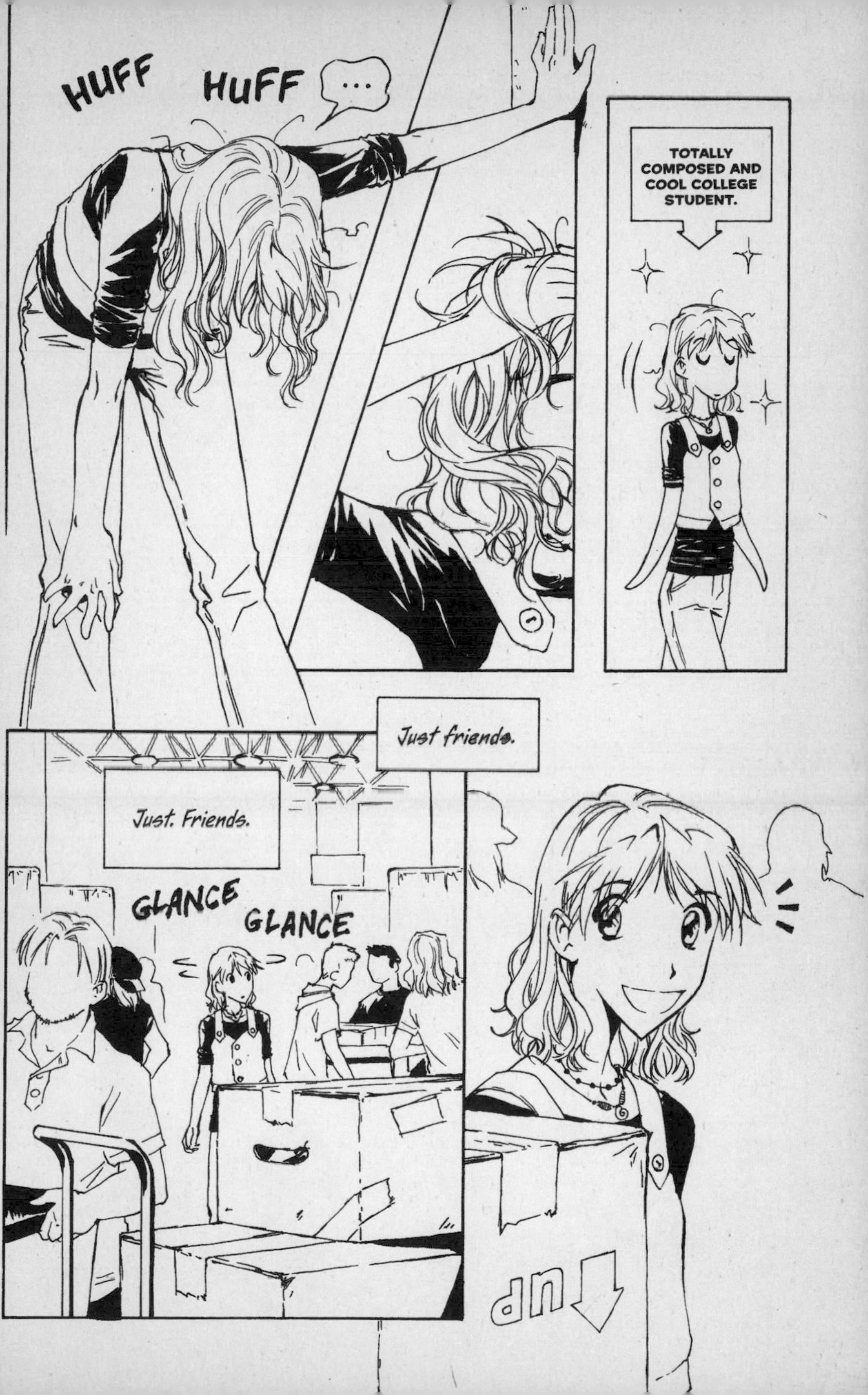
HUFF
HUFF
...
TOTALLY COMPOSED AND COOL COLLEGE STUDENT.
Just friends.
Just. Friends.
GLANCE
GLANCE
UP

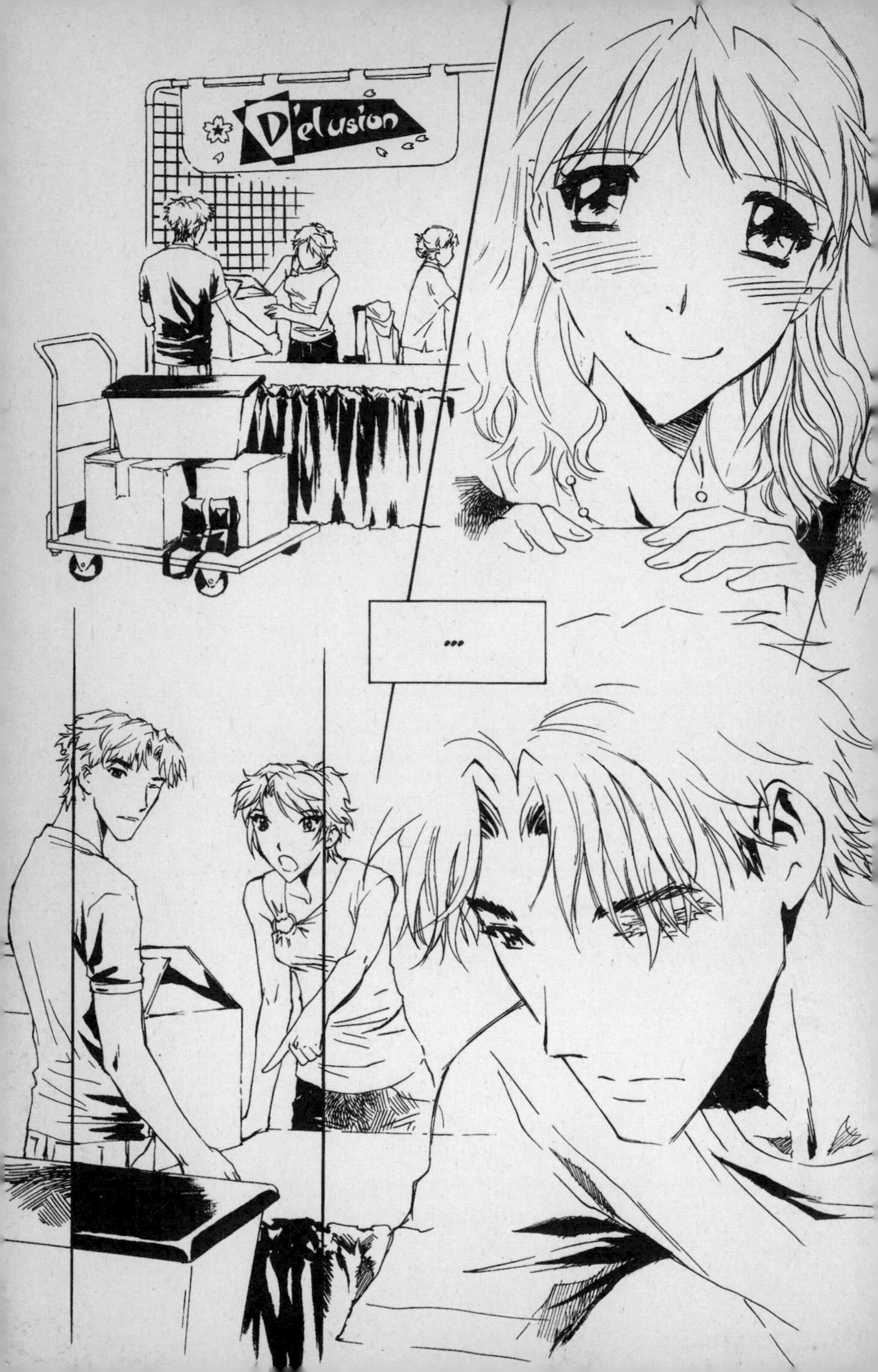

D'elusion
...

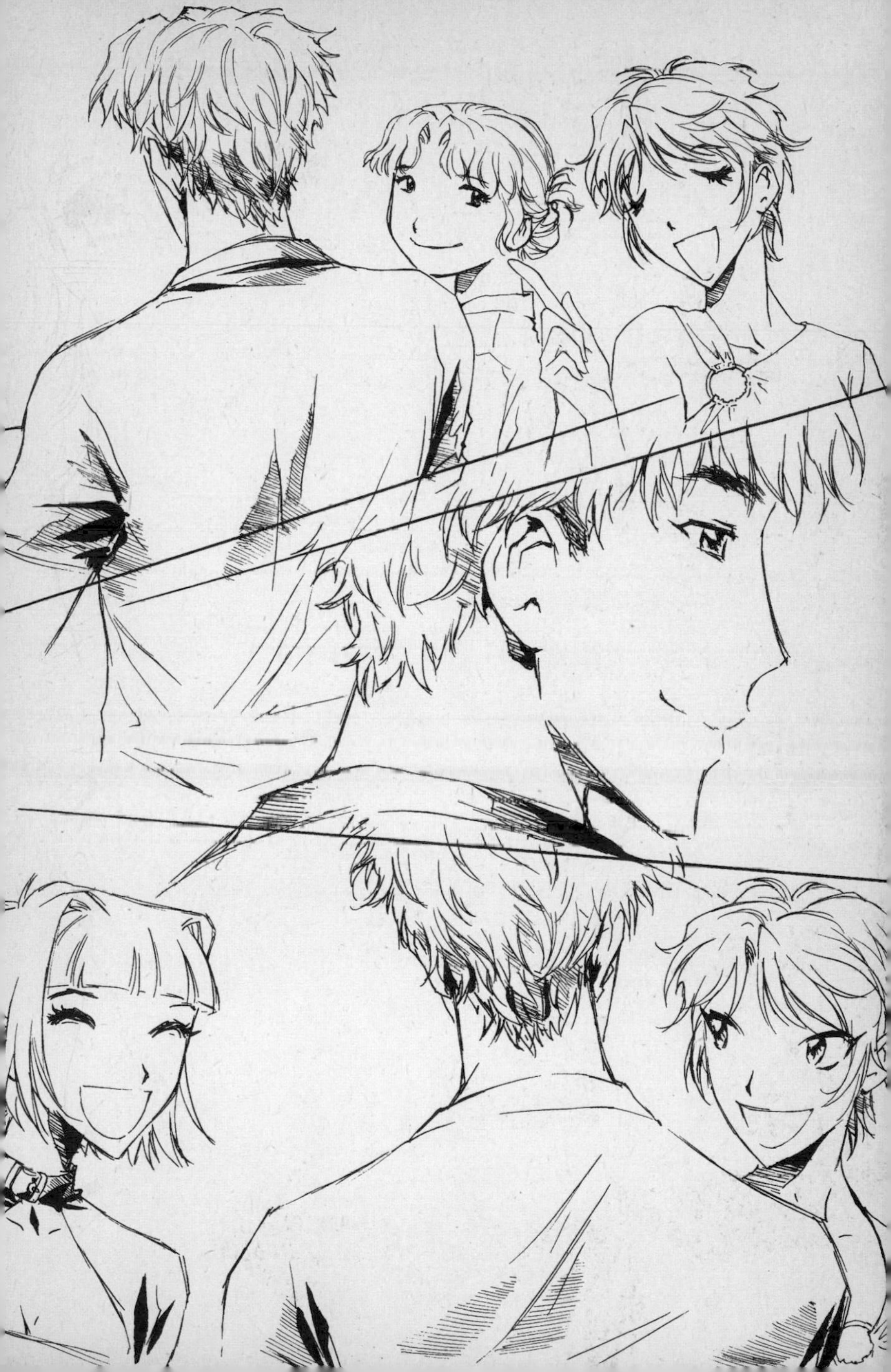

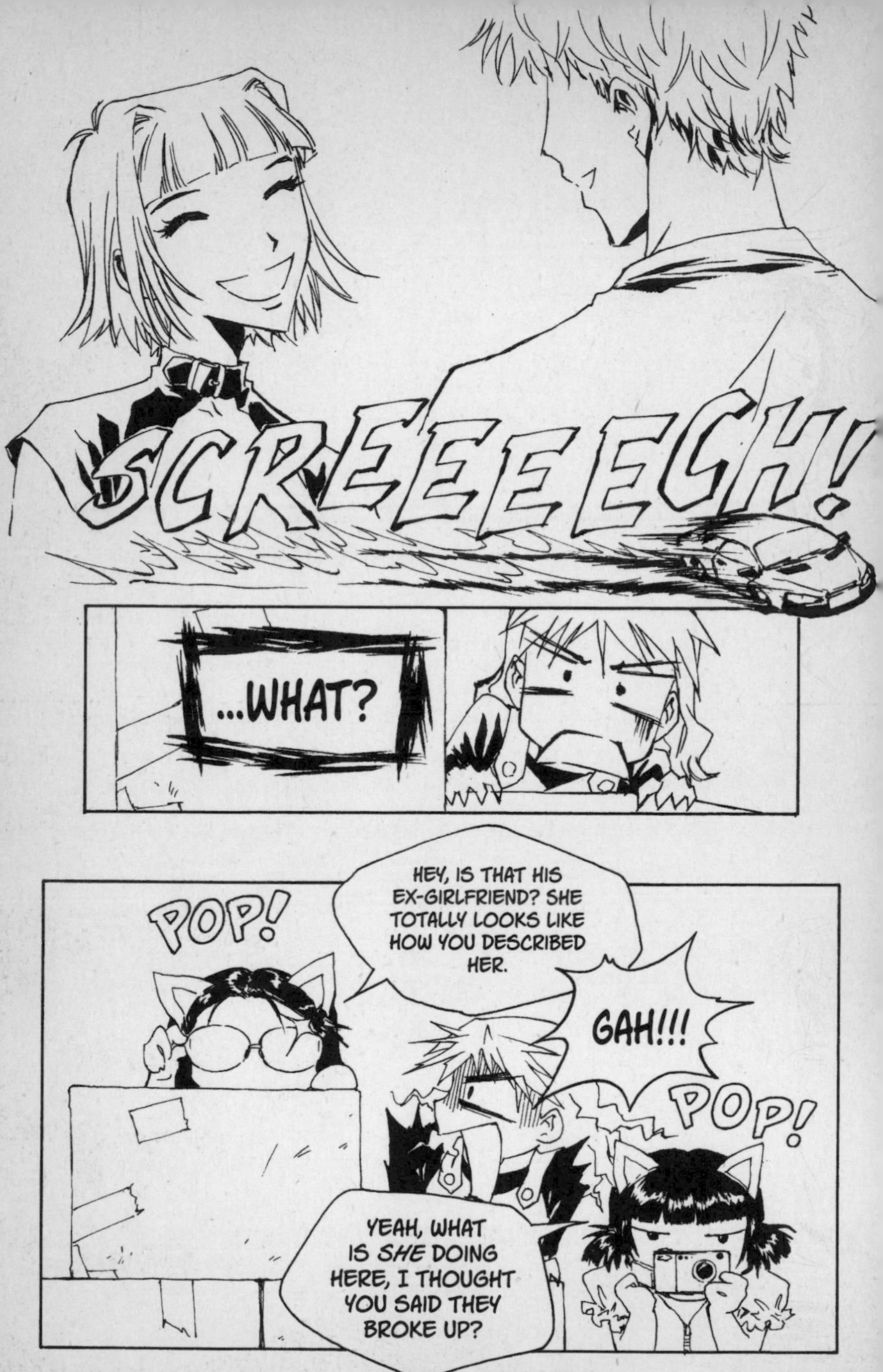
SCREEECH!
...WHAT?
POP!
HEY, IS THAT HIS EX-GIRLFRIEND? SHE TOTALLY LOOKS LIKE HOW YOU DESCRIBED HER.
GAH!!!
POP!
YEAH, WHAT IS *SHE* DOING HERE, I THOUGHT YOU SAID THEY BROKE UP?

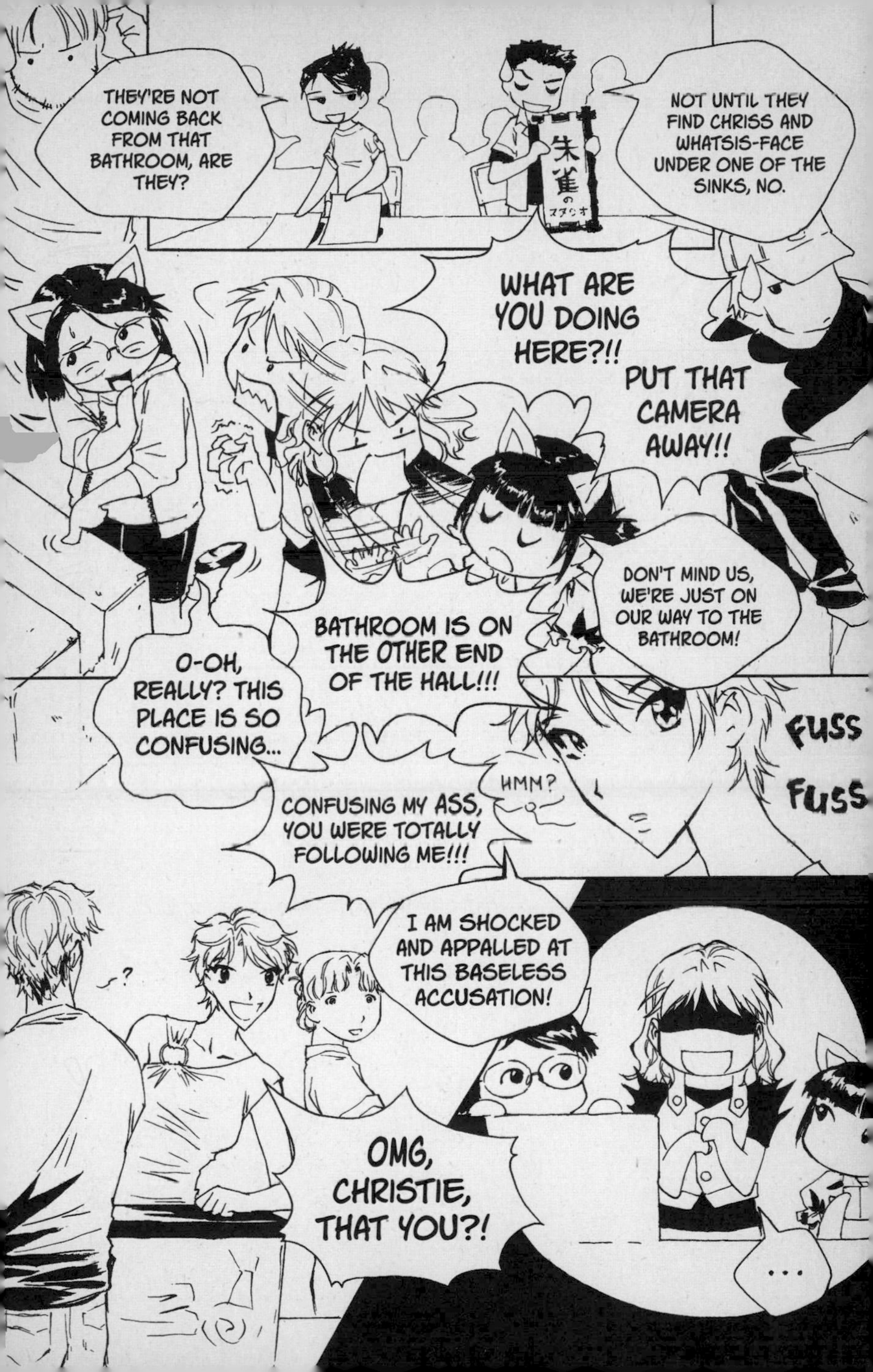
THEY'RE NOT COMING BACK FROM THAT BATHROOM, ARE THEY?
朱雀の
NOT UNTIL THEY FIND CHRISS AND WHATSIS-FACE UNDER ONE OF THE SINKS, NO.
WHAT ARE YOU DOING HERE?!!
PUT THAT CAMERA AWAY!!
DON'T MIND US, WE'RE JUST ON OUR WAY TO THE BATHROOM!
BATHROOM IS ON THE OTHER END OF THE HALL!!!
O-OH, REALLY? THIS PLACE IS SO CONFUSING...
FUSS
FUSS
HMM?
CONFUSING MY ASS, YOU WERE TOTALLY FOLLOWING ME!!!
I AM SHOCKED AND APPALLED AT THIS BASELESS ACCUSATION!
~?
OMG, CHRISTIE, THAT YOU?!
...

A Sneak Preview of

KARMA CLUB

Vol. 1

D.J. Milky

CHAPTER 1:
CLUB SUSHI, COME IN!

Club Sushi to all Karma Club agents: Do you copy?"

What's this? A message for all five agents? Kemmy leaned in toward the Plasma Phone on her wrist. She knew something was up.

"Come in, agents. Come in now!" A deep voice blared through the early afternoon sky as Kemmy cruised between neon skyscrapers on her SkyBoard.

"This is Kemmy," she said into the tiny television-like watch on her left wrist. "What is it, Ed? I've got five trays of fresh maguro, salmon, and egg rainbow rolls to deliver."

Kemmy had moved to MegaMallopolisuika only just over a year ago, but she already was used to the various nicknames and slang everyone used.

In her first week after moving from her home planet, which was way less citylike and urban than these new digs, she noticed that nobody used the proper name for the city: MegaMallopolisuika. Instead, this incredible metropolis—which was the most populated of the four remaining MegaMall planets in the United MegaMalls (UMM)—was called simply "the Big Melon."

"I've got to be at BMCC by four," she said confidently. As a recent transplant from the backwoods planet MegaMallopolisticks, a.k.a. "the Sticks," Kemmy felt proud that she could rattle off the codelike nicknames, such as BMCC and maguro. When she'd first arrived, she'd felt like such a hick when even dorks from the Big Melon knew things she didn't, like that BMCC stood for Big Melon Convention Center and maguro was the sushi term for tuna. But now Kemmy was in the know.

As she zipped between buildings, one hand grasped the handle of her SkyBoard while the other communicated on her Plasma Phone with Club Sushi's leader, Big Ed.

"You mean you haven't delivered those yet?!" His deep voice boomed through the Plasma Phone speaker.

Ooops, Kemmy winced, *busted again*. Now Big Ed definitely would know she'd stopped by the B-ROK store to scope out the new Jolted Jades. Kemmy wanted to call them "sneakers," but she knew that was another hick term. In the Big Melon, they called sneakers "athletics."

"Kemmy!" Big Ed was getting frustrated. "Stop daydreaming and pay attention. *Now*." Big Ed's bushy eyebrows started to twitch——a hairy cue that alerted anyone who knew him that Big Ed was losing patience. "We have a crisis on our hands," he said soberly, "and I need all agents to report for duty."

"Sorry, Ed," Kemmy said while pouting her bottom lip and trying her best to look cute for the Plasma Phone.

"Okay, okay, fine, Kemmy." Big Ed's brows relaxed. He couldn't ever stay mad at Kemmy for long. "The important thing is that you neutralize the situation."

"Me? Why me?" Kemmy whined, thinking about the plans she had to do some shopping once she'd completed her sushi delivery duties. "What about the other agents?"

"Kemmy, this is more serious than you realize," Big Ed explained. "I haven't seen misconduct and crime like this in the Big Melon since the time of the Armageddon. It's making me worry—*really* worry."

Kemmy had never seen Big Ed like this before, even though she had just hit her one-year mark working at Club Sushi. She was employed as a peacekeeper, but the job usually was more about her cover activities, which were delivering sushi and playing music with the other four agents. What a gig!

Kemmy snapped into agent-readied mode, flipping her mental switch from fashion-loving girly-girl to crime-fighting superteen.

"Okay, Ed," she said with conviction. "You can count on me. Just program the crisis location into my SkyBoard auto-navigation, and I'll be on my way."

"That's 'auto-navi,' Kem, and you got it." Big Ed smiled at his favorite Sticks MegaMall transplant as he uploaded the location.

Kemmy blushed. Then she realized this was officially her first *real* crime mission. She was totally trained, but . . .

"Oh, um . . . Ed?" Kemmy asked quietly.

"What's that, Kemmy?"

"Please try to get one or two agents over to help, okay?" Maybe it was the serious look on Ed's face, but Kemmy suddenly wasn't so sure she could handle this on her own. She wanted everyone from Club Sushi on high alert.

Club Sushi was the cover operation for the Karma Club, a special five-member unit of peacekeepers for the Off-Center Intelligence Agency (O-CIA), the secret government organization dedicated to keeping the UMM peaceful. Club Sushi was a perfect guise because there were dozens of sushi restaurants in the Big Melon—and hundreds of uniformed teens delivering sushi on SkyBoards in airways, on streets, and inside buildings. Posing as Club Sushi employees, the Karma Club could go anywhere without raising suspicions.

The five Karma Club teens weren't just selected because they would blend in with other sushi types, though—their age was very important. Kids have pure souls, but teens are kids who are *almost* adults, making them pure *and* responsible, an ideal combination for ensuring good Karma or, if necessary, fighting any evil that threatened the peaceful order of the UMM.

Kemmy had been an agent for a year, but she hadn't actually seen a truly threatening Karma breach. She wondered, *Why now?* And she worried whether an ex-hick from the Sticks could handle a real situation.

"Don't you worry," Big Ed replied, soothing her. "I just got Shay on the other line. You won't be alone. Club Sushi out."

The crowd of people gathering on the street corner was growing larger. A frenzied chorus of panic erupted among the frantic onlookers. No one could believe the horrendous acts of mischief they had just witnessed.

While more than fifty people squeezed together to get a look at the crime scene, the victim—a tiny, white-haired old lady—was sprawled on the sidewalk, clutching her left leg.

"That mean, horrible kid on his SkyBoard," she cried. "And his friends! How could they do this to me?" The old lady's purse had been ripped in half, and only the straps remained.

"Are you okay, lady?" a large, imposing man hollered. "What happened?"

"Oh . . . I, uh . . ." She was almost in tears. "I was just walking down the street, heading toward the shopping plaza," she explained in a shaky voice. "All of a sudden, two hooligans came diving down toward me on these bright yellow SkyBoards. They were yelling and laughing like *maniacs*. Um . . . then . . . then another one came out from around the back of the building— that one lurched down and *attacked* me."

"This is unbelievable! Here, in the Big Melon!" cried a young mother as she clutched her baby tightly to her chest.

"I tried to turn around and duck, but . . . but . . . but he was too fast," the old lady bellowed as she clutched her injured leg. "Before I knew it, that kid had grabbed my purse, ripped out the inside, and then flown away with the other two *criminals*. They were high-fiving each other. It was horrible. How could this happen . . . ?"

The old lady burst into sobs. The crowd's murmur of disbelief grew louder. Crime was unheard of in the Big Melon.

✺

KARMA CLUB VOLUME 1
AVAILABLE NOW!